Way Past Legal

Also by Norman Green

Shooting Dr. Jack

The Angel of Montague Street

Way Past Legal

a novel

Norman Green

HarperCollins*Publishers*

HarperCollins books may be purchased for educational, business, or sales promotional use. For information, please write: Special Markets Department, HarperCollins Publishers Inc., 10 East 53rd Street, New York, NY 10022.

FIRST EDITION

Designed by Jaime Langione

Printed on acid-free paper

Library of Congress Cataloging-in-Publication Data
Green, Norman.
Way Past Legal: a novel/Norman Green.—1st ed.
p. cm.
ISBN 0-06-056454-7
I. Title.
PS3607.R44H37 2004
813'.6–dc22

2003056994

04 05 06 07 08 ❖/RRD 10 9 8 7 6 5 4 3 2 1

For Christine

Acknowledgments

I would like to thank my friends from down east for their contributions to this book and to my life, chief among them D. W. Terrell, who has always managed to be both a Yankee and a rebel. Thanks also to George Harris, skipper of the *John G*, for being generous with his time and his knowledge. I have taken liberties with the geography of Washington County, Maine, but not many, and I have done my best to stay true to the spirit of the place. I have also made the Old Sow in this story larger than she is in real life, but the Old Sow has, in fact, devoured both boats and men.

I need to thank Marjorie Braman for her patience and persistence. She and her colored pencils have made this a better story and me a better writer. And, as always, thanks to Brian DeFiore for his encouragement and his belief in me.

Finally, my apologies to Kluscap and his friends for whatever violence I have done to one of his legends. I heard the story long ago, and memory is a frail thing, but it might have happened my way after all.

Way Past Legal

Prologue

It was centuries before they got their white man's names. At first it was only him, paddling down the St. Croix, though there was no one there to call it that. He was looking for the right place to leave his children. He was almost to the mouth of the river, the place where it emptied into the ocean, when he decided to pull his canoe up onto dry land and camp for the night. He was, in fact, in the act of doing so when he saw them. The moose was pregnant, the deer was not, and they were both out in the cold water swimming with the strength of fear, oblivious to the power of the current. The wolves ringed the spot on the riverbank where their quarry had entered the water, hesitating, and then, as if tethered to a single will, they leaped in to continue the chase. He stood there with the freezing water swirling around his ankles, watching with mixed emotions. It was right that the deer and the moose should flee, right that the wolves should follow, but it was wrong that the bay should kill them all. Even as he thought this the current seized the group of swimming wolves and sprayed them out into deeper water, where the currents ran even faster. Already it was too late for them.

He closed his eyes and waved his arm slowly to stop them all where they were, then opened his eyes to see what he had done. The large ungainly humpbacked one, closest to shore, that was Moose Island. Out in the current, low and green, that one was Deer Island, and the smaller ones, farther out in the bay, fanned out from one another and from the larger islands, those were the Dog Islands. He waited there on the bank until sunrise to make sure that the thing he had done was right. When he was sure, he got back into the canoe and paddled away, leaving his children there on the bank behind him, almost as an afterthought. But the bay, denied its prey, had its revenge. At flood tide, the juxtaposition of the islands and currents created the phenomenon that came to be known as the Old Sow, a howling vortex of malevolent sea, a devourer of canoes, ships, and men.

But by flood tide, he was far, far away.

1

Time, a guy once told me, ain't nothing but one goddam thing after another. I met the guy in Ossining, New York, last time I was up there. I was a guest of the state, and so was he. He was like me, I suppose, a little too smart for his own good. Not smart enough to figure a way out of the life, not stupid enough to enjoy it. I heard he got shanked after I got out. I never found out why. I suppose it doesn't really matter. These things happen. Right?

The reason I remembered the guy, I was trying to figure out what got this whole thing started. You never know, when it happens, what's going to change your life, what's going to bounce you out of the rut you been in, send you flying off in some new direction. It might have been that guy and his theory of time, it might have been that I was worried about Nicky growing up to be like his old man, it might have been that I didn't want to have to kill Rosey, because we'd sorta been friends for too long, but I really think it was Leonid.

I don't know who he was, the paper didn't say. They named a meteor shower after him, though, I read about it in the *Post*. I know, another bad habit. The *Post* said it was the last time any of us would see it, because it wasn't coming around again until 2099, by which time I will be dead, and so will you, along with everybody you ever knew. I don't know why it bothered me. I mean, shooting stars, who gives a shit. Right? But I couldn't get it out of my head, this idea that tonight, this thing is coming by, doesn't matter if it's a big deal or not, you, my friend, and I are both gonna be worm food before it happens again. Little Nicky might make it, if he lives to be a hundred and five, but growing up in foster homes in Bushwick, you gotta figure his chances are not good.

Rosario is this guy that I work with from time to time. I was just a burglar before I met Rosey, not a great one, but pretty good. I did all right. Rosey was more of an armed-robbery guy. First thing we did together, it was a card game down in Canarsie, it was just him and me. They ran the game on Friday nights, we watched the game four Fridays running, make sure nobody too heavy was there, then on the fifth Friday, we hit them. We wore ski masks so none of them would know who we were, and it went down easy even though it was just the two of us, mostly because Rosey's a scary guy whether he's got a mask on or not. He's slightly taller than I am, maybe six foot two or three, and he's a few pounds heavier, he probably goes around two-thirty-five or two-forty. He got his physique for nothing—as far as I know, Rosey has never had to lift a weight or run a mile. Everything I have to work hard for, he gets for free. The thing that sticks in your mind, though, is not his build. I guess you would have to call it his aura. They say God gives you the face you're born with, but you earn the one you die with. Rosey had eyes that looked like they had seen a lot of pain, though how much of it he bought and how much he sold is anybody's guess. It's not just in his eyes, either, it's in the way he holds himself, it's on his face, it's in his bones. You meet the guy, you know instinctively you gotta watch him. People shake hands with Rosario carefully, and I've known him long enough to know that he's worse than he looks. Rosey's one of those people who believes that you were put here on this planet to be miserable, to suffer, and to die. It's almost as though he knows he's predestined for trouble, so he's never surprised to see it coming, and he never runs away from it. Rosey looks like he's right on the edge, all the time. You just know, he thinks he needs to pop you, he's gonna do it. He won't have to think about it much, not until it's over with.

So anyhow, when you hit guys that know how to hit back, you have to be careful, you have to be absolutely certain you can't be recognized, you have to plan thoroughly so nothing goes wrong, and you can't go stupid afterward, either, buying jewelry for your favorite hooker. Most guys in the game find those rules too restrictive, believe it or not.

The last job I did with Rosey, there was this brokerage house run by a couple of Russians. They had a stock scam running, it was your basic Ponzi scheme, and they were getting ready to pull the plug. The trickiest part of a scam like that is cashing out, okay, because everybody is worried about getting screwed or going to jail. Most of the money we couldn't touch because it's already in some bank in the Cayman Islands or someplace, but there are certain elements involved that don't trust banks of any kind, they got to be paid off in cash. Now the brokerage house is in Manhattan, but the Russians are running it out of an apartment house in Vinegar Hill, which is this neighborhood down on the Brooklyn waterfront, used to be mostly factories but half of them got people living in them now. The place is too big for me and Rosey to take down by ourselves, so Rosey picks up three other guys, one guy to drive and two to handle the exits while Rosey and I go in. I'm only twenty-eight, right, already I'm getting gray hairs from this shit.

So we go in, and right away two things go wrong. One, there turns out to be way more money there than we thought there was gonna be. I mean, way more, the kind that comes with serious heat. We weren't even out of the place and I'm hearing the wheels turning in everybody's head. And two, the doorman must've called the cops, because we were just a couple of blocks away when the sirens started up. We got away clean, but now you got the cops looking at the Russians and the Russians looking at the cops and all of them looking for us. One whisper of this gets out, one little peep, and it's all over. We dumped the car we used over in Fort Greene, down by the projects. We transferred the money into a van we had parked there ahead of time. The three guys Rosey picked up to help out, their eyeballs are spinning, they're all excited, they never seen so much money. They had agreed beforehand to a flat fee of ten grand apiece, but now that's out the window. They're looking at each other, then at Rosey and me—man, I can practically smell it coming.

The thing is, a job where the payoff is too small is actually better than a job where it's too big. Five guys and a bunch of cardboard boxes full of money in one van, we had achieved critical mass. That's when you get too much fissionable material in one spot, right, once the chain reaction starts, it's not gonna stop until it runs out of fuel. Rosey climbs into the back of the van. "Mohammed," he says to me. "You drive."

What can I tell you, street names tend to be dramatic.

I'm driving down Flatbush Avenue, I hear him bust open one of the boxes. The shit's in all denominations, but they got it banded into ten-grand bundles. I watch him in the mirror, he's got this box cradled in his arms, he looks like a proud papa, he's in love. He hands each one of those characters one banded stack of hundreds. Half-inch thick, ten grand, that's what they agreed to, but now they're all disappointed, we're screwing them. He should have given them one of the fatter bundles, made up of tens and twenties instead of hundreds, it would have made them happier. As it was, it started to look like the whole thing might blow right then and there. I still had the piece I used in the stickup. I started looking for a place to ditch the van in case one of these guys decides to renegotiate. Rosey got them calmed down, though. "Look," he said, "me and Mo, we got to stash this money in a safe place until the heat is off. What I'm giving you is just for now, it's just to tide you guys over, you hear me? Then, when it's safe, we gonna make a good split. Don't worry, I gonna take care of you all." We were supposed to ride them down to Red Hook, this neighborhood where one of them lives with his mother, but I pulled over on the corner of Flatbush and Fulton Street.

"Okay," I told them. "Out."

"Why you leavin' us way over here?" It was one of the two that had gone up with us. "You 'posed to drive us home."

"You're a rich man now. Take a fucking cab." I'm half turned in the driver's seat, I've got the pistol in my hand but I'm not showing it.

"Hey, bro," Rosey says to the guy. "Gimme a break, okay? We din know there was gonna be this kinda money in there. We gotta get it under cover before the heat comes down. Every cowboy in Brooklyn gonna be all over this, it ain't smart to be drivin' aroun' with this shit. We don' got a lotta time. You unnerstan'?"

"Yeah, yeah." They weren't happy about it, but they got out, slammed the side door to the van closed behind them. Rosey climbed back into the front passenger seat. He rolled the window down and stuck his head out.

"Listen," he said, "you muthafuckas keep your mouths shut, you hear me? Don't say nothing to nobody, not your momma, not your baby's momma, nobody. I gonna call you in the morning." I pulled away, looked back at them standing there on the corner, watching us.

The storage place was this old warehouse way the fuck down near Coney Island. We had already rented a stall there. The building was an old printing plant, fourteen stories high, poured concrete, bars on the windows, metal doors. It was on a block where the other buildings had all been torn down, the neighborhood was all chain-link fences and weeds, just this one big art deco–looking warehouse, nothing around it. Our stall was on the twelfth floor. Rosey grabs a few more stacks of money out of the box he had broken open, he hands me a couple, sticks the rest in his pocket. "We did it, Mo." He's grinning ear to ear, first time I ever saw him do that. "We did it, muthafucka. We rich now."

"We ain't in the clear yet."

"Don' worry," Rosey said. "Everything gonna be fine."

Rosey showed his ID to a security guy behind a bulletproof glass window. The guy checked it against a paper list, opened the door and let us in. We piled the boxes on a wooden pallet. I was trying to do the math in my head as we went. I figured there was about four hundred pounds there, give or take. I tried to guess how much in each box, and how much altogether, but without sitting down and counting it, there was no way to tell. The guy fired up a forklift, picked up the pallet, we all rode up the freight elevator. We got it all put away, right, locked up, the place looked pretty secure. I guess that's why Rosey picked it. We got back in the van, Rosey held up the key to the storeroom. "Look," he said. "I got an idea. Just so nobody gets any bad things in his head, okay, let's leave this key in a hotel safe somewhere. We'll tell the guy we need two claim tickets, he has to get them both back before he gives up the key. Time comes, we both gotta go back together for it. That way, we can both feel comfortable. You okay with that?"

"Yeah, sure." I felt like a guy buying a new car, he knows he's getting fucked, he just doesn't know how. That's the way we played it, though, we dumped the van, and we left the key in the hotel safe at the Omni on Fifty-third Street in Manhattan, just the way Rosey said. We separated on the sidewalk outside. Rosey gave me that shit-eating grin again, walked away looking like a winner. I put the claim ticket in my pocket, went home to catch some sleep. I had a feeling I was gonna need it. I had the thought then, I should have settled for one box. I should have taken one box from the van, let Rosey drive away with the rest, but I hadn't thought of it in time.

I slept most of that next day away, woke up in the early afternoon. I took the twenty grand Rosey had given me out of my pocket and laid it out on the kitchen counter, and I put that claim ticket on the counter next to the money. I didn't want to think about it, I didn't want to have to go where thinking was going to take me. I wanted to trust Rosey. I wanted to believe that the two of us would meet in a week or so, split the money, and go our separate ways. I couldn't, though. What's that old rule? Do unto others? I remembered a big hit some guys pulled off back in the seventies. People still talked about it, it was like Captain Kidd's treasure was buried in Brooklyn someplace. What happened, a bunch of guys, maybe ten or twelve, took down a cash shipment out at JFK. The take was just short of six million. Talk about critical mass—over the next year, all of those guys came up dead except for one, and he died in prison, of cancer, couple years later. If anybody knows what happened to the money, they ain't talking. Six million, whatever it was, it was too much to handle. I don't know if it says anything about the guys involved. Maybe not. Maybe there was just no safe way to cut it up and walk away. Bad things had to happen, and they did. It was inevitable.

The claim ticket lying on my kitchen counter was never going to buy me anything, I knew that. I remembered it as I sat there, it's an old scam, they used to call it the pigeon drop. It was Rosey's idea of getting fancy, switch the real claim ticket for another one he had in his pocket already, he winds up with the two tickets the attendant would need to give up the key, and the one I had gives you the booby prize. That was why he picked the Omni, he must have gone there ahead of time to get a third claim ticket, which was the one he'd given to me. It was touching, in a way. Rosey was giving me an out. As long as I had that ticket, he didn't have to kill me. I could walk around with it in my pocket, all happy and shit, and he could take care of business. That way, he gets away with the money, and I live to talk about it.

Ah, but there it is, there's the rat turd in the oatmeal. I'm still alive, right, I can still talk. When they come looking—and brother, they will—I can say, guy you're looking for goes by the name of Rosario Colón, about so tall, all of that. My guess was that Rosey hadn't followed the logic that far yet, and I was safe until he did. But Rosey was no dope. It wouldn't be long. I went into the bathroom of the place where I was living and looked at my face in the mirror. You talk yourself into it yet? That's what I wanted to know. You all right with it yet? It would really be self-defense anyhow. Right? But I couldn't tell, from that face looking out at me, much of anything at all.

It isn't just your face that forgets how to smile. For a long time, growing up, I hadn't found a hell of a lot to laugh at. And that expression you wear on your puss all the time, sour or hostile or resentful or whatever it is, it sinks in, it seeps into you, it prints itself on what you are inside, and then it's not a mask anymore, because you can't take it off. It's you, you're it. I got all the excuses you want, but they don't mean shit

It was in the *Post* the next morning, same day as the meteor shower, right, cops found three dead guys in a Dumpster out in Queens. Rosey was as good as his word, he had taken care of them. I took the train into Manhattan, wondering if I was going to be in time. Rosey might have moved the money already, but if he thought I'd bought his scam, he might have just left it where it was. I went into a big sporting goods store up near Union Square, a place where they sold serious mountaineering gear. I spent about twenty of those nice clean hundred-dollar bills on rope, a climbing harness, some cam-lock tensioners sized for a three-inch crack. I also bought two of the biggest duffel bags I could find, green, like army surplus, big enough for me to fit in myself. You had one of them to put your dirty clothes in, you wouldn't have to do laundry for a month.

It was not quite dark when I parked the U-Haul truck behind the warehouse. It hurt me to actually rent the thing, but it seemed the smart thing to do. The warehouse looked like it was built back in the twenties. It was an industrial building, but it had a certain elegance to it, a kind of a solid dignity. It was still a factory, but it was built back when they gave a shit about factories. You could have had pride that you worked there. There were vertical grooves cast into the concrete of the outside wall, the grooves led up to the tenth floor, where there was a terrace, a flat ledge about four feet wide, and then the building went up four more floors to the roof. I waited another half hour until it was dark enough. It was an easy climb, actually. The cam-lock tensioner locks securely into the vertical groove, you rope yourself in, reach up as high as you can with the other one, lock that one in, pull yourself up, and so on. I put on the climbing harness and went right up like a spider. It might sound scary, but it's not. It's a hell of a lot easier, and saner, than walking into a room full of desperadoes and taking their money. The only thing I needed to worry about was a couple of places where the concrete had gotten a little crumbly. I thought, while I climbed up, This is the kind of shit I should have stuck to. No partners, no scams, no guns. I popped a window on the tenth floor, took a stairwell up to the twelfth. It probably took more time to open the boxes and transfer the money into the duffel bags than it did to climb up. I thought about leaving a few bucks behind, just to fuck with Rosey's head, but I didn't do it. When I was finished I closed the door on all those empty cardboard cartons and humped the bags down to the tenth-floor ledge. Too bad the stuff wasn't all in hundreds, it would have made for a much smaller package. As it was, it took me two trips. I counted the bundles as I was packing the money, and put it right at two million. About two hundred pounds per duffel. I lowered the bags down first, climbed down after them. I dumped the climbing gear in one of those used-clothing boxes in a strip mall somewhere in Brooklyn. It always bothered me to do that, but if a cop caught me with that stuff, he'd take one look at me and throw my ass in jail. Good thing I tossed it, too, because a cop pulled me over just as I crossed the George Washington Bridge into Jersey. The guy nearly gave me heart failure, but he just wanted to tell me that the truck had a taillight out. I showed him the rental papers, told him I had just picked the thing up, which I had. He looked at my license. The name on it was Emmanuel Williams. Manny is clean, he doesn't have any convictions yet, no points on his license, he even has a good credit rating. I spent a lot of time and money setting him up. Call it an unofficial pardon. I always figured, I survive long enough to retire, I could be Manny. I guess it was my lucky night—the cop didn't feel like writing me up, so he let me go.

I stayed in a cheapo motel in Hackensack that night, took the duffel bags into the room with me. The next day I rented a storeroom of my own, stuck the bags inside. I paid the guy for six months up front. It was still hard for me to believe that I was actually gonna get something out of this, other than a bullet. The guy in the office of the storage place gave me a paper grocery bag, and I took a hundred thou with me when I left. I don't know why, it wasn't like I really needed it, I hadn't even spent the twenty Rosey gave me. I guess I did it just to prove to myself that it had really happened. It was late in the afternoon when I got the truck back to the U-Haul guy.

"Hey, buddy," I told the guy. "Fix that taillight, will ya? You almost got me a ticket."

"Yeah, yeah, sure," the guy said. "You leave the key in the truck?"

I dropped off the paper bag at the place where I was living, but I couldn't stay there, I was too keyed up. I decided I had to go look at the Leonid thing that night. The paper said you had to get out of the city, go out where it's dark, so I took the subway up to Brooklyn Heights to steal a car. I boosted a Volkswagen GTI, which is one of my favorite cars. Guy bought the four instead of the six, the cheap fuck, but at least he got the five-speed stick. I jumped on the Brooklyn-Queens Expressway and headed back for Jersey.

If you cross the George Washington Bridge and head north on the Palisades Parkway, there's a lookout up on the state line, up on the cliffs. It's got to be a couple of thousand feet up above the Hudson. It's a great place to go and look at the city at night, also great for watching migrating eagles, hawks, falcons, and so on. It was dark when I got there, maybe about one in the morning, but the parking lot was full, there were more cars than I had ever seen there before. I got out and laid on the car hood, and as the engine cooled off I started freezing. It was colder that night than I expected it to be, plus there's usually a pretty good wind up on the bluffs.

They came in bunches. You'd see two or three shooting stars together and the crowd of people up there in the dark would ooh and aah and then there would be nothing for a few minutes. In the crowd there was one example of the common tufted Jersey blowhard, this one was a male, and he's going on in the stentorian bellow native to the species, "Orion is right over there, and that's the Big Dipper, and if you follow the handle out you can see . . ." and like that. I listened to it for a while, but he just kept it up, they always do, and finally I felt obligated to point out to the guy that he should shut the fuck up before someone from Orion went over there and kicked his ass.

I suppose I've been spoiled by video games and computer-generated dinosaur movies. They were just quick streaks in the sky, maybe three of them in the space of an hour and a half were what you'd call memorable, big enough to leave a sort of afterglow, a neon green streak that took thirty seconds or so to fade out, but it's something, when you think about it. This stuff has been flying through space for six or seven billion years, if you believe what they tell you, and it's dying tonight, burning up, and the only ones watching are a bunch of loonies from Jersey and one thief from Brooklyn. I wasn't thinking about that at the time, though. I was wondering how pissed off Rosario was gonna be when he opened up his rented storeroom, whether or not he was already trying to find me, also whether that chickenshit crested Jersey gasbag was looking around the parking lot, seeing if there were any cops in attendance. I didn't need the attention, I was already a two-time loser. Next time I go away I'm gonna do serious time. And how stupid would that be, get away with two million bucks and then get busted for hassling some loudmouth asshole in a parking lot? I left while it was still dark.

I really didn't want to go back, and I drove down the parkway wondering what Leonid was really all about. In primitive societies they would probably know, the old men would probably stay up all night watching, they would probably attach some spiritual significance to the event, fast for a few days, start looking for a virgin to sacrifice. I paid the toll at the bridge, asked the guy if he had seen Leonid, but he didn't know what I was talking about.

I dumped the car back where I got it. Hey, I try to be a good guy when I can. By the time I got back, though, my head was all fucked up. Last thing in the world I wanted to do was get back on the train and go home. There was a little park a few blocks away from where I left the car; it runs over the top of the BQE behind some brownstones. I had done a few B&E's in the neighborhood, but nothing recent, so I went over and sat on a park bench. You can't watch the sunrise from there because it comes up behind you, but I stayed there while it got light. You can see the whole of Upper New York Bay from there. It made me wish I had brought my binoculars along. It ain't much of a place to watch for birds, though, mostly what you see there are herring gulls, cormorants, and your basic assortment of ducks. There's supposed to be a nesting pair of peregrine falcons that comes back to the Brooklyn Bridge every January, but I've never seen them. You wanna see birds, the best place to go is Central Park, as insane as that sounds. Think about it: New York City is right on the migration path, right, the bird's doing his thing, he gets tired, okay, all he can see for miles around is fucking buildings, then all of a sudden he sees this big green park, got its own lake, trees up the ass. Stands to reason, right?

Life is much less of a bitch if you can distract yourself with shit like that. Didn't work for me that morning, though. I sat there and went through my whole sorry fucking history, feeling like shit. I don't think I was looking for excuses, not really, I think I was just trying to understand what to do. History repeats itself, even when you ain't got much history. I never knew my parents, some sanitation guys fished me out of the trash in front of a building in Williamsburg. I don't remember that, naturally, but I heard the story often enough.

One of my earliest memories is having the shit beat out of me by a gang of kids in the basement of some institutional building, some government place made of cinder-block walls painted yellow, fluorescent lights, gray asbestos tile floor, white panels in a suspended ceiling. To this day, I am uncomfortable in those places. I don't remember if I cried or not. I might have, at that early age. It doesn't work, though. You learn, early on, not to indulge in it. Anyway, when kids are left to their own devices, they seem to bunch themselves in gangs, and rival gangs take turns working you over until you join one or the other. I don't know where that impulse comes from, maybe the gangs satisfy those shadowy cravings for family and acceptance, but that's just supposition on my part, I have no real information on the subject. I was never a joiner, so I had no other option than to take it until I could build myself up into someone who would make them think twice, send them in search of softer prey. I remember seeing Jack LaLanne on some television talk show, it couldn't have been too long after that first beating, and I only saw him that one time. He was wearing a fruity-looking blue jumpsuit and fucking ballerina shoes, but I remember thinking, I bet nobody fucks with him. From that age on I worked at getting bigger, getting stronger, getting faster. I sought out the gym rats and the iron heads, I attended the academies of the street, and I did my postgrad work at Rikers and Ossining. I didn't do it out of nobility or virtue. It was just easier, for me, than subjecting myself to another set of rules, putting up with shit from another self-important authority figure. To me, the only difference between a gang and any other institution was the color of the uniforms.

So make your left hand into a fist. Hold it out away from you, roll your shoulder and twist forward at your waist. Now hold your right up next to your jaw, somewhere about halfway between your chin and your right ear. I have kept you all at least that far away. That's my comfort zone. If you get too close, it will cost you. Get past the left and I've got the right waiting. Once, I saw a tape of Teofilo Stevenson, the great Cuban boxer, fighting a succession of Romanians and Bulgarians during the Olympics. Three-round fights, right, and they all thought they could survive. They would dance around and throw pitty-pat punches, piling up points while they tried to avoid that left jab. Stevenson, like a giant praying mantis, would wait patiently until they forgot themselves and got too close, and then he would drop that right hand like the hammer of God, and that would be that.

So now I'm two years shy of thirty, more or less. I can't give you an exact birthday. I do know the day they found me in the garbage. I'm six foot one, I stay right around two-twenty. It's a little heavy for a burglar, but it's my best weight. My hair is jet black, when I let it grow in, and my skin fades to a yellowish olive when I've been out of the sun for a while. I've got tattoos from my wrists to my shoulders. They were not the smartest choices I ever made.

I wasted a lot of time wondering where I came from. I don't mean the curb in Williamsburg, I mean the people. Could have been anything, anybody, almost any ethnicity. I mean, I'm pretty sure I'm not a pygmy, okay, but I've seen kids from black families whose skin was as light as mine, and there are a lot of Jews in Williamsburg, and a lot of Spanish, too. And who's to say that my mother, whoever she was, didn't take the subway so she could dump me a safe distance from wherever she lived? Genetically, I could be a part of any one of those groups, but in reality I lack the credentials for any of them.

It's funny, though, when you look at all this ethnic shit from the outside. All of these convenient categories, white, black, Hispanic, Oriental, they only have meaning when you are standing too far away to see any detail. Get up closer and all of those terms become worthless. Chinese guys get pissed off if you mistake them for Japanese, the Japanese look down on the Koreans, and nobody can figure out the Tibetans. The languages don't even help much. The Mexicans can't understand the Cubans and the Cubans can't understand the Guatemalans and nobody can understand the Puerto Ricans. Get closer still, even those divisions break down into smaller subsets. You take two Mexicans, one guy from Mexico City and an Indio from Oaxaca, put them in the same room, they might kill each other. The same principle applies to white, black, and whatever other group you might care to name. I used to know a cracker from Alabama, okay, he got stationed in England when he was in the army. Pissed him off no end that everyone he met over there called him a Yankee.

I suppose I have given up on the idea that I could figure out, somehow, whatever subspecies of human being to which I belong, that I could compare the shape of my fingers, say, or my ears, or that some clue to who I am lies buried in the unconscious patterns of my speech. And even if I knew, even if I did figure it out, I wonder if I would feel any different. When I hear the word "we," I accept that it never includes me unless it is used in a limited and mercenary way by some guy like Rosey, with whom I may have formed a temporary alliance in order to better separate some fool from his money. I am the other guy. I suppose I should feel happy I didn't get tossed into the garbage truck. Anyway, you can probably guess the rest of it, except for the part about my son.

Little Nicky, I call him, five years old, he is the most beautiful fucking kid you ever saw. I know, everybody says that about their kids, right, but in my case it might be true. Little Nicky looks like Elvis and Sophia Loren had a baby. He's got curly brown hair and this smile, Jesus, it could break your heart. I don't generally make a great first impression on women, but when Nicky's with me, they swoon, man, young, old, and in between, they just melt. Everybody wants to stop and say hello, and Nicky will talk to them all. The only woman I ever met that didn't love Nicky is the Bitch who runs the foster home he's in. I guess she is more in love with the money the state gives her to take care of him.

"Poppy!" That's what he calls me, and he yells it out every time he sees me, which isn't all that often, "Poppy!" and he'll come running, wrap himself around my leg. I'm not supposed to hang around where he lives. The Bitch doesn't want me visiting, so she got an order of protection on me to keep me away.

Nicky's mother and I never married. I mean, we talked about it, went to the parenting classes and the whole bit, but that was when I got sent upstate for the second time. She got into crack while I was away, she was dead by the time I got out, the state had Nicky, and that was that.

I'll tell you what a supervised visit is like. Somebody's office, right, another one of those government buildings, cinder-block walls, fluorescent lights, all of that. I'm uncomfortable, they bring Nicky in, he's uncomfortable, we got this woman sitting there watching us, we can't go anywhere or do anything. I can't give him money, but I can bring a toy, or a T-shirt, something like that. Nicky isn't really interested in presents, he just sits right up next to me as close as he can get, talks to me in a voice so quiet I have to lean down close to hear him. It's fucking torture, I love this kid, man, but I hate seeing him like this, it puts me in a rage. I really want to kill the Bitch for doing this to me, and I know Nicky can sense that. The half hour blinks past and it's gone, Nicky tries not to cry when they take him away, and so do I. I walk out of the place cursing the Bitch, God, Nicky's mother, and everyone else who's had a part in this, but I never once look at myself. I always want to skip these visits, but I can't. I want to do the right thing, but I don't know what it is.

Once in a while you get one moment when you can see the future, it's like a present from God, "Here, asshole, here's how it's gonna play, and what are you gonna do about it?" That morning on the park bench I could see it all. If Rosey didn't get me the Russians would, either that or my luck would run out and I'd wind up back in Ossining, and this time they weren't gonna let me back out until I was old and gray. And the worst of it was that Little Nicky was coming up the hard way, just like I did, and he was gonna turn out just the same, maybe worse. I did not want to sit in some fucking jail cell and think about that.

That was when I decided I was gonna steal him and run.

* * *

I didn't have a fixed address. All I really had was two regular-sized duffel bags and a laptop. I paid my bills on-line, I carried a cell phone, and I lived in sublets. The way it worked, there are Web sites for people who want to rent their place out while they're away, and I would log on to one of those and find something I liked, usually just for a month or two. Sometimes you could even work the whole thing out without ever meeting face-to-face—people's faith in their fellow man can be astonishing. I used a variety of cover stories. Usually I would claim to be an artist or a musician or a college student, and if I had to meet someone to pick up a key or drop off a check I would wear a long-sleeved shirt to cover the tats, and maybe a beret, grow a little goatee. If I managed to look boho enough they almost always trusted me. Hard to figure. And anyway, I never robbed any of the places I stayed in, though a few times I would hit a different apartment in the same building. I always left the places I'd stayed in nice and clean, though, everything intact.

The place I was living just then happened to be in a very nice building in Cobble Hill. I had been keeping my eye on this little old lady down the hall. She loved jewelry, she had like ten different watches she liked to wear, Cartier and Patek Philippe and Rolex, plus diamond earrings and bracelets, very old and very nice. Problem was, she was a sweet old bat. I carried groceries up for her a few times and she would always try to give me something to eat. She kept a pair of binoculars next to her patio, but the only birds she was interested in were the ones living in the building across the courtyard. She had this little dog, and she took him out for a walk every day. It was almost criminal not to, but I couldn't bring myself to do it, she was too nice. I thought I might hang around for a while, though, see if she croaked.

So I'm walking back that morning, the morning after Leonid, and I'm feeling very jumpy. I'm thinking about Little Nicky, I'm worrying about the deal with Rosey, I want to get away with the kid and the money, both. Anyway, I notice some vans I hadn't seen on the block before. Two big Ford cargo vans, the kind tradesmen use. They had the windows blacked out, both of them had the engines running and one of them was bouncing around a little bit, like there were guys inside, moving around. I turned back when I saw that, went off to think about it.

I could have just walked away. That's what I had been telling myself, that was one of the reasons I was doing the nomad thing to begin with, but I found out I was wrong. That paper bag with the hundred large was up there on the kitchen table, but it was not worth getting killed or busted for, I mean, there was plenty more where that came from. Aside from that, all I had up there was just, you know, personal stuff. But it was mine, you know what I mean? I didn't like the idea of someone I didn't know going through my shit, whether it was cops or the Russians or even the people I was subletting from. I got a flash then, how all those people I had ripped off must've felt, but I put it out of my mind. I knew I would have to deal with it sooner or later—once it comes up you've got to decide what you're gonna do about it—but just then I was too worried about getting back into that apartment. See, there were two things up there that I wanted. I know it sounds stupid, but I really wanted that laptop. It was nobody's business how much I spent on food or dry cleaning or women and it was all right there in Quicken, I hadn't even bothered to put a password on the file. And the other thing was my life list, which I had folded up in the front page of my copy of the *Sibley Guide to Birds*.

A life list is a record of every bird species you have personally seen and identified, and mine isn't even official because you're supposed to have someone with you to verify your sightings, is that a cedar waxwing, yes, by God, mark it down. That would have ruined it for me, this was a thing I had to do on my own, don't ask me why. I had never spoken a single word about it to a soul. But it was up there, and I had a lot of birds on it, too, everything from house sparrows to a great big beautiful son of a bitch of a barn owl, what he was doing in Brooklyn I'll never know, but I wanted that list. No way was I gonna start all over again.

There were some kids shooting baskets in a schoolyard not far away, and I hung out and watched them for a while. I picked out two of them. They were both tall, looked like they could run, and I gave them twenty bucks each to go put a couple of bricks through the back windows of one of those Ford vans. It was pretty funny, the way it went down. The kids come walking down the sidewalk, boom, there go the windows, they take off, the doors of the van burst open, the guys inside are cops and they can't help themselves, they come boiling out and go chasing after the kids, guy in the front seat hops out, he's red-faced, yelling at his guys to come back, and right then a car that I hadn't noticed which had been parked just up the block pulls out and goes screaming away, had to be Rosario waiting for me. The other Ford van jumps out and goes after him, and after a few minutes the cops all come back and get into the one with broken windows, and they take off, too.

Makes you wonder. Maybe Rosey just wanted to talk, maybe the cops wouldn't get him, maybe he wouldn't roll over on me when they did, maybe the Russians were too busy running for the hills themselves to come chasing after anybody. Right?

Sure. I was in and out in fifteen minutes. I grabbed an old Toyota out of the garage under the building. Hey, it was an emergency. I left it in front of some hotel in Queens, took my bags, and jumped into a cab. That way, I figure, dude gets his car back, the guys in the impound yard won't mess with it too much because it's an old crock, not even worth cracking the trunk open.

When you have to run, the toughest thing in the world is to think about it first. I kept going over it on that ride to Manhattan, Rosey sitting there waiting on me, not noticing the cops waiting on him. That's what he was like sometimes, so focused on what he was doing that he couldn't see what was going on, and I began to wonder if I might not be guilty of the same sort of blindness, so busy running away that I didn't look for the trap. Rosario had to be on fire, man, he'd had all that money right there in his lap, and now it was gone. He wouldn't even consider that he'd been ready to screw me out of my cut, and put me in the ground when I found out. He was the offended party now. He could take me up to the roof and throw me off, and who would blame him? Maybe he'd feel sorry for it afterward, add my death to his list of regrets, but that wouldn't do me much good.

I made a few calls on my cell phone while the cab was stuck in traffic. They had a vacancy at the Halloran House on Lexington, so that's where I wound up. That's not the name of the hotel anymore, but Halloran House sounds much cooler than the Sheraton or whatever the hell it is now, so that's how I always think of it. That must be what it's like to get old, you keep seeing things the way they used to be instead of how they are now.

I sat in my hotel room eating room service and watching television while I tried to figure out what to do. The movie *The Fugitive* was on. Tommy Lee Jones knew that Harrison Ford was going to be running downhill, knew how fast he could run and how far. I had to think about that. My first impulse had been to head for Miami—Miami is like Brooklyn with palm trees, and there are a lot of guys there that look like me, I could fit right in. If someone was looking for me, though, if they knew me and wanted me bad enough, Miami would be a good place to start. I liked the place and had been there a few times. That's how they get you. They watch how you move, they keep track of what you've done before, assuming that's something like what you'll do next time. So what would Tommy Lee Jones expect from me? He'd expect me to head south in someone else's car.

It took me a few days to put it together. I went back out to Jersey, there's one place about ten minutes from the George Washington Bridge, has to be the center of the used-car universe. There's even a place that specializes in exotics, Maserati, Lotus, Vette, Ferrari. I was sorely tempted, I got the money, right? But I wound up buying a Ford minivan from the guy across the street. It's the last thing anyone would ever expect me to drive, but I'm running away from Tommy Lee, right, and I'm going uphill. I paid the guy cash, told him what I wanted, and he was more than happy to take care of the whole transaction, tags, insurance, and all.

The next day I had an appointment to see a guy named Michael Timothy Buchanan. Dude is supposed to be a lawyer, that's what it says on his office door. You wouldn't want him making out a will for you,

though, or closing a real estate deal, or much of anything else. He was a crook, and a good one. The cops have never bagged him. I don't think he's ever even shown up on their radar screen. I had dealt with the guy twice before, and both times I worried if this deal was gonna be the one that put us all away. What Buchanan did was solve problems. You take a guy like me, my problem is that I got cash, and I need to get it into the system. Cash is just one kind of money, but it can be inconvenient. The other kind of money is the kind that doesn't really exist except for a row of numbers on a piece of paper, a check or a statement of some kind. Changing cash to the other kind of money is a common problem. Uncle Sam keeps a sharp eye out for guys trying to do that. They watch banks and casinos and brokerage houses, and if you start moving large amounts of cash through a place like that you will be visited by a couple of guys who will ask you a lot of questions about where you got it. I worked for it, motherfucker, but any time Uncle Sam's minions catch you with a fat wad of green they automatically assume you got it from some nefarious activity, and they take it. You want it back, you got to demonstrate to their satisfaction that you earned it in some socially acceptable fashion. How is that fair?

What Buchanan does is broker a deal with two other crooks who have different problems. You take a guy that owns a used-car lot or a candy store, say it's worth a half a million bucks, and the guy is looking to sell. He sells it straight up, the IRS is gonna want about a hundred and fifty grand from him in taxes after the deal is done. So the guy goes to someone like Buchanan, says, "I want a hundred and fifty regular and three and a half in cash." Okay? But it costs me a hundred and fifty thousand in legitimate dollars and four hundred thousand dirty ones. Plus, what the hell do I want with a candy store? Buchanan goes out and finds some guy who really does want it, maybe he offers it to the guy for something less than market value, say, four and a half. So, on paper, I bought something for a hundred and fifty grand, turned around and sold it to some other guy for four and a half. What I actually did was launder my money. I get my original hundred and fifty back, plus three hundred thousand more that I can put into the system in any fashion I choose,

transforming myself in the process from a crook to a man of substance and independent means. I gotta pay some tax on the capital gain, but hey, I'm a citizen now, right? Buchanan gets a percentage, plus, you can be relatively sure he is screwing everyone involved, but that's not my business, and it beats the hell out of going to jail. It doesn't have to be a candy store, either, it can be anything from Liberian freighters to office buildings, and sometimes the deal can be ferociously complex. The only safe way through something like that is to be totally clear on your own end of it. Here's how much I give you in this form, here's how much I better get back from you in that form. You yield to temptation and get drawn in any further, especially if it has anything to do with real estate, you will get gutted like a fish.

Buchanan had an office in a suite with a bunch of other lawyers in a building right off Union Square. I don't know if he was partnered in with those other guys or if he was just a carbuncle on their ass. I don't know what any of the other lawyers did. He was in when I called, though, and he agreed to meet me at a coffee shop around the corner from his building. I got there ahead of time, sat in with a bunch of Jamaicans who were hanging on the corner across the street from the place. Buchanan showed up about five minutes late, looking like he always did. He was a pale white guy, always wore a three-piece suit, always, white shirt with French cuffs, tie, shiny shoes. His hands always shook, he sweated like a coolie even in the dead of winter, so much so that the collar of his shirt was always wet. He was deep into the process of drinking himself to death. Too bad. Smart bastard like him, you gotta wonder what he could have been, he didn't have that monkey on his back. I didn't see anybody following him, so after a few more minutes I crossed over.

I sat down across from him. He didn't offer to shake hands, and neither did I. "Hello, Michael."

"Mohammed. I heard you were dead."

"Did you really?"

"No. I did hear that there is a contract out on you. You and that Puerto Rican gorilla you run with."

"Wow." That was fast. "No kidding. How much?"

Buchanan laughed, shook his head. "You want me to find out?"

"No. I want to do a transaction, just like last time, only bigger. Two million, this time." The number did not impress Buchanan at all.

"How much time do we have?"

"I don't know. I'm not staying in town, I'm only in for the day. How much time you think you're going to need?"

He shrugged. "At least a couple of weeks, maybe more. I might be able to give you details in a few days. Is there someplace I can reach you?"

"No. I'll call you."

"All right," he said. He stood to go. No small talk for him. "Try me in about a week. Call me at the office, around ten. Call too early and I won't be there. I'm not always available after noon." He smiled once, a quick mechanical grimace, and he turned and walked out. He must have been getting worse. Last time I dealt with him he didn't start drinking until after five in the afternoon. That's the way alcohol addiction gets you, though, like a beaver working on the base of a tree, it keeps chewing off pieces of you until it takes you down.

Two days later I'm sitting in the minivan, parked on Flushing Avenue outside the Bushwick Houses—that's the housing project where the Bitch lived. Nicky didn't come outside that day, but I wasn't worried—you can't keep a kid like Little Nicky inside for long, he'll drive you out of your mind. Sure enough, the next day he came outside, he was chasing leaves around the dogshit-speckled patch of grass between the buildings. I slid back the side door of the van and sat in the opening watching him. When he finally noticed me he came tearing over, screaming, "Poppy!" Nobody noticed, nobody was watching, nobody gave a fuck. After a few minutes he detached himself from my leg and looked up. "Poppy," he said. "You got a haircut."

I had been wearing dreads for a while, but after the job with Rosey I'd gotten them chopped off, and now my hair was not much more than a painted shadow on my skull. "Yeah, I did. How you feeling? You doing okay?"

He looked down at the sidewalk and shrugged. Didn't want to talk about it.

"You wanna come with me?"

He looked up, eyes wide. "To stay?"

"Yeah."

He looked around. "Mrs. Hicks is gonna get mad."

"She'll get over it. Come on, let's go."

We made it as far as Haverhill, Massachusetts, that night. I still don't know anything about Haverhill, it was just one of those places on the way to where I was going. We got out on that wide, flat, endless American interstate, it got dark and I got tired, I saw the sign that said Haverhill, and I got off. Nicky and I slept in the same motel bed that night. He was scared and he cried, I comforted him the best I could. It was tough for me to understand his tears. They couldn't have been for his mother, he didn't really remember her, nor could they have been for Mrs. Hicks, God forbid. Me, I had plenty to cry about, and I did it, too. New York City was lost to me now. She had cast me out, left me in these strange backwoods, I thought she was closed to me forever, this beautiful hideous bitch goddess whore mother of a city had turned her back on me and left me out here with Opie and Dorothy, River City before Harold Hill, Jesus, who wouldn't cry?

Little Nicky got over it and fell asleep tucked up next to me, his arm stretched out onto my stomach. Every time I moved he would grab and hang on, and that really said it all.

That sense of urgency left me sometime during the night, and in the morning we lay in bed while Nicky watched *Barney* on the motel television. I wondered, for a while, what *Barney* was doing to my son's head, but it was something he knew. He watched, rapt, sang along with the idiotic songs in his little boy's voice. He even tried to explain to me, distractedly, what the hell they were singing about. I should have done this long ago, I thought, I should have come for him as soon as I got out. We shut the television off when *Barney* was over, and Nicky stood on a chair in the bathroom, brushed his teeth with my toothbrush, washed his face. I watched him, wondering how in the world I was going to do this. What could I teach him? I didn't know anything myself. Nothing good, anyway.

There was a huge shopping mall on the other side of the highway from the motel, and there was a pancake house in one corner of the parking lot. I've never been a breakfast guy myself, I always thought the only civilized time for breakfast was about two in the afternoon, preferably with a few Bloody Marys up front. Nicky was bouncing in the front seat beside me. He didn't say anything, but little kids gotta eat, even I knew that. I pulled into the parking lot next to the pancake house and shut the car off. He got nervous when I opened my car door.

"Where you going, Poppy?"

I pointed at the pancake house. "Me and you are gonna go have breakfast in there."

"Breakfast?" He looked out his window with his mouth open, wonderment plain on his face.

"Yeah, breakfast. Lock your door, push that button down. Okay, come with me."

I probably should have put him next to me in the booth so that I could help him out, but I was new at this. He climbed up and got onto his knees on the bench so that he could lean his elbows on the table the way I did. When the waitress came, she handed me a menu, but she spoke to Nicky.

"You want a booster seat, honey?"

"No, I'm okay," he said. "Do you work here?"

"Yes, sweetheart," she said, smiling. She glanced over at me. "Coffee?"

"Yeah."

Nicky recaptured her attention effortlessly. "Are they good to you here? They treat you nice?"

She smiled again, wider this time, looked over her shoulder in the direction of the kitchen. "Well, you know," she said, "sometimes they do, and then sometimes they don't. You want something to drink, honey?"

The two of them turned and looked over at me like I knew something. It took me a couple of seconds. "You want a glass of milk?"

"Milk?"

"It's that white stuff goes on your Cheerios."

He gave me a look, like, Okay, buddy, and turned back to her. "You got chocolate milk?"

"I don't know, honey," she said. "I'll go check." She walked off chuckling, shaking her head. I've got to learn how he does it, I thought. I knew that part of it was his looks, but still, he had a way of connecting, of opening people up and making them want to talk to him. He'd been able to do it ever since he'd learned how to talk, and I had no idea how it worked. Put me in a room full of strangers and I will be guarded and defensive until I figure out who's who and how much compensating I have to do to make up for what I am, you know, no education, jail, and the rest of it. Put Nicky in the same room and he'll walk out a half hour later friends with everybody in there, he'll remember their names and everything they talked about. Jesus. He should be helping me eat my breakfast, not the other way around.

They didn't have chocolate milk, so he settled for the white stuff. I don't think he'd ever had pancakes before but he didn't let on, he watched me carefully and did what I did. He had some trouble cutting them into manageable portions, so after a while I woke up and helped him with that, and then he did okay, aside from getting maple syrup all over his face, hands, and shirt. I think he was pretty worried about how I was going to react to that. When we were done we went to the men's room and hosed him down. After I got him more or less clean he stood there with his face upturned and his eyes squeezed shut, getting blasted by the hot-air machine. Jesus, God, I thought, I know this is my job, but I got no idea what the fuck I'm doing, You got to help me out, here. It struck me then that he had no other clothes, he had nothing in the world except what was on his back.

The stores in the mall were open by the time we left the pancake house. Nicky and I went inside and wandered around for a couple of hours. I bought him a knapsack almost as big as he was, then we went into Baby Gap and filled it up. I watched him work on the ladies who staffed the place, and then I took one of them aside and told her I was taking him to camp for the first time but I had forgotten to bring his stuff, I didn't want to ruin things for him, could she fix him up with all the normal kid stuff?

She put a hand on my shoulder. "It would be my pleasure," she said, hardly looking at me at all. She and the other women fussed over him for what seemed an eternity. He sucked up all the attention like a camel drinking water after a long dry trip, and I watched, feeling inadequate. What had made me think I was qualified to be anyone's father? I knew the answer to that one, though. When you get a hard-on, the blood rushes out of your brain and into your dick so you can't think at all. Otherwise, the human race would have died out long ago, because who would be so egotistical that they would do this on purpose? "Oh, yeah, I can handle this." Sure you can, pal.

We walked out of that mall with Little Nicky looking like all the other suburban yuppie kids, Little Lord Fauntleroy, ready to inherit the world. You're gonna have to change your style, too, I told myself. Urban street rat chic is not going to cut it. As soon as we hit the highway, Nicky fell asleep clutching his knapsack. See, I thought, you're learning already. Wear his ass out first, then drive.

I got off the highway when we hit the Maine state line. I was sick of it by then, it seemed pointless, speeding through the countryside in a big hurry, particularly in light of the fact that I didn't know where the hell we were going to begin with. There was a big sign, "Scenic Route, U.S. 1," so that's the way we went. For quite a while, "scenic" seemed to mean tourist traps, giant liquor stores, souvenir places, and outlet shops, but gradually they tapered off and we began to see more of the Maine shoreline, rocks and pine trees and wide wet mudflats that smelled strongly of salt and clam shit when the tide was out. We passed through a few small towns on the way and I looked carefully at the inhabitants, wondering how I was going to blend in up here. I didn't know anything about my heritage, but it was a pretty safe bet that my forebears did not come from Maine. These people looked rugged, but they were white, baby, white, with lots of red faces, yellow hair, and blue eyes.

I called Buchanan from a pay phone outside a diner in Gardiner around ten the next morning. "What do you have?"

"I got something sweet, baby, I got a guy the SEC is after," he said. "Nice deal, clean and neat."

"How does the guy help me if the SEC is after him?"

"That's what makes this work," Buchanan said. "He's holding stock in a small pharmaceutical company. They're going to get FDA approval on a new boner drug."

"Say what?"

"A new boner drug. You suffer from limpus dickus, it makes you seventeen again."

"I thought these guys were trying to cure cancer."

"More money in hard-ons. Anyway, he can't hold the stock. He's got to sell before word of the approval gets out. The SEC thinks he uses inside information, which he does, but if he sells early, before the stock goes up, he can say, 'Hey, look at the bath I took,' and they'll back off."

"So how does this work?"

"He sells, you buy, sometime between now and three weeks from now, current market price. You got any trades in the past twelve months?"

"Yeah."

"How'd you do?"

"Don't ask."

"Better and better. They look at you, they got to figure you work on the monkey and the dartboard theory, you finally got one right. So you buy the stock from him, right, you put your cash in escrow with me. After the FDA approval becomes public, you ride it up and then dump it, you're nice and clean. He takes his end out of the cash you put up with me."

"How are you getting yours?"

"You're getting a free ride on this one, Mo. Once I know the name of the security, I'm jumping in on the open market."

"Serious?"

"I like this one, Mo. This guy is golden. Listen, you got a broker or do you make your trades on-line?"

"I do everything on-line."

"What's the total value of your account?" I told him. "Wow," he said. "You're not doing so bad."

"Job security," I said.

"Yeah, sure," he said. "Look, here's what I want you to do. Sell everything you're holding, and start messing around with some pharma stocks. Buy a bunch of Merck, hold it for a week, then sell it all and buy Abbott, or something like that. We want to establish a pattern of trades in the time we've got left until it's time to jump into this new stock. Can you do that?"

"Yeah, sure."

"How can I reach you? It will take me a few days to get set up with this guy, but I've got to get to you before the FDA goes public."

"You can leave a message on my voice mail." I gave him my cell number.

"Okay, great," he said. He was actually beginning to sound excited—usually, talking to him was like talking to an undertaker. I guess the guy loved making deals. "How do you want to handle the cash end of this? I'll need to have it when he gives me the word."

I pictured it, inside those two big green bags, sitting on a table inside that storeroom in Hackensack. "It's out in Jersey," I told him. "You tell me the day and the time, and I'll meet you there. You can do a count, and after that it's yours." And your problem, I thought.

"Oh, man," Buchanan said, "I hate New Jersey. Can't we do this in Manhattan?"

"I don't want to move it again. It's too dangerous. There's too many things that can go wrong. You want my opinion, leave it where it is. I'll give you the key and walk away, and then when it's time to pay your boy, you give him the key and do the same thing." Working with Buchanan depended on trusting him. Now I would find out if he would trust me not to go back and rip him off.

"All right," he said, after a moment. "We can do it that way. I'll call you when it's time. Meanwhile, don't forget to make those trades."

I hung up the phone and went back to where the van was parked. I'd left it in a spot on a concrete bridge spanning a good-sized, fast-moving stream. Nicky was glued to his window, watching the water cascading down the hillside and passing underneath on its way to the Kennebec River. It was a weird feeling, letting go of that business with Buchanan, getting my head back to me and Nicky, and Gardiner, Maine.

"Pretty, huh?"

He turned to me and nodded, but he didn't have words for it, and I guess I didn't, either.

Back out on the road, Nicky and I made up a game to pass the time. It was called "bird." If Nicky spotted a bird and I either missed it or didn't know what it was, he got a point. If I knew the name of the bird, I got a point. The game got more complex as we went along. He didn't believe me when I identified a seagull as a great white bug-eating stinkbird, so he got ten points for that one, and I got penalized a hundred points for making up stories, not that it mattered, because Nicky was keeping score and his math system was idiosyncratic, to say the least. He got bored with that game after a while, so we made up another one, the "what color is the ugliest car" game. He could pick out ugly cars with no problem, but he really didn't know the colors too well. That game went on a lot longer than the bird game. His attention would flag from time to time, and he would start telling me about cartoon characters or the people in his building, but he always seemed to go back to the color game. Kid's five years old, right, already he's playing catch-up. See, that's the way it goes. You grow up the way I did, the way Nicky had been, you're on your own in a lot of ways, and of course no kid can make up for the lack of an interested adult. You wind up deficient, and that's not a value judgment, it's just how it is. You reach school age, one of the first things you learn is that you're not like the other kids. As a matter of fact, you're way behind, and you begin trying to compensate, you have to try to be cooler than anyone else, or tougher, or wilder, you start doing everything you can think of to catch yourself up to where you think you are supposed to be. I had been playing that game for as long as I could remember, and of course you can't win. In fact, it gets worse as you go along, because you lose track, the gap between what you were supposed to be and what you are becomes wider instead of narrower until you can no longer see any way across. You wind up with the conviction that you might somehow cross the finish line if you keep dogging along, but no way you're winning any prizes, bro. I was really hoping Nicky was young enough, that I had gotten to him in time for him to be spared that, but there's no way to know that, and besides, there were still plenty of things that could go wrong. I mean, I was just making this up as I went along, and on top of that, Tommy Lee Jones might be right around the next corner.

2

The Maine coast gets wilder and more beautiful the farther north you go. I had been a street rat my whole life, had grown up thinking there was only two kinds of trees, Christmas trees and the other kind. Nicky and I found plenty of places to stop and lots of stuff to look at, and we had no problem finding motels with vacancies. We bought matching plaid flannel shirts at L.L. Bean, we climbed the hill above Camden and looked down at the boats in the harbor, we rode a ferryboat over to Vinalhaven Island and back, we drove to the top of Cadillac Mountain. I don't know what I was looking for, and I began to doubt myself, you know, maybe I should have had more of a plan before I jumped into this, but I knew in my heart that if I had stopped to think about things too long I would have wimped out. By the time we hit Washington County, up at the northern tip of the Maine coastline, we were way past the tourist zone, the radio stations all played hillbilly music and gospel, there were deserted houses with peeling tar paper in the middle of fields of tall grass, and I halfway expected to see Jed Clampett somewhere, except it was too damn cold up there for the way he dressed. We were a couple of hours north of a town called Machias when a CV joint in the front end of the minivan let go. I coasted to a stop over at the side of the road, feeling lucky to get there, because I'd suddenly lost all influence over the van's direction. I got out, cursing, kicking the front fender. There was not a house in sight. As a matter of fact, I could not remember exactly how long it had been since I'd seen human habitation. I looked up and down the road, but there weren't any cars around, either. Nicky climbed into the driver's seat and rolled down the window.

"Poppy," he said, sounding worried. "What happened?"

"Sit down, Nicky. Everything's gonna be all right."

He looked around doubtfully. "Are we gonna have to sleep in the woods?"

"Wow, wouldn't that be fun, huh?" He blinked at me a few times, so I went over and rubbed his head. "Don't worry. We won't have to sleep in the woods, I promise. Just sit down and be cool, okay?"

"Okay." He climbed back over to the passenger side, sat down and hugged his knapsack.

And then it was my turn to look around and start worrying if we'd have to sleep in the woods. They stretched as far as you could see, pitching and rolling over the low hills that marched off to the horizon. Not a single restaurant, not one gas station, not one 7-Eleven, not a single goddam thing to eat except for the seagulls, and good luck catching one of those. I had been driving through this landscape for what seemed an eternity, and it had not occurred to me until that very minute what a desert the place could be. I mean, you can't eat the trees, can't eat the grass, can't eat the rocks. What else was there?

I cracked the hood of the van and propped it open. Might as well advertise.

I heard the sound before I saw the vehicle. From far off it was just a low rumble, but as it got closer it sounded like a farm tractor with a bad muffler. I saw it going down a hill in the distance, coming south, and it seemed to be moving very slowly for a motorized vehicle. I couldn't quite make out what it was, some kind of a pickup truck.

It was a Jeep, green, white, and rust-colored. I guessed it had to be from the early fifties. I leaned against the minivan and watched it make its calm and unhurried way down the road. It stopped when it reached us, right in the traffic lane, and a white-haired guy with leathery brown skin looked out the window.

"You evah notice," he said, "they nevah seem to break down anywheyah convenient?"

"I noticed it this time."

"Ayuh. Any idea what's wrong with her?"

"I think it's a CV joint."

"Now just what in the hell is a CV joint?"

"Constant-velocity joint. It's what this thing has instead of a front axle."

The guy shook his head. "Theyah making cahs too damn complicated anymowah. Too many things to get frigged up on ya. Computahs, plastic and metal thin enough to open with nail clippahs. You fellas like a ride?"

"That would be great."

"Well, lemme pull off the road heah fore I get run ovah by a pulp truck." He clunked the thing back into gear and pulled behind us onto the shoulder, tail to tail with the van, then he got out and walked back. He looked to be in his sixties, maybe five foot ten, lean, as though the wind and cold weather had eroded away all the superfluous parts of him. He had the letters "USMC" tattooed on his forearm in faded blue.

Nicky was standing up in the driver's seat. "Hey theyah, young fella," the guy said, going over to the window. "What's yaw name?"

"Nicky."

"Who's that guy?" He nodded his head in my direction.

"Poppy," Nicky said. "That's my dad."

"Well, I'm pleased to meet ya, Nicky. I'm Louis." He turned in my direction.

"Friends call me Manny."

"Well, Manny," he said, "I guarantee you ain't gonna find no CV joint noth of Ellsworth. I'll ride ya down ta see Gevier, an' we'll get him to come give yah a tow." I locked up the minivan and we climbed into the Jeep.

Louis's truck was even noisier from the inside, but I didn't want to say too much, since it was running and the minivan wasn't. I sat in the passenger seat and held Nicky in my lap. There were, needless to say, no seat belts—such frivolities came along a decade or two after the truck was built. The ride was beyond harsh, and you could see the road going by beneath your feet through holes in the floor pan. And every so often the truck would hit a bump and take a funny sort of sideways hop.

"That feels a little weird," I shouted to Louis over the clatter of ancient metal. "You feel that, every once in a while, when you hit a bump just right?"

"Ayuh," Louis said. "She slides around a bit. The old girl ain't much of a piece anymowah. Body sits on the frame like a hat on a bald man's head. Long's we don't go too fahst nor the wind blow too hahd, she be fine."

"How'd you ever get this thing to pass inspection?"

"Inspection?" Louis looked at me like I was nuts. "This heah's a fahm vehicle. Kinda like a tractah. Don't need no stickah." He winked at Nicky. "She don't got no CV joints, though."

"Just as well," I said.

I suppose I really should say something about the way down easters, or some of them, talk, because it is a strange and anachronistic tongue which cannot properly be reproduced in speech or in ink, and if I continue to try, I will drive both you and myself crazy. It is one of those things which must be experienced to be appreciated, let alone understood.

The most basic element of this puzzle is the complete loss of the letter *r*, except in places where it does not belong. "Whore," for example, is no longer a simple monosyllabic term with a concrete definition, it is "ho-ah," and you, me, Richard Nixon, and Mother Teresa are all sons of whores, as is your minivan when it breaks down, and your decrepit Jeep pickup when it does not. No judgment, either good or bad, is implied. And while the capital of the state of Maine is Aguster and Hong Kong is part of Chiner, out-of-state yuppies tend to drive Beemahs and a man too tight with a buck is a pikah.

Certain expressions, as well, like endangered species that may be found here and nowhere else, are best understood in context. For example, if a Mainer tells you that last night he got "right fucking sideways," his meaning may be deciphered if you notice that he is severely hungover, and if you are too dim to figure that out, he may later refer to you as "nummah than a pounded thumb."

I could go on at length but I will not. From now on I will only reproduce the pronunciations when I can't help myself. One final word: While a family whose members exhibit a consistent lack of judgment, ambition, and financial acumen may be called "a bunch of swamp Yankees," a Yankee, by and large, is a baseball player from the remote and foreign isle of Noo Yok. You, however, are "not from round heah," and should pull yaw christless Winnebago over to the side of the road once in a while, you son of a ho-ah, and let people who got to get to werk go on past. Ya bahstid.

Gevier's garage was about ten miles south of where the minivan had broken down. I had driven past the place on my way north, but I had taken no note of it on the way by, apparently, because I had no memory of it when Louis pulled his wreck of a Jeep off the road and into the yard. The yard must have been paved once upon a time, because traces of the blacktop still remained, and crushed stone filled in the holes where it had worn away. The building itself was made of concrete blocks unadorned by paint or siding, the roof was galvanized metal, and there was one oversized garage door that fronted on the yard, with a personnel door off to one side. An amazing array of vehicles was parked on the fringes of the yard, along the sides of the building, and among the trees out back. Some of them looked repairable—older American sedans, station wagons, and pickups—and there was a big green amphibious assault vehicle on black tires. But for the fading paint, it looked untouched by time. A lot of the other stuff was done for, though still interesting, like the '57 Nomad that had weeds growing up through the empty engine compartment.

When I opened the door of Louis's pickup to get out, Nicky grabbed my arm and held on. I am the only thing in this kid's entire universe that looks familiar, I thought. If I were in his shoes I would be shitting my pants. I took him by the hand and helped him down out of the truck.

Gevier hadn't shaved or washed his face in a while, or changed his clothes, either. Forget about a haircut. He had his feet up on his desk in his amazingly cluttered den of an office while he watched an afternoon soap opera on a black-and-white television that used a long piece of wire for an antenna. He had a fire burning in a wood stove fashioned out of two fifty-five-gallon steel drums.

"Damned hot in heah," Louis said to him. "Gonna burn all your wood up before it gets cold. Whattaya gonna do when winter comes?"

Gevier did not move. "Don't you worry about me," he said. "End of September, you ain't got a stick of firewood cut yet. I'll bet you're gonna be burning green wood all winter long, just like lahst yeah. And the yeah before that."

"No, sir," Louis said. "I'm changing my ways, I'm gonna get it all cut in time this yeah. I got almost a cord left over, anyhow. Listen, I brought you a customah. This is Manny, and his van is broke down about five mile noth of heah."

Gevier dropped his feet to the floor and looked at me. "What happened?"

"CV joint," I told him.

"Get her off the road?"

"Yeah, I was lucky."

"No steerin', all of a sudden, and when you step on the gas she revs but she don't go nowheyah?"

"Yeah."

"CV joint," he said, nodding his head, "most likely. What is she?"

I told him the make and the model, handed him the spare key. "You want some money up front?"

"That's all right," he said. "If I got ya cah, I don't guess you'll get too fah off." He looked at Louis. "Where ya gonna put 'im up?"

"I was thinking he could stay up to Gerald's trailah. Won't be no one using it till hunting season."

"How is Gerald these days? I ain't seen him in a while."

"No, he don't get up to visit too often. He got laid off that air-freight place in Boston and had to go back doing long-haul driving. No telling where he is right now."

"Well, that's a hell of a note." He looked at me. "All right," he said. "I'll go get her, drag her back here, find out what we need. Then I'll call Ford, see what they say. I'll give a yell, tell ya the bad news."

We got back into Louis's pickup and headed back north. I looked over at him.

"Who's Gerald?"

"My son," he said. "Ain't no jobs up here, unless you want to work at the mill. Working at the mill can be discouraging, because you can see where yo-ah gonna be and how much yo-ah gonna make for the rest of yo-ah life, and it ain't enough. Gerald lives down in Massachusetts. I give him the sixteen acres next to my house, and we put a little trailah on it. We're gonna replace it with a cabin, but we can't do it until Gerald saves up the money." Louis shook his head. "He'll get a union pension in another twenty years, and Social Security, if there's any left. He had a 401(k), but the economy has ate that up. My grandson is going to college, so Gerald is gonna pay for that, too. It's hahd, you know. You have a little dream, you think it's just out of reach, but all the time it's running faster than you are, you lose ground on it every day."

"So you rent out his trailer?"

"Ayuh," he said. "Fishing season and hunting season, 'lantic salmon and deer. Gevier's daughter Edna takes care of the place, cleans it up and whatnot. You'll like it."

"I'm sure I will. Better than sleeping in the woods. Ain't that right, Nicky?"

Nicky was sitting in my lap, looking out the window at the trees going by, swiveling his head to catch the occasional patches of ocean visible from the road, not paying any attention to the two of us. He looked up at me, no suspicion, no wariness, no fear in his eyes. He was trusting me to take care of him. "Yeah," he said, nodding his head, unaware of what he was agreeing to. He was with his Poppy, and everything was gonna be okay. I felt uncertainty gnawing at my stomach, and I wondered if Louis's son Gerald had that same feeling, worrying about college tuition.

"You think Gevier can handle the van? I don't know how many CV joints he sees."

Louis grinned. "Well," he said, "he's a bit queeah, I'll give ya that. He was the smahtest person evah went to school round heah. Went off to college aftah high school, we all thought he'd be a rocket scientist or somethin', but he come back up after twenty yeahs or so. You think that garage was a sight, you ought to see where he lives. He's right downstreet from me, lives with his dottah Edna. Best damn mechanic I evah met, though, and I've met a few. He'll take good care a ya."

Nicky got very still when he saw the police cruiser. It was parked on the shoulder behind the van, lights flashing. Louis pulled his truck over and stopped behind the police car. "We shoulda grabbed yoah bags befoah," he said, staring out his windshield. "Now we gotta deal with this son of a hoah."

"I'll talk to him," I said. I felt Nicky tighten up in my lap.

"His name is Thomas Hopkins," Louis said. "He's got the disposition of a bay-ah with a bad case of hemorrhoids."

"All right." I gave Nicky a squeeze. "You stay here with Louis, okay?"

"Okay," he said, in a small voice.

Hopkins got out of his car when he saw me coming. His yellow hair was cut boot-camp style, and he had pale blue eyes in a square face. He was about a head shorter than me but he was not a small guy—even without the bulletproof vest he was a big son of a bitch. Some guys never get over the fixation with height, though. You can build strength, you can build quickness, you can do the martial arts thing, carry a cannon, stick needles full of steroids in your ass and turn yourself into a monster, but if the other guy is taller than you, you still gotta look up to him. Hopkins was doing that now, and he did not look happy about it. Maybe it's just the alpha male thing. "This yoah cah?"

"Yeah," I said. Hopkins was looking at the tattoos on my forearms. I was wearing a sweatshirt, and I had the sleeves shoved up to my elbows. "I broke down, and this gentleman was nice enough—"

"You got any ID?"

"Yeah." I watched him as I slowly reached for my wallet with my left hand. Hopkins was not theatrical about it, but he got ready for me to do something rash. He rose up on the balls of his feet, looking like he was hoping I would take a swing at him. I got the feeling then that if Hopkins and I had met in a bar, one of us would definitely have had a bad night. Maybe both of us. I came up with my wallet, fished out Emmanuel Williams's license, and handed it to him. He glanced from the picture to my face.

"Wait here for one minute, please." He left me standing there, went back to his car, and talked on the radio for a minute. Back in the Jeep, I could see Louis mouthing the word "asshole." Nicky's eyes went from me to the cop and back. I winked at him, but he missed it.

Hopkins didn't find anything on Manny, Manny was cool. He came back and handed me the license. "Do you mind if I take a look through yoah cah? You have a right to refuse permission, and if you do, we will all wait right heah for a search warrant."

I watched the muscles working in the side of Hopkins's jaw. I reached into my pants pocket for my keys, handed them to him. "Knock yourself out."

He looked at me, reached around behind him for something on his belt. It was my turn to bristle. No way this cocksucker is putting me in cuffs. He seemed to think about it, then change his mind. "Wait over here by the cruiser," he said.

"All right."

He walked up to the passenger-side door, glanced back at me, then went to work. Back in the Jeep, Louis was shaking his head in disgust, but I was beginning to sweat. Suppose whoever owned this van before me left a roach under the seat? Then it hit me. I had a hundred and twenty grand, more or less, wrapped up in a paper bag in one of my duffels. There might not be a law against it, but there's nothing I can tell this bastard that will keep him from slapping those bracelets on me and taking me and Nicky to some police station until he's satisfied I'm nothing more than a rich guy who likes to keep a lot of cash around, and not a bank robber. Or a burglar.

I couldn't believe I'd been so stupid.

I didn't even need the money. I'd been doing pretty well, as burglars go, and I had never developed the sailor-on-payday mentality that a lot of crooks get. I had a little better than thirty-five thousand bucks in a bank account in Emmanuel's name, and I could access it through any ATM. I had taken the cash out of impulse, and now it was going to cost me. Maybe everything. I could see them sticking me in a cell, I could see Nicky, confused and losing hope, thrown back into the state machinery that would slowly grind him down, turning another lost child into someone like me.

How could I have been such an idiot?

Hopkins finished with the glove box, the console between the seats, the space under the front seats, and he moved on to the passenger compartment. All right, the guy is armed, he's ready, and he looks tough, but I can handle him. Fuck, I have to handle him. When he gets to the bag the money is in, I'll jump him, and then I'll cuff him and leave him in the cruiser, I'll take Louis's keys, I'll grab Nicky and we'll take off. I'll dump the van in Machias, right, boost a car. . . .

The van doesn't work, Einstein.

Okay. I'll never get far in Louis's truck. I'll cuff Hopkins, leave him with Louis. I'll toss Louis's keys into the woods, steal the cruiser. You can't leave Hopkins with a gun, either. Oh, this is great, man, this is fucking brilliant. But what choice do I have? I'm not losing Nicky, not after all this.

All right, I'll bribe Hopkins with the money. That's got a chance. What can the guy make, thirty-five, forty grand a year? It's cash and it's good, take it and drive away, buddy. . . . He might go for it. If he doesn't, though, I've just made him a lot more difficult to handle, he'll be expecting me to make some kind of move. Fuck it, I can still handle him. I better be able to handle him. . . . Okay, grab the police car, dump it in Machias, hope nobody notices an inconspicuous motherfucker such as myself, with a kid, driving a police car, leaving it someplace, stealing another car. Hey, it might work. And then what? Head for the Canadian border, maybe. If I remember the map right, we've gotta be about an hour from Calais, which is the first place you can cross. Maybe two hours. Do I have two hours? Louis or Hopkins might be able to walk to a phone in that time. And the van is registered in Emmanuel's name, so if they get to a phone before I get across, I'm fucked. How about if I head for Ellsworth instead? I could dump the second car there, boost another one, head west instead of north, but now I don't have a good ID anymore, so I'll have to forget about Canada. Shit.

There was nothing in the passenger compartment, so Hopkins moved back and opened the rear hatch. Three bags, two of mine and Nicky's knapsack. Which one was the money in? I couldn't remember. I glanced back at the Jeep, felt Nicky's eyes on me. Hopkins grabbed one of my bags and unzipped it. I could feel my heart picking up speed and my mouth went dry. I got ready. Hopkins turned back to me, a condescending smile on his face. He had something in his hand.

"What the hell is this?"

I could barely talk. God, if you're there, I owe you one, man. Another one. "It's a spotting scope," I croaked.

"What's it for?"

"I'll show you." Hopkins stepped to one side. I wiped my hands on my jeans, hoped they weren't shaking too much. I fished my tripod out of the bag, set it up, mounted the scope. I sat on the end of the van, scoped the far end of the field across the road from where we were parked. "All right," I said. "Take a look."

I moved out of the way, and Hopkins peered through the scope. "What?"

"Red-winged blackbird."

He straightened up, looked at me, incredulous. "You got this thing for looking at birds?"

"Oh, yeah. I also got a digital camera that mounts onto it. Say I got a bird I can't identify, okay, I can capture the image of the bird, download it onto my laptop, then compare the image to *Sibley*. That way—"

"*Sibley*? What is a *Sibley*?"

I reached into the bag, pulled out the fat hardcover edition.

"Oh," he said. I could see the transformation in him. I was no longer a threat to his manhood, I wasn't a tattooed ironhead freak itching to find out if I could kick his ass, I was an eccentric, a harmless dork. A bird-watcher. "How much did all this crap cost you?"

"The scope was about eight hundred, the camera was about a grand. I don't remember what I spent on the tripod. Then, you know, there's books, binoculars, not to mention the cost of trips and stuff."

He stared at me for a minute. He shook his head once. "All right. You can put all of this stuff away, Mr. Williams. I'm going back to have a word with Louis Avery." He walked back to the Jeep.

I broke the scope and the tripod down, stuck them back in the duffel bag. The paper bag with the money in it was at one end of the bag, underneath some shirts. My hands were shaking again as I thought about how close we had come to disaster. Stupid, man. No matter how careful I try to be, I still do something moronic at least once a day. . . . I got everything stowed, then turned and sat on the tail of the van and watched Hopkins back at the Jeep. Louis was wearing an expression of distaste. Hopkins, looking at Nicky, asked questions. Nicky, a true son of Brooklyn, looked at the floor and either shrugged, shook his head, or gave one-word answers. Attaboy, Nicky. Don't tell him shit. After a while Hopkins got tired of it and came back up to the van.

"Well, Mr. Williams," he said, not looking at me, "I'm sorry for taking up yoah time. We've been having a lot of problems with the drug traffic in Washington County. I thought maybe I'd gotten lucky." Hopkins avoided eye contact, looked like he despised apologizing, but someone must have told him he had to do it.

"Drug traffic? You're kidding me."

He shook his head. "Nope. I spend more time on OxyContin than just about anything else."

"Oh, yeah. Hillbilly heroin. I heard of that."

"I wish I hadn't," he said, and a little bit of that short-guy resentment came back into his voice. "Enjoy yoah time in Maine," he said, and one corner of his mouth lifted in what I would consider a sneer. Another time I would have called him on it. I don't like unfinished business. Prison had given me this attitude, you know, you got a problem with me, let's work it out right now. I didn't say anything, though, I swallowed it. You got away with one stupid mistake, I told myself. Don't make another one. Hopkins got back in his cruiser and fired it up, shut off the lights, pulled a U-turn, and drove away. I carried the bags back to the Jeep.

"What a jerk," Louis said when I got back in. Nicky climbed back into my lap.

"Yeah," I said. I was flooded with relief. I didn't care about Hopkins. You've got to be smarter, I told myself. You came this close to losing everything.

Louis went on, oblivious, shouting over the noise of the Jeep. "Ya know, the trouble with a fella like that, ya give him a nickel's worth of authority, right away he wants to hit somebody with it." He squirmed in his seat, warming to his subject. "Bookman says Hop is the smahtest officah he's got, and he might be right about that, but Hop is too much of an ahshole to be walking around with a gun, you ahsk me."

"Who's Bookman?"

"County sheriff. Hoppie married one of the Pottle girls, but he smacked her around once too often and she run off to New Hampshah, left his sorry ahss. Now theyah ain't a female up here with any sense will go out with him, he's gotta do his laundry by hand. Serves him right."

"He said he had to go through all that back there because you guys have been having trouble with drugs. OxyContins, he said."

"Ayuh," Louis said, "well, that much is true. My wife, Eleanor, is on that stuff. It's the only thing will handle the pain spells she gets. Costs me almost two hundred a month. I've bought houses for lower payments than that. And ya practically need an escott when ya got to pick it up, because of how many addicts being so desperate for it. Probably don't cost the drug company squat to make it, either. Anyhow, ya run across Hoppie again, wise man might keep an eye on him. Don't call him Hoppie, neither, unless yo-ah ready to do battle. He don't like it much."

* * *

Louis made a right turn off Route 1 onto a small two-lane road that meandered more or less westward along the bank of something too big to be a stream and too small to be a river. The surface of the water was still, with patches of green lily pads here and there. The forest beetled down close upon the water on the far side, mostly fir and spruce. On the side we were on, the woods were mostly hardwood, the leaves long gone except for the brown oak leaves that were hanging on stubbornly. Here and there you could see an evergreen, stark against the bare branches of its neighbors. Even the trees self-segregate, I thought. They're most comfortable with those like themselves, except for the occasional odd duck who insists on living far away from his relatives.

Louis braked, downshifted to second, and turned up a steep gravel driveway. "I really appreciate your doing this, Louis."

"Nothing to it," he said. "Used to be a motel 'bout fifteen miles noth, but she burnt down a couple yeahs back. Hate to see anybody get stuck, so far away from home, with no place to stay. Besides, you can give me a couple days' rent on the trailah."

"It's a deal."

There was a tall yellow house on the knoll at the top of the driveway, high narrow windows, peeling paint, front porch with no railings, two sheds appended single file to the back of the house, connected to a large barn of weathered gray wood spotted here and there with touches of red paint. You could see through the side of the barn and out the back because some of the siding had been removed and a few of the beams were gone, and the back third of the structure looked like it was thinking about laying down.

Louis opened his door, paused. "Mrs. Avery ain't been out of the house in a long time," he said. "She loves company, other than mine, mowah than just about anything in the world. You'll be doin' me a favor, give her another couple sets of eahs to chew on for a while." He winked at Nicky. "Besides," he said, "yo-ah son ought to get a taste of country living while yo-ah up heah. Do him good."

There was a tall oak tree in the side yard. Two blue jays were flying in and out of it, calling to each other raucously. I took a couple of steps over and watched. I didn't see any other birds, just the jays flapping around and making a racket up where the first big branches of the tree met the trunk, about twenty-five feet from the ground. There was some bird shit around the base of the tree, though, and a little furry gray ball, maybe half the size of a golf ball. Nothing exotic about blue jays, but in my mind they are no less beautiful for being ordinary, brightly colored, opportunistic, fearless, and smart. Louis saw me looking.

"He out?"

"He who?"

"Scritch owl," he said. "Lives in a hole up in that oak. Jays get all upset when he comes out in the daytime." He walked over, shading his eyes and peering up into the tree. "Don't see him," he said, "but he's hard to see, anyhow. Feathers just the color of tree bark, he blends right in. That ought to tell you what business he's in." He kicked at the little gray ball. "Hocked up a bunch of mouse hair and bones." He looked at me and grinned. "That's the way to do her," he said. "Swallow yo-ah dinnah all at once, then just heave up what don't agree with you and be done with it."

Houses inform on their inhabitants. A place long heated by a woodstove will have a particular smell, even in late September when the stove has been cold for six months. It is a comfortable smell, maybe even primal, because I had never experienced it before I walked into Louis's house, but I still knew what it was. She baked bread in there, too, another good smell. Of course, I was assuming it was her that did the cooking, and that she was his wife.

There was a cast-iron Franklin stove right in the center of her kitchen, with a brick chimney standing behind it. Cupboards lined the walls, going from floor to ceiling on three sides. On the fourth side, the one abutting the main part of the house, they only went waist high, topped by a soapstone counter. Eleanor Avery was a compact woman, gray hair pulled straight back, round wire-rimmed glasses, pale skin unadorned by makeup of any kind, strong hands, ice blue eyes. She might have been about sixty, but it was hard to tell. She reserved judgment when she met me but she lit up when she saw Nicky. Louis made introductions, explained about the broken van. "I thought they could use the back bedroom for tonight," he told her. "Too late to bother with the trailah now, but theyah gonna stay for a few days, 'till Gevier gets the cah fixed. Otherwise, he'd have to rent a cah and drive all the way up to Calais. We can move them ovah to the trailah tomorrow."

"Of course," she said, looking over at me, smiling at Nicky. "That trailah's gone empty too long. Nice to have someone use it once in a while. But you'll stay with us tonight. I'll just go make up the bed." She held her hand out to Nicky. "Would you like to come help me?" He was still hanging on to me, doubtful. "After, I'll take you out to see the animals. If your father says it's okay."

"Animals?" He looked up at me with his mouth open, relaxed his grip on my leg.

"You wanna go see the animals?" He let go of me then, went over to her with that look of wonder on his face.

"Why don't you put some coffee on first, Eleanor?" Louis asked.

"I think you can handle that," she said, steel in her voice. "And go turn on the water to the back bathroom."

"Yes, ma'am," Louis said, winking at me. "Right away, ma'am."

"Don't get smaht with me," she said, glaring at him. I couldn't tell if she was serious or not.

Louis winked at me again. "If I'da shot her thirty yeahs ago," he said, "they'da let me back out by now."

Nicky was so excited when they got back that he couldn't stand still. "A hoss!" He started telling me about it at the top of his lungs. "They got a hoss! A great big one! You gotta come see it!"

"No yelling in the house," I told him.

He tried whispering. "They got a hoss, and they got chickens, too, and some cats. Come and see 'em! You gotta come see!"

"How do you know it's a hoss?" I asked him, mimicking his pronunciation. "How do you know it ain't a moose?"

He pointed at Eleanor. "She says it's a hoss. And mooses have horns, silly. Like Bullwinkle."

There was no holding him back. We went through the back door of the kitchen into the shed, and out of the back door of that into the Averys' barn. I am not going to admit to being afraid of horses, okay, but they are way bigger than I am and there's no way of telling what the hell they're thinking. I watched from a safe distance while Eleanor, Nicky, and the horse made friends. It didn't matter anyway, Nicky was so entranced and his enthusiasm was so infectious that neither he nor Eleanor paid any attention to me at all. Louis was right, this was going to be good for Nicky. I was almost glad the damned van had broken down.

And there was something about Eleanor Avery's cooking, too. At least I thought so. Maybe it's just me, but institutional food is institutional food, you know what I mean? It fills the hole, and it'll keep you alive, but it tends to make eating into another chore you have to do before you can go to bed. When I am out on my own, I mostly eat in restaurants or delivery, like Chinese or pizza. Eleanor made a deer-meat stew. I sat there and watched her do it. She took things out of glass jars and mixed them up in a pot, she didn't once look at any kind of recipe, she shook and dusted different spices without seeming to pay any attention to what she was doing, there's no way she could know what this was going to taste like. That's what I thought. I was wrong, though. Like I said, maybe it was me, but that had to be the most amazing meal I had ever eaten.

I washed the dishes, after. She didn't want me to, then she said I could dry, but I didn't know where anything went so I won the argument. Louis told Nicky he thought one of the cats had just had kittens, and that if he could refrain from shouting and stomping around like Jim Kelly's ox they might be able to see them. After the two of them left, Eleanor looked at the tattoos on my forearms. You gotta roll up your sleeves to wash dishes, after all. Tactical mistake.

"He seems like a wonderful child," she told me. "Does he take after his father?"

Smooth, I thought. Nice way to do it. "No, he doesn't. He is a special kid, though."

"His mother, then? Where is his mother?"

"She died when Nicky was two. She had a bad reaction to some medicine she was taking."

"Oh," she said, "I'm sorry. So all he has is you."

I grinned. "Ain't that a thought? But it's true, all he has is me."

She laid a hand on my forearm. "I'm sure you're a great father. What is it that you do, Manny? I hope you don't mind me asking."

"I don't mind. You ought to have some idea what kind of character you got sleeping in your spare bedroom. I work with computer software."

"Is that right? I wanted Louis to get us a computer, but he says no one ever explained to him why he needed one."

"Well, you don't need shoes, either, strictly speaking, but it's a little hard to live without them once you've had a pair."

She laughed. "I can see that," she said. "I guess Louis and I are behind the times." She sounded wistful. I felt myself warming up to her in spite of myself.

"I have a laptop in my bag," I told her. "Would you like to see what the Internet looks like?"

"Oh, I'd love to," she said. "Can you do that from here? Don't you have to do something with the phone company?"

"You guys have a telephone?"

"Yes."

"That's all we need. I don't know how far away the server is, though. Probably not a local call. You think Louis will mind?"

"Oh," she said, "Louis doesn't need to know every little thing that goes on."

She really was a bright woman, she was intuitive, she asked good questions, she had an organized mind, and she wasn't afraid to try new things. I found out she'd been a history teacher, and it wasn't long before she was doing it all by herself, chasing her curious nature all across the Web. Louis and Nicky came in after a while and stood watching us, but neither of them was very interested in what we were doing, and they wandered off to amuse each other some other way. After a couple of hours, Eleanor looked down at her watch.

"Oh my," she said. "I have to stop. My head is spinning." She stood up. "Does this cost a lot of money?"

"Doesn't have to," I told her. "If you don't mind reading ads, all you really have to pay for is the phone service."

"Don't computahs cost thousands of dollars?"

"Hundreds."

"I've got to get this." She looked at me. "Louis is going to be seriously pissed off at you."

A couple of things kept me awake that night. The first one was what I'd seen after Eleanor gave me back the laptop. I logged on to a site in Denmark that permits truly anonymous surfing, and then I looked at the *Daily News* Web site. The Bitch, the woman at the foster home, surprised me. She must have reported Nicky missing, because there was a short item and a picture of him that was probably a year old. He'd had shorter hair, but that face was pretty recognizable. Kids go missing all the time, their faces show up on posters and flyers and milk cartons, and whoever looks at them twice? But Nicky had one of those faces that jump out at you.

There was another story, too, a bigger one, about the Russians and their stock market scam. I didn't really care what happened to the Russians, but there was a line at the end of the story, how a gang had ripped them off just before the SEC got around to shutting them down. Yeah, right. What bothered me was the line about the cops seeking two men for questioning about the holdup. They didn't have names or pictures, so I assumed Rosey was still one step ahead of them. I believe in riding your luck, but I was beginning to feel like I was out on a fine edge, here. And then, just before he fell asleep, Nicky asked me when we were going home. I had a cold shiver run up my spine when he said that. "Home" is one of those loaded words. I never know what to think when I hear it. It's like when someone asks me where I'm from, I'm tempted to tell them I'm from a curb in Williamsburg, down on Broadway, a couple of blocks from the bridge. It's as good an answer as any. Home, like, where do you really belong?

No such place.

I laid there for a while after Nicky fell asleep, but I was feeling antsy, so I eased out of the bed and put my pants back on. He stirred, rolled over, and sighed. I went over and pulled the blanket back up over him, and he seemed to settle back down into sleep. As I looked at him, I wondered what went on inside that head. He put himself in my hands without hesitation, he trusted me in a way I had never trusted anyone in my life.

I grabbed my binoculars, sneaked through the kitchen, and stepped out into the Averys' yard. I closed the door behind me as quietly as I could. He was there when I glassed the oak tree, I could make out his shape among the branches, right where the blue jays had been fussing him out a few hours earlier. He knew I was looking at him, I could swear his head swiveled in my direction as soon as I put the glasses on him. You can't sneak up on a predator that hunts by sound. There's no way I could stay quiet enough for him not to notice me.

He took off then, an unlikely shape in the darkness, ear tufts on a big head, stubby body, short pointed wings. I doubt he was afraid of me. I doubt any predator is truly afraid of a human being. When an animal sits at the top of his food chain, what does he see when he looks at you? You're either too big to eat, not to his liking, or dinner, nothing more. I figured the owl took off because I was making too much noise and spoiling his hunting. I followed the wagon track up the hill behind the Averys' house, past the barn and the fenced-in garden, in the general direction the owl had taken. I wanted to mark him down on my list, but I couldn't, not yet, I had not really seen him, just his outline, just his shadow. I couldn't take Louis's word for what he was, either, that's not the way this thing works. It wasn't that I didn't believe him, it was just that, if you're going to cheat, what's the point?

The wind picked up as I climbed the hill. I turned and looked back. The shape of the buildings came and went in the darkness as the moon played hide-and-seek among the cloud cover. A sudden scattershot of big drops sprayed me as I stood staring. The wind began gusting then, and I could almost see the big trees whirling and dancing just beyond the edge of the field. I knew then that the owl was not going to show himself to me again that night. That's the way it goes sometimes: you get one quick chance, and if you fumble it the moment passes by and is lost. Damn, you think, damn, I had him, I had the bastard but he slipped away, and it's no good going back and writing "eastern screech owl" on your list when you know in your heart he could have been any one of a half dozen different birds.

I turned and continued up the hill. Very quickly Louis's house and barn faded from sight. The wind tore at my jacket and splattered me with raindrops again as though it held something against me personally. "Who are you, you fuck, and what are you doing up here? You better watch your ass. . . ."

The wagon track reached the tree line, and the utter blackness of the night woods stopped me. Where the hell are you going, Manny? What do you really want? I don't know why but right then it seemed like it was the first time I had ever asked myself that. I guess when you spend most of your life running you don't often wonder where you're headed. Something is trying to catch you, either that or something you desperately need is fast receding in the distance and you've got to haul ass, you've got to go right now, shake your moneymaker, Jack, you don't have time to sit mooning.

Nicky had changed all that.

What did I want? I really had no clue. It was almost as if those questions were so foreign to my way of thinking that I had no real way to go about answering them, because I did not understand the underlying premise. Is it really possible, does anyone really sit down and decide, Hey, I want to be a nuclear physicist, and then set about becoming such a thing? How can you when you're already dancing up on the wire, with no net to catch you if you make one mistake? If you go hungry when you can't scare up dinner, next month's rent becomes a long-range goal.

I had been riding that horse for a long time, though. Maybe it really was time for me to get off it, to quit feeling sorry for myself. Making the rent was no longer an issue, the money I had stashed in that Jersey warehouse had kicked financial insecurity off of my list of excuses. Stop thinking like a loser, I told myself. You got to start being a father now, not just a progenitor. If you want Nicky to have a chance, you had better start thinking about growing up yourself.

You could feel the rain coming, the air held a pregnant dampness and the wind was flexing its muscles. I headed back down the hill feeling like a foreigner, like none of the survival tricks that Brooklyn had taught me would serve in this strange place.

3

The little bastard woke me up at five o'clock in the morning.

"Poppy!" he bellowed. I came instantly awake, bolt upright in the bed, my heart pounding as my brain struggled to remember where the hell we were. "Poppy, the hoss!" I might have known. "He's getting away!"

"Jesus Christ."

"Poppeeee . . ."

"No yellin' in the house. Didn't I tell you that already? You probably woke up the whole damn neighborhood." I could hear Louis Avery in another room somewhere, chuckling. "Lemme see," I said, and rolled out of bed and went to kneel next to Nicky in front of the window. The horse was standing in the pasture behind the barn. In the early-morning light it looked cold outside. The storm or squall or whatever it had been had blown on past during the night. At the back of the pasture, right up next to the wagon track I had walked up last night, the storm had ripped a huge tree from the ground, roots and all, leaving a big black gout of exposed earth behind where the tree lay sprawled in the grass. "The horse is not running away, he's eating his breakfast. Did you brush your teeth and wash your face and hands and all that stuff?"

"No." He stood at the window, looking like he wanted to fly right through it, down to the pasture to go visit that stupid horse.

"Well, why don't you go do that? Then we can go look at the horse."

Might as well resign yourself, I thought. No way he's letting you get any more sleep this morning.

Louis met us in the kitchen. "You lost a tree," I told him.

"Red oak," he said. "Seen it when I let the hoss out. Guess I'll have to cut her up for firewood. I was leaving that one, she was too pretty to cut down." He shook his head, looking like he'd lost some old and good friend.

"You need a hand chopping it up?"

"Kind of you to offah," he said. "Let's go take a look." Nicky was over at the window, peering out. "Come on, Nicholas," he bellowed, his voice as loud as Nicky's had been, "come on, let's get going."

I was thinking what a forgiving soul Eleanor Avery must be, all that noise in her house so early in the morning. I paused when I went through the door, looking down at the stairs to the Averys' yard. Some nocturnal drama had played to the sleeping house sometime during the night, leaving three small bloody footprints on the wood of the bottom step. Louis paid them no attention on his way past. Perhaps such markings had been a common occurrence in his life and therefore unworthy of comment, or maybe a guy who spends his life in the country is better acquainted with the base realities of existence and thus accepts as normal things which somebody like me does not, insulated as I have been from the real world by the amazing construct of steel, glass, concrete, and imagination called New York City. In my mind I had, up until that point, divided living beings into four convenient categories: humans, vermin, animals in the zoo, and animals on television. Birds didn't count.

We humans kill each other with numbing frequency. We do it because we are fucked up, deficient mentally or morally or both. We do it because we want the other guy's money, or his wife or his car, or because he made our son sit too long on the bench at Little League, or because he cut in front of us on the highway, or maybe he just pissed us off. Or for the rush, you know, for the hell of it. All of that is common knowledge, publicly reenacted every day, repeated so often that no one bothers to keep score. You have to either target a celebrity or else do something truly gaudy or vile to rate much notice. But that's just us, just the humans, and it's understandable because we are assholes, most of us, rash, ruled by our passions, blinded to our better natures by greed or stupidity. I know that you and I would both like to believe otherwise, but the facts are beyond dispute, really they are, all you have to do is pick up the newspaper.

My problem was, I had always assumed it was only us, that the natural world was better than we were, that peace or at least some kind of coexistence was the rule, that we were an aberration, that life was different, that if we could only open our eyes we would see it, that we could transcend our present travails and animosities, become nobler beings and live as God or Nature had truly intended. But there it was, right under my feet. It was the same old story, history written in the blood of the loser.

Louis came back to see what I was looking at. "Raccoon," he said. "Musta got a chicken." He went off into the barn to look, came out a minute later. "Don't see none missing," he said, shrugging. "You ready to go?"

Avery handled his chain saw like an artist. He hopped up on the trunk and walked its length, holding the saw one-handed and nipping off the small branches. When he got to the end he jumped down and went to work in earnest, filling the air with noise and smoke and small wood chips. Nicky watched from a safe distance, the way I'd told him to, his interest more or less evenly divided between the horse and Avery's chain saw.

Those of us who earn our living sitting on our asses, or even climbing up drainpipes to second-story windows, cannot truly appreciate the physical demands of doing a chore like cutting firewood. I found out that morning that lifting weights and working Nautilus machines is no substitute for wrestling with four-foot sections of tree, bending down, getting one end up in the air, leaning the thing against your shoulder, grabbing the bottom end and standing up, humping the surprising weight over to the truck, laying it down with enough care that it does not punch a big hole in the rusted bed of the truck, grappling over and over with objects supposedly inanimate, but which seem to take sadistic pleasure in ripping the skin from your hands. I got into it, though. I hadn't seen the inside of a gym since a couple of days before I bought the van. It felt good, even though I knew I was going to be sore the next day.

"Son of a ho-ah," Louis said, wiping his forehead and sitting down on the log he'd been cutting. "I can't keep up with you young fellas anymoah. You know how ta handle a standid?"

"A standid? Oh, drive with a clutch. Yeah, sure."

"Wiseahss," he said. "Why don't you run that last load on down the hill while I set here and catch my breath."

Louis's Jeep had no power steering, no synchromesh transmission, and the clutch engaged right at the bottom quarter inch of pedal travel, but I got it down the hill okay. I was shoving the logs off the back when a big Ford pickup about fifty years newer than Louis's turned into his driveway and powered smoothly and silently up the hill. "Calder's Blueberries" was stenciled on the door. A bearish-looking guy got out and ambled over. He was an inch or so shorter than me, but round, with thick black hair on his arms, a barrel chest, ample stomach, Coke-bottle glasses, short black beard, black hair thinning on top. "Sam Calder," he said, reaching out a hand. "You must be Manny."

I must have looked surprised shaking his hand.

"Small towns," he said with a rueful smile. "Word travels fast. We've got nothing better to do, you would think. I heard your car broke down, and that Gevier ordered the parts for it yesterday, and he thinks they'll be here day after tomorrow. And I know you have a little boy with you, whose name is Nicky."

"Jesus."

"Don't think poorly of us for it," he said. "All we have to talk about is each other."

"How come you don't have the accent?"

"I went to Columbia for six years," he said, looking wistful. "I lived on One hundred fifth and Riverside Drive."

"You sound like you miss it."

"Something wicked," he said. "I go back as often as I can manage. At least two weeks a year, that's what it takes to keep me sane." He looked at the pile of four-foot tree sections over by the entrance to the barn. "Louis working up in the woodlot?"

"No," I said. "He's cutting up a tree in the top end of his field, out back there. You need him?"

He nodded. "I have to talk a little business to him."

"You want a ride up?"

He looked at the Jeep. "In that?" He shook his head. "Louis is going to kill himself in that thing someday. He has to be the most stubborn man I've ever met. Suppose we walk."

"All right. Why do you say he's stubborn?"

Calder glanced back at the house, then at me. "He could afford a better truck if he wanted it. I've been trying to get him to come work for me for a good ten years. A regular job, with a steady paycheck. He's a smart guy, he's dependable, resourceful, just the kind of man you'd want to put in charge of, say, plant maintenance. He won't hear of it, though. He would rather scratch for a living on his own, you know, cut pulp logs and Christmas trees, rake blueberries, dig clams, put a new roof on somebody's barn once in a while. He works his ass off when he can find something profitable to do, and he starves the rest of the time. No pension, no health insurance, and he drives that wreck of a Jeep. Grows most of his own food, shoots deer out of season. . . . It's his life, I suppose, but Eleanor deserves better. Not that anyone asked me. He'd be much better off working for me, though, and I could really use him."

We started up the hill. "You come out to make another pitch?"

"Nah. Waste of breath. No, he owns a piece of property up in Eastport, and I've been trying to get him to sell it to me."

"That right?"

"Yeah. My father's trying to buy it to put together a development deal, and I don't want it to go through. We don't need any more damned industry up here. You want to live around developments, you should move to the city." He glanced at me. "I don't mean to bore you with local gossip."

"That's all right. You think Louis will sell to you?"

Calder shook his head. "Louis Avery is a stubborn, stubborn man.

Actually, I don't care that much if he sells it to me or not. I just want to make sure he doesn't sell it to my father."

Louis was still sitting down on what was left of the tree, the bottom part of the trunk that had gone from the ground up to where the first branches had split off. It looked too big to cut, but I didn't think Louis would leave it there to rot. Just because I didn't know how to get the thing whacked into pieces small enough to burn in his woodstove didn't mean that he couldn't do it.

"Hello, Louis."

"Hi, Sam. How are you."

"Finestkind," said Sam. I assumed he was trying to sound indigenous. "I hope I'm not interrupting your work."

"No, no," Louis told him. "The boy's got me worn right down to the nub. A man shouldn't have to work this hard before he's even had his breakfast. I guess it takes a lot of wood to heat Noo Yok City. What can I do for you?"

Calder heaved a sigh. "I think my father's getting ready to make you another offer. You know I don't want him to go through with this, Louis. Between you and me, I want to match whatever he offers you."

"That right? Manny, you and Nicky want to go have some breakfast? I might have to slap old Sam around a little here, and it won't be pretty to watch."

Calder looked at me and rolled his eyes.

"C'mon, Nicky, let's go eat."

Eleanor was looking out her kitchen window at Sam Calder's truck, clucking her tongue. "Good morning," I said. "I hope Nicky didn't wake you up too early this morning."

"Oh, no," she said. "I was awake. Is Sam junior up there yammering at Louis about that damned field up to Eastpoht again?"

"Yeah. Says he doesn't want him selling to his father."

"Everyone has an opinion," she said. "I wish they would just leave us alone about it." She looked at Nicky. "Dear, would you like some breakfast? Do you like bacon and eggs?"

Nicky nodded. "Yeah," he said.

"You mean 'Yes, please,' " I told him.

"Huh?"

"Say 'Yes, please.' "

He looked at me, mystified. "Yes, please."

"Not to me, I'm not cooking your breakfast."

"Oh." He looked at Eleanor. "Yes, please."

"Why don't you have a seat right over at the table," she said to him. "Manny, would you like some coffee?"

"I'd love it." I saw Nicky give me a look. "I mean, yes, please." I felt a little weird about her waiting on me, though. Here I was, with my son, mooching off two people so broke that their only transportation was a horse and a Jeep about twenty years older than me, but there didn't seem to be much I could do about it right then. Eleanor handed me a cup of coffee.

"Milk and sugar?"

"No, this is fine, thanks."

She looked out the window at Calder's pickup truck. "That Sam," she said. "He sure is windy."

"You figure he's making any headway?"

She shook her head. "You can't talk Louis into doing something he doesn't want to do." She turned back to her stove. The sounds and smells of bacon and eggs cooking began to fill up the kitchen. "Sam's father wants to build an oil terminal up in Eastpoht," she said. "Up on the bay. He wants to unload tankers. Got some refinery company interested. It would mean work, so there's a lot that would like to see it happen. It's hahd to make a living this far up, you know. Most of the children who grow up here have to leave when they get out of school, go off and get a job somewhayah else. But if they build it, they would have to put in a big tank fahm, and pipelines and so on. There'd be big trucks hauling oil out of there all hours, and that would mean noise, and pollution. A lot of folks think that it would ruin everything, spoil the town and the bay, both. Tourists might stop coming, not that we get flooded with them now. But why would you drive all the way up heah to see oil tanks and whatnot? Anyhow, they can't build if Louis doesn't sell. And believe me, we could use the money, but neither of us wanted to be in the position of making the decision about whether or not the terminal gets built. That's what it seems to boil down to, though."

"Do you think they should build it?"

"I don't know." She thought about it while she flipped eggs. "Hahd to watch yo-ah children leave, go off to the city. You only get to see them once or twice a year. . . . But you know if they build the terminal, it'll be up on that ridge spoiling the view and stinking up the breeze for the next hundred years. Think of all the people who would go by and curse whoever put it there. I can't imagine that would do your karma much good."

"So why not sell it to Sam junior? He says he doesn't want to see any development."

"What Sam junior doesn't want is development that he doesn't have his fingers into," she said. "This isn't about development anyhow, not with him. He wants to get control of the Calder family trust away from his father, so he'll do anything he can to put some stones in the road. As soon as Sam senior is cold in the ground, Sam junior will start building something up theyah to make himself moah money. Might not be an oil terminal, but it would probably stink just as bad."

Eleanor poured two more cups of coffee when Louis and Sam junior came tramping through the kitchen door. "Oh, I can't stay," Sam said, but he took the cup anyhow. He shook his head. "My father is going to be apoplectic."

"You work for your father?" I was surprised, given that they seemed to be at cross-purposes.

"I work with him," Sam said. I could see Louis suppressing a grin. "It's a family business. We were going to call it a co-op, but it's more like an unco-op. He hates it when I'm late."

"He don't like it much when yo-ah on time," Louis said.

"Louis," Eleanor said with a warning tone in her voice.

"Yeah, yeah," Louis said. Nicky giggled.

"Listen," I said, to nobody in particular. "Is there a car-rental outfit up here someplace? If I'm going to be here for a few days, I'd kind of like to be mobile."

"Nope," Sam said. "Not if you're talking about something like Hertz rent-a-car. If you ride up to Lubec with me, though, I can fix you up. I'm sure the guy who takes care of our vehicles has something you can use, if I ask him."

"I would appreciate that. You don't use Gevier?"

"No. Nothing wrong with him, it's just that he's too far south. Lubec is north of here, Gevier's place is south. He's a good mechanic, though. You don't need to worry about your car." He took a slug of coffee and handed the cup back to Eleanor. "Thanks, Eleanor, I really have to go."

"You sure you won't stay for breakfast, Sam? I'm cooking for Louis anyhow, I'd be happy . . ."

He grinned at her. "You love to cause trouble, don't you?"

"Well, I don't get out much," she said. "I have to take advantage of whatever oppahtunities come my way."

"I'll give my father your regards."

Nicky stayed behind. He wanted to come along at first, but I was no match for Louis's horse, and his cats and his chickens. I tried to remember what I had been like at Nicky's age, but I couldn't. I couldn't have been like Nicky, though. He was more adept socially at five than I was at twenty-eight. Maybe something had happened to set me back, I don't know. No profit in sweating about it now.

Sam junior was a deliberate driver. He kept near the speed limit, came to a full stop at intersections, waited for oncoming traffic to clear. He did talk to me almost the whole trip, too. I was beginning to understand what Eleanor had meant when she called him "windy." And in a funny way, he talked almost as though I weren't there, not in any real sense. It was like he didn't need me, he just needed a pair of ears, so I didn't pay much attention to what he was saying, I just made appropriate noises once in a while.

The trip took about thirty-five minutes. We passed a small airport, then some houses, and then the outskirts of a town, where the dwellings ran a little closer to one another, together with a post office, liquor store, grocery, VFW hall. Just when I thought we were just about to reach the downtown, the center of the place, the Atlantic Ocean cut it off, as though it had slashed the bigger half off of some larger, livelier, and more prosperous town, leaving the smaller, quieter section standing. What passed for a downtown was really only one long block butted up against the waterfront. There was a large island a hundred yards or so offshore, and the water ran hard enough in the rock-lined channel between to make you think twice, look down at your feet and make sure they stayed safely back on the sidewalk. You fell in, you'd be halfway to England before you could even yell for help. Calder's office was in a stately old Victorian a block off the town's main drag. Sam junior parked his pickup out front.

The offices of Calder's Blueberries were decorated in tasteful shades of powder blue and gray. A woman sat behind a desk, talking on a telephone. She looked blankly at me, waved to Calder. Just then a door in the back burst open and a short old guy came fuming out. He looked like he'd been pickled in his own malevolence. He had a small pot stomach, and when he stood with his hands on his hips he thrust it forward belligerently, along with his chin. "You couldn't leave it alone, could you. You had to go out there."

"I don't want to have this debate again," Sam junior said.

"Goddammit, Sam! I'm trying to do something to build this company back up again, and this community, and instead of helping me out, you stab me in the back." He turned on his heel, took two steps back toward his office, turned back again. "What a piece of shit you turned out to be." He turned again, stomped back where he'd come from, slammed the door behind him.

Calder looked at me. "My father," he said, looking bleak. "My father. Come on, let's go get you that car."

"Roscoe, you seen Hobart?" Roscoe, Sam junior had told me, was a French Canadian guy who worked at Hobart's garage. Roscoe was exploring the mysteries of a Holly four-barrel that he had sitting on a workbench. He was a dark-haired guy, five eight or so, and solid, looked like he was ready to fight you. He looked up from what he was doing, a wide grin on his face. He reminded me of Teddy Roosevelt because you couldn't be sure if he was smiling, grimacing, or just showing you his teeth. "Over da smokehouse, maybe," he said. "De old man call over here. Look for you, aye?"

"He got me already," Sam said sorrowfully.

"Someday," Roscoe said. "Someday you ask him if his pee-pee reach his asshole, aye?"

"You think I ought to tell him to go fuck himself?"

"He wait for dat, I tink." Roscoe shook his head slowly, still grinning, or showing his teeth, or whatever it was he did. His accent was much different than the down east accent. "Dat old man too mean to die," he said, "too old to fight, too ugly to fuck. I tink you maybe stuck wit him. Check over da smokehouse, I tink Hobart over dere."

The smokehouse was across the street on a wooden pier that stuck out into the vicious currents of what was called Passamaquoddy Bay. The back of it was a long red barn-looking thing with vents in the roof, and the front was small, no bigger than one room, white clapboards, and cedar shingles on the roof. We stopped on the sidewalk to let a single car pass by. Whoever it was driving waved to Sam, and he waved back.

"Hobart own the smokehouse, too?"

"Yep. Maine multitasking. Most men up here have to wear a lot of different hats to make one living. There's not enough business to be just one thing."

The door to the white building was unlocked, but there was nobody inside. We went back out and around to the smokehouse. There was a row of low, door-sized openings that ran along the length of the place, and there were piles of sawdust on the floor inside, smoldering. Rows of wooden poles bridged the upper part of the place, and what I found out later were herring fillets hung from the poles. They averaged about eight inches in length and were a dark, dark brown, almost black color. Calder stuck his head into one of the openings. "Hobart!" he yelled. "You in there?"

A tall guy with unruly white hair stepped out of the far end of the smokehouse. He was taller than me, maybe six three or so, broader through the shoulders than I am, and sinewy, made you think of a lifetime of hard work and exposure. He wore suspenders to keep his pants up, probably because his bony ass didn't have enough shape to give a belt any purchase. He had an air about him—maybe it was the sparse white beard, the kind old guys grow when they're bored with shaving, or maybe it was the wrinkled shirt, the unkempt hair, or just the look on his face, but I would have bet you then and there that this guy was beyond caring, that everybody who'd loved him was gone. He was just playing out the hand.

"Right heah," he said. "No need yellin'."

"Hobart." Sam turned in his direction and started telling him how my van was broken down, how I was staying out at the Averys' and needed a car for a few days. Hobart walked up, stuck his hand out, and I shook it. It felt like I had a handful of what I'd spent the morning wrestling out of Louis Avery's pasture, rough, no inner warmth of its own, covered with hard bark. He didn't squeeze in that adolescent way that some guys do, but I got the feeling he was taking my measure somehow, and more out of habit than interest.

"How's my old friend Louis?" It struck me as an odd question to ask, in a place so small. How could you avoid running over the guy every other day?

"Seems fine to me. You want me to say hello for you?"

Hobart chuckled. "Long as you can do it when Eleanor ain't around. She thinks I'm a bad influence."

"That so?"

"Ayuh," Hobart said. "Tell the Frenchman to give you the Brat."

It was a Subaru Brat, sort of a miniature pickup truck, fiercely rusted and seriously cramped for a guy my size. I wondered if Hobart had chosen it out of some sadistic impulse, but Roscoe told me the thing was the most dependable piece of shit they had. It started with a roar and ran raggedly, stood there on the lot in front of Hobart's garage and quivered like a dog who'd been in cold water too long. Roscoe told me, while we waited for it to warm up, that his band was going to be playing at the VFW that night, and that I was invited. Sam Calder made his way back over to his office to resume the cockfight with his old man. You assume, when you're on the outside looking in, that families tend to be, you know, love, caring, mutual support, all that shit. Maybe not exactly the Brady Bunch, but everybody on the same side, at least. Right then I got an image of Sam and his father: two cats with their tails tied together, thrown over a tree branch. No matter what their motivations, they would only continue to slash at each other, each unable to help either himself or the other guy. How do you get into something like that? Was I, even now, taking the steps that would lead to Nicky and me being thrown across that same branch?

Jesus.

Roscoe seemed genuinely pleased when I told him I'd probably see him at the VFW.

All the other drivers waved at me on the way back to the Averys'. I mean, all of them. They did it in the minimalist way Mainers have, nothing very demonstrative, just a quick flash of one open hand. Hobart's vehicle, it seemed, had given me entrance into some private club, and even though they were probably waving to the Subaru and not to me, I found myself waving back, Hey, how are you, hello, whoever you are. It got me in the habit of looking at whoever was riding inside the cars, not just at the outside of the vehicles. These were people out here, individuals, not just cars in my way, slowing me down.

I took a wrong turn somewhere on my way back to Louis's house. I knew right away that I was on the wrong road, because the stream was missing. I didn't turn around, though, I followed the road as it twisted and turned past what I assumed were abandoned farms. There weren't any farmhouses, just a decaying wooden shed here and there, and fields of tall yellow grass banded by rock walls. It was impressive, in a sort of melancholy way, because of the sheer volume of backbreaking labor it must have taken to build those walls. Some poor bastard busted his ass for what had to be decades to hump the rocks out of his fields, and now the fields were empty and untended. In some places the woods had taken over, the stone walls ran through stands of trees, and not skinny ones, either, these were mature, thick at the bottom. I didn't know how long it took to grow a tree that big. A hundred years? More? And the poor son of a bitch that cleared the fields to begin with, built those walls, wrestled his living from that hard ground, he was long gone, dead, forgotten, nameless, while the fucking rocks endured. Didn't seem fair.

A truck came around the curve in front of me, a pale green GMC pickup truck with oversized tires, looked like a '74 or '75, two teenagers in it. The kid driving it was going way too fast and using most of the road, so both he and I were very busy for a couple of seconds. It was a good thing the Subaru was on the small side—there was room for it in the ditch. The GMC's horn bleated at me, and I jerked the Subaru back on the road, none the worse for wear, it appeared. I looked in the rearview mirror just in time to see the pickup round the corner behind me and vanish from sight.

Stupid kids.

It was hard to stay mad at them for too long, though, because I wasn't that far removed from being a stupid kid myself.

A few miles farther on, I slowed down, began looking for a place to turn around. That's when I saw the guy. He was huge, bigger than me, bigger than Rosario even. He had straight black hair, sloping shoulders, sleepy eyes. It was hard to tell his age, I would have guessed early twenties. He was carrying a bicycle under one meaty arm. The front wheel of the bike was badly bent, some of the spokes were broken off, and the rubber tire hung loose from the metal rim. I pulled over to the side of the road, intending to ask directions, and the guy looked down at the ground, not at me. I rolled the window down. "Hey, buddy. How you doing?"

He glanced at me, just a quick flick of his eyes, then he looked back at the ground and shrugged his shoulders. I wished that Nicky were with me, I was no good at this shit. Nicky would crack this guy open in a second, he'd hop out of the car. . . . I shut off the Subaru and got out, held out my hand. "Hi, my name is Manny."

He looked at my hand for a second or so before reaching out slowly with his big mitt. "Manny?" His voice rumbled deep in his throat.

"That's me. What's your name?"

"Franklin." He was still looking at my hand, or maybe the tattoos on my forearm, not my face.

"Is that your bicycle, Franklin?"

He looked at the bike, nodded slowly.

"What happened to it?"

He glanced back over his shoulder then, back in the direction he'd come from. "Pickup truck," he said, looking back at the ground again. "Scared me off the road."

"Well, that's a hell of a thing."

"Don't cuss," Franklin said. "Cussing isn't nice."

"You're right, Franklin, I apologize. So what happened when you went off the road? You hit a rock?"

"Tree."

"That's too bad. Messed your bike up, but you can fix that. Did you get hurt?"

"Just my ahm."

"Let me see. Can I see your arm, Franklin?"

He set his bike down, leaned it against his leg, held his other arm up for my inspection. His denim sleeve was shredded, and he had some road rash on his hairy forearm, it was scratched up pretty good, with blood seeping through in places.

"That doesn't look too bad, Franklin. Just a little scrape. Let's put your bike in the back of my truck here, and I'll give you a ride home."

It took him a long time to answer, like he had to think of the words one by one, line them up in a row before he spoke. "My dad says I'm not supposed to take rides from anybody."

"Well, your dad sounds pretty smart. How about if we call him up? Do you know his phone number?" Franklin shook his head. "How about your number at home?" Same response. "Well, this is kind of an emergency, Franklin. I'm sure your dad would think it was all right." He looked doubtful. "I'll drive, okay, but you can tell me which way to go. How about that?"

He looked down at the bike, thought about it. "All right," he said.

I took the bike from Franklin and put it in the back of the Subaru. He squeezed himself into the passenger side, and it was a tight fit. The first time he tried to slam the door, it thunked him in the ass and didn't latch. He sighed, hitched himself over as far as he could, and tried again, with more success. He looked uncomfortable as hell. "Roll your window down if you want, Franklin. It might give you more room."

He looked at the window crank by his right knee. "Okay."

"Which way to your house?"

He was looking at the floor, but he pointed over his shoulder with his thumb. "Other way," he said.

Franklin must have gotten around pretty good on his bicycle, because it was something like six miles to his house. It was your basic suburban raised ranch, I don't know who came up with the design but you see them everywhere. There was a Ford station wagon parked in the gravel driveway. I couldn't tell the year of the wagon, but it was from back when they were making them the size of Noah's ark. A small dog with short, curly gray hair ran around in circles, barking at the two of us. Franklin lumbered out, ignored the dog, and stood by while I got his bike out of the Subaru. He took the bike from me and carried it over to the side of the house. He tried to make it lean on the kickstand, but it wouldn't, because of the bent rim. He fussed with it for a minute, then sighed, gave up, and laid it down in the grass.

The front door to the house opened and a woman came out. She was short and sort of round, and her hair was the same color as Franklin's. She looked afraid—her eyes were wide, and she clutched her hands together in front of her. She was much smaller than Franklin, who was out of sight around the side of the house. "Can I help you?" The dog ran over to where she was standing, barked at her, too.

"Franklin had a little accident."

He came around the corner just then, stopped, glanced at her, then at me, and shook his head. He seemed to know that the aftermath was going to be worse than the event.

"Franklin! What happened?"

"I hit a tree, Ma."

She sucked in a big breath, hustled down the steps, and went over to him. "You hit a tree? Oh, my God. How did that happen?"

He didn't seem to want to tell her the story. He shrugged. "Went off the road. Hit a tree."

"Franklin, you're going to be the death of me, you worry me so much." She had that sixth sense mothers have, in a half a second she was looking at his arm, holding it up to the light, shaking her head and clucking in consternation. "Go on in the house and take that shirt off. I'll be right in to clean that up."

"It's just a little scrape, Ma." He glanced at me when he said it, and I thought I saw a little bit of amusement on his face.

His mother wasn't having any. "Go on, now." The dog finally got her attention, and she snapped. "Scruffy, shut up!" The dog stopped barking, finally, but he growled and showed me his teeth when he looked at me, as if to say, I may be afraid of her, pal, but I ain't afraid of you.

"All right." Franklin ambled over to me, stuck out a huge mitt. "Thanks for the ride, Manny."

"You're welcome, Franklin," I said, shaking his hand. I winked at him. Out of the corner of my eye I could see his mother watching me in disbelief. "You take care of yourself now, okay?"

"Okay." He let go of my hand, took a step toward the house, and stopped. "You take care of yourself, too."

"Thanks, I will."

His mother watched him go through the front door. "He must like you," she said, looking at the front door, shaking her head. "Honestly, I'm so surprised. Normally he's so shy, he never talks to strangers. He hardly talks to the people he knows. Thank you so much for bringing him home. Did you see the accident?"

"No. He was walking down the road, carrying his bike, and I stopped."

"Where did it happen? Do you mind me asking?"

"I don't mind at all, but I can't tell you where it was. I could show you, I guess, if I could find my way back there. I was actually going to ask him for directions. I'm staying with the Averys, and I took a wrong turn. I don't know the name of the road. It's five or six miles away from here."

"He worries me so much," she said. "Can I ask you to come in, Mr. . . . ?"

"Manny Williams. No, thanks, I think I really need to get back."

"You're staying with Eleanor and Louis?"

"Yes."

She came over and squeezed my hand. "Thank you again, Mr. Williams. You don't know how much I appreciate this."

Louis wasn't there when I got back to the Averys' house. Eleanor said he'd had to go off to fix a broken toilet at someone's summer camp. She told me the place was owned by some people who lived down in Massachusetts, and one of Louis's gigs was taking care of the place for them. She looked a little frazzled telling me this. "He was going to go open Gerald's place up for you," she said, "but that might have to wait until tomorrow, if you don't mind."

"Are you kidding? Of course I don't mind. Would you like me to take Nicky out for a ride somewhere, get him out of your hair for a while?"

"He does have a lot of energy," she said, and she sighed. "I guess I'm not as young as I used to be."

"I'll try to wear him out a little bit. Do you know a good place we could go?"

"Oh, sure," she said. "Would you mind picking up a pound of coffee for me while you're out?"

I followed Eleanor's directions to a lake up in the woods about fifteen miles west of the house. You had to follow some dirt roads to get there, and the last one wasn't even a dirt road, just a grassy set of tire ruts under the overarching trees. I would never have attempted it in a car, or at all, I suppose, if Eleanor hadn't assured me we wouldn't be trespassing on anyone who cared. "The timber companies own everything up in there," she'd told me. She dosed Nicky and me with bug repellent before we left. "Might be a few blackflies still around," she said. "And they don't suck blood, either. They eat meat."

The only thing that kept me from chickening out that last half mile was the knowledge that I'd have to back all the way out because there was no place to turn around. Finally, the track opened up into a clearing, just as she'd told me it would. You could see where other vehicles had parked in the grass, although there weren't any there now. On the far side of the clearing an opening in the trees showed you the lake, sunlit blue and beautiful, unspoiled, it seemed to me, because there were no houses or cabins, no boats, even. There was a trail that meandered between the trees along the shoreline, though. Eleanor said you could follow it all the way around, though she herself had never done so.

Nicky was hesitant. I walked around, opened the door for him. "Whose . . ." He looked around. "Who lives here?"

"Nobody. This is like the park. People can come here and walk around if they want to. Mrs. Avery said so."

"She did?"

"Yep."

"All right." He jumped out.

"You forgot the book. Do you want to carry it, or do you think it will be too heavy?"

"I can do it," he said, and I reached in and got it for him.

We spent a couple of hours there. For a while I tried to teach him how to use the binoculars to look at things, and he tried to do it, but I think he was really too young for it, and he was probably looking through them mostly just to shut me up, so I stopped trying to teach him and just let him explore in his own way.

The most amazing thing about the place, to me, was the utter silence. I guess I'd never experienced such a thing before, never heard it. In Brooklyn, where I grew up, there's always noise, all day and all night, all year long. You get so you don't notice it, you tune out the cars, planes flying overhead, people shouting, talking, laughing, music coming from a radio somewhere, always and forever. Up here the only human noises were the ones Nicky and I made walking through the leaves. Everything else was the wind or the animals. A crow, once, staccato, yelling for his friends, the breeze banging empty tree branches together, something chirring softly in the brush. I didn't know if it was some kind of a bird or maybe a raccoon or squirrel. I tried to see it, but it was too shy for me, whatever it was. There were some ducks on the far side of the lake, a couple of overloaded barges in miniature, riding low in the water. I thought they might be loons, but they were too far away for me to be sure without the spotting scope. I was too distracted anyhow, watching Nicky. Come back, I told myself, come back and look for them another day.

"You ever hear of Daniel Boone?" I asked him.

"No," he said. I made up a story about Daniel Boone and told it to him. I left out the ugly parts, him and the Indians shooting at each other, Boone's inner knowledge that white guys were gonna follow him there and take it all away, cut down the trees to make room for houses, roads, and all the shit that comes after. He must have hated it, that had to be the reason he was out there on the hard edge, he had to know that time and civilization were going to spoil it all. I left all that out of the fairy tale I told Nicky. I just told him about the explorer wearing deerskins, the first guy to come looking, who never got lost.

When I was about Nicky's age I was in this foster home for a while, the guy living there had a lot of books. That was where I found out about Daniel Boone. I have always had problems sleeping, and they would turn off the television at a certain hour and make you go to bed. I would cop a book, hide it under my pillow, and then pretend to be sleeping until they all went to bed. Then I would lie awake reading by the faint glow of the hallway light. Reading became my first addiction. It was my first, and maybe best, escape. It's magic, when you think about it, how some dusty artifact made of paper and dried ink can transport you off to Skull Island, or out to the purple-tinged plains of the Southwest. It's very seductive, you know. I got caught up in it, and I have never really recovered. Anyplace but here, right? Any life but mine.

It's the same thing that makes me look at real estate every time I go someplace new. What would it be like? What if I did not live where I do, what if I were not who I am? I kept picturing log cabins back in the woods while I watched Nicky play by the water's edge, and it was that same old thing, you know, that itchy discontent, that restless spirit inside, always asking What if? Life seemed so much easier back when I had nothing, because back then it didn't matter what I did, nobody gave two shits, least of all me. But now life, or nature, or God, if you prefer, some cruel spirit had given me Nicky, suddenly I wanted things I had never cared about before, and the castles of my imagination seemed far beyond my poor capabilities. I wondered then if every parent feels this way, if even old man Calder might not be skewered on this same spit, roasted over these same slow flames. I could picture what I wanted for my son in a thousand variations, not for me, God, really. . . . But in all my capacity for fantastical thinking I could not picture any of it coming to pass.

Nicky got tired, finally. I was beginning to think that would never happen, either, but it did. I had to carry him back out, but he insisted on hanging on to the book, and we hung the binoculars around his neck so I wouldn't have to carry them, too. The only weight I felt was Nicky, and I was happy to bear him back to the clearing where I had parked the Subaru. That, at least, was something I knew how to do.

It probably won't come as a complete shock to find out that I don't like cops. Part of it, I suppose, is just an occupational bias, but you have to admit that it is difficult to like a guy whose job largely consists of driving around looking for someone to fuck with.

I should have passed the place up when I saw the police cruiser parked out front, but I remembered Eleanor had asked me to get her some coffee, and the little convenience store was the only place I'd seen on the way to the lake that looked like it was open. I didn't want to have to drive all the way to the grocery store up in Lubec, so I pulled in.

It was Hopkins, the same guy who'd searched the minivan. He'd parked out in front of the place, next to the gas pumps, and he was out of the car, having an earnest conversation with some female, although it wasn't really a conversation. He was talking, she was listening, white-faced. Nicky and I got out and went into the store. Hopkins glanced in my direction, but he gave no sign that he recognized me. I got Eleanor's coffee, and then I wandered around in the place for a while, picking out stuff I thought the Averys might need. I took my time, figuring I would stall until Hopkins left. They didn't have carts in the place, so I just kept carrying stuff up to the counter and giving it to the girl working the register. She didn't say anything to me, she just rang it up, but she was watching Hopkins and the woman outside by the gas pumps. Nicky got tired of following me around, I guess, and I lost track of where he was. I finished, finally, and watched the girl putting all the stuff into plastic bags. She didn't look at me, though. She was more interested in the soap opera unfolding outside.

"Friend of yours?" I asked her.

She nodded once, leaned forward. "Hopkins is a pig," she said, keeping her voice low. "Brenda never should have went out with him."

Just then I felt Nicky pulling at my pant leg. He had some kind of intuition, he always knew when someone else was in trouble or hurting. You can make something out of that if you want. All I know is, the pains he had endured in his short life had given him some kind of special antenna.

"Poppy," he said. "That policeman outside is hitting that lady. Make him stop."

Nicky was right. Hopkins had the woman backed against the cruiser, and as the girl behind the cash register and I watched, he grabbed the woman by the hair and whacked her head against the car. He did it very quickly—if I hadn't been watching for it, I might have missed it.

"Poppy," Nicky said. "You have to make him stop. He's hurting her." I looked down at him, thinking that he had a purer sense of right and wrong than I did, mine being polluted by years of thievery and an overdeveloped instinct for self-preservation. The girl behind the counter made a frightened squeak and picked up her telephone, dialed 911. "Don't worry," Nicky told her. "My dad can take that guy."

The sound of Hopkins yelling came right through the plate-glass windows. Nicky pulled my pant leg again. "Poppeeee . . ."

I looked at the girl. "Watch my kid, okay?" She nodded, holding the phone to her ear, waiting for someone to answer. I looked down at Nicky. "You stay right here, you understand me?"

"Okay," he said.

I took two of the bags of groceries and carried them outside, put them in the back of the Subaru. Hopkins stopped when he saw me. I leaned on the back of the truck. I remembered the nickname that Louis Avery had said Hopkins hated. "No, go ahead, Hoppie," I said. "I want to see how you do it. Maybe I'll learn something."

Hopkins's face turned a furious red. "Go on back in the store. Mind your own business."

"Yeah? You want me to watch from inside?"

He was so mad his whole body was shaking. He half turned in my direction, and the woman he had up against the car flinched, as though she were going to run away. He was quick, though, he spun back and held his finger out at her. She froze.

"C'mon, Hoppie, this is stupid. You can't do your business out on the street."

He turned completely toward me then, took a step in my direction. "Goddam you! Go on and leave me alone!" The woman behind him saw her chance and made a break for it, but Hop was way faster than she was, he had her before she'd gotten four steps. He dragged her back and threw her up against the car.

I applauded. Hopkins froze at the sound of me clapping. "Way to go, Hop. Be careful, though. You don't want to mark her up. Might bust a finger that way, too. You got to hit 'em in the soft parts." The woman held her hands up to her face and began to sob loudly. Hopkins let go of her and dropped his hand, and his shoulders slumped. "Go ahead, Hoppie. Show her you're a man."

"Oh, shit," he said to her, ignoring me. "I'm sorry. Oh, Jesus, Brenda, I'm sorry. . . . Brenda, come on. Stop. Brenda . . ."

"Go fuck yourself, Hop," she said, but she said it without any heat. She pushed herself away from the car and stomped off into the store. Hopkins made no move to stop her.

Maybe I shouldn't have rubbed it in. "That was fucking pitiful, man."

That reignited him, and he walked slowly in my direction, his hand fluttering down by his pistol and his face twisted in anger. "Get over theyah," he said, his voice low and vicious, "and put yoah hands on the hood."

I was still leaning on the Subaru, and I didn't move. "I don't think so, Hop." He took another step in my direction, put his hand on the holstered gun. He looked like he was going to burst. "What are you gonna do, asshole, shoot me?" I pointed at the store, where the two women, and my son, were watching through the glass. "You got three people watching, you moron. Besides, you're too close. Don't they teach you country-ass hillbilly cops anything at all? I could break your fucking arm before you ever cleared your piece."

"Is that what you think, you son of a hoah?" He was so pissed off he could barely spit the words out. "Is that what you think?" He took a step back away from me, took his hand off the gun, unbuckled his belt. "You think I fucking need this?" We both heard the siren then, faint in the distance, and he knew it was over. The air seemed to go out of him, and he turned away from me, walked over slowly, and stood with his head down, over by his car.

The other cop shut his siren off before he got to us and coasted to a stop with a minimum of drama. He got out of his car and stood there, looking from me to Hopkins, and then he saw the two women inside the store. He was a tall guy who looked to be in his early fifties, he was on the heavy side, with bland gray eyes in a mild face, and thinning brush-cut hair. I think he had it all doped out before anybody said a word, or maybe the cashier had told the dispatcher what was happening. He opened the back door of his car, gestured to Hopkins. Hoppie walked over wordlessly and got in, and the guy shut the door on him. He looked over at me. "Who might you be?"

"Manny Williams."

"Could I see yaw drivah's license, Mr. Williams?"

"Yeah, sure." I got it out and handed it to him, but he only glanced at it and gave it back. The guy had the down east accent, but it was slightly different from the one I'd been hearing from everybody else.

"That yaw boy, in the sto-ah?"

"Yeah."

He looked over to where Nicky and the two females were still watching, and he sighed. "Would you mind waiting heah for a few minutes, Mr. Williams?"

"Not at all."

"Thank you," he said, and he walked over and went into the store. Nicky tensed up, and when the cop went through the door he came tearing out. He ran over to me and grabbed on to my leg. The cop stood inside and watched, then turned and started talking to the two women. I could feel Nicky shaking as he held on to me. He pulled at my sleeve, and I leaned over so he could whisper in my ear.

"Poppy," he said. "Did they come to take me back?"

"No," I told him. "Nobody's taking you away from me. Shh, now."

He wasn't finished. "Are they gonna put you in jail?"

"No, shhh. Nobody's going to jail. That guy over there just lost his temper, that's all." This is all I need, I thought. I'm gonna get ratted out by my own kid. "Look, I want you to sit in the car and stay out of trouble, okay?" I walked him over to the Subaru, and he reluctantly got in the passenger side.

"You're coming back, right?"

"I'm not going anywhere, you can watch me the whole time. Now just sit there and be quiet, okay? Can you do that?"

He nodded, and I closed him in, went back to where I had been standing. Inside, the cop had teamed up with the girl who'd been working the cash register, and they were both working on the other female, but she had her face in her hands and she was shaking her head, no, no, no. . . . They kept at it for a long time, but they couldn't break her down. Eventually the cop gave up, left her there, and came back out to talk to me.

"Mistah Williams," he said.

"Manny."

He nodded. "Manny. My name is Taylor Bookman, and I'm the sheriff of this county. I appreciate yaw patience."

"That's okay."

"I apologize for the actions of my deputy ovah theyah, Thomas Hopkins."

"That's all right, Mr. Bookman, I—"

He was shaking his head. "No," he said, "it isn't all right. This is not the first time this has happened, but that fool girlfriend of his refuses to press chahges. Again. That kind of ties my hands, Manny." Bookman talked very slowly, and his deadpan expression never changed. He looked at the groceries in the back of the Subaru, and then at Nicky. He's taking it all in, I thought. Filing it away. I made a mental note not to let Bookman's verbal slowness lull me into thinking he was a dope. You better watch your mouth around this guy.

"Thing is," he went on, at his unhurried pace, "Hop is a very bright young man. He's done some good work with the kids up heah, and that has helped the depahtment make some inroads on our drug problem. I know it might be hahd for you to appreciate right now, but he is a good man, when he isn't thinking with his glands. He has got the makings of a fine officah, if he would just grow up some. But Brenda, ovah theyah, she's nevah going to do what needs to be done, she don't have the backbone for it. But you might be able to help me out."

"Yeah?" I didn't want to have anything to do with this, I just wanted to be on my way. "How's that?"

"Well," he said, "if you'd be willing to come on up to Eastpoht and swayah out a complaint, that would give me just what I need to put a twist in Hop's nut sack, if you get what I mean."

"Mr. Bookman, I really don't want to get anybody into trouble."

"Oh," he said mildly, "you won't be getting anyone into trouble. You'll be helping me stop trouble befoah it gets out of hand. Won't be nothing to it. Just fill out a fohm, and I'll keep it between you, me, and him. You'll be doing both of us a big favah." He turned and looked at the guy, sitting in the back of the cruiser, head down. "You see, the thing is, Hopkins has nevah had anyone to teach him how to act. Don't mean it's too late for him to learn, though. If you help me get to him, I can teach him how to get pahst this kind of meanness." He looked back at me. "It's the right thing to do, Mistah Williams."

"Manny," I said, looking at him, and he nodded. I found I could relate to Hop's problem, getting by on bulldozer tactics and muscle, knowing it was wrong but unsure of the alternatives. It struck me then, a normal guy, a regular Joe citizen, would have no problem trusting Bookman, and would not be afraid to walk into the police station to sign a paper for him. I could feel his bland eyes watching me, I could almost sense him wondering about the source of my reluctance to do what he wanted. "All right, Mr. Bookman. If you think it's best."

"Good. Good." He clapped me on the shoulder.

"Wouldn't it be easier to take him back to the station and beat the shit out of him?"

"If I thought that'd werk," Bookman said, "I'da done it long ago. Believe me."

Somehow, I didn't doubt him. He fished a business card out of his shirt pocket and handed it to me. "Just give a call befoah you come," he said, "and I'll be theyah. You staying someplace local?"

"With Louis and Eleanor Avery."

"That right," he said. "Well, I'll expect to heah from you, tomorrow or the next day."

I nodded. "No later."

"Excellent," he said. "Good thing I was close by."

"Good thing for me or for Hopkins?"

He looked at me, shook his head. "Hahd saying," he said. "But you can believe that's what the foolish bahstid is sitting in theyah thinking about."

Nicky was subdued on the way back. Part of it might have been fatigue, but part of it had to be our encounter with the cops. I didn't know what to make of his silence, and I didn't know what to say to him. I had not yet found it difficult to get him to talk, but when I asked him if he was okay, he just nodded his head. A few minutes later, he crawled down on the floor and fell asleep with his head on the seat. It didn't look very comfortable, and the Subaru was anything but smooth, but he went out like a light. He didn't wake up until I turned into the Averys' driveway. Louis's Jeep was parked at the top of the hill. I pulled the Subaru up next to it. Nicky got up and looked around.

"You want to help me carry groceries inside?"

"Okay," he said. He didn't seem over it yet. Wherever he'd gone in his head, he was still there.

Louis was in a funk.

Eleanor tried a few times to get him talking as she fussed around her kitchen, putting away groceries. "Look at all this stuff he bought," she said to him. "All I asked him to do was buy me a pound of coffee." Louis didn't answer.

"I forgot what you told me to get."

"Hmmph," Louis said. He was sitting at the kitchen table playing solitaire, with actual cards. It had been a while since I'd seen anyone do that. Nicky had been hanging on to me ever since we'd gotten into the house. It struck me that this was the first time in either of our lives that we had spent so much time together. We had known each other by sight, I guess, and by that weird connection related people have, that free-floating, undefined sense of obligation. On my end there were some bad feelings, too—the kid had gotten saddled with a fuckup for a father—and then close on the heels of that I would go through my normal run of justifications, you know, who isn't a fuckup in some way, you're doing the best you can, and so on, and that would last only a second or two before the guilt would come back again. But beyond all this surging mess of unfamiliar emotion I realized that I was getting to know my son for the first time, and one of the first things that struck me was that sixth sense he had for when other people were suffering, and how different his reaction to that was from what mine would have been, if I had even noticed. He'd been sticking close to me, within arm's length, but he walked over to Louis then, stood at his elbow, watched him play cards. Louis looked down at him, and Nicky stood on his tiptoes to whisper in Louis's ear. Louis bent down to listen.

"All right," he said, gathering up his cards. He patted the deck square and put it on the windowsill. "Let's go look. Maybe if we're real quiet, we'll do better this time." He stood up and took Nicky's hand, and the two of them headed for the barn. Eleanor and I both watched them go. I was wishing I understood better, and maybe she was, too, but then, she was an old hand at this family shit, and I was a rank beginner, so what the hell did I know about what she thought.

"They're a little bit alike," she said. "My husband and your son." She stood at the kitchen counter with her back to me, making supper.

"You think so? Why?"

She glanced at me over her shoulder, then went back to what she was doing. "It takes a certain amount of cussedness to get through, sometimes. I'm not sure that either Louis or Nicky has enough of it." She looked back at me again. "Does he miss his mother?"

"I don't know if he remembers her. He hasn't had it easy, though. I guess we both had a couple of tough years after she died."

"I imagine," she said. "But you've got enough cussedness, Manny, I can tell. You get knocked down, you come up swinging. Am I right?"

"I haven't had much choice in the matter."

"Sure you have," she said. "There's a million ways to give up. Somehow I don't see you quitting." She turned around, leaned her back against the counter. "The problem is, the older you get, the more difficult it becomes. Getting back up again. Louis and I, we've had it too easy out here for the last few years, living apart like this. And Louis has that same thing I see in Nicky. When life takes a poke at him, it hurts him more deeply than it would you or me. And it isn't the punch that does the damage, it's the intent behind it."

Something must have gone wrong, I thought. She and Louis must have hit some kind of bump in the road. She doesn't want to tell me what it was, but she wants to talk about how she's feeling. "Seems like a good life out here, still and all."

"Very peaceful," she said. "I've never been to Noo Yok City. So many things I'd like to have seen. Isn't that a funny way to put it? But that's the way it is. I couldn't go to see it now. Maybe I don't have enough cussedness left, either. I guess it bothers me too much when life tramps with big feet through my nice little garden." She turned around, went back to her work.

"Why should you have to struggle anymore? You've found a nice quiet place here." I was thinking of those log cabins back up in the woods, the ones I hadn't managed to dream into existence. "A refuge, almost."

"Oh, well, that's true enough," she said. "Manny, can I ask you something? Would it be all right if we forgot about moving you and Nicky over to Gerald's trailah?" She looked over her shoulder, in the direction Louis and Nicky had taken. "I think I'm falling in love with yoah little boy."

I don't think I had ever loved anybody before, or any thing. All I knew was, the longer I stayed with this kid, the more my guts knotted up every time I thought of him. It had been bad enough back in the city, when I saw him only once or twice a month, but that had been mostly guilt, I think. I didn't know what it was I was going through now. It hadn't occurred to me that it might be love, because I thought that was supposed to make you feel good. Jesus. "We would be happy to stay with you, Mrs. Avery. I think Nicky's having a great time here with you guys."

"Well, that's nice," she said, turning away from me. "I'm glad."

Over dinner, I told Louis and Eleanor about my encounter with Hop and his current love interest at the convenience store. I included the fact that Bookman wanted me to swear out a complaint against Hopkins. I had intended to ask them about Franklin, but it slipped my mind. After dinner, Louis told me he had a problem with his truck. "Manny, why don't you come outside and look at my Jeep for one second. I busted a shackle on her, and I think I'm gonna have to get it welded. Come see what you think."

"Okay." Nicky got up from the table and followed me to the door.

"Nicholas," Louis said, "do me a favor, stay here, all right? Keep Mrs. Avery company."

"I wanna go too, Poppy." He hung on to my leg with determination.

I was beginning to understand him a little bit, but it was clear that Louis wanted to talk to me out of Nicky's earshot.

"I'm not going anyplace," I told him. He started to whine. "Look. Come right over here by the window. You can watch me the whole time."

"All right." He stood there, but he wasn't happy about it. "You're coming back inside, right?"

"Absolutely. We're just gonna look at Louis's truck, I promise."

Louis leaned against the tailgate and looked at the pile of red oak logs in front of the barn door. "Listen," he said. "One piece of information you should know. Bookman ain't one to observe the formalities. He's old school, if you catch my drift."

"Yeah? He thinks I did something, he'll string me up in a basement room and let the boys go to work on me with rubber hoses?"

"It wouldn't be the first time," Louis said. "Mind your manners when you're dealing with him. He takes the direct approach to problem solving."

"Good to know," I said. "I'll be careful. Tell me something, Louis. Is everything okay with you and Eleanor? You both seem very quiet this evening."

"Ah, well," he said, and he waved his hand as if shooing away a mosquito, which he might have been doing, because they had located us. "Eleanor's pain spells were getting worse, and I took her in to the doc a couple or three weeks ago. They done some tests and so on. She was pretty ugly about it, seeing how much she loves getting out of the house. Anyhow, this aftahnoon the doc called, said we gotta come in again some day next week. Evah since she found out, she's been giving me the picked end of the stick."

"Oh." I didn't know whether to be relieved or not.

Louis squatted down and peered under the back of the Jeep. "My eyesight ain't what it used to be," he said. "Take a look at this damned shackle before it gets too dahk to see it. Tell me if you think it's busted."

It was just light enough to see. "Yeah, Louis, it split up at the top, and it spread out so the spring assembly is all loose. And your shock absorber is bent all to hell."

"Son of a hoah." He said it calmly.

"Might be time for a new truck, Louis."

He shook his head. "Ain't in the budget."

"Wouldn't take a lot. Even that piece of shit I rented from Hobart would be a serious upgrade. I bet he'd sell it to you for two or three hundred bucks."

"No, he wouldn't," Louis said. "Give it to me, though, if I wanted it."

"So?"

He shook his head again. "Had this truck a long time," he said. "She might be about used up, but she ain't dead yet. I don't like to go letting myself want moah than what I got. I'll wind up just like old man Calder, mean and ugly, thinking bad about everyone I know. If you'll give me a hand tomorrow mohning, we'll push her downstreet to Gevier's house, see if he'll bring his weldah home from the garage and patch her up again."

"Be glad to help, Louis. If you got a piece of chain, we'll tow her over first thing in the morning, before I go up to see Bookman."

"Don't forget what I told you about him," Louis said. He looked away from me, out into the growing darkness. "Sometimes I do wish," he said, "that I could just write a check and solve all my problems. Course, you know what they say: Wish in one hand, piss in the other, guess which one fills up the quicker." He slapped at his arm. "Christless mosquitoes," he said.

I waved away the one that was trying to bite my ear. "Ain't these things supposed to be gone by this time of year?"

"Worse in the spring," he said. "These ones are just the survivors. First hard frost'll kill 'em. Let's go inside."

Later that night, I sat in the chair with my feet up on the bed. I could hear either Louis or Eleanor snoring in the other bedroom, and I could just make out the shape of my son underneath the covers. Most nights were like this for me. I have never needed as much sleep as everyone else. Sitting up alone in the dark, night after night, had always reinforced what I thought was the solitary nature of my life, the essential aloneness of anybody's life. I might have had that lesson beaten into me at an early age, but these other people had to learn that eventually, didn't they? Every man for himself, isn't that what they say? Dog eat dog. Devil take the hindmost. But now I could feel the connections between me and these people around me in the dark, and I was worried about Eleanor and whatever her physical ailment was, about Louis and his financial problems, and my son—Jesus Christ, what's going to happen to my son? What kind of life would he have, how could he be normal, growing up with someone like me for a father, who didn't even know what that word really meant?

There's no one to tell you what the right thing is, there's nowhere you can go to look it up, you have to feel for it on your own, in the dark.

4

We used the Subaru and a twenty-foot piece of chain to tow Louis's Jeep over to Gevier's house. Nicky rode in the Jeep with Louis. He was getting attached to both Louis and Eleanor, and followed one or the other of them everywhere. Eleanor had started teaching him the alphabet and some rudimentary arithmetic. I appreciated her efforts, but now the kid's head was filled with a million questions. "What's that word, what's this mean, what's that sign say?" Jesus. I was glad to see it, in principle, and I kept reading and spelling and so on for him, but he could get on the nerves of a plaster saint. Once he realized that all those numbers and letters meant something, he went insane with curiosity. Let him ride back there with Louis, drive him nuts for a while.

Gevier lived with his daughter in what had once been a trailer, but you couldn't see the trailer part of it anymore. Louis told me about the place the night before, trying to prepare me ahead of time for what was coming. Gevier, during the years he'd been living in the place, had added onto it, following the dictates of his own inner voices until the thing had morphed beyond recognition. I found out that morning that if you asked him about the design, he'd explain the logic to you, but you had to have a lot of patience and a good vocabulary to follow him. A lot of it supposedly had to do with heat loads, overhangs calculated to let the sun in during the winter and keep it out during the summer, due south being the primal attitude, round being from nature, Satan hiding in corners, and shit like that. If you closed your eyes and listened you might be persuaded that he was a genius and everyone else was building his house to outmoded ideas, but open your eyes and look at the guy one time and the illusion was destroyed, because when you looked at him, you had to know the guy had to be fucking whacked. I guarantee no professor in the history of MIT ever had hair like that. Some of what he said was probably right and some of it was probably bullshit, but I was never sure which part was which.

Building, trailer, whatever it was, it sat about thirty yards back from the road. You wouldn't call the space between the road and it a front yard, necessarily, there was no grass and no trees, just dirt, flattened and beaten down hard, oil-soaked in a few spots. You couldn't tell what was out behind the house, either, because there was a chain link fence on either side of the building that ran parallel to the road. It had green plastic strips woven into the open spaces, so all you could really see was a few trees poking up here and there.

White trash, that's what you'd think. I admit that's what came into my mind when we pulled up in front. Gevier came out—I swear he had on the same shirt he'd been wearing the day I met him—and stood blinking in the sun. Nicky popped out of the Jeep and walked on up to him. "Hi," he said. "Remember me?"

"Of course I do," Gevier said, watching Louis and me. "Hello, Nicky. Hello, Louis, and . . ." He looked at me, uncertain.

"Manny."

"Yeah, Manny. Fohd sent the right part, but for the wrong side of the van. I did a little screaming and yelling, they're gonna rush the other one out. They say. Supposed to be heah Monday. If it is, you should have yo-ah van Monday night. You fellas want to come inside?"

No, I thought, hell no, but Louis walked right up to the door. "Sure," he said. I've probably been inside the homes of at least a hundred people, mostly as what you might call an uninvited guest, and there are few things that fascinate me more, but I was a little worried, going through Gevier's front door, anticipating what I was going to find.

Man, was I off.

I don't always enter through the door the residents of the place habitually use most often, but when you do that, you almost always see a set piece. This is what they'd like you to think about them. They may be accountants or dentists but they love art, or they have a million pictures of their family (see, I do love them), or they're big Yankee fans, or whatever. I broke into a loft in Chelsea once, guy actually had a kayak hanging from the ceiling just inside his front door. I had been inside only two houses in Maine so far, so my sample was limited, but in both cases you walk through that door and you're in the kitchen. I guess that's because the kitchen was central to the lives of the people who lived there. In the domiciles I was used to invading, the kitchen was peripheral, off to one side.

Gevier's kitchen didn't have your normal kitchen layout, there's a shock. No cabinets, for one thing, the place was floor to ceiling shelves. One wall was devoted to food—canisters, jars, cartons, and all that. The wall next to that one was bare, the space taken up by the woodstove and the shiny copper-jacketed water heater. I wasn't sure how the water heater worked. All I know is that it had pipes running through the woodstove, two more that ran up to the solar panels on the roof. I didn't see a gas line, and there were no wires going to it. And the pipe that carried smoke out of the woodstove didn't go straight into a chimney like the Averys' did, either, it made a circle around the top of the kitchen and then ran off down the hallway. Gevier watched me looking at it the way a scientist might watch a rat that had displayed some unexpected trait, unusual intelligence or a gift for abstract reasoning, maybe. Not up to his level, of course, but beyond what he'd expected.

The other two walls were lined with books, a lot of thick, fat ones, too, a set of encyclopedia, engineering manuals, books of all kinds, some in what I took to be Latin and Greek. Louis told Gevier his tale of woe while Nicky and I admired the library. Nicky was too busy taking it all in to ask a lot of questions, which was a relief.

There was a certain order to the place. I started to pick it up after a while, even though I could not make out the logic behind it. The thing is, just because a guy is smarter than you does not mean he isn't crazy.

You had to keep your eyes open when you talked to Gevier, you had to hold on tight to the context, or you wouldn't be able to use anything he told you. Rosario, my partner from Brooklyn, was just the opposite. With him you had to close your eyes. Sometimes I would picture his words typewritten in the air in front of me, all context removed, because Rosey had a serious Brooklyn accent, and he tended to chew up his words before he let go of them, plus he had this thing in his eyes, you wouldn't be surprised to see guys sneaking up behind him with a net. He was actually a pretty smart guy, but unless I could separate what he was saying from the way he looked and sounded I would always tend to discount it because he came across like such a maniac.

A girl came out of a back room. She looked like she was right on the edge of adulthood—it's that look that baby birds get when they don't know yet if they're going to be able to fly, so they stand there on the edge and look out with an intensity that the rest of us old crows have forgotten. She bore a certain resemblance to Gevier, but not too much, lucky for her. She was tall and thin and she had the kind of muscle tone you have to work for. She wasn't what you'd call beautiful. Handsome, maybe, if your taste ran that way. She had circles under her eyes. I'd never seen them on a person so young before.

"Edwina," Gevier said, "I want you to meet Manny and his son, Nicky."

She considered him icily. "My name is Edna." She turned in my direction. "If you ever call me Edwina, I will clean your clock."

Nicky couldn't say "Edna." "Hi, Ed . . . umm, Ed . . ." He shrugged. "Hi, Eddie. Do you live here? Did you read all of these books?"

She looked at me and shook her head. "I can't win," she said. She walked over and shook Nicky's hand. "I've read most of them," she said, "except the ones on rebuilding motorcycle engines." She glanced at her father in disgust. "We've got more in the other room," she said, turning back to Nicky, "better ones than in here. Would you like to go look at them?"

He looked over at me. "Can I go?"

"Yeah, sure," I said. "Don't break anything." I couldn't get used to him asking me permission for things, and I felt strange giving it. Funny how a five-year-old kid can feel the shape of a relationship before an alleged adult can. I watched the two of them go. She had a fine, taut rear end, but I didn't know if she was past the age of consent yet. I wasn't sure I wanted to go there anyway, you might come away bleeding. Better to admire from a safe distance.

"How's the bike coming?" Louis asked.

Gevier glanced in the direction his daughter and my son had taken. "Come on," he said. "I'll show it to you." He looked nervously in Edna's direction again.

"She give you a hahd time about it?" Louis asked him.

"A hahd time? A hahd time? She's making my life a living hell." He looked at me. "When I got out of Thomaston Tech, nine yeahs and some ago, one condition of my parole was no motorcycles. I get done with probation in eight moah months. I told Edwina, eight moah months and I'm bohn again, my scoot will be ready befo-ah that and I'm going. She ought to be off in college by then, if she's as smaht as they all say she is." He puffed a little. "Couple of schools offered her a full scholarship, all's she has to do is quit bitching and say yes to one of them."

"She don't wanna go?"

He shook his head. "Sweahs she ain't going. Says she'll stay right here and stahve to death when I leave. Trouble is, she's just about stubborn enough to do it. C'mon, let me show you the bike."

It was in a workroom at the end of the building. I've never been into bikes, there's enough ways to get killed in Brooklyn without looking for another one. Besides that, most of the bikes I'd seen were fancy, shiny, chromed fashion statements, usually owned by some orthodontist or lawyer doing the midlife crisis thing. Go get a bike, a tattoo, a leather vest, and a goatee. Give me a fucking break.

Gevier surprised me again. It was an old Triumph, not a Harley. The frame was black, no chrome on it anywhere, the front end was raked out about a foot farther than normal, no front fender, no front brake that I could see. The carbs were over on a bench in pieces, and there was no exhaust.

"You got the engine in her," Louis said. "What comes next, the tank?"

"I guess. I'm trying to stretch the job out, Louis. I could have her done in a weekend, but I'm afraid to." He looked back down the hallway toward the main part of the building. He shook his head. "I got to get Edwina settled before I can go."

You never know what guys are going to get hooked on. "Would you really chuck everything and take off on that?" I asked him.

"No," he said, lowering his voice. "But don't tell Edwina that or she'll stay right heah until she's a dried-out old prune. I don't know what's wrong with her. I suppose I never did understand her." He shook his head. "Anyhow, I thought I might take a ride down to Daytona one time, though, and maybe out to Sturgis, though I hear they're both getting pussified. Just to see if any of the guys I used to run with are still alive."

"Why don't you just look for them on the Net?"

"I ain't on any goddam Net. I been trying to get less connected, not moah. Besides, it ain't like I know any of their Christian names." He grinned. "You were looking for a guy named Dog-Eating Duane, you ain't gonna find him in the phone book."

"Dog-eating Duane?"

"Hungry and broke will make you a desperate man."

"No doubt. What year is this thing?"

"Engine's a sixty-three. Frame is original, modified by me. Front end is a Hahley springah, unknown vintage. Rest of it come from heah and theyah."

"You really think you can get this thing to run?"

"Had her running already, bettah than new." He launched into a long speech about the virtues of English engineering and the shortcomings of English manufacturing. After a while he must have noticed my eyes rolling back in my head, and he stopped. "Well, Louis," he said, "how are we gonna get yoah truck up to the garage? I could ride my bicycle up theyah and bring down the tow truck. . . ."

Louis shook his head. "Don't know that she'd survive a tow," he said. "I was hoping you could bring your buzz box down heah and patch her together with some angle iron."

"Still have to ride the bicycle up to get the truck," Gevier said.

I took Hobart's keys out of my pocket and tossed them to Louis. "Take the Subaru," I told him.

"Well, then," Gevier said. "Let's go take a look, see what we need."

"How come he calls you Edwina?"

She was watching Nicky, who was sitting on the floor by her chair, paging through a picture book. "He's trying to get me mad," she said. She looked at me without expression. "He thinks if I get mad enough I'll go off to school and leave him alone."

"Would that be a bad thing?"

She gave me a little head bob and an openmouthed look of complete disbelief, like, How could you be such an ignorant jackass? "You saw him," she said. "Can you imagine him living on his own?"

"Looked way past twenty-one to me."

She had her mouth agape. "The man believes in astrology," she said, staring at me. "He plants his garden at night, under a full moon. Next thing you know he's going to be channeling Peter Fonda. I can't just go off and leave him."

I noticed that she had almost no trace of a down east accent. "Fonda's not dead yet."

"You think that matters?"

"I think your father has every right to hide out in the woods and do his hermit routine if that's what he wants, but it's stupid for you to do it with him."

"Oh, what do you know about it? Who the hell asked you, anyway? Besides, what would you do if it was your father?"

I looked down at Nicky, who looked lost in his book. I had no idea what he knew about where he came from, I didn't know what the Bitch might have told him, and I didn't know if he was listening, anyway. "I don't know. I never met the man."

"Oh," she said, surprised. She went on in a softer tone. "Your mother, then."

You think you've been through it all, felt everything there was to feel, you think you're done with it, but I suppose you never are. All I could do was shake my head.

"You didn't know her, either? You're an orphan?"

I watched Nicky for a minute before I answered. He was looking at pictures of desert landscapes, fiery sunsets over sand and cactus. His mouth was open, and he was touching the pictures with a finger, almost caressing them. "I, ah, I don't know who they were. Someone found me on the street, on a curb in Brooklyn. That's all I know."

"That must be so hard," she said. "You're the first person I've met who had it worse than I did. Were you adopted?"

It was safe for me to look at her by then. "No. I never caught on anyplace. I don't know why." I tried to laugh. "I thought I was over it. You know what I mean? I thought I was done with wondering where I belonged, and all that shit. How did we get into this, anyway?"

"I don't know," she said. "I'm sorry." She gestured at Nicky. "He's your whole family."

I just nodded. "Did you know your mother? Tell me about her."

She smiled then, but with only half of her face. "My mom," she said.

"It's all right if you don't want to talk about it."

She shrugged. "It's okay. I guess I don't mind. No one up here ever asked me about her." It was her turn to watch Nicky for a minute, to see if he was preoccupied. "I lived with her until I was ten. Down in Connecticut. She was nice, sometimes, but she drank a lot, and she had . . ." She sighed. "I guess she was manic depressive. You never knew, when you got home from school, if she would be winging dishes at you or trying to hug you and stuff. Then, when I was ten years old, she drove her car into the river. I never knew if she had an accident or if she did it on purpose. . . . Anyway, my dad had gotten out of jail about a year previous, he was living up here, so I came up." She looked at me, and some of her fierceness came back. "That's when it started, that's when they first wanted to send me away. When I transferred to the school up here, I brought a transcript with me from the school in Connecticut. I had been a pretty rotten student. Ds and Fs, but it wasn't my fault! What nobody understood was, I never had any time to study. My mom didn't do the laundry, she didn't clean the house, she didn't cook, she was either in bed with the covers pulled over her head or she was out spending money she didn't have." She stopped for a minute. "I guess it wasn't her fault, either. She was sick. But when I got up here, I had to take a test before they'd let me in school. IQ and all that stuff. Anyway, I've always tested well. I probably should have sandbagged a little, I guess, but I got interested in it, and I did better than I intended to. The guy who had given me the test, the vice principal, he came storming out of his office with the test in one hand and my transcript in the other, he was almost purple." She widened her eyes and screwed her face into an exaggerated scowling imitation of the man. "'You don't deserve the God-given gift you've been given. . . .'" She was shaking her head. "They've been trying to send me away someplace ever since. Well, I'm not going."

I looked around. "Well, I can see why you wouldn't want to leave. . . ."

"Oh, listen, buddy—"

"I'm only kidding. Who wanted you?"

"BU, Columbia, Seton Hall."

"Damn, Columbia, you could live in Manhattan. How old are you?"

"Seventeen."

"Oh, shit. Oh, God, seventeen years old, beautiful, all alone and living in New York City." I threw my head back and howled like a wolf. "Awrooooo . . ."

Nicky looked up from his book and laughed. "Don't mind him, Nicky," she said. "He's crazy." Nicky patted me on the leg and went back to his book.

"So now Columbia's offering you a free ride, and you don't want to take it? That's like somebody putting a hundred and fifty grand in a bag and handing it to you. You can't give it back. When someone offers you that much money, if you don't take it, man, that's a sin that God cannot forgive."

"You stole that from Zorba."

"I adapted it." There's an old salesman's trick, they use it when the mark keeps coming up with lame excuses why she can't buy the vacuum cleaner. I decided to give it a shot. "Tell me the real reason," I told her. "I won't tell a soul. Nicky won't, either. Tell me the real reason you won't go."

She stared at the floor for a full minute, then looked up at me. "How would you feel," she said, "if you were some hick from the sticks? Suppose you lived half your life out here on the far side of the moon? I can't even fit in with the kids up here, how the hell am I gonna make it in New York City?"

"That's not good enough," I told her. "I can get you around that one in ten minutes. You gotta do better than that."

I heard the sound of Gevier's tow truck pulling up next to Louis's Jeep. "They're back," she said, sounding relieved. "Don't you think you should go help out?"

I figured Louis didn't have any money to pay Gevier, but I owed him a couple days' rent, so I settled up with him while Gevier patched the Jeep back together. He used some scrap steel and a shock absorber that was a long way from new, and it took him almost no time at all to get the truck fixed. He tried to get Louis to let him go further and beef up the bed where it had rusted through, but Louis, it seemed to me, preferred living on the edge of crisis. Gevier didn't want to take Louis's money, he said that all he'd done was weld some small pieces of scrap steel onto some larger pieces of scrap steel, which did not change the essential nature of the finished product at all. Louis pretended to be insulted. They worked it out after a while, and then Gevier drove his tow truck back to the garage, and Louis followed him in the Jeep to save him having to ride his bicycle back. Nicky went with Louis, and I headed for Eastport.

If you hold your hand up in front of you with your fingers spread apart, Lubec is at the end of your thumb, and Eastport is at the end of your forefinger. The space in between is one small corner of Passamaquoddy Bay. Louis and Gevier lived down by your wrist somewhere. The point being, although you can see Eastport from Lubec, and vice versa, it is not a short drive from one to the other. Eastport is bigger than Lubec, too, and it doesn't have that half-finished air that Lubec does. It's actually on the end of Moose Island, and you drive over a long causeway to get to it. They call it a city, there's a sign that says so on your way in. Maybe so, but you could fit the whole damn thing in the subway yards in Jamaica, Queens, and have room left over.

They had only a couple of cells in the building where Taylor Bookman had his office, but a couple is enough. In fact, all it takes is one. Let me tell you, there is nothing on earth like the clang when that metal door slams shut on your ignorant young ass. I can hear it now, and I don't ever want to be on the wrong side of that sound again, in fact, I don't want to be anywhere in the neighborhood, which is why I was nervous, looking for Bookman's office. Tell you the truth, I was shitting my pants. They had some kid in the lockup, you couldn't hear him through the thick steel and glass door but you could see him huddled up in the corner, sweating and shaking and crying. I was following the deputy, but he wasn't Hopkins, he was a different guy. He stopped to look through the window at the kid in the cell.

"What happened to him?"

"OxyContin cowboy," he said without looking at me.

"You guys ever heard of a detox?"

"This is a poor county," he said. "No money for that shit up here." He shook his head. "This kid's father used to be a friend of mine."

"Fucking drugs." I had my own story on that topic, but I didn't think he wanted to hear it. Actually, neither did I.

He turned and looked at me then, his face etched with anger. "We caught this dumb son of a whore headed south with two bags of OxyContins in his car. A hundred beans in each bag. This is going to tear his family apart."

"I guess he'll be going away for a while."

The guy shook his head. "He's just a mule. We need to get him to tell us how they're coming across the border. If he'll do that, he might still have a life."

"You think he'll do it?"

"Who knows," he said. He didn't sound optimistic. "C'mon, let's get outta here." We went on by, leaving the kid to suffer through on his own.

Bookman's office had a big window, and you could see over the tops of the few little downtown buildings in Eastport to Passamaquoddy Bay. The water never seemed calm. Every time I saw it, the currents seemed to be fiercely ripping in one direction or another, and sometimes both ways at once, downstream out in the channel, upstream near the shore, constantly worrying away at the stone that made up the islands. I don't know anything about boats or the sea or anything like that, but I do know that it doesn't make a hell of a lot of difference if the tide is in or out when you go to the beach in Brooklyn, I don't remember noticing it one time in my entire life there. The vertical rise of the tide might be three feet or so, tide goes out, you might get twenty yards of extra beach to lie down on at Rockaway or Riis Park, should you so desire. But if you tie up your boat to the pier at high tide in Eastport, you'd better use a strong piece of rope, brother, because the son of a bitch will be hanging there like a bauble on a Christmas tree when the tide goes out. And they don't have sand beaches up in Eastport, or any use for them, either, the water is too goddam cold to do anything but look at. They do have clam flats, though, and the water might be right up next to the road at high tide and a half a mile away at low. Twenty-three feet of rise is what I heard they get, and that's a hell of a lot of salt water. I guess that's why the currents always look so busy. Makes sense, given the amount of work they have to do.

And seagulls, everywhere you look, you see seagulls. Stand out in the road anytime and look straight up, and as far up as you can focus you'll see seagulls soaring. Mostly herring gulls and great black-backed gulls, maybe a stray laughing gull, wondering which way it is to Brooklyn. They have a lot of the other shorebirds you see in Brooklyn, too, cormorants, sea crows, ducks, and so on. The herring gulls are the most fun to watch. They are the jet fighters, acrobatic fliers, fast and beautiful, and they seem almost human to me, fighting, squabbling, eating, and flying with what seems to be great relish. Walking down a street, you hear a loud, hollow metallic *bonk*, some seagull a mile or so up in the air has taken a shit and hit a car trunk, I always picture him up there thinking, Damn, missed him again.

Taylor Bookman was sitting behind a metal desk, his back to the window, watching me look out. "How do you get any work done?" I asked him.

"That's what deputies are faw," he said, deadpan. "Have a seat." I sat down across the desk from him, and he looked at me in that way of his. "How long you been out of prison?"

My heart stopped. I knew it, I fucking knew it. "You got me confused with some other guy," I told him, trying to keep my face as blank as his.

"Manny," he said, and he grimaced slightly, just for a fraction of a second. "We may be a long way from Noo Yok, but I don't live in a cave."

"I never thought you did." I turned my left arm over, looked at the back of my wrist where the black snake's tail came out from under my sleeve and wrapped around the space where you would normally wear a watch. "I grew up on the street," I told him, and it was true enough. "I got most of these as a teenager."

"You paht of a street gang?"

"When I was young. The Poppy Chulos." That last part was a lie. The Poppy Chulos that I knew ran over in Sunset Park, which is a neighborhood in Brooklyn. Their name is Spanish for "cute guys," and I never met the admission criteria.

"So? You didn't stay with them? Why not?"

I looked out the window for a couple of minutes. "Well," I said, rehearsing some bullshit story to give him, and then I decided I didn't need to. "There was five of us, growing up, hung out together. Time I was twenty, I was the only one left. They were the closest thing I ever had to a family, Mr. Bookman, and they were all gone." I ticked them off on my fingers. "One overdose, one shot and killed during a robbery, two buried in a cell somewhere, doing life plus. And me."

"You saw the light and decided to go straight. Nice to know that can still happen." He lifted one eyebrow a millimeter or two, curled one corner of his mouth up. It was probably his equivalent of a belly laugh.

"You know, when you're a teenager, it's like playing Russian roulette with no bullets in the gun. Nothing can happen, you're a minor, there ain't shit anybody can do to you."

"Noticed that."

"I bet. You turn eighteen, though, they put a bullet in the gun. But you're still immortal, you're Superman, right? Five out of six is still pretty good odds, that's what you think when you're that age. But the longer you play, the more bullets they put in the gun."

"How many in yaws?"

I shook my head. "Couldn't tell you. I quit playing years ago."

"Glad to heah that," he said. "I worry about folks like the Averys sometimes. There's such a thing as being too kindhahted. Did you know it ain't safe to pick up hitchhikahs any moah?"

I nodded my head.

"Louis Avery," he went on, "used to be an awful rakehell, back befoah he found the baby Jesus." His expression did not change. "Thought maybe good living might have clouded his thinking. But Eleanor, now, you'll nevah get much past her. She told me she thought you was probably all right. Said you'da nevah raised that little boy up as good as he is if you didn't have some finah points."

"I appreciate the vote of confidence."

"I trust her judgment," he said, "up to a point. Why don't you read ovah this statement, see if you agree with what it says." He handed me a couple of typewritten pages. As I took them from him, he picked up a newspaper that had been lying on his desk. It was a copy of the *New York Daily News*, a couple of days old. I was pretty sure it was the issue that had had the story about the Russians and the stock scam in it, and the story about Nicky going missing in Bushwick.

It was hard to concentrate on the statement, but I did the best I could while Bookman paged idly through his paper. After a few minutes I handed the pages back to him. "Says here he punched her in the face, but he didn't. All he did was whack her head against the car."

"A fine distinction," he said, putting down the paper. "Hold on, this won't take a second to change." He came back with a new printout a minute later. He handed the sheets to me, picked up his paper again.

"I 'magine those tattoos ah kind of a handicap for a guy like you, ain't they?"

"I'm a software designer," I told him. "They don't handicap me at all, I just get tired of the questions."

He was nodding. "That's right," he said. "Eleanor Avery told me that, but I forgot." He rolled the paper up and tossed it into his trash can. "Don't know how you can live down to Noo Yok," he said. "People robbin' each othah all the time. Don't seem natural." He was staring at me.

"You get used to it."

"I 'magine," he said. "None of my business, what you do to each other, down to Noo Yok or Boston. I got enough to do right heah. You know what I mean?" He regarded me calmly, giving me a minute to think about it, then cleared his throat. "Wife told me you was out to the house yesterday."

"Out to your house?"

He turned around one of the framed pictures on his desk so that the image faced me. It was a picture of Bookman and Franklin, the big kid with the broken bicycle. The two of them had their arms around one another, and Bookman squinted into the camera while Franklin looked at the ground. "Ah. He's your son."

He nodded. "My son. Funny thing about him. He don't talk a lot. He won't say a word about who it was run him off the road, and I really need to know who done it."

"Nobody likes a rat."

He stared at me. "Populah misconception," he said.

"I didn't see the accident. I saw a pale green pickup truck, seventy-four or seventy-five GMC, with two kids in it. Mile or so later, I saw Franklin."

"All right." His face betrayed no emotion at all. "I appreciate you coming in like this. I'm gonna tell Hop to stay the hell away from you. He don't, you let me know."

I guessed that he knew who the kids in the pickup were, and would administer justice in his own way and in his own time. "All right."

"I had a visit from a private investigatah this mawning. Russian guy, from down to New Jersey. Checked in with me, just like he's supposed to."

Man, this guy was a laugh a fucking minute. "Is that right?"

"Ayuh. Said he was tracing some guy jumped bail on an ahmed-robbery chahge in Bayonne. Guy name of Mohammed something. That wouldn't be you, would it?"

"I never even been to Bayonne."

"Figured that," he said. "I nevah liked private investigatahs myself. Most of 'em ah just bottom feedahs, you ask me. Anyhow, I'm gonna leave that paypah, and all them stories in it, right theyah in the trash bucket."

I think my heart had stopped beating. "What is it that you want from me, Mr. Bookman?"

He shook his head. "Nothing at all," he said. "I want you to have a good time while yaw with us. Gevier ought to have yaw cah fixed tomorrow or the day aftah. See if you can stay out of trouble in the meantime."

"I'll do that."

"Good," he said. "Thanks for coming in."

I stood up to go.

"Manny?"

"Yeah?"

He turned the picture of him and Franklin back around to face him. "You notice how nice and quiet it is up heah? We like it like that."

I thought about protesting my innocence, but I didn't. I just walked out.

I wanted to run away.

I hesitate to admit it now, but I did, I wanted to run, I wanted to take off. Looking out Bookman's window, I could see Canada right across the water, for Chrissake, I knew I'd have to drive about thirty miles up the U.S. side of the St. Croix and cross at Calais, Jesus, I can't tell you how bad I wanted to do it. Bookman was letting me slide, maybe because he decided Nicky was better off with me than in some foster home, maybe because I had picked up Franklin and given him a ride home, or maybe it was just because he didn't feel like filling out the paperwork. I didn't want to push my luck with the guy, though, I wanted to be gone, I wanted to go grab Nicky and run.

I drove Hobart's Subaru over the causeway that links Eastport to the mainland, past the Passamaquoddy Reservation, the fucking Subaru barely broke ninety but I was in full flight mode, I promise you. Then I had this thought: All I need is one small thing to go wrong on this relic, this rusted collection of steel, paint, iron oxide, and rubber, and they'll be scraping me up off this fucking road with a shovel. Where would Nicky be then? It's like when you hear someone say, "I would have killed myself but I was too much of a coward." I got to the end of that road, the end point, where it butts up against U.S. 1, and I wrestled with that. I sat there at the stop sign, there was no reason not to, there was no one behind me and no one coming. Easy enough to get away, if that was what I wanted. I could call Gevier and tell him to chop the van and sell the parts, leave some money with Louis, tell him to pay Hobart for the Subaru, grab my kid and take off. I wouldn't be fooling anybody. I might buy myself enough time to cross the border and get lost, but Bookman would find out in a day or two that I'd run away, and Louis and Eleanor would know it, too.

I found that I cared what these people thought of me. And worse than that, I didn't want my kid living with some guy whose coping skills consisted of running away every time the shit got a little funky. Still, part of me thought I was losing my edge, going soft. How did this make any sense? Nicky's too young, he won't remember anything. . . .

I couldn't do it.

I turned left, headed back to Louis's house.

There was a big yellow Mercedes parked up next to the Averys' yellow house. I stopped as soon as I noticed it, maybe a quarter of a mile away, and pulled the Subaru over to the side of the road. I fished my bird-watching glasses out from behind the seat, thinking, From now on, everywhere I go, they go. I got out and glassed the place. All I could tell was that the car had Maine plates and there was nobody in it. S 500, maybe four years old. I have never understood Mercedeses' popularity, they're too heavy and too slow for my taste. They do what they're made to do, though. You might as well wear a sign. "Hey, I'm a rich old guy." It struck me then, I was rich, but I wasn't old yet. The Mercedes still looked like an old Checker Marathon to me.

I waited for about half an hour but nobody came out of the Averys' house to get into the car. I couldn't see through the windows, either, not at that distance, and there wasn't much cover between me and the house. I got back into the Subaru and fired it up, drove on past.

After you go past the Averys' horse pasture the road curves, and between that and the trees in his woodlot I was very shortly out of sight. Before you get to the Gevier estate there's a little path on the right leading up into the woods, another narrow, overgrown wagon track where the trees come right down next to the road. I slowed down there. I couldn't see either the Geviers' or Averys' house from that spot, and they couldn't see me. I turned the Subaru into that wagon track and drove up in between the trees.

It was smoother going than I had expected. The Subaru was made for this sort of thing, I guess, with its low-torque engine and four-wheel drive. I was almost starting to like it in spite of myself. I mean, it wasn't like I'd ever wanted one. If I got a sport-ute, I wouldn't go for an old crock like the Subaru, I would pick something that had AC, a CD player, two sunroofs, three-hundred horsepower, and a ten-grand custom paint job. Of course, then I'd be afraid to take it up into the woods, where it would get all scratched.

The track ran uphill into the trees about a hundred feet and kind of petered out. You couldn't see anything from in there, not the main road and neither one of the houses. I parked the Subaru in what seemed the logical place and got out. I headed through the woods, in the general direction of Louis's house. I was distracted, defending myself from the onslaught of mosquitoes, so it took a few minutes, but I came out in Louis's pasture, closer to the road than I had intended. It was just dusk, dark enough so that I thought I could sneak up next to the house without much chance of being noticed, especially if I approached from the front of the place, where nobody much went. I checked for the horse first, and then I went for it.

I saw him just before I got to the corner of the house. He was an eastern screech owl, no doubt about it, I had looked up the listing in *Sibley* the night before. Smallish for an owl, mottled brownish gray, ear tufts. The tufts look like ears but they are not, they're just little bunches of feathers on top of the owl's head. The owl can lay them back like a cat or point them up if he wants to, but his ears are actually openings on the sides of his skull under the feathers, one higher than the other so he can triangulate on the sounds his dinner is making before he catches it. I don't know why he had the ear tufts, I can't think of a possible survival advantage they gave him, or why some owls have them and others don't. Maybe a lady screech owl would never look at you if you didn't have them, who knows. He heard me coming, of course, and he flew away, but I got him before he did. I can't really describe the feeling that gave me, it was almost a physical chill. I don't understand why I was so interested, either, but I can tell you that right then, that owl was fucking beautiful. For a fraction of a second, just an eyeblink, I was tempted to forget everything else, follow the bird and watch him hunt, but instead I just watched him fly away.

It was Sam Calder Sr. sitting in the Averys' kitchen. He was on one side of the kitchen table and Louis was on the other, Eleanor standing behind her husband with her hands on his shoulders. There was one more woman in there, too, I couldn't see her but I could hear her voice. I assumed it was Sam's wife. I couldn't tell what any of them were saying, I could hear only murmurs. Louis was agitated, though. I could tell from the tone of his voice and the way he sat in his chair that he was not happy. Eleanor stood calmly, patting Louis once in a while. She loved him, you could feel it coming right through the wall of the house, she loved the fucking guy. Jesus. What would I have been if I'd had a woman to love me like that? Shit.

I followed the edge of Louis's pasture down to the road, then followed the road around to where the wagon track up into the woods started. Long way around, I know, but I'd had it with the Leatherstocking routine, at least until I got some bug spray. I got back to where I'd left the Subaru, fired the thing up, and drove back down out of the woods. I turned my cell phone on, but I couldn't get a signal, so I drove to the convenience store where I'd seen Hopkins romancing his girlfriend and called Louis from the pay phone. I told him I wanted to go hear Roscoe's band at the VFW, and he said that he and Eleanor would be glad to look after Nicky. I could hear Sam Calder Sr. in the background, and Louis didn't seem in any hurry to get back to him.

"Is that Sam senior I hear?"

"Ayuh," Louis said.

"He still harassing you about that field up in Eastport?"

"Ayuh."

"Why don't you throw him the hell out?"

"Can't," Louis said, with a trace of sadness in his voice. "Events have conspired against me."

I remembered that Louis had seemed kind of dour the night before, and I wondered what had happened.

There was a different woman working behind the cash register in the convenience store. She probably thought I was nuts. I bought gas, and a whole bunch of other shit, too, maps, a flashlight and batteries, bug dope, some chocolate bars, Poland Spring water, a big hunting knife to go under the seat, and so on. You'd have thought I was going to the North Pole. I had picked up a bunch of new mosquito bites, though, and in a classic case of locking the barn door after the horse was dead, I doused myself with repellent. The bugs had reminded me, Maine is not New York City. You got to be prepared up here, or something will start chewing on your ass.

I've never been into music. People look at me and assume I'm into rap, but I'm not. To me, rap ain't nothing but some guy talking shit, and you can get that for free anytime. It's interesting, though, you look at kids who go for that, they usually live someplace where it's okay to go around blowing smoke out of your ass. Where I come from, you never make threats, it's not safe. You're gonna do something, you either do it or you keep your mouth shut and you step out around. A lot of the places I've sublet, though, people are really into their sound. Old dudes from the sixties hang on to those old LPs, I been inside places where they had boxes and boxes of them. I imagine them blowing reefer and putting that old crap on the turntable, remembering back when they were gonna change the world. My thing is, I'll go out somewhere to hear guys play, but I'm not gonna start buying their stuff and lugging it around with me. That's in the city, though, where you can go hear music any night of the week. Not so easy out here in the boonies.

I guess that's why I decided to go hear Roscoe's band. There was a pretty good crowd when I got there, the parking lot was almost full, about half cars and half pickup trucks. I had to park the Subaru way out back, down in a dark corner. I could hear the music as soon as I got out. It was, I guess, country and western, but with a twist, with a French Canadian accent, you might say. I would call it an improvement over the original, because the guy's girl might have broken his heart and left him for you, okay, but instead of whining about it, he was gonna come over to your house and kick your ass.

There was an old soldier at the door, white hair and sad eyes. He took my five bucks and nodded me inside. The place was one big room and one small one, the small one being the bar. Roscoe's band was set up at the far end of the big room, and they were dressed like shitkickers, white shirts, black ties, jeans, cowboy boots and hats. They were loud and energetic—Roscoe's shirt was soaked with sweat. He played the fiddle. He didn't have it up under his chin, though, he had it jammed into his belt and he was wailing on it, man. You might not like his style but you couldn't fault his enthusiasm. A half dozen couples were jumping around on the dance floor in the middle of the room. Roscoe looked at me over their heads, nodded at me, and flashed that Teddy Roosevelt grin of his, but then he was lost again, submerged in what he was doing. There were round tables scattered around the edges of the room, about ten chairs each.

I noticed Franklin first. You couldn't miss him. He was sitting at a table on the far side of the room, next to his father. I saw him glance at me and I waved to him. He looked down at the table but he waggled three thick fingers at me. Bookman caught the motion, saw me, and waved me over, motioning to an empty chair next to his son. I made my way around the perimeter of the room, nodding at the few faces I'd seen before. More than ever, it seemed to me, I stood out in the sea of plaid flannel shirts and white faces, different in every aspect. They tolerated me well, though, smiling and nodding in spite of my brownish skin color, black leather jacket, and running shoes. Ex-cop I used to know liked to call them felony boots.

I sat down next to Franklin. He stuck his hand out to me, looked down at the ground while we shook. My hand is not small but it was lost in his dry leathery mitt. He didn't squeeze too hard, though, there was a gentleness in him you would never expect, looking at the guy.

"Hi, Franklin." I had to shout to be hear over Roscoe's band. "You like the music?"

"Too loud," he rumbled back at me. "Hurts my ears."

I leaned forward and looked over at Bookman. "Your son is an honest man."

"Yes, he is. How are you?"

"Thirsty. Can I get you something from the bar?"

He nodded, waggling an empty Budweiser bottle.

"How about you, Franklin? Can I get you something to drink?"

He glanced at me and looked down. It was the most eye contact he'd ever give you. It was incongruous that this huge bear-child could be so shy. "I don't drink," he said.

"How about a Coke?"

He looked up at me then, almost a full second before he looked away. I could see his father out of the corner of my eye, leaning in to hear. "You want to buy me a soda?"

"Yeah, Franklin, I do."

He thought about it. "All right," he said. "Ginger ale."

"Coming right up." I slapped him on the back as I stood up, thinking, This guy is freaking huge, then remembering. Franklin was a navy destroyer piloted by a little boy.

I walked through the door from the big room into the small room where the bar was, pausing to let my eyes adjust to the relative darkness of the place. The bar itself was an oval-shaped affair in the center of the room, stools around the perimeter, TV in one corner with the sound turned down. They were showing a Red Sox–Yankees game, and I never cared about the Yankees, so I ignored it. I leaned on the bar and nodded to Hobart, the guy who'd rented me the Subaru. He was sitting on the far side. He nodded back, then pointed down the bar with his chin. Thomas Hopkins was at the far end.

Hop was drunk. There were three guys clustered around his stool, watching the baseball game. Hop was in civvies, drinking shots and beers, and he had that slow-motion, unfocused, fog-brained look that guys get when they're deep into a run. The bartender came over to take my order. He was an older guy with a gray brush cut and a navy tattoo on his forearm. Hop's eyes followed every move the man made as he went to get my two Buds and the ginger ale. My guess was that Hop's drinks were getting low and he didn't want to run dry, not for a minute. I been there, that's the place where there's something rising up inside you and the only way to keep it down is to keep hitting it with something, alcohol or dope or sex or whatever it is that works for you. Hop's eyes passed by my face once or twice but he didn't seem to remember me. I paid the bartender, left him a couple of bucks, but as I turned to go, I saw recognition dawning on Hop's features. I thought I saw alarm in the bartender's eyes, but Hobart sat and watched, impassive. I glanced his way as I turned to go, and I thought maybe he was amused by the two of us, Hop and me, just a little bit.

Bookman stood up when he saw me coming. Franklin started to rise but Bookman leaned over and said something in his ear. Franklin nodded and sat back down. I handed Bookman his beer and put the ginger ale on the table in front of Franklin. "Thank you," he rumbled, and when I didn't reply, I heard him say, "You're welcome," softer, to himself. I stopped then, admiring Bookman for teaching his enormous kid that it made a difference how you talked to people. I patted Franklin on the back again, silently apologizing, I suppose, for my uncouth ways, and resolved to myself that I would be more careful from here on out, at least around him. Bookman caught my eye, jerked his head at the back door. He patted Franklin on the shoulder. I couldn't hear him but I could read his lips.

"Stay here, I'll be right back."

Roscoe's band was getting louder as the night wore on. The two of us stepped through a side door. I watched Bookman look back at his son before the door swung shut, leaving us in the relative gloom and quiet of the parking lot. He'd noticed me watching.

"I probably shouldn't worry about him," he said.

Must be like worrying Godzilla is going to hurt himself, I thought, but I didn't say it. "That's your job."

"I guess it is." He took me by the elbow, led me a few steps away from the building. "I made a few phone calls this aftahnoon," he said. "That Russian's name is Alexander Postrozny. His cahd says he's from Jersey City, so I talked to a detective from theyah. Guy told me Postrozny is a scumbag. His word, not mine. Said Postrozny's a hiyed gun, they suspect he's tied to the Russian mob." He stared at me. "You ready to tell me what this is all about?"

The side door to the VFW opened, then, and Bookman and I were briefly bathed in light until the door swung shut behind some kid and his fat girlfriend. She was shorter than him, and she was fat in a muscular way, sort of like a hippopotamus, I guess, like if she caught you, she could rip your liver out and eat it if she wanted to. "G'night, Sheriff," they both said, and waved at the two of us. "G'night." She had a huge butt that rolled back and forth when she walked. Bookman and I watched the two of them cross the parking lot and get into an ancient pickup truck and drive away. It has to be pheromones, or something like that. A man gets a sniff of the right one and something terrible happens to his brain.

"Nicky's mother is dead. I don't have legal custody." You start with the truth, or a small piece of it, and then you build your structure on that. "She was Russian American. Her father's brother is in the Russian Mafia. The family wanted to take Nicky away from me, and there's no way I could compete with that kind of money. So I took him." It was a good lie, especially for something I came up with on the fly. I had to do it. Bookman wanted a story, but if he found out I had two million bucks that I took off some Russian scam artists, and that I was keeping it in a storeroom in Hackensack, I'd be lucky if I ever saw Nicky again. Maybe with a thick sheet of Plexiglas between the two of us.

"Postrozny gave me the name of a motel down in Machias as a local address," Bookman said, "but when I called down theyah, they didn't know who I was talking about. I can't exactly put out an APB on the son of a hoah, he's not wanted for anything. If you was smaht, you'd stay out of sight fah the next few days."

"I'll do my best. Thanks for the heads-up." He looked at me then, and again I could feel myself being scrutinized, and I wondered what was really going on behind that bland expression. "How you making out with your reconstruction project?"

"What's that?"

"Hopkins."

"Oh," he said. "Well, I got his attention, I can tell you that. Might take a day or so, but he'll come around, he's too smart not too. Not always easy to grow up, you know. Generally involves a little discomfit." I didn't have anything to say to that.

We went back inside and sat down. Roscoe's band filled the air with French Canadian voices that were by turn pleading, mournful, angry. I was surprised by the number of people who got up and stomped their way across the dance floor, swirling and shouting in time to the music. I felt like I was on a small island of relative peace, sitting next to Franklin and his father, surrounded by noise and furious activity.

I asked Franklin if he wanted another ginger ale. He lumbered to his feet. "I'll get it," he said. On his far side, Bookman's eyes went wide in surprise.

"You sure?" I asked him.

"Yep," he said, without looking at me. "My turn." He gathered up the empties.

"Franklin, you got money?" his father asked him.

"Course I got money," Franklin said, and he headed off toward the bar. Bookman stared at me across Franklin's empty chair.

"I don't know what you did to that kid," he said. "Sometimes days will go by befoah I get that much out of him."

I shrugged my shoulders. I didn't know what I had done to him, either, but I felt good for having done it. "I don't know," I said to Bookman. "Maybe he was ready."

Bookman shook his head. "Maybe," he said. I was getting to like the guy, and I had to keep reminding myself that Bookman was a cop, a policeman who could ruin my life, take Nicky away from me, put me behind bars for the foreseeable future if he found out the truth.

Franklin came back, looking pleased with himself. He plopped the bottle down in front of me. "Budweiser," he said.

"Thank you, Franklin."

"You're welcome," he said.

The two of them got up and left soon after, and they took that island with them, that small patch of tranquillity. I finished the beer Franklin had bought me, got up, and walked through the back door of the place into the parking lot. From the outside, you couldn't hear music, all you got was the thump of the bass and muffled shouting. It was a clear and cold night. I leaned against a pickup truck, watching a bunch of swallows feeding in the airspace over a field adjacent to the parking lot. Swallows flying always remind me of movies of World War II dogfights, Messerschmitts and Spitfires.

Behind me, the door burst open and Thomas Hopkins stepped out into the night. His three friends were behind him, and they looked somewhat more sober than he did. One of them had Hopkins by the elbow, but he tore himself loose. "There you are," he slurred, "you son of a hoah. Goin' round, stickin' your nose where it don' belong. Fix you."

The guy who'd been trying to restrain him took another stab at it. "Not now, Hop, this ain't the right—"

"Fuck away from me," Hop snarled, turning on his friend and shoving him away. The guy held his hands up in surrender, looked over at me and shrugged.

"You want me to go call Bookman?"

"Nah. Hoppie's too fucked up to do anything," I said. "Ain't that right, Hoppie?"

Hop shook his head unsteadily. "Bassard," he said. "Take you drunk or sober."

"You sure you want to do this, Hop? Nothing good can come from it." He didn't say anything, just shuffled a couple of steps closer to me. I didn't react, I just watched him, because he'd looked too drunk to walk on his own, but then he lurched at me, threw a left uppercut that was surprisingly quick. He didn't miss me by much. I danced back out of the way. "All right, all right," I said. "Hold up." I shrugged off my leather jacket. Good thick leather, it'll slide right off you. Hop tried the same thing with his woolen jacket but it bunched up around his elbows, trapping his arms behind him. "That was probably a mistake, Hoppie," I said, and I took a step in his direction and threw a nice stiff left right onto his nose. It rocked his head back sharply, and he staggered back. Not having his arms for balance, he tripped and went down.

I hadn't been sure about the other three, but what they did was start laughing. "Way to go, Noo Yok," one of them said.

Hop was pissed, though. He rolled around on the ground until he had his knees under him, then he jumped back up to his feet and got his jacket back up over his arms. He rushed me, making incoherent noises in the back of his throat. He paid no attention to the blood that was running out of his nose and down his face. He seemed much more sober than he had just seconds ago, and he started throwing quick hard punches. The guy had hands like rocks, but I got my arms up in time, and his punches bounced off my elbows and shoulders. Hop's friends started laughing harder, which only made things worse. Hop changed tactics then. He grabbed me by my shirt and started grappling for my head. I tucked my chin and cracked him on the nose with my forehead. I knew it had to hurt, but he showed no sign of it. Even drunk, the guy had a horrible strength, and he had me by the head and left arm. His friends were still laughing, probably at both of us now.

My right arm was free, though, and I was starting to get angry myself. I held him straight up with my left arm and hit him in the guts with four of the best right hands you ever saw. He let go of me and staggered back, holding on to his midsection. His eyes went wide and his legs got rubbery, then suddenly he pitched forward. I caught him by the back of his collar just in time to keep him from planting his face on the bumper of a parked car.

"Noo Yok's got quick hands," one of Hop's friends said. Hop threw up convulsively right then, splattering the car he'd almost hit. The three of them howled.

"Hey," I said, holding Hop away from me. "One of you stooges want to take over for me here? He's your guy, not mine."

One of them stepped forward. It was the guy who had tried to restrain Hop a half a minute earlier. "Thanks for catching him," he said. "His face is bad enough as it is."

"It was reflex. I had time to think about it, I might have let him kiss that car."

"Ayuh," the guy said. "We would'na let him hurt ya, if things had went the other way."

For whatever reason, I believed the guy. "Well, thanks. You better get him looked at. I think his nose is broke."

The guy grabbed Hop by the head and rolled it back, looked like Michael Jordan palming a basketball. "Oh, Christ," he said. "Eric, bring your pickup around, we'll throw Hop in the back and ride him over to Doc's." He looked back at me. "Hop's gonna be some ugly in the mawnin."

One of them jogged off to get his coat. "C'mon, Jimmy," the guy holding Hopkins said. "Muckle on, ovah heah." The third guy stepped forward and grabbed Hop's other arm, and the two of them dragged him away.

I went back inside, looked at myself in the mirror in the men's room. I was going to have some bruises on my shoulders and arms where Hop's punches had landed, and there was some blood on my forehead, but it was Hop's, and it washed right off. I was going to leave, but Roscoe's band was taking a break, so I sat back down. Roscoe was making the rounds, shaking hands. He stopped at my table. "T'anks for coming, aye?" he said. "You like da music?"

"Too loud," I told him. "Hurts my ears."

Roscoe laughed. "Yeah," he said. "Franklin, he tell me dat last time. We play loud, by God."

"I was kidding, Roscoe. You guys are all right."

"T'anks," he said, nodding. "I hear you popped old Hoppie pretty damn good."

"Damn. Word gets around fast."

He shrugged. "He had it coming. Maybe you make a few friends tonight, aye?"

He leaned in, lowered his voice. "You be careful now, aye? Old Hop, he's a backshooter from away back. Okay?"

"Thanks, Roscoe." I watched him walk away.

I was thinking about leaving when two Russians came through the door. I'd never seen either one of them before, but I knew who they were right away because they had my old partner Rosario with them. His face was gray and sweaty, and if you looked close you could see how carefully he was walking. The crowd had gotten a little thinner—the saner portion had gone home during the break, and I began to wish that I had, too. The Russians were both big, beefy guys, thick necks, wide shoulders. One of them had a vertical scar on one side of his face, ran from one cheekbone up past his eye into his hairline. The other guy looked like he was the one in charge of the brain. He was still in decent shape, but you could see the ghost of Boris Yeltsin in his face, he had already started down that booze highway. The three of them made their way over to an empty table and sat down.

Yeltsin leaned over and said something to Rosey. Rosey nodded, and then he made a show of panning the crowd. His eyes passed mine without stopping. A few seconds later, he looked back at Yeltsin and shook his head. Yeltsin said something, he must have wanted Rosey to be sure, because Rosey did it again, looked at all the faces carefully, shook his head again. The Russian bent closer, looked into Rosey's eyes, saying nothing. Rosey leaned back away from the guy. I could see he was afraid. He shook his head, No, the guy ain't here. Yeltsin sat back, disgusted, looked around for the bar. He said something to Scarface, got up, and walked into the back room.

Rosey wiped his forehead with a shaking hand, dried it on his shirt. Scarface watched him for a minute before he turned away, showing his contempt by twisting in his chair so he wouldn't have to look at him. Very slowly, Rosey leaned his elbows on the table in front of him, steepled his fingers, and glanced up at the ceiling like he was praying. Then he looked over his shoulder for Yeltsin again before glancing across the room at me.

I stared right at him.

He looked around for Yeltsin again, then pantomimed holding on to a steering wheel. I nodded to him. Yeah, I get it. He put his hands palm down on the table just as Scarface turned to check on him.

We're all human. No matter how tough you think you are, you've got fears, you've got emotions, you've got nerve endings. Rosario was a bad motherfucker, but the Russians had reduced him to a sweaty, shaking husk of what he had been. I read somewhere that we're all born with two fears, the fear of loud noises and the fear of falling, all the rest of them we pick up as we go along. I mentally added those two Russians to my list.

Two tables down, the people got up to leave. I waited until they passed by where I was sitting, then I got up and mixed in with them. One of the women in the party looked like she was still in her teens, she had long blond hair and she wore jeans that could not have been any tighter. Who would look at me when they could look at her? I got out the door just ahead of them.

I took a quick tour of the parking lot. There was a late-model sedan with a National Car Rental sticker on it, and I assumed that it had to be what the Russians were driving. There were a bunch of empty spots in the lot from the people who'd already gone home, so I moved the Subaru to a place where I could watch both the car and the doors of the VFW. They stayed about another half hour. I guessed that Yeltsin must have been juicing himself pretty hard during that time, because he looked unsteady when they came out, and Scarface looked pissed. Rosey walked slowly and carefully, as he had before. I didn't want to think about what they had done to him.

It's not all that hard to follow someone in an urban setting. There's usually plenty of other cars around, nobody's gonna notice one more. Here, though, it was just the two of us, my car and theirs. They pulled out of the lot, and I gave them about thirty seconds before I started in their wake. I thought about that, and I lagged back maybe three quarters of a mile. They seemed to be heading more or less due west. I tried running without my headlights for a while, but I don't know how smart that was. When there aren't many houses with lights on and there are no streetlights at all, it gets real hard to see the road. I had to slow down too much to keep from killing myself, so I turned the lights back on.

They turned south when they got to Route 1. I was about a half mile behind them, but I saw their brake lights, and the left-hand turn signal blinking. I had to wait when I got to the stop sign, and a southbound pickup truck got between me and the Russians. I thought that was a good thing at first, but the guy in the pickup drove too slow, and the Russians began gaining on me. I couldn't get past the son of a bitch, either, because he would speed up every time the road straightened out, and the Subaru just didn't have the horses to take him. I guess the driver thought I was questioning his manhood, I don't know. We were headed toward Louis's house, and I was beginning to learn that section of Route 1 pretty well, so I hung back until we got to one long curve, and then I stood on the gas all the way around it, caught up with the bastard, and passed him at the beginning of the next straightaway. I must have pissed him off, he stayed right on my ass until we hit the next curved section of road, but I had other things to worry about. Rosario hadn't given me up. Maybe he really did think I could rescue him, or maybe he was worried what the Russians would do to him once they found me. But they had definitely squeezed him, and I couldn't be sure how much more of that he could take.

I saw them take a right turn and head west. I thought it might have been that same road where I'd first seen Franklin, but I wasn't sure, and again, we were back to two cars, one following the other through the middle of nowhere. After about three miles we ran out of pavement. The Russians had to slow down, and so did I, but I was feeling less and less comfortable with the situation. These guys would have to be complete idiots not to have noticed me. I shut my lights off as I got to the top of a hill. The dirt road dropped away in front of me. I could see the road going down the hill, but I couldn't see any taillights, so I stopped and waited. It occurred to me then that I was being much more cautious than was normal for me, and I wasn't sure if I liked that, but then I realized that I had a hell of a lot more to lose now than I'd ever had before. I didn't know what to make of it: I sat there feeling like a coward for a few minutes, even though there were two of them and one of me, and they were sure to be armed while all I had was a hunting knife and a can of bug spray. I saw their lights come back on—they had pulled over into the trees to see if someone really was on their tail. I sat there and watched their taillights wink out of sight, wondering what to do. There must be a difference between courage and stupidity, that's what I told myself. Rosario was going to have to take it a while longer.

Nicky was asleep, right in the middle of the bed, his arm stretched out over to my side, reaching out for someone who wasn't there. I was afraid to move him—I didn't want to wake him up. I wasn't all that tired anyhow, in spite of the hour. I sat in an overstuffed old chair in the corner of the room and watched him. One thing about him, he went to bed without complaining and he slept like a dead man. Little bastard got up early, though. Just the opposite of his father. "Father," Jesus, there's a word for you.

Coming from where I did, it's tough for me to understand people who are so desperate to have kids when we don't know what the fuck to do with the ones we already got. You see it in the paper all the time, and I don't get it. Surrogate mothers, in-vitro fertilization, egg donors, sperm donors, fertility drugs that make women bear children like litters of baby mice, and all the time I'm growing up, I'm yelling, "Hey! What about me?" I guess it's in the genes, nobody really wants to just raise some kid, what they want is to procreate. Yeah, I'm a real winner, kid, and I'm gonna give you my DNA so you can be a winner, too. Just like me.

And yet, there he was, you know, this beautiful little person, this natural con artist, sleeping right in the middle of the bed in Eleanor Avery's spare bedroom, and what was I supposed to do with him? He didn't need to live out of a knapsack, sleep in motels and spare bedrooms. No matter how well intentioned I might be, no matter what a great kid I thought he was, if I wanted him to turn out better than me, I needed to start doing things different. Fuck me, it's bad enough you got to be responsible for yourself, okay, I'm a crook, I'm this and I'm that, go right down the fucking list, I don't really care, I'll cop to it all, but now I've got this kid, and if I don't find him a place where he can have his own room, and a bicycle, and a school to go to and all that shit, then it will be on me how he turns out. When he hits eighteen, he could be in college or he could be in prison, and I couldn't get away from the premonition that the decisions I was making right then were going to make the difference between the two.

Even Louis had done better than me. His son had grown up in a house, it was his bedroom that Nicky and I were sleeping in. Okay, maybe the guy wasn't Bill Gates, but he was a regular person, a guy with a job, and whatever the possessions were that he had managed to scrape together, they were his, the cops would stand between him and whoever it was that wanted them, he didn't need to worry about some bastard with a warrant, or two Russians from New Jersey, showing up in the middle of the night to take his shit and his family away from him.

I wondered if it was Bookman who had sold me out. I couldn't think of another way the bastards could have gotten so close so quickly. There was no way they could have traced me on their own. I hadn't used a credit card, I had been paying cash for everything. Even though the money had quite recently belonged to them, or to whoever had hired them, they had stolen it from someone else first. Cash doesn't tell stories, anyhow, it's never clean or dirty, only the hands that hold it. I had gone on-line from Avery's telephone, but I couldn't think of a way they could have traced that, either. They would have to know, in advance, what sites I would be looking at, they would have to know my on-line identity, and nobody knew that name but me. I cover my tracks, man. There's nobody any more paranoid than me. The only person I could think of who could put the pieces together was Bookman.

And why would he do it? What kind of game was he playing? Even if the Russians were offering some kind of a reward, I couldn't picture Bookman going for it. Cops go to cops, that's what they're used to. He didn't seem like that kind of guy, anyway. I hated to admit it, but I kind of liked the guy, even if he was a cop.

I put my feet up on the corner of the bed. Nicky stirred when I did that, mumbled something in his sleep. He liked this place, he liked Eleanor and Louis, and he loved that stupid horse. The kid had never had anything of his own, never in his life. I knew that was more my fault than anyone else's, but I couldn't change it. I couldn't go back into the past and give him a different family, and to be honest, I don't know if I would have done it if I could. He was mine, you know? Blame it on the DNA, he was part of me, and I was part of him, for better or worse.

It came to me then, what I needed to do. And it's funny, you know, you hear this shit all of your life, and I don't know about you but I would never listen. I already knew everything, why the hell would I pay attention to you? But those voices had been right. I needed to stop taking the easy way out, stop sneaking out the back window, stop running away. I always thought I was so fucking smart. I still do. So go on, genius, figure it out. Find a way to take care of the Russians, deal with Bookman somehow, clean up your goddam mess for once. I had never lived in a house before, never in my life. Well, the big house, but that didn't count. I had never lived in a normal place, like Louis's, with a yard full of green grass outside, and a cat, never mind the horse and the chickens and all the rest of it. Even when I had gotten to the point where I was about as successful as burglars get, I still never had anything real, I still lived in apartments, people upstairs, downstairs, and on both sides, and not even that much was mine, the apartments had always belonged to someone else. Maybe things could work out here, maybe we could stay. If I could manage to give Nicky something real, maybe he could grow up to be something real himself.

5

I woke up wondering if the Russians were the kind of guys who would go to church. Funny, the things your brain worries about. It was Sunday morning, my ears were still ringing from Roscoe's music, and my back was stiff from sleeping in the chair. Nicky had gotten up before me, of course, but he'd stayed quiet. He was sitting over by the window, watching Avery's horse. When I got up, he followed me into the bathroom, and the two of us washed up together. He did not seem to question the bond between us, somehow he accepted what I had such a hard time comprehending. You couldn't write it off, either, couldn't say that it was because he was young and didn't know any better, you couldn't say it was because I hadn't hurt him yet, hadn't let him down. I had already done all of those things, in spades, and yet he still trusted me. And even more than that, Nicky expected me to be the good guy. He had faith in the image of me that he held in his head, and I felt the weight of that faith and those expectations, and I was no longer comfortable being the unprincipled rat that I had once been. It was a new experience for me, being the subject of another person's uncritical positive regard, knowing for sure there was another human being out there who worried if I was going to be okay. I suppose I'd never had occasion to think about it before, maybe I'm emotionally retarded, stunted from a lack of water, but in my mind I always associated the word "love" with getting laid, you know, like in rock-and-roll lyrics. I'll tell you, though, those few minutes first thing in the morning, holding Nicky up so that he could make faces at himself in the mirror while he brushed his teeth, the hug that he gave me for no particular reason when we were done, that was worth everything to me. It was what I stood to lose if the Russians won.

Louis went to church that morning. He was already dressed to go when Nicky and I got downstairs. He was wearing a suit that had to be twenty-five years old, but it was clean, his shoes were polished, he was polished too, he was into it, man. He got that light in his eyes that religious people get, you know, and he asked me if Nicky and I wanted to tag along. Hell, no, I wanted to say, but I declined politely. Maybe next time. Eleanor, Louis told me, was having one of her pain spells, and was staying in bed. I promised Louis that Nicky and I would be quiet.

Nicky and I had cereal for breakfast, and then I got him settled in front of Avery's television. I plugged my laptop in and went on-line. I looked at MapQuest, trying to figure out where the Russians had been headed the night before. It looked to me like they had taken the back way toward Calais, as if they had wanted to stay off Route 1. They couldn't be staying far away, so I did a search for motels within a fifty-mile radius. I was surprised how few there were and worried for a while that I wasn't getting them all, but I searched a few different ways and kept coming up with most of the same names. I quit when I was happy with my list. It had about twenty names and phone numbers.

My phone spiel was pretty straightforward. Do you have a Dubrovnic party registered there? Oh, are you sure? Mr. Dubrovnic and his cousin are up there on a fishing trip. . . . Maybe they registered under his cousin's name. Oh, gee, you know, I don't remember his cousin's last name. Big guy, though, and Russian. Might have a third guy along. . . . Nobody like that? Sorry to bother you.

I made a mental note to myself to leave some money with Louis for the phone bill. I was three quarters of the way down the list when I hit pay dirt, sort of. "Oh, yes," the lady said, "I know who you mean. I'm afraid you missed them, though. They checked out this morning."

"Oh, no," I said. It was not too hard to sound distressed. "Oh, this is terrible. I've got to get a message to Mr. Dubrovnic right away, his wife went into labor earlier than expected, and if I don't get ahold of him, she's going to kill him and me both. Did they give you any idea where they were headed?"

She lowered her voice. "Well, they didn't say anything to me, but I did overhear one of them on the phone in the office, making arrangements to rent a cabin somewhere out near Grand Lake Stream. I don't know what good that will do you, though, they didn't leave the phone number."

"Oh, my," I said. "Well, I'll have to figure out something. Thank you so much for all your help."

I was up getting another cup of coffee when Avery's phone rang. It was Bookman, looking for me.

"Louis go to church?" he asked me.

"Yeah."

"Look," he said. "Howevah those Russians sniffed you out, the leak is on yaw end, not mine. Now you listen to me carefully: I don't want any dead Rooskies turning up in my jurisdiction. Do you understand me?"

"Bookman, you got me all wrong."

"Yeah, I 'magine. By the way, what did you hit Hopkins with?"

"My good right hand. Listen, the guy's a nutcase, I got the right to defend myself."

"Relax, I heard all about it. Stupid bahstid looked like a raccoon with a white nose this mawning, two black eyes and a big bandage in the middle of his face. I put him on unpaid leave for taking aftah you. Hop has had this coming for a long time, and I think that when it's all said and done, he'll be the better for it. If he's half the man I believe he is, he'll learn from it, but if you go stirring him up, he won't get the chance. I told him to stay away from you. I'm asking you to do the same."

I was beginning to get the impression that Bookman had a blind spot when it came to Hopkins. They say loyalty is a good quality in a person, but I didn't have much experience with it. "Bookman, I got nothing to prove to Hoppie or anybody else."

"'Hoppie' is one of those red-flag words." I could hear the disapproval in his voice. "Be helpful if you could go along with me on this."

"I am the soul of cooperation." He snorted disgustedly. "Listen, Bookman, I need you to do something for me. I checked around this morning, those two Russians were in a motel up in Calais, but they checked out this morning. The clerk said they rented a cabin up near Grand Lake Stream. Is there some way you could help me out? I'd feel much more comfortable knowing where they are and what they're doing."

He didn't say anything at first, and I wasn't sure if I'd pushed him too far or not. "I'll see what I can do," he said finally, and he hung up.

I didn't know what to think about Bookman. There were too many layers to the guy. He was too good at misdirection for you to take him at face value. He wore that chubby doofus exterior like a jacket, but his eyes belonged to a much different creature. He never told you enough, either, never said exactly what he was after. What had he done with me, that day in his office? He fed me a few scraps of information, and then he sat back and watched me jump to conclusions. I knew the first time I met him that he had to be smarter than he looked. Question was, how much smarter? I believed him, though, when he said that it wasn't him who'd ratted me out to the Russians. He just didn't seem to be that kind of guy.

I started thinking about the Russians again. Obviously they knew I was up here, but they didn't seem to know exactly what I looked like or what my name was. They couldn't know where I was staying, either, or they'd be coming through Avery's door already. They had Rosario, but he couldn't give them a lot, he only knew me by the street name I used in Brooklyn. I had to assume they were pretty good, though, because they'd bagged Rosey and broken him, and that could not have been easy. It's one of the bad things about being a crook: you make a big score, all of a sudden you're a target, the headhunters start coming after you, including the ones you thought were your friends. Hey, what are you gonna do, call the cops? I started getting antsy, started watching through the windows and shit.

"Hey, Nicky, you want to go for a walk?"

We stopped at the Subaru first and slathered ourselves with bug spray. I strung my binoculars around my neck and we started up the hill behind Avery's house. Two gulls flew overhead, one chasing the other. The pursuer was a great black-backed gull. They're easy to spot because they're bigger than the other gulls, plus, as you might guess, their backs and the tops of their wings are black. Usually. I mean, you might get one that's all white, and you might get one with gray wings, but this one was basic black. The other one was probably a herring gull, white body, gray on the back and the wing tops, but I couldn't be sure, because there are a dozen or so other kinds of gulls that can look almost exactly the same, ring-billed gulls, glaucous gulls, Iceland gulls, lesser black-backed gulls in a gray phase, forget about hybrids, and the immature gulls all look the same to me. Gulls are a pain in the ass. You have to go on small differences: either black or white on the wing tips, pale spots in the wing feathers when seen from below, small black bands on the tail, maybe a black ring on the beak, or a red spot, all while the son of a bitch is running for his life, wheeling and diving to evade the bigger one chasing him. The black ones will kill and eat the other gulls sometimes, grabbing them in midair and shaking them hard enough to break their necks.

Nicky was getting used to my fixation with birds, and he stopped next to me. We watched the two gulls until they were out of sight. "Why is the big one chasing that other one?" he wanted to know.

"The small one probably caught a fish, and the big one is trying to take it away from him."

"That's not fair. Why doesn't he go catch his own fish?"

"I don't know. Maybe he's no good at catching fish. Maybe the fish hide when they see him coming."

"He should go catch his own."

"Yeah, you're right." He seemed satisfied with that answer, and we went on up the hill. It's hard not to think of what animals do in terms of good and bad. It's a mistake to do that, they say, animals just do what they do, there's no morality involved. Nobody says why it doesn't work the other way around, though. I knew what the Russians were gonna do if they caught me, and it had nothing to do with some abstract set of rules about the politics of coercion. It was just who they were, what they did. No less true, I suppose, when I got the money to begin with, or when the guys I stole it from got it before me. Everything depends on where you're standing when the shit goes down.

Nicky and I messed around up in Louis's woodlot for an hour or so. We stayed away from the hole where the red oak had gone down, went farther up the hill into the woods. You could see where Louis had dropped a tree here and there, and there were piles of small branches lying around, making their slow way back down into the dirt. Louis didn't cut his firewood the way I imagined most people did, start with the closest trees to his house and work his way back, chopping down everything thicker than a pencil. He took one here and another one there, left the better-looking ones standing. I could hear a woodpecker drilling for his lunch but I couldn't spot him, he kept moving around. Kept his distance. Smart bird.

After a while we came back down the hill. I stopped Nicky just inside the tree line and glassed Avery's house. There was someone in the pasture next to Louis's house, next to the horse. "I wonder who that is," I said, mostly to myself.

"That's Eddie," Nicky said.

"Eddie? Oh, you mean Edna. How do you know?"

"She comes over during the day sometimes when you're gone. She helps out when Mrs. Avery isn't feeling good."

"Wow, Nicky, you got good eyes. Let's wait up here for just a minute, okay?"

"Okay, Poppy."

I watched her through the glasses. She was wearing construction boots, jeans, and a plaid shirt with the sleeves rolled up. If I had met her in the city, I might have assumed that she batted from the other side of the plate, but up here in the boonies, it's tougher to tell. I was used to people who wore clothes for what they said, but out here, people wore them for what they did.

"We going down?" Nicky was getting restless.

"Yeah, we are," I told him. "Just one more minute." My paranoia was in full bloom, and I wanted to make sure she was alone. I didn't know what difference it made, but I tend to listen to these inner voices.

Nicky tugged at me. "C'mon, Poppy."

"All right, let's go." If there was anyone inside the house, they weren't going to come out carrying a sign to let me know who they were, anyhow. We headed down the hill. Nicky, who had been showing signs of fatigue in our last half hour in the woodlot, started bouncing up and down next to me.

"Can I go? Can I run, Dad?"

"Don't fall and hurt yourself." He turned and grinned at me, patted me once on the hip, for luck, I guess, and tore off down the hill. The horse must have heard him coming—she raised her head to look. Edna turned then and saw us. By the time I got down there she had Nicky up on the horse's back, and he was grinning so hard I thought his face was gonna break. I didn't go into the pasture with them, but leaned on the outside of the board fence and watched. Edna said something to Nicky, and he nodded, patting the horse's neck. She came over and stood next to me, inside the fence.

"Hi," she said. "What did you do to Hoppie?"

"Well," I said, "we had to have a conversation about nonaggression and mutual respect. Man, I gotta say, the grapevine up here is pretty muscular."

"Yeah, no kidding," she said. "Really, what happened?"

"I went to hear Roscoe's band. Hop was there, and he was tanked. Just as well, I guess, it made him easier to handle. He came after me, and I had to dissuade him."

"I hear you did some job of it."

"Do I need to worry about him coming back for a rematch?"

"You bet your ass you do. Hop always has to get the last word in, always." She looked at me. "If I had someone like Nicky to think about, I would get far away from here." She looked down at the ground. "It's none of my business, but I hope you're not into beating your chest and showing everybody what a tough guy you are. Tangling with Hop would be a serious mistake."

"I'm not into posing. Listen, he came after me."

"I know. I'm not trying to tell you what to do." She glanced over at the house.

"How's Eleanor?" I asked her.

"Not too swingin'." She looked over at Nicky sitting on the horse, and then she led me a few steps farther away. "How much have they told you?"

"How much have they told me about what?"

She stared at me for a minute, and it struck me how much older than her years she seemed, and then the next thought was that old male thing, you know, she's old enough, or at least she's big enough, and she seems interesting as hell. . . .

"About her tumor."

That got my attention. "Tumor? Nobody said anything about a tumor. Louis said she gets pain spells."

"That sounds like Louis," she said, pursing her lips in disapproval. "Never admit when you're in trouble, never ask for help." She shook her head. "Eleanor gets pain spells because she has a tumor in her stomach. Louis has been taking her to a doctor in Machias, and Eleanor hates to go because she's agoraphobic."

"Afraid of sweaters?"

She glared at me. "That would be angoraphobic, you moron. Agoraphobia, she never leaves the house."

"I kinda noticed that."

"So anyway, the doctor said she's got a tumor, and if they operate on it now and get it before it gets any further along, she might have a good chance of survival. The problem is, Medicare won't cover the operation. Louis told me the doctor said Medicare would jerk him around for another year, and by the time they're finally convinced she needs to get it taken out, it'll be too late."

"Jesus."

"Yeah. The problem is, even with the surgeon kicking in his fee, it's going to cost about forty grand, and Louis doesn't have it. Might as well be forty million."

"No shit. What about that piece of property up in Eastport that Sam Calder wants to buy?"

"He doesn't want to buy it anymore. He must have heard that Louis is over a barrel, and now he only wants to buy a right-of-way to cross it. He's offering twenty-five thousand. Either way, whether he sells that or not, Louis is worried that he's probably going to lose his house."

"Damn." No wonder Louis and Eleanor were willing to put Nicky and me up, let us invade their home until the van got fixed. They were going to need every cent they could lay their hands on.

Edna was looking down, kicking the ground with a booted foot. "Anyhow, can we get off that? Can we talk about something else?" She glanced at the glasses hanging around my neck. "Your son tells me you were up in the woods looking for birds. Are you a bird-watcher?"

"Yeah, I guess. I been to therapy for it, but I think I'm a hopeless case."

"How did you get into that?"

"I don't really remember." That was a lie. The first birds I really paid any attention to were the ratty little dark brown ones that used to hang around the yard in prison. They were starlings, though I didn't know that at the time. It seemed to me then that they didn't give a fuck what the rules were, they went where they wanted to go and did what they wanted to do, they weren't interested in what anybody thought. I was wrong about most of that—birds generally lead lives as regimented as any convict's—but by the time I found that out it was too late, I was hooked.

She turned around, leaning on the inside of the fence. She called out to Nicky. "You all right, honey? You want to get down yet?"

Nicky shook his head, still grinning. I guess there was no place in the world he would rather be. She turned back to me. "So that's what you're doing up in Maine? Looking at birds?"

"Nah, not really. I look at birds no matter where I go." Think, Manny, why are you up here? You've got to come up with something halfway believable. . . . "Nicky's mother died a couple years ago. We've been living in Brooklyn since then. Can you imagine a kid like him, cooped up indoors all day long? I want to find something better for him."

She shook her head. "There's no jobs up here, Manny. You won't be able to work."

"I'm a software designer. I could probably work from just about anywhere, you know, with some limitations. I guess I'm up here trying to figure out what the right thing is."

"You'd give up New York City, for him?"

"Whoo. What a thought." Oh, but I would, man, yeah, now that you mention it, I would give up everything for Nicky. That wasn't a decision I came to, it was something I woke up to just then, maybe because Eddie asked me about it, I don't know. What a strange idea, anyway, what an odd sensation that was, that I would sacrifice my life, give up myself for another person, even if he was related to me. I felt it washing over me, almost like a spell of dizziness, and for that moment I was close to losing it, which went against every instinct I had. If you have a weak spot, you never dare to show it in public, do you? I swallowed it, tucked it away so that I could look at it again when I was all alone. "Maybe I can sneak back for a visit once in a while."

She smiled at me then, and we watched Nicky sitting on the horse, caressing its neck, talking to it softly. Change the subject, I thought. "So you checked on Eleanor this morning?"

"Yeah," she said.

"I've been thinking that I should take Nicky out for a ride or something. You know, try and give Eleanor some peace and quiet. Nicky makes a lot of noise when he's been cooped up inside for too long."

"Good idea," she said. "If you thought you and Nicky would like a boat ride, you could call up Hobart, the guy you got the Subaru from. He has a lobster boat, and he takes it out most Sunday afternoons. I'd bet he knows more about the bay than just about anybody. See if he'd take you guys out. It might be fun."

"Thanks, Eddie. Maybe I'll do that."

* * *

Hobart recognized my voice. "How's the Subaru working out?" he asked.

"Fine," I told him. "Listen, I'm trying to get my son out of Louis and Eleanor's house for the afternoon. I was told, if I wanted to see Passamaquoddy Bay, you're the guy to talk to."

"Yeah," he said. "I was gonna go out and dub around, I guess. You wanna come along, I could probably use the company." He told me how to find the boat, and we agreed to meet there. Before we left, I checked the voice-mail box on my phone, but there were no messages.

He kept his boat tied up at a long-legged pier that perched high above the water of a round inlet called Bailey's Folly. The place was outside of Passamaquoddy Bay, south of Lubec, and out through the narrow mouth of the inlet you could see the cold water of the southern reaches of the Bay of Fundy. There were a couple of houses on one side of the place, and a dog somewhere barked as Nicky and I made our way over to the pier. There was a long walkway on one side of the pier that tilted down to a square wooden platform that floated in the water next to the pier, and as the tides came in and out, the platform, with Hobart's boat tied to it, rose and fell with the water level. There were piles of wire-mesh lobster traps stacked on the platform, bits of dried seaweed and barnacles stuck to them.

The boat itself was fiberglass, green on the outside, white on the inside, maybe twenty-three, twenty-four feet long, with a sort of half shelter built around the steering wheel and the throttle. I guess it would keep you a little drier in the rain, as long as the wind wasn't blowing too hard, which it generally was. The thing looked exactly like a million other lobster boats up and down the coast. Nicky and I climbed down onto the platform, over behind a pile of lobster traps, and sat down. With my binoculars, I could see out through the mouth of the inlet, out to where a bunch of seagulls sat in the mad, churning, swirling rush of water, riding the insane currents, eating something that floated near the surface. Nicky got down on his hands and knees next to the water, reached down, and put his hand in. "Cold," he said. After that, he came over and sat down beside me, and I gave him the binoculars to play with.

"Turn that little wheel on top," I told him. "Turn it back and forth until you can see something." I showed him how it worked. I don't know if he got it or not, but he seemed happy enough to sit there and mess with it.

About fifteen minutes after I sat down, I heard footsteps coming down the walkway. Had to be him—there were no other boats there. I stood up.

"There you are," he said. "Come ahead."

"This is my son, Nicky. Nicky, that's Captain Hobart."

Nicky's mouth went wide. "Captain?"

Hobart chuckled. It was the first real sign of emotion I'd seen in him. "Hello, son," he said. "You ready to go for a ride in my boat?"

Nicky's mouth went wider still. "Is that your boat?"

"Yep. C'mon aboard." I handed Nicky over to him, then climbed aboard and sat down on the doghouse that covered the engine back by the stern. Hobart climbed out onto the dock and untied a rope at the front of the boat. After that, he got back and started up his engine. He pointed back at me. "Cast us off, there," he said. "Let go that line."

There was a rope holding the stern of the boat to the dock. I started looking for the end, where it was tied to the boat. "T'other end," Hobart said. "She's wound around that cleat on the dock there." I got it loose. Hobart put the thing in gear with a thunk, pushed his throttle forward. He spun the wheel and the boat chugged away from the dock. He looped a piece of rope around one of the spokes on the wheel. Autopilot, I guess. "Nicky," Hobart said, "we got to get you to put a life vest on. Okay?"

Nicky, enthralled, nodded his head slowly. Hobart fished around in a wooden locker, came up with a child-sized life vest. It had a ring on the back, with a piece of rope tied to it. Hobart glanced over the side. I guessed that he was satisfied we weren't about to run into anything, and he knelt down and fastened the vest around Nicky. "This piece of line, here," he said, "is a safety line. We want to make sure we don't lose you, okay?" He looked up at me. "Some kids don't like the line, makes 'em feel like a dog in the backyard, but you gotta have it. He went over the side, even with a vest on, it'd be hell getting him back. You'd be asking a lot of him, just to try to keep his face out of that cold water."

"You don't mind, do you, Nicky?" I asked him. He looked up at me, no idea what we were talking about. "You all right?"

He nodded his head again.

"You want to sit down on the back or you want to stand there?"

He closed his mouth, finally, and swallowed. He looked around, then back at me. "Here," he said, pointing at his spot on the deck. I think he was blown away. I think the boat, the water, the noise of the engine, the smell of the bay, had all overloaded his inputs. I think he was doing that thing that only little kids can do, when they're wide open, taking it all in.

Hobart shoved the throttle forward a little more, and the boat picked up speed, but not much. It was a workboat, and its only speeds were slow and slower. "I appreciate this," I told him. "I've never been out in a boat like this before."

"Well, there it is," he said, a small waggle of his hand encompassing the whole scope of the water and islands around us. "There's the bay. It's a hungry place. Every living thing you see out here is looking for something to eat. Dolphins, over in the channel."

"Where?"

"Ahead, and to your left, headed up into the channel between Lubec and Campobello Island, into the bay." He pointed at some fuzzy neon green shit on a small sonar screen in front of him. "That there's probably a school of herring. That's what the dolphins are chasing, like as not."

I looked up where he pointed, and a minute later they broke through the water's surface, sleek rounded shapes topped by smallish dorsal fins. "I see 'em. How about that?"

"Poppy."

I looked down, and Nicky was peering through the glasses. "What?"

He pointed unsteadily, trying to hold the glasses to his face with one hand and point with the other. "There's a bird," he said. "Over there."

I looked where he was pointing, but all I saw was a small rocky islet sticking out of the water. It had a small patch of green on the top, looked like a toupee several sizes too small. I guess that was what was left showing when the tide was in. "I don't see a bird."

"Ten points for me," he said. "He's sitting up on that rock."

I squinted. "Oh, yeah. Good job, Nicky. I can't tell what he is, he's too far away."

"We can go see, if you want," Hobart said. "Shags like to stand up theyah and dry their wings out so that they can fly again."

Nicky handed me the glasses and I looked through them. "Too big for a shag, I think. Too big for a hawk, even. Big hook on the beak. You got eagles up here?"

"Plenty. Probably fifty bald eagles within a ten-mile radius of right here. Sometimes you'll see a whole row of 'em, scaling."

"Scaling?"

"Yeah, just hanging there in the wind, you know, still, over the water."

It was an eagle, an immature first-year bird without the distinctive white head it would get if it survived into adulthood. It was big, though, as big as it would get. It got nervous when we approached, arched its wings, and hopped off to another rock farther away. Hobart jerked his head at the wooded island looming on the far side of the island the bird was on. "Nest over there in the spruce trees," he said, spinning the wheel and turning us into the current. "You wanna go see it?"

"Nah. Leave 'em alone."

"Awright."

I checked my cell phone's voice mail again, still nothing. "How long you lived up here, Hobart?"

"My family moved here when I was ten years old."

"No kidding. Man, if this place is quiet now, it must have been desolate back then."

Hobart shook his head. "You're wrong about that," he said. "There was still a bunch of sardine canneries in business then." We had made it up into the channel between Lubec and the big island to the north, and the bay opened up in front of us. The sky was overcast, giving the surface of the water a fog-colored sheen. The wind raked at us, it never stopped, it was like the currents of the bay, ceaseless, unpredictable, cold. Hobart pointed at the town of Eastport, farther west along the southern shore of the bay. From the water it looked like a row of two- and three-story buildings maybe three blocks long, built on a ledge by the shore, with a couple of wharfs in the water and some houses in the trees on the low hill behind the town. Picturesque as hell, but dead quiet. "Used to be fish canneries cheek by jowl, right along the waterfront, over theyah. Every little cove had a factory building. I seen this whole bay full of herring, one giant school seven or eight miles across, and everything that eats herring was in here after 'em. Cod, pollack, big bluefin tuna, dolphins, seals, sharks, whales . . ."

"Whales? Serious? What kind?"

"Finback," he said. "And minke. And you know something? The old-timahs were complaining then that there was nothing left. They used to tell stories about halibut as big as this boat. Cow halibut, they used to call 'em. Lobstahs, four foot long, dredged up in a net."

"You believe them?"

"Yeah," he said.

"So what happened?"

"In the old days, fishermen went out in sailboats, wooden, fifty or sixty feet long. Didn't have no refrigeration, just salt. They went fishing in the places where they'd been lucky befowah, or where their fathers had been lucky, that's all they knew. That's all the technology they had. By the end of it, twenty yeahs ago, we had factory ships from all over the world just offshore, processing and freezing right on board, and a thousand fishing boats keeping them busy. Didn't need to guess where the fish was, neither." He rapped on his sonar screen with his knuckles. "If there was fish there, you could see 'em, and you could go catch 'em."

"Too bad. All gone now?"

He shrugged. "Fella like you, never seen it back when, you'd still think the bay was perfect. I seen a tuna just last week, he had to be a good five or six feet long, he had a bunch of herring drove up into the cove just around from where we were tied up this morning, and he was right up in the shallows eating 'em, in about a foot of water. Bet he went six hundred pounds easy."

"No kidding."

"And we still get some of the rest, pollack, a whale now and then, seals and dolphins. Ten-thousand-dollar fine for shooting a seal."

"Why would you want to shoot a seal?"

"You might be tempted if you seined him up along with your fish and he was about to tear a hole in your net and cost you twenty-five grand in damage and lost catch." He glanced over at me. "You really cayah about any of this?"

"I'm interested."

"Awright. That's Lubec, to your left, and Eastport, up ahead there. On the right, that's Campobello Island. Everything on that side is Canada. FDR had a summah house over theyah, you can drive across that bridge from Lubec and go see it if you want. This channel we're in is called Friar's Road." He spun his wheel to the left and we headed over toward the Canadian side. "Right in the water at the foot of that bluff there, that's Friar's Rock." From a distance, it did look like a thirty-foot statue of a monk in a robe, a finger of rock rising out of the water at the foot of a cliff.

"Up across there, on the fah side of the bay, you got Deer Island and Indian Island, and the channel down between them is Indian Road. Eastport is built on the end of Moose Island, they got a causeway out to it, but you know that. Them small islands around the side of Moose Island are the Dog Islands. Now you got four hundred feet of water out here in the middle, you got the St. Croix flowing down between Moose and Deer Islands, you got the current coming down the Indian Road, and you got the tide sweeping in and out of Friar's Road, here. Twenty-three feet of tide, normally, but sometimes you'll get a lot more. I don't know what causes it, the moon or the planets or what, but sometimes you'll get what we got now, low tide five or six feet lower than normal, and high tide five or six feet higher than normal. Figure twice the normal volume of water in and out of here, twice a day. Now, you see that mahkah over there on Deer Island?" He pointed at it, a large white triangle over on the far shore.

"Yeah."

"'Nother one on this side, just opposite, but we can't see it from here. Well, that stretch between the mahkahs is called the Old Sow. Usually it looks like a big boiling pot. You'll get big boils of water come up there five foot high out of the water, up out of nowhere from the currents all swirling around. Looks pretty rugged out there now, don't it? But we're on the ebb tide now, and what you see now is nothing. On a flood tide, from about an hour after the tide starts until about an hour before she turns, you'll see whirlpools right out there in the middle, out there in those tidal streaks in the center. In forty years, the biggest one I seen was twenty-five feet across and maybe twenty feet deep, and the tide wasn't near as bad that day as it's been for the last few days. You can hear 'em growl, all the way over on the shore. These last few tides have been worse than anything I can remember. I wouldn't want to guess how big they'll be on the next few flood tides. You get out there on a flood tide, son, you might learn more about Passamaquoddy Bay than you wanted to know."

"Not now, though."

"Nah. Ebb tide, just what you see, just a little churning around." What he called "a little churning around" looked bad enough to me. Gulls, sitting in the water, went ripping past us, carried along by the current. You went overboard here, they'd have a bitch of a time catching up to you. Provided you didn't get eaten by something in the meantime.

On the way back, just outside Bailey's Folly, I saw a strange bird, like a gull only ten times bigger, although it's hard to gauge size against a backdrop of empty ocean and sky. It had impossibly long, slender wings, and it flew like it was tired, wingbeats like the strides of a marathon runner. I didn't get a good look, and I didn't get my glasses on it until it was too far away, but it might have been an albatross. You don't see them often in the North Atlantic, and I had never seen one before. I have heard that there have been a few windblown vagrants. What happens, an albatross needs wind to fly, so occasionally one will ride up on a storm from the Southern Hemisphere. Once he's up here, he can't get back, he can't get back across the doldrums on his own. You wonder if a bird can miss his mate and all the places he knew, you wonder if he knows he can never go home again.

I picked Nicky up. I told myself it was so that he could see better, but maybe it was so that I could see better, I don't know. He put his arm across my shoulders and stared out across the water. He still had that look of wonder on his face. A minute later, he turned and looked at me. "You like boats, Dad?"

"Yeah, I like boats."

"Me, too," he said.

I went out that evening after dinner because I was feeling a little squeezed. I told everyone that I wanted to see the screech owl again, and I suppose I did, but the real reason was that I was having some trouble breathing. I had been used to a certain level of solitude most of my life. Funny, when you think of living in the city, you think of the inescapable pressure of so many people crowded together. The fact is, you can walk down any street in New York at rush hour and be totally alone. There was something perversely comforting about that, being surrounded by millions of people and knowing that none of them can touch you, none of them have any connection to you at all. And yet, here I was, up in the middle of nowhere, living in this great big house with only three other people, and I could feel the web of invisible nerve endings that held the four of us together. I could actually feel Eleanor's sorrow over the thing growing in her stomach and how it was upsetting the fragile balance of the life she and Louis worked so hard to live, I could feel Louis's worry about her and his sense of helplessness and fear, I could feel Nicky's heart, not small and hard like mine, but growing and opening up in this place. It was more input than I knew what to do with, I felt like a drowning man inhaling water. It wasn't that they were asking anything from me, either. Eleanor was feeling better, she'd gotten up and was surfing the Web on my laptop, Nicky was watching television, and Louis was sitting at his kitchen table, drinking Jim Beam out of a coffee cup and playing solitaire. Eleanor had gone pale and haggard when she saw him break out the bottle, but she hadn't said a word. None of my business. I sat watching Eleanor, thinking about what Eddie Gevier had told me, wondering if Eleanor was going to die for the lack of a lousy forty grand. And then I began to wonder if I, too, might be carrying the seeds of my own death, lying quiet inside me somewhere, waiting for their time. I began to wonder if there was something wrong with me, some reason why I couldn't handle caring about someone other than myself. I found, shortly after that, that I needed to get outdoors. I needed to be by myself for a little while, until I could catch my breath.

I stopped at the Subaru for my glasses and some bug spray, then settled into a comfortable spot on the far side of the yard. I was as quiet as I could manage, not that it mattered much. Even if I lay completely still the owl would hear the sound of me breathing. An owl can hear a mouse walking across hard ground from thirty yards away, and he can pinpoint the mouse's exact location from those faint noises. If I really did want to see the owl again, I had to pay attention. He might hear me, but I would never hear him. Owls are engineered to kill in complete silence. Their feathers are different from the feathers of other birds, there are no hard edges on them anywhere, and when they fly, they are as quiet as death. I just hoped he wouldn't be interested in me, that he would go about his business and not mind my attention. As it got progressively darker, the bugs came out. The repellent kept them off my face and hands, but mosquitoes and the odd blackfly would land on my shirt and jeans and wander around looking for a weak spot. A mosquito pierced one of my socks and bit me on the ankle. You learn as you go along, I guess—next time I'd use bug spray down there, too. They say only the females bite you. I couldn't spare her any attention, though, I just hoped none of her sisters were as smart as she was.

I got distracted anyway. A pair of bats began working the airspace over the Subaru and Louis's Jeep. I guess they were eating the bugs attracted by the dim lights of the house. I watched them until it got too dark to see them anymore. It was a clear night with no moon, and even with the blue light of Louis's television in the background, it was darker than any night I could remember experiencing before. The stars came out, hard and cold, they seemed much closer to me that night in Maine than they ever had before. To tell you the truth, I had never paid them any attention. Even when I'd gone up on the Jersey Palisades they'd just been the background to what I was looking for, just wallpaper. For most of human history people lived this close to them, though, thought they might mean something, looked up there for portents, clues that might help them decipher their own course. I could easily have gone my entire life without really noticing the night sky at all, let alone wondering if it had anything to tell me. We're so smart now, we know at least something about everything, but still, nobody can tell you which of those pieces of information are important.

I wasn't thinking about Louis and Eleanor, but some inner voice got through. If she was your mother . . .

She's not my mother, I thought. I don't have a mother.

Yeah, so? You got the money, you cheap fuck.

Hey, man, people just don't go around interfering with other people's lives like that. Besides, if it was me that was fucked up, nobody's lining up to help out my ass. That's not the way the world works. I'll kick in a couple Gs for the cause.

Okay?

The voice was silent, but I could feel the cold weight of disappointment laying on my chest.

6

I still hadn't heard from Bookman, and I was trying to come up with another way to find out where the Russians were staying when he called me the next morning. "Talk to Chris Johnson," he said. "He's an Indian, lives up on the Passamaquoddy Reservation near Grand Lake Stream."

"You think he can find these guys?"

"He knows everything that goes on up there, and if he doesn't, he'll know how to find out. You're gonna have to hire him. Be better for you if you didn't mention my name."

"He don't like you?"

"Hahd to believe, isn't it? We may have worked at cross-purposes in the past, but it's authority he doesn't like, not me personally. Nice enough young fella, for all of that. He's a guide, takes rich people from Noo Yawk fishing and hunting. Gets a hundred a day, they tell me."

"How do I find him?"

"He don't have no phone, I don't think. Take a ride on up there, stop in the tackle store and ask. They're the ones that do his bookings, so they should know where he is."

"Thanks, Bookman."

"Just you remember what I said: no dead Rooskies in my county."

"I'll dump 'em up in Aroostook."

Bookman exploded. "Goddammit, Manny! I already got one dead man on my hands. I don't want any more problems than I already have.

You better not be more trouble than you're worth."

"Don't worry, Bookman, I ain't a violent person. Who's the dead guy?"

"That stupid kid we picked up with the OxyContins. Last night he aspirated his own vomit and choked to death."

"Jesus."

"He was a good kid, once upon a time. Now he's dead, and whoever the bastard is, bringing that shit over, he can keep right on doing it."

"I don't know, man. There's not a lot of people up here. Somebody's bound to know who your guy is. Maybe this will piss them off enough to give you a name."

"I keep telling myself that. Remember what I said about them goddam Russians." He hung up.

I asked Eleanor if she would watch Nicky for me. "I'm embarrassed, how much he's with you and how little he's with me."

She patted my hand and smiled. "I don't think you realize how lucky you are, Manny."

"Well, I didn't want to just assume . . ."

She shook her head. "Your son is a joy."

Then I went and asked Nicky if he minded staying with her. I guess I was trying to treat him like an adult. I didn't know how you were supposed to treat kids. He took it seriously, too. "You're coming back, right?"

"Course I'm coming back."

He nodded gravely. "Can I come with you next time?"

"This is not a trip for fun. I have to go take care of some things. Anytime I go somewhere for fun, I'll take you with me. Okay?"

"Okay."

"In the meantime, you promise to mind Mrs. Avery?"

"Yep."

"You'll do what she tells you to do?"

"Yep."

He followed me up the stairs, stayed close to me while I grabbed a few things out of one of my duffel bags, and he followed me back downstairs again. God, I felt rotten. Every time I left him with someone I felt worse than the last time. He gave me a hug before I left, and that made it even harder. I had to get out of there before I started blubbering. Jesus. What I needed was to find a safe place to be with my kid, where he would have a chance to grow up and be normal—I realized it as I drove the Subaru down Louis's driveway. It was Mohammed's fault, it was that fucking guy from Brooklyn. I promised myself, if I ever got loose of him and his business, I would never go back.

There was a store in Grand Lake Stream that sold, among other things, bait and tackle. I myself have never been fishing. You can buy a fish in a store if you want one, or order it cooked already in a restaurant, am I right? The guy had lots of gear for sale in the place, though, rods and reels and flies and special clothes, all sorts of crap. Sometimes I think accessorizing is the real point of any sport. There was no point to my fascination with birds, either, it was never gonna make me any money, and every time I hear about a new gizmo, a new scope or better binoculars or another book, you know I gotta have it.

I picked out a bucket hat, one of those stupid-looking things that fishermen wear, got a brim going all the way around to keep the sun off you, and I took it up to the register. The guy behind the counter was the only other person in the place, and he was watching some celebrity news show on a small television. "Find everything you were looking for?"

"Actually I'm looking for a guy, name of Chris Johnson. I was told he's the best guide around here."

"He's very good," the guy told me, "but you're out of luck. He's up the Alleagash, taking some naychah photographahs to see the river."

"Damn. I got lousy timing."

"I can fix you up with another guide, if you want."

"Chris came highly recommended." It wasn't fish or deer I was after. I would have to talk to Bookman. I couldn't just take some guy at random.

"Well," the guy said. "He's been gone 'bout ten days, I imagine he'll be back fairly soon. Why don't you go ask his mother? She would prolly know bettah than me."

"You know her phone number?"

"She don't have a phone, but she lives right up the road." I paid for my hat, wrote down the directions to Chris Johnson's mother's house.

She had some serious pine trees around her house. Who knew those things got so freaking huge? Some of the branches seemed so large and so high, if one broke off in a storm it would crush her house like an egg crate. The house itself was very small, and under the corners you could see the cement blocks that held it up off the ground. It was green, with a reddish brown roof, more what you would call a cabin than a house. It had a deck at one end, gas grill in the corner. There was a carpet of pale brown pine needles everywhere, on the roof, the yard, and the deck. I parked the Subaru out front and knocked on the door.

The lady who answered was a short, broad, roundish woman, brown skin and eyes, black hair pulled back from her face in a bun. She looked vaguely Oriental to me. "Hi," she said. "If you're selling something, I'm too broke to even pay attention."

She had a soft voice, and her accent was different from the ones I had been hearing. "I'm no salesman. I'm looking for Chris Johnson."

"He isn't here," she said. "Come on inside and I'll take down your information so he can get back to you." She stood holding the door open. The central room was the living room, dining room, and kitchen. The walls were knotty pine, and the floor was linoleum with an oval rag rug. It felt like a comfortable place. I took the seat she offered me at her kitchen table. "Are you trying to arrange a fishing trip?"

I hadn't bothered to think of a scam to run on her, and I couldn't think of one now. "Not exactly." She took a seat across from me and waited. "You know Taylor Bookman?"

She nodded. "Sure."

"He told me to ask for your son."

"Didn't think you looked like a rich white man after a trout."

"There are two guys up here somewhere," I told her. "Two Russians, gangsters from Brooklyn. I've got something they want, and I can't let them have it. Plus, I think they're holding a friend of mine against his will. They were staying in a motel down in Calais, but they moved. They're supposed to be in a cabin near here, but I don't know more than that."

"Why don't you go to the police? Won't they help you?"

"I haven't had much luck with the police in the past." That was sure as hell the truth. "I think I need to find out more information before I involve cops."

The expression on her face never changed, but her voice did, just a little bit. "Did Taylor Bookman tell you that my son could help you do something to these men?"

I shook my head. "Not my style. No, what I'd like to do is see if there's some way I could steal my friend away from them, let them think he got loose on his own. That way, they'd have to go chase him and leave me alone."

"A coyote," she said, "and not a wolf. Nothing wrong with that, I guess. Well, Chris won't be home until next week. I tell you what, if you pay me his day rate, I'll help you find them, but if you do something bad, I'll help Bookman find you. Deal?"

"Bookman was the one who sent me here to begin with." She waited, said nothing. "Deal," I said.

"Okay," she said. "First I'll have to make a few phone calls, just to find out where they are. Do you have some quarters for the pay phone?"

"I got a cell phone in the car."

"You get a signal up here?" She sounded surprised.

"It comes and goes. We might need to stand outside."

"All right," she said.

We went out to the Subaru. I had my binoculars and a *Stokes Field Guide* on the front seat. "Coyote," she said. "Are you a birder?"

"I'm just learning," I told her. I figured out what it was about her speech, she used the proper words and diction and all that, but she did it like a person who has learned English as a second language. No slang at all, and no street, but there was the vague presence of another tongue underneath it all, another world, another life.

She picked up the glasses and scanned the woods around her house. "Aren't we all," she said. "Where's your notebook? Did you get a grosbeak yet?"

"I don't have a notebook. Where do you see a grosbeak?"

"You have to have a notebook. You need to know the date, the time of day, was it raining, was the bird in flight, what color were the primaries, how about the secondaries and coverts? What color were the feet, and the beak? You can't remember all that." She handed me the glasses. "Right over there in those alders. Three feet off the ground on a branch, black head and back, red throat, white belly. Male rose-breasted grosbeak."

I found him, half hidden in the brush. "God, he's beautiful." I handed the glasses back to her. "You are really good."

She shook her head. "This is my home ground. I saw him at one of the feeders out back. I knew he had to be around here somewhere. Did you find that phone?"

I came reluctantly back to the real world. "Yeah, I got it."

She leaned her butt on the hood and made a series of phone calls. She could have been calling her grandmother in Texas for all I knew, because while she would greet in English whoever answered—"Hello, Willie," she said to the first one—the rest of the conversation was in what I assumed was her native tongue. When she was done she shut the phone off and handed it back to me. "Handy little gadget," she said. "Well, Coyote, I've got good news and bad news. The good news is, I know where they're staying. The bad news is, it won't be easy for you to get close. Get in, I'll show you the place."

We took off. She leafed through my field guide while I drove, following her directions. She hardly looked out the window. She reminded me of Hobart, in the way she seemed to be of this place. I wondered what that must be like, to have some special part of the world where you belonged. "So tell me," I asked her. "You live up here your whole life?"

"No," she said. "I used to live in Queens, back before my husband got killed."

I almost drove off the road. "No shit! Queens?"

She smiled then, but I could tell from the look in her eyes that she was evaluating me. "Do you think I'm like a tree, planted up here?"

"Hey, I didn't mean nothing, I'm just surprised, that's all. What made you pick a place like Queens?"

"My husband was a steelworker. We moved down to the city so he could find work. We thought we could save up some money. Get ahead."

"What happened?"

"One night on his way home from work, someone pushed him in front of the subway train. Take the left up past that gas station."

"Jesus. I'm sorry to hear that."

She shrugged. "Are you religious, Coyote?"

"No."

"Neither am I, but it would be nice if one of them was right, though, wouldn't it? Left again, right up ahead there."

It was about a half hour's ride from her house. "Pull over here." We were on a narrow two-lane road, forest on one side, fields on the other, sloping gently away from us. There didn't seem to be a farmer attached to the fields, they were pastures with no cows, growing tall yellow grasses that swayed with the rhythm of the morning breeze. More of those rock walls. In the field closest to us there was an iron farming implement of some kind rusting away, looked like something you'd tow behind a horse or a tractor to scrape the dirt into rows. A pair of ruts in the grass ran down the edge of the field next to a rock wall, leading down toward a narrow lake that was maybe three quarters of a mile away. "Down there," she said. "There's a cabin on the far side. That little road you're looking at is the only way in. I don't think you could get in there without them seeing you. There isn't even anyplace you could hide this little truck and walk in."

I looked at the place through my binoculars. The exterior told me nothing. Just a cabin by a small lake in the middle of nowhere. "I see what you mean. What's up behind there?"

"Woods," she said, looking at me like I was an idiot.

"I can see that. But if you went back far enough, you'd have to hit a road or something eventually. No?"

"I guess you would," she said thoughtfully. "Do you think you could come in from the back?"

"It's an idea."

"It might be a long walk. Okay, turn around, go on back the way we came."

The road we took was unpaved, and it seemed almost like a tunnel of pale greens and quick patches of yellow. Tall fir, spruce, and hemlock filtered out most of the sunlight. When we first turned onto the road we passed a sign warning us that the next twenty-eight miles were seasonal and unmaintained, and I slowed the Subaru down to keep it from rattling apart. There were no power lines or phone lines, either, no houses, no other cars. In one spot a small creek covered the road with a couple of inches of ginger ale–colored water. We were nine miles in from the sign when she had me stop.

"Find a place to pull over," she said. "You'll need to get right off the road because logging trucks come through here sometimes, and they don't go slow. How about over there, past those oak trees? Did you bring some bug dope with you?"

"I got OFF. That okay? It's behind the seat."

"That's good for this time of year," she said. "The spring is another story, though. How about a compass?"

"Nope."

"Didn't think so. Native Americans such as myself, we don't need no stinking compass. City boy like you, you should probably pick one up." I was trying to figure out if she was yanking my chain when she started laughing. "Come on, Coyote," she said, shaking her head. "Bring your glasses and bug dope."

My first trip through that place was hell. In an old-growth forest, the trees are huge, ancient, and therefore very tall. They shut out most of the light, which means nothing much grows on the forest floor unless one of the giants goes down. When that happens there is a riot of competition among various plant forms until one of them wins and fills up the hole in the canopy overhead, at which time the rest of the undergrowth dies off again. Mrs. Johnson told me all that while I did my best to follow her through the second-growth forest, which was choked with a tangle of fucking puckerbushes that all seemed to have it in for me personally, doing their best to scratch my face or arms or trip me and knock me on my ass. The bushes liked her better than me, they must have, because she didn't have the same problems with them, even though she was broader of beam than I was. She just moved resolutely forward in her calm unhurried fashion while I tried to keep up. "You should have brought boots," she said after I stepped in a wet spot and filled my sneakers with mud.

Once we got through the first half mile or so, we got past the marshy section, and the going got marginally easier. She stopped to point out different things: piles of furry brown marbles she said were deer shit, scratch marks on a tree she said were made by a black bear, and a bird she identified as an eastern towhee, but I missed it. By that time, I don't think I would have cared if the entire population of *Sibley* had been sitting in the same tree wearing ID tags. I just wanted a beer, and a nice bug-free tavern to drink it in. I promised myself never to come here in the springtime.

After what seemed to be untold hours of struggle, we finally made it through the slough of despond and up over the steep ridge of fucking aggravation and we were sitting halfway down a wooded hillside, looking through binoculars at that same cabin by the lake. We were probably five hundred yards away from the place. The long driveway I'd seen from the road that morning dead-ended at the cabin, and below us, at the foot of the ridge behind the cabin, there was a rusting U-Haul truck, sunk to its axles into the ground. I watched the cabin through the glasses, but there was no sign of life.

"What's with the truck," I asked her.

She shrugged. "The story I heard was that somebody stole it years and years ago and left it right there. Are you going down there?"

"No. Not right now. Those two guys might live in Brooklyn, okay, but they won't be all that easy to sneak up on. I'm gonna have to think about how to do this, and then come back."

"All right," she said.

* * *

The trip back to the Subaru wasn't as bad, I guess because I'd been through it all once already and I wasn't slogging into the unknown. I don't know why that makes it easier, but it does. It was still a relief, though, when we got back to the Subaru.

"Do you think you can find this place again? Here, where we parked?"

"Yeah. Little over nine miles in on this road, just past this stand of oaks."

She smiled her crooked smile. "Not bad, Coyote. Have you ever used a compass before?"

"No."

"Okay, here's what you do. This is your direction, right here." She drew a line in the dirt with her foot, glanced up at the sun. "East-northeast, more or less. That's the line between here and that cabin back there. Okay? So you stand here, you line up your compass so the needle points at north on the scale, and that will tell you exactly what direction this really is."

"Okay. Stand like this, find north, then follow that direction. Right?"

"Almost right. What you do, you go one or two degrees to the south of this line, okay, that way, when you hit that ridge we were on, you know you have to go left a little ways."

"Oh. Very smart."

"You do the same thing coming back. Go one or two degrees one way or the other, so when you hit this road you'll know which direction you need to turn. Otherwise what happens, you might get close to where you want to go but you won't be able to see it, and then when you wander around looking for it, you get lost. Getting lost in the woods up in here could be fatal."

"Ouch. Okay."

"Suppose you do get lost. Try to follow the water. That little swamp we went through turns into a creek, that's the creek that's washing out the road back there. Do you remember when we drove through that?"

"Yeah, I remember."

"Even if you don't find this road, keep following the water and eventually you'll come to a road or a river or something."

"Okay."

"Do I need to worry about you, Coyote? If something happened to you in here, it might bother me a little bit."

I took my soggy sneakers and socks off and threw them into the back of the Subaru. "I'll be fine," I told her.

It was late afternoon by the time I got back to Calais. I stopped at a sporting goods place and picked up a compass, some dry socks, and a pair of waterproof hiking boots. I was starting to look at that kind of stuff with a different eye. Before that I'd always looked at a sporting goods store as the kind of place you bought a jersey with John Starks's name on it, but I didn't see anything like that in this place. This was the kind of place that sold you stuff you needed to do things, not to go watch someone else do them. I wandered around in there for a while, trying to think if there was anything else I would need. I already had a hunting knife. I looked at the pistols for a while, but I settled for a vest instead. It was a mesh kind of thing, I guess it was intended for fishermen, and it had a lot of pockets. I thought long and hard about a pistol, though. There are a couple of problems with pistols. One is that they tend to make you overconfident—it's easy to forget that the thing is just a gun, it's not a magic wand that will get you out of trouble if you wave it around. Another is that having a pistol greatly magnifies the chances you'll get shot yourself. I didn't know that I really wanted to shoot anybody, and I sure as shit didn't want anybody shooting me.

There was a young guy working in the place, he looked like Maine's version of a juvenile hard-ass. He wore his hair greased back, he had a few chin whiskers trying to pass for a goatee, and he wore a Leatherman knife clamped to his belt. I palmed him a ten, asked him if he knew where I could buy a few M-80s.

"Whatcha need them for?" he wanted to know.

"I might need them for a distraction, that's all. Nothing to get anybody in trouble."

"Awright," he said, and he gave me a guy's name and directions to his house. He glanced at his watch, a big black one with a lot of buttons on it. "He won't be home from work for another hour or so. His brother ain't working, though, see if he'll give 'em to you. His brother's name is Vince."

It took me an hour to find the place, and then Vince spent the next ten minutes professing not to know what the hell I was talking about. I finally had to wave a fifty in the guy's face. Fifty bucks for a couple of firecrackers, Vince must have thought I was the biggest dope in the state. At the very least, he thought he had a fish on the line, because he tried to sell me all the other ordnance he had. Again I was tempted to go for something more serious, but in the end I thanked him for his kindness, took my M-80s and left.

I followed the directions in reverse to find my way from Vince's brother's house back to Calais. There was probably a quicker way to get where I was going, but it was getting dark and I couldn't find anything on the map. I didn't want to get lost.

Maine surprised me again—they didn't have a Starbucks in Calais. I could understand it, though, once I thought about it for a few minutes. You will find precious few down easters willing to pay four bucks for a cup of coffee, no matter what kind of fancy shit you put in it. Sixty cents at McDonald's, bro, and that's probably pushing it. And the stuff in the pot at five-thirty in the afternoon, you gotta know it's been sitting there getting meaner and more vile since about two. It didn't matter, I bought a couple cups anyway. I figured I was going to need the boost. Normally, I might have looked around for something a little more serious, not to mention easier on the stomach, but I had wasted enough time on the M-80s already.

I had tried calling Louis on my cell phone a couple of times while I was driving around, but I kept losing the signal. I tried again in the McDonald's parking lot, but the line was busy. I gave it five minutes and tried again, got the same result. They won't worry too much, that's what

I told myself. They know me by now, and they love Nicky. I was sure they wouldn't mind putting him to bed. I told myself I would call again when I got to Grand Lake Stream.

I was better prepared this time. I drove back in, watching the odometer. It wasn't hard to find the place where I'd parked the Subaru just hours earlier. I had my new boots on, and I had the vest. The M-80s and the electrical tape went in one pocket, the knife went in another, flashlight in a third, and so on. I checked the little window on my cell phone, but there was no signal. I turned the phone off and put it in a pocket. I found the mark Mrs. Johnson had made on the ground and took my sighting. East-northeast, she'd been right on the money. I coated my bucket hat with bug spray, put it on, and started out.

Even now I'd have a difficult time guessing at the distance. It had taken something like three hours to get in that morning, and the same to get back out, and that was with Mrs. Johnson leading the way—I hadn't had to stop every five minutes and look at a compass.

Guilt is funny stuff. I hadn't had a lot of experience with it before then. I mean, I'd been guilty of a lot, I admit that, but I'd never felt it much. Justice is generally what you want for the other guy. You don't want to pay the price for what you do, nobody does. When a cop pulls you over for speeding, you don't want the ticket, you want to skate. Right? It's all right for the other guy to go to jail, but they ought to let you go, send you on your way properly chastened, smarter, maybe, or at least more careful, if not more honest. The thing was, I had to admit that Rosario's ass was in a sling because of me. I could have done things different, and in retrospect, maybe I should have. Maybe I should have left Rosey's half of the money in that storeroom. I had been pissed off because he was going to try to swindle me, but how could I hold that against him? The guy was only human. I kept seeing him at that table at the VFW, looking like he was praying, and I knew I had to do something. I mean, I could have justified it, I could have talked myself out of this stupid expedition, but I didn't want to have to go around feeling lousy about whatever was gonna happen to Rosario.

And it's funny, too, because Rosey was one of those guys that have horrible problems with guilt. He came up Catholic, and when he got drunk or fucked up he would cry, and all of his pains and regrets would come flooding out of him. Me, I grew up in the machine, and I didn't have any illusions about some cosmic system of retribution that would somehow make everything come out even.

It got gradually darker as the sun sank lower in the sky, and when it hit the horizon it seemed to pick up speed, it was almost as though you could see it move, getting smaller and smaller as it dropped past the far edge of the world. Burglars do a lot of their work after the sun goes down, but the woods look a lot different in the dark. I stopped every little while to look at the compass again, and I had to slog straight through some of the obstacles that Mrs. Johnson had led me around earlier in the day. I started to worry about the flashlight, too. It was possible, if you thought about it, that my life depended on the thing. Say the batteries crap out, or the element in the bulb goes, I'm out here in the dark, and I'm fucked, with a capital fuck. That thought made me a lot more careful not to drop the light, and I only turned it on when I had to, when I needed it to see my way around something or to look at the compass. And then, you know, the woods have animals and shit, not just birds, either. Presumably the bears that made the marks Mrs. Johnson showed me were still around someplace, and they could probably hear me stomping around out there. I know that black bears are not as big as horses, okay, but I sure as hell did not want to make the acquaintance of one. I guess I hadn't needed the coffee to rev me up, after all.

I got to the ridge a lot quicker than I thought I would. I went up and halfway down the other side and turned left, the way Mrs. Johnson told me to, and it worked—after a couple hundred yards I saw the lights from the cabin windows. I felt flooded with relief, since I wasn't lost after all, not yet, anyhow.

I made my way down there as quietly as I could. There was an outhouse behind the place, just a tiny little shack knocked together out of old planks, looked rustic as all hell. Smelled pretty rustic, too. I hadn't noticed it before because it was on the far side of the U-Haul truck, about ten yards from the tree line. I stopped when I saw it, waited for a few minutes. If someone was in there, I wanted to give him time to come out. No one did, though, so I eased over to the cabin.

The light inside the place wasn't an electric light, it was one of those gas things that campers use, looks like an old hurricane lantern with the glass chimney, little green tank on the bottom with a tiny pump attached that you use to pressurize whatever it is the thing burns. The three of them were inside. The one that looked like Boris Yeltsin was asleep in a chair, his head back and his mouth open. The other guy, the one with the scar on his face, was sitting at the table drinking beer and playing cards, and he did not look like he was enjoying his game very much. Rosey was tied to a chair, head down, his chin on his chest. He didn't look like he was having a great time, either. He had a piece of duct tape over his mouth. The cabin was really crude. I made my way carefully around the outside, looked through each window. There was just the one big room, and it held everything. Two beds, a sink with an old-fashioned pump handle, an icebox, the table Scarface was at, and that was it. Just those two assholes and Rosey. I went back to the edge of the woods to think it over.

I sat down on a rock and fumed. Part of me wanted blood, maybe a lot of me, you know, the hell with it, just go kill those two pigs. Stupid, though. Blind rage is an unguided missile, and you never know if it's going to circle around and get you instead of the people you're after. After a while I cooled off and started to think.

Scarface was the real problem. I was willing to bet that Yeltsin was shit-faced, that I could walk in there with a brass band without waking the guy up. A guy who slept like that, snoring openmouthed, he was down for the count, at least until his body's thirst for alcohol woke him up in four or five hours. I had to think of a way to get Scarface out of there, though, because it seemed like tempting fate to walk in there with the two of them both present, asleep, drunk or not. This wasn't going to be like burglarizing some yuppie's house. I went back over and watched Scarface through the window.

He got up once, moved out of my line of vision, came back opening another beer. This guy seemed to be pouring a lot of liquid into himself, and it struck me that sooner or later he was going to have to pour some of it out. I could wait by the door with a rock, knock the guy in the head when he came out. . . .

I would do that if I had to, but maybe I didn't have to. Scarface looked, to me, like a guy who was too much of a control freak to piss indiscriminately in the grass. I went back behind the cabin, over to the outhouse. It smelled seriously bad over there, and the ground was a little marshy. I put it out of my mind, both the odor and the thought of what I might be tromping through, and as quietly as I could, I pushed the thing over backward. It turned out to be easy enough, it wasn't heavy at all. I dragged it straight back about six feet and stood it upright again. Then I went over by the U-Haul truck, where the ground was drier, and I felt around until I found a half dozen rocks that were about the right size, maybe half as big as a baseball. I took out the M-80s and the electrical tape, and I taped one M-80 to each rock. I stuck two of them in my vest pocket and lined up the other four on the truck tailgate. I cursed myself for thinking I didn't need a gun, and then I knew that I had been right not to bring one. I didn't want to get into a firefight with these two assholes, and odds were, one or both of them had to be a better shot than I was. I found another rock, a little bigger than the others, just in case I needed to whack Scarface in the head after all, and I went back over by the cabin door to wait.

Motherfucker must have had a bladder like an elephant's. I wasn't wearing a watch, so I had no way to judge the passing of time, but the guy drank four more beers before he finally got up to piss, and it seemed to take hours. I watched him come through the cabin door. I had been wondering, while I waited, if he would just walk four or five paces away from the door and piss in the grass after all, and I got ready with my rock, but he didn't, he headed for the outhouse, walking down the path in the dark, secure in the knowledge that he'd been there before, and had nothing to worry about.

I didn't see him fall into that stinking pit, it was too dark, but I heard it happen. An incoherent yell from a guy who speaks English sounds different from an incoherent yell from a guy who speaks some other language, but the meaning was clear enough, and another time it would have been funny. I went through the cabin door, watching Yeltsin while I listened to Scarface. I had the knife out, Rosey looked up and saw me coming with it, you could see from the look on his face that he knew he was going to die. Bastard thought I was going to stick him. Maybe once I would have done it, I don't know, but I held a finger to my lips. He nodded, and I hacked the ropes that bound him to the chair. Yeltsin never moved, not even when Rosey stumbled on the way to the cabin door, and we were out.

Rosey's legs weren't working real well, and I could feel him shaking, I could sense his fear as I dragged him around the far side of the cabin. Scarface had gotten himself out of the shit by then and he was bellowing as he ran for the cabin, probably swearing but it still sounded like incoherent rage. Rosey and I kept moving, circling around behind the place. We stopped when we got to the U-Haul truck. Rosey's hands were still tied together, but I didn't think I had time to cut him loose. I could hear Scarface over in the cabin, screaming at Yeltsin. I stuck my head close to his ear. "Don't move," I whispered to him. "Stay right here." I went over by the tailgate where I had lined up the four M-80s, took a deep breath, and then I lit all four fuses at once. I threw them quickly, as hard as I could, high over the cabin. An M-80 makes a hell of a bang, especially in the relative quiet of a Maine night. Three of them went off close together, out on the far side of the cabin, *pow-pow-pow*, and then the fourth maybe a second later, *pow*. I would have laughed if I hadn't been so freaked out, I could hear the sounds of breaking glass, and the staccato cracking of two semiautomatics firing away blindly in the darkness. I got behind Rosey, feeling for the ropes that bound his hands together. I could hear the Russians crashing around in the dark, but I couldn't tell where they were, and I had to be careful with the knife or I'd wind up cutting off one of Rosey's thumbs. I finally got him loose. I leaned up and whispered in his ear again.

"Can you walk?"

He wrapped his arms around his chest, but he nodded.

"Okay. This way."

I could still hear one of the Russians floundering around on the other side of the cabin, but I didn't know where the other one had gone. I found him, though, or he found us, because when Rosey and I got back to the edge of the woods, Yeltsin was there waiting for us, and he was pointing a pistol at my chest.

"I knew you'd come," he said harshly in thickly accented English. "Put that knife down or I shoot you now."

Sometimes you win and sometimes you lose. It's like when the cops put the manacles on you, you have to recognize when it's over, and that fighting them only makes it worse. They got you, sucka, so you may as well relax, the ride's gonna be the same whether you're kicking and screaming or not. Why make it harder on yourself than it has to be? My head told me that for about a half a second, even though I knew that these two assholes were going to work me over the way they had done Rosey, until they got what they came for. I could almost accept that much, but what really pissed me off was the realization that they would put Rosey and me in shallow graves when it was all over, leaving Nicky well and truly alone, with absolutely no one on his side. Maybe that gave me the extra little bit of desperation I needed, I don't know, maybe it gave me the courage I needed to face the fact that this was the best chance I would get, that I had to go up against this guy and his gun right then because once he got me inside that cabin and tied to a chair I would never get odds as good as this again, no matter how bad they looked. You're better than he is, anyway, I told myself, drunk, stupid, ignorant pig-fucker. . . .

I half turned in his direction, and the anger I had been feeling up till then was nothing compared to what came surging through me, I could feel my face twisting up with it, but Yeltsin didn't notice, maybe he was too drunk, maybe it was too dark. I had one hand in my vest pocket, wrapped around one of the two rocks that had an M-80 taped to them. I tossed the knife in his direction, I saw his head turn, following the glittering trajectory of the knife, and in the same motion I spun the rest of the way around, brought the rock out of my pocket and fired it in his direction.

I probably would have made a good infielder. That rock sizzled through the distance between the two of us and it hit Yeltsin right in the forehead. He went over backward, but he must have fired out of reflex, and I felt some invisible giant hand swat me down. Stupid, going up against the gun, but sometimes stupid is the best you've got. I didn't feel any pain, but as I struggled to get up I discovered that my left arm didn't work anymore. I didn't want to look at it, it was too dark to see much, anyhow. I went looking for the knife, nagged, I guess, by that same doubt that had made Rosey sure I was going to kill him. Rosey came over behind me, he was staring down at Yeltsin lying on the ground, he wanted to kick the Russian in the face, I could feel it in him, but he was too far gone, he didn't have the energy to spare for it. I found the knife, scooped up the pistol that lay in the mud where Yeltsin had dropped it, stuck them in one of my vest pockets, and we headed up the ridge behind the cabin. I didn't worry about the karma attached to the gun. Seeing how I'd already been shot once, I didn't figure taking it would do me any harm.

The hill we had to climb seemed a hell of a lot steeper than it had before. I heard a few more shots then, Scarface banging away in the darkness, but this time he was firing in our direction. I could shoot back at him, but I knew I wouldn't hit anything, not at that range. Meantime, Rosey had been working at the duct tape on his face, and he finally got it off. "Mohammed," he said. "Mohammed, you fucked me."

"Shut up, you asshole." I bumped up against his rib cage and he cried out in pain. Below us, I heard another flood of frustrated and angry Russian invective, and I figured that Scarface had found his friend at the edge of the trees. Rosey and I kept climbing, trying to get some distance between us and the Russians, but we had to stop and sit down before we got to the top of the ridge. Both of us needed a rest. Rosey's breathing sounded hoarse and convulsive, and my left arm and shoulder were starting to hurt like hell. Rosey had his arm wrapped around me, and he must have gotten some blood on his hand.

"Mo, you're hit."

"I know. Not so loud."

"Sorry. Let me look at it. You got a light?"

"Yeah." I fished out my flashlight and handed it to him. "Get around downhill from me, we don't want that asshole down there seeing us."

"Okay." He moved around in front of me, clicked the light on and then quickly off. "Upper arm, gash jus' below your shoulder," he said. "Lucky, I thin' the bullet jus' crease you, half inch deep, maybe." He clicked the light on and off again. "Bleeding like a mofucker, though. You still got that knife?"

I was not giving Rosario my hunting knife. "No."

"Shit. I gonna tear off your shir' sleeve, wrap it aroun' you for a bandage. We got to stop the bleeding."

"Wait, wait." I could see the light flickering below us. My guess was that Scarface was looking at Yeltsin. The light started moving after a minute, going raggedly back toward the cabin. Scarface was probably dragging his friend back inside. "Okay, do it now. Try not to make much noise." Rosey was inordinately strong, but it seemed to take him forever to get my sleeve torn off and tied around my upper arm. When he flicked the light back on to check his work, I could see the sweat pouring off his face.

"Slowed it down, I thin'. Sorry, Mo, tha's the bes' I can do."

"All right," I said. "What kind of shape you in?"

It was a minute before he would answer me. I sat listening to the ragged sound of him breathing. Below us, the light came back out of the cabin and started moving slowly in our direction. "They fuck me up good, Mo. I got bussed-up ribs on both sides, an' my abs hurt so much, man, I can harly stan' up." He got a wounded tone in his voice, then. "Why you fuck me, Mo?"

"What are you talking about?"

"You took my money, man, you wen' away, don't say nothing. . . ."

"I seen what you did to those three guys. You think you fooled me with that bullshit routine at the Omni? With that claim ticket? Besides, I haven't fucked you yet. The money is still safe."

"Oh, man." You'd have thought I'd saved his mother's life. "Oh, man. Where is my money, Mo?"

"I got it someplace safe, and it's gonna stay there until this bullshit is all over with. Don't worry, I'm gonna take care of you. I'll make sure you get yours." I should have phrased that in a different way—that was almost what he had told those three guys that wound up in the Dumpster. "What did you tell those two Russian assholes?"

"What could I do, Mo? I tol' them you had it."

"You prick. Why the hell you do that?"

"Mo, you don' know what they do to me. They fuck me up good, Mo. I thought I was gonna die. What was I suppose to do?"

"All right, forget it."

Below us, the Russian's light started up the hill, slowly weaving back and forth as it came. "You might live to spend your money yet. That guy is following the blood trail. We should be able to stay ahead of him, though, as long as neither one of us passes out. You ready?"

"No, man, I'm not. Less go."

I can't tell you a hell of a lot about that trip back through the woods. What I remember is that it was the hardest thing I've ever had to do in my life. Rosey did pass out a couple of times, and I had to get him up on my back and across my good shoulder to keep going. I kept seeing the Russian's light now and then, but it got weaker and weaker, finally I didn't see it anymore. My guess was that his batteries went dead. I also remember thinking about giving up, I'm not proud of it but it did cross my mind, you know, find a nice, comfortable place to lie down, rip that bandage off and let it all go. I didn't do it, though. What kept me going was Nicky, just the idea of him, you know, and that I wanted to see him again, I wanted to watch him brush his teeth in the morning, I wanted to feel him put his arms around me, and like that. I'm pretty sure I cried about it, but it was dark out, and Rosey and I were both covered with blood and dirt and shit, so it didn't matter.

Brother, it was forever before we hit that fucking dirt road. I laid Rosey down in the weeds and sat down beside him. I was starting to get light-headed, and it took me a while to figure out if I had to go left or right to find the Subaru. I thought about laying down next to Rosey for a nap, but something told me I better not, if I did that it might be the whole ball game, so I got up and trudged off in search of the car. And it was a bitch of a long way off, too, I guess I'd gotten careless with the compass, and there are some days when you just can't catch a break. I had begun to doubt myself, wondering if I'd fucked up and picked the wrong direction. In fact, I was seriously considering whether or not I should turn back, go looking in the other direction, when I finally saw those oak trees in the early predawn gloom, the Subaru parked underneath them.

I had some candy bars and some Poland Spring water under the seat. I ate two of the candy bars, drank some warm bottled water, and I got going. I almost forgot Rosario, believe it or not, I almost turned in the wrong direction. I didn't, but I did realize that my head wasn't working right. I drove, one-armed, back to where I'd left him. He came out of it long enough to help me get his ass belted into the passenger seat. It was a good thing he did, because unconscious, he was like a two-hundred-fifty-pound bag of shit. I don't know if I could have done it by myself. Rosey's a big guy, bigger than me, and he barely fit.

I remember driving back down that dirt road, I remember nodding off and jerking back awake, the fear bringing me back around for a while, I remember driving past that tackle shop in Grand Lake Stream, all closed up and dark. The last thing I remember is cracking the Subaru into one of those big pine trees in front of Mrs. Johnson's house, and then everything went black.

7

I came to in a room painted pastel green. The place had that unmistakable hospital air about it, the sharp tang of disinfectant, the muffled downcast voices of relatives waiting on the sick and the dying. My left arm was swathed in bandages, and a tube ran from the inside of my wrist up to a bottle of clear liquid hanging on a stainless-steel rack. The sun was pouring through a big window. Chris Johnson's mother was sitting in a chair next to the window, reading a book. When she heard me stirring, she marked her spot with a finger and looked up.

"Coyote," she said, a look of amusement dancing across her round face. "How are you feeling?"

"Like shit," I told her, and I tried to sit up. I was surprised at how much effort it took. Inside my head, I felt that wild, dancing elation—I made it, I did it again, but that was tempered with the shock of being so weak. "Damn," I said. "Where am I at?"

"Calais hospital," she said.

"How long have I been out?"

"Two days."

"Oh, Jesus." I'd left Nicky with Louis and Eleanor, and all three of them were bound to be worried about me by now, but at least Nicky was out of harm's way. "Does Bookman know I'm in here?"

"I don't know," she said, shrugging. "I didn't tell him."

"What about the doctor? Don't doctors have to report gunshot wounds to the cops?"

"What gunshot wound? You were in an accident, Coyote, and you cut your arm. Your friend broke some ribs. That's the official story." She smiled. "You shouldn't drive when you're that tired."

"You hear anything about the two Russians?"

"I don't know anything about any Russians," she said. "I do know some poor man was lost up in the woods, got bit up something wicked by mosquitoes, no-see-ums, blackflies, and so on. Looked like a pincushion, they tell me, face and arms got all swelled up. He got disgusted, went on back where he come from. Some other guy fell down and hit his head on a rock, got a concussion. He isn't fit to travel yet because he's still seeing two of everything." She stood up, put her book facedown on the chair. "I better go tell someone you're awake. Don't go anywhere, okay?"

"Yeah, okay. What kind of shape is the Subaru in?"

She shook her head. "Done for. My cousin towed it to the junkyard."

"Damn." I looked around my bed. "Don't they have any phones in this place?"

I could see amusement in her bland expression. "You have to pay extra for that."

"Oh, great. Is my phone in here somewhere?"

"Your stuff from the little truck is all here in a bag." She reached into a cloth bag on the floor next to her chair, pulled out the rock with the M-80 still taped to it. "Except for this. That cannon you had is still in your vest pocket."

"That rock with the M-80 taped to it was a diversion. I took the pistol away from that guy who hit his head on the rock."

"I wasn't worried about the gun," she said. "The only person who seems to have gotten shot is you."

"Funny how that works. Anyway, what I need right now is the phone."

"All right." There was a large paper bag, the kind they use in grocery stores, in the closet. She fished around in it. "One cell phone," she said, pulling it out. "Here you go. I'll be right back."

* * *

There was no answer at the Averys' house. I dialed the number twice, listened to it ringing for a minute or so each time with no result. I felt a pang at the pit of my stomach. Don't worry, I told myself. Maybe Louis is working, maybe Eleanor and Nicky are in the barn looking at the horse. Maybe they went for a walk. Maybe they're working in the garden.

I couldn't buy it, though, I couldn't see Eleanor going outdoors without a damn good reason. Plus, I had been missing for a couple of days. Wouldn't they be worried? Wouldn't Nicky be driving them crazy, asking them every five minutes when I was coming back? I tried their number again, waited a longer time, picturing in my mind someone who could hear the phone ringing but could not, for some horrible reason, get to it. Eleanor, tied to a chair the way Rosey had been.

Shit.

I checked the voice mail, found I had one message from Buchanan, back in New York, and two from Bookman. Buchanan could wait, and I didn't want to talk to Bookman until I found Nicky and the Averys. I always had the feeling that I was on thin ice with Bookman, and I didn't want to make it any worse than it was. Gevier lived right next door to the Averys, and I was sure he would know what was going on. The phone number for his garage was stored in my phone's memory. He answered on the sixth ring, out of breath.

"Gevier, this is Manny. There's nobody home at Louis's house. Do you know what happened to them?"

"Well," he said, "Louis is resting comfortable."

"What are you talking about?"

"He's in jail. Bookman locked him up for drunk and disorderly, assault with a deadly weapon, who knows what else."

"Are you kidding me? Louis, assault? Holy shit! What the hell happened? Where are Nicky and Eleanor?"

"Well, Louis took Eleanor down to Machias to see the doctor, and the doctor put her in the hospital. He come back without her, and he's been drunk ever since. He went into the VFW but they wouldn't serve him on account of he was already loaded, so he went out to his truck, come back inside with his chain saw, and cut the bar in half."

"Oh, fuck me. Did he have Nicky with him?"

"Yep. Louis put a nice straight kerf in that bar, top to bottom, right through the glass top and all. Set the saw down on the bar, said, 'Give me a bourbon.' And, by God, they did."

"When did this happen?"

"Night before last."

"Oh, shit. What happened to Nicky?"

"You know, I'm not sure. You'd have to ask Bookman, he was the one that arrested Louis."

Great. "Anybody make bail?"

"Well, you know, I think his old partner Hobart was going to, but Bookman talked him out of it. Thought he might be better off inside there for a few days."

"Jesus Christ." My stomach rolled over. "I gotta find my kid." I remembered that I had smacked up Hobart's Subaru and was currently without wheels. "Listen, Gevier, did you ever finish fixing my van?"

"Be done in a half hour," he said. "I had to come out from under to answer the phone."

"Sorry. What would you charge me to tow that van up here and leave it in the hospital parking lot in Calais? Could you do that tonight?"

"Yeah, sure. It would take me a couple hours. Figure an extra fifty bucks."

"Great. Do that for me, will you? Leave it unlocked, stick the keys under the passenger-side floor mat."

"All right," he said. "Good enough. I'll put my bill on the driver's seat. Why don't you stop down the house and pay Edwina."

"She in charge of the money?"

"She's in charge of everything," Gevier said. "It's her world. You and me, we're just visiting."

I laid there with that telephone in my hand, thinking about all the terrible things that my mind was telling me had happened to Nicky while

I was out of it, and all the terrible things that were going to happen when I talked to Bookman. I was past worrying what Bookman thought about me, except that, if his opinion got low enough, he might make it tough for me to get Nicky back. I felt like throwing up, but I had to call him anyway. I dialed his office number.

"Sheriff Bookman is not in," the lady told me. "May I take a message?"

"Not in?" You gotta be kidding me. "What do you mean he's not in? I have to talk to him. Is he home? Do you have his home number?"

"I'm afraid I'm not allowed to give that out, sir. . . ."

"Oh, man. Listen, I have to talk to him, and he's definitely gonna want to talk to me, I promise you."

"Maybe I could take your number, sir. I'll try to get in touch with him and let him call you back. Would that be all right?"

It sounded like the best deal I was going to get, at least from her. "Sure. My name is Manny Williams." I gave her my cell number. I hung up, then listened to the two voice mails Bookman had left for me. He hadn't said much, just dryly wondered where I might be, left his office number. I could probably get his home number from Gevier, and I was about to do that when the phone rang.

It was Bookman. "I 'magine you want to talk to yaw son," he said.

"Yeah! Is he there?"

"Nope."

"C'mon, Bookman, what are you doing to me? Why you torturing me like this?"

"That's what you done to him," Bookman said calmly. "Three days now, the poor little kid don't heah from his fahthah, sleeping all by himself in a strange bed. . . ."

"It ain't my fault, Bookman, I just woke up a half hour ago. One of those Russians creased me with a slug a couple nights back. I was out for two days. I left Nicky with Louis and Eleanor, I thought I was going to be back later that same night. What are you talking about, a strange bed? What the hell did you do with him?"

"When I put Louis in jail for being a drunk pain in my ass, he had yoah boy in the truck with him," he said. "The Maine Depahtment of Human Services is responsible—"

"Oh, Jesus Christ! Bookman, what did you do?" That was all I needed. "The Maine Department of what?" I'd already stolen him once, now I could picture myself having to do it all over again, and a kid disappearing in Maine was sure to draw more attention than one that went missing in Bushwick. "Fuck me, Bookman! Why don't you just fucking shoot me? Why don't you—"

"Calm down, calm down," Bookman said. "I said they were responsible, I nevah said I give him up to them. Nicky is down to the creek, fishing with Franklin. You can't talk to him because they ain't back yet." I laid back in the bed, felt relief wash over me. I wiped my forehead on the hospital's ratty cotton bathrobe.

"Oh, Christ, Bookman . . ."

"No need to get religious. If yaw up in theyah with a gunshot wound, how come I wasn't infommed?"

"It's a long story."

"I 'magine it is," he said. "I look fohwahd to hearing all the details. What'd you do to the Rooskies?"

"One of them went home, and the other one was sleeping like a baby, last time I saw him."

"That so." He took a minute to think about that. "When ah you getting out?"

"I'm leaving tomorrow morning. Gevier's got my van fixed, he's gonna drop it in the parking lot tonight. Where should I meet you?"

"Go on back to Louis's. Call me when you get theyah. I'll call this numbah when the boys get back from the creek, let you talk to yaw son."

The doctor who came to see me was taller and leaner than Mrs. Johnson, but he had that same black hair, same brown skin and brown eyes. "Mr. Coyote," the guy said, smirking. "How are we feeling today?"

"Terrific," I told him. "How soon can I get out of here?"

He started unwrapping the bandage on my arm. "You in a hurry to leave us? You lost a lot of blood, you know."

"Can't you fill me back up? I got business."

"We already filled you up." He took the last of the bandage off. "Hmm," he said. "Well, I'm afraid the snake on your arm is going to have a scar on his head."

"It hurt me worse than it hurt him."

"I'll bet it did." He glanced at his watch. "It's almost four in the afternoon," he said. "Too late to do any business today. Why don't you stay with us one more night, see how you feel in the morning?"

I didn't want to stay, I wanted to get out right then, but I was feeling pretty shaky. Maybe staying another night was the smart thing. "If I have to. How's my friend Rosario?"

He looked at me. "Let's stop bullshitting one another, okay? You took a bullet in the arm and your associate was severely beaten. I sincerely doubt he'd had anything to eat in days before he was brought in here. There's something worse going on here than someone falling asleep behind the wheel. Mrs. Johnson is a good friend, and she asked me to patch you up and keep my mouth shut, so I did that. But I wouldn't want to think you were going to involve her in something that would put her in jeopardy."

"I wouldn't like that myself, Doc. Rosario and I were both in the wrong place at the wrong time. The sooner I can get him far away from here, the better off we will all be." It was true, I had to get him away from the Russians, and I didn't want Bookman asking him a lot of questions, either.

"That might be so, but it's not going to happen tonight. Your friend had a collapsed lung, and he's going to have to stay right where he is for another four or five days. The best I can tell you is that I'll stop in on you both in the morning, and then we'll talk about what I find. Okay?"

"All right. Thanks, Doc."

* * *

Mrs. Johnson came back in, gathered up her stuff. "I'm going home, Coyote," she said. "Do you think you're going to be all right now?"

"I'll be fine. I don't know how to thank you."

"Don't worry about it," she said. "You did okay in those woods. That was a big son of a whore you carried out. I don't know many men who could have done it."

"Fear makes you strong."

She shook her head. "Fear just makes you afraid. Did you find Nicky?"

"My son? Yeah, I did. I guess I talked about him in my sleep."

She was nodding. "Yes, you did." She looked at me, impassive. You'd have to spend your whole life up in this place to be able to read the faces of the people who lived up here. "You talked about a lot of things. Don't worry, though, no one heard you but me, and I know how to keep quiet. Besides, if you're a coyote, it's no good pretending you're a pussycat." She started to leave, but she paused at the door. "I bet you've got some stories to tell, Coyote. Someday when you got time, I'd love to hear 'em."

There was a hole in the room when she left, it was a colder and meaner place, and I was not so content to lie there. The bathroom was about twelve feet away from the bed. I made it over there okay, I was pretty shaky but not bad, considering. I could feel how empty my stomach was, though, and I could tell that I really needed a shower. I was on my way back to the bed, dragging that rack with the bottle swinging on it behind me, when a nurse came into the room. She was an older lady, gray-haired, all business. In no time at all she got that bottle unhooked from my arm, got me into the shower, got food ordered. She went off to locate Rosario for me. I made it back to the bed, feeling much more human, but weak, for such little exertion.

Hospital food is what it is, you know, if you're hungry enough, you'll eat it. I was more than hungry enough, and after I got it down, I began to feel better, like I could make it down to Rosario's room and back without incident. Before I finished eating, though, my phone rang. It was Bookman.

"Hold on," he said. I heard the phone passed from one pair of hands to another, heard breathing in the phone.

"Hey, Nicky," I said, trying not to sound guilty, which was what I felt. "Is that you?"

"Hi, Poppy." I could hardly hear him.

"Did you have a good time with Franklin?" There was no answer for a minute, and I could hear a female voice in the background, telling Nicky that I could not see him nodding.

"Yes," he said, in that same quiet voice.

"Are you being a good boy?" I got the same answer, in the same tone. God, this was terrible. I wanted to reach through the phone lines and put my arms around him. "Did you catch a fish?"

"I caught a pickerel!" he said, in the shout he reserved for truly exciting events like horses running away. "Franklin said it was a pickerel, and it was all slimy, and it had big teeth!"

"Did he bite you?"

"No." I could hear him laughing. "Silly."

"Did you eat him for dinner?"

"No. We let him go. Franklin says they got too many bones."

"Oh. Okay. Don't go fishing in the morning, all right? I have to stay here tonight, but I'll see you in the morning. Is that okay?"

"Okay." He was back to that faint voice.

"You be good, now. Bye-bye."

"Bye."

Bookman came back on the line. "All right, Manny," he said. "Call me in the morning, when you get to Louis's house."

"Will do." I had the distinct impression that he wanted to say something else, but he didn't, he just hung up.

Rosey was lying in bed, pale, watching television. I came in and sat in the chair next to him. He must have been awake longer than me, because I could tell by looking at him that he'd had too much time to think. He looked surprised to see me when I walked through the door, and then immediately resentful and petulant, wounded at heart, suspicious. I suppose I would have felt the same way. It was a bad situation to be in: dependent, unable to move, out of your native habitat, and the crook you used to work with has your money. "How you feeling, Rosey?"

He reached for the remote and turned up the volume on the set so we could talk without being overheard.

"You save my ass," he said, looking at the tube. "I owe you."

"Damn straight you do."

He craned his neck to look past me, make sure nobody was standing in the corridor, listening. "And you owe me, muthafucka. You owe me." I could see him putting on that wounded face again, going back into character. He looked like a woman who'd just caught her husband in bed with her sister. "Why you hadda take my money, Mo? I thought you and me was friends."

I put my hand on my chest. "Rosey. I can't tell you how much it hurts me to hear you talk like that."

"Oh, fuck you, man. . . ." He started to rise from the bed, but his eyes went wide and he grunted in pain and laid back down on the pillows. It took him a minute to recover. "You are a cold son of a bitch, you know that?"

"Hey, Rosey, no bullshit. Did you really expect me to fall for that switch you pulled with the claim tickets? You really thought I was that stupid? Besides, I know what you did to those three guys you picked up. Tell the truth, Rosey. I was gonna get the same. Ain't that right."

"Oh, man, c'mon. I couldn't talk to them, when I met them the next day they got all unreasonable and shit. They wanted a half a mill apiece. I couldn't give them that. . . . So I gave them something else instead." He had not lost any of that hurt and resentful expression on his face. "How much was there, Mo? Can you leas' tell me that?"

"One point eight million." I had to sting him, at least a little bit.

"You see? You see? I was tryina take care a you, Mo. I give those three guy a half apiece, how much would that leave for you an' me?"

"Rosey, I'm touched, man, really. I never had another friend like you."

"Oh, fuck you, man, you fucking piece of fucking shit." I really thought he was going to cry. "Why you come here, Mo, you come down here to fucking laugh at me, you come to piss in my fucking face, you know I gotta lay up here in this fucking bed like a fucking baby. . . ."

I waited a minute after he stopped. "Rosey, you're a smart guy."

He took a couple of breaths, let go of the jilted-lover act. "Yeah, so what." No false modesty there.

"You see me sitting here. What does that tell you?" He wouldn't answer, he just lay there staring at the television. "Think about it, Rosey. If I wanted to keep your money, I could just walk out of this place and leave your sorry ass stuck in this bed. Why didn't I do that, Rosey?"

He continued to stare at the television, his distrust plain on his face. It was because he'd been ready to do it. I'd had the suspicion before, but now I knew it for sure. There was no way he could have brought himself to split it with me. He'd have had to kill me. "You tell me, Mo. Esplain to me why."

"All right, Rosey. You believe in karma?"

He glared at me. "I'm Catholic, Mo, you know that. I believe God gonna send you and me to hell."

"Maybe he will. But the way I look at it, I got three ways to go here. One, I wait until you're sleeping, okay, and I come down here and put some rat poison in your IV, you die screaming, and God puts you in hell tonight. Okay?" Rosey was staring at me, wide-eyed, looking, once again, like an outraged housewife. "I coulda done that already, and you know it. Or two, I could just take off, keep it all. But then I gotta go around worrying about you coming up behind me for the rest of my life. That ain't no way to live. Or three, I can give you your cut, and we can both walk away from this. The first two choices got too much bad karma on 'em. So I'm gonna pick number three. All you gotta do is lay up here in this bed and keep your fucking mouth shut."

His face was drawn, haggard with doubt and suspicion in the flickering light of the television. "You wan' go get it for me? Look at us, Mo. I don' gonna trus' you, you don' gonna trus' me. You still don' gonna tell me where my money is at."

"If I did, you couldn't leave it alone. You knew what was going on, it wouldn't make any difference how good it was, you would have to get on the phone and fuck it up. Besides, how long could you hold out if the Russians picked you up again? Or some different ones, maybe? Look at you, man, you ain't going anywhere for a couple of days, anyhow. By the time you're ready to walk out of here I can have everything taken care of. After that, you'll be able to go anywhere you want. As long as you stay the hell out of New York City, you can die a rich man."

He opened his robe and looked down at his chest. He was wrapped from his collarbone all the way down to his waist. He looked at me, considering, nodded once. "What you gonna do?"

"I told you, I'm gonna take care of it. Couple more days, maybe a week, your money will be nice and legal, sitting in your brokerage account."

"Oh, great, you gon' give it to my useless fucking piece of shit broker."

"It will be in your account. He can't do anything with it without your say-so."

He rubbed his face with both hands, grunting with the effort it took him. "Yeah," he said. "All right." He said it with an accusatory tone in his voice, like he knew he was getting screwed somehow, and he was putting up with it because he loved me.

"But I want you gone, you understand? Your money in your pocket, on a beach someplace far away."

"Like Puerto Rico," he said.

"You got relatives there?"

"Yeah."

"Puerto Rico's no good, then. Think about it, Rosey. You got a big dollar sign on your back now. You gotta go where nobody will think to look for you."

He laid back on his pillows, looked thoughtful. "I see what you mean," he said, and he considered it for a minute. "Thass why you come up here. You knew all this shit gonna happen."

"How did those goons know where to look for me?"

"I thin' maybe somebody from here call down there, tell them to come get you."

"Somebody from up here? You sure? Somebody up here ratted me out? They tell you that?"

"They tell me shit, man, but they keep on talking about some guy, he say, you know, 'I hear you looking for this guy, about so big, look like dis an dat, got a kid with him, come up here and get him.' I thin' maybe the guy tell them the town, but maybe not like the house where you was at. Maybe the guy tell them Eastpor', 'cause they spen' a lot of time looking over there."

"Eastport? All right. Who are they, anyhow? They work for those Russians we knocked over?"

"I don' thin' so, Mohammed. I thin' these guy, they hear about you an' me from somebody up here, they put two an' two together, they wanna come get the money. One a your new fren' from here call down to find somebody to come make trouble for you. Because those guy we rob, they too busy right now. They got plenty money, anyway. *New York Time* say fifty, sixty millions, say the SEC don' know where is it. Those guy don' thin' too much for you an' me."

"Good. That means we can still pull this off. But when you get outta here, you gotta go someplace where nobody knows you. If you wanna be a rich man, you're gonna have to be a smart one, first."

He was nodding. "Never been to Greece," he said.

"Don't tell me."

He looked at me sadly. "An' you don' gonna tell me where you go from this place."

"That's the way it is. That doctor comes around, you tell him you feel wonderful. Two, maybe three days, you gotta be ready to go."

He looked down at his chest, swathed in bandages. "Mo, I tell you sonting. From a few day ago to now, I feel fokking great."

"Listen, Rosey, I think one of those Russians is in this hospital somewhere, so you be careful. Stay out of trouble."

"Which one?"

"The one that drank."

Rosey's face went dark with anger, but at least it was not directed at me. "Where the other one at?"

"I was told the other guy gave up and went home."

"All right," he said. "You come back for me, you sommanabitch. I be ready."

"All right. Who's your stockbroker?"

His eyes filled up with suspicion again. He had to think about it before he told me. "Charles Schwab," he said. I guessed he had decided to trust me.

"You know your account number?"

He nodded. He gave it to me, but he did not look happy about it.

By the time I got back to my bed, I felt like the needle on my tank was back down into the red zone. I felt like I had used up whatever energy I'd gotten from the hospital food. Maybe I really did need a good long sleep.

Buchanan's number was not in the phone's memory, but it was in mine, and therefore just a little bit harder to retrieve. My brain gave it to me after a little prodding. I didn't think there was any way possible he would still be in his office this late in the day, but I figured I would leave him a message, let him call me back in the morning. I was wrong, though. A woman answered, said, "Just one minute." Twenty seconds later, he came on the line.

"Mohammed," he said. "God, am I glad to hear from you." He had an unusual amount of animation in his voice. "I was beginning to think you had forgotten all about our, ah, arrangement."

"I didn't forget. I was laid up for a few days. Sorry."

"That's all right, forget it." I could hear the relief in his voice. "You still want to go through with this? You all ready?"

"Yeah, we're still on. Am I all ready for what?"

"Well," he said, "we still have some details to take care of. You're going to have to put your funds in escrow with me, for one thing, and you'll need to take a position in the security in question. And, of course, there will be some paperwork."

"All right."

"Can you meet me tomorrow?"

"I don't think so. How about the day after?"

"All right," he said, "but make sure you get here. We don't want to cut this too close. It would be a crime to mess this up, Mohammed. This is looking better and better all the time. I'm telling you, a deal like this one does not come along every day."

"I'll be there. Day after tomorrow, say, early afternoon? I've gotta drive in, I'll call you around one."

"I'll be waiting."

I remembered Rosario. "Listen," I said, "would it be possible to cut this transaction in half, and do it under two separate names?"

"Anything you want," he said. "But you've got to decide all that before me meet. After that it will be too late to make any changes."

"I can give it to you now." I told him Rosario's name and account number. If he found this late change of heart strange, he didn't say.

"Done," he said a minute later. "See you in two days."

8

I woke up around five o'clock that morning. It took me a minute to wake up, to remember where I was, and where Nicky was. I missed him, man, I missed him bad. I wanted to make one of those deals with God, you know, "Get me through this, get me and Nicky out of here and to some safe place and I promise I'll never steal anything again, man, really, I won't. . . ."

My left arm and shoulder were throbbing. At least they had a pill for that, and they gave it to me when I got breakfast. And breakfast was a real treat, too, all healthy stuff. First thing I was doing when I got out of there was stop for an Egg McMuffin or two.

I was almost insane by the time the doctor came around a little after nine that morning. He looked at my arm, took my temperature, did all that stuff that those guys do. I could barely sit still. "I guess you're still in a hurry to leave us," he said, wrapping that blood pressure thing around my arm.

I wanted to tell him how much I missed Nicky, how lousy I felt for exposing the poor kid to all this craziness, how sorry I was for being such a rotten fucking father. I really did want to tell somebody, but I didn't think I could do it without crying, and anyway, he wasn't the guy. "Yeah," I told him. "I really gotta get going."

"Well," he said, "that arm is going to hurt for a while. I'm going to give you something for the pain, and something else to fight infection.

Take the pain pills when you need them, and take the other ones twice a day until they're all gone. I suppose I'd be wasting my breath if I told you to get lots of rest."

"I'll be good, Doc, I promise. What about Rosey?"

He shook his head. "It's like I told you," he said. "You're going to have to leave him with us a while longer. He's not ready to travel. Even if his lung was all right he couldn't take the pain unless you sedated him."

I thought sedating him might be a good idea, but I didn't say that. "Can I go see him before I go?"

"Of course. Did you get anybody to bring you some clean clothes?"

I shook my head. "Never thought of it."

"Not much left of your shirt," he said. "We'll find you something. The rest of your stuff is a bit funky, but it ought to get you by."

"Thanks," I said. "I want to ask you a question that might put you in a bad position, ethically. Feel free to tell me to go to hell, but can you tell me anything about a guy from Russia with a concussion?"

"Don't know," he said. "Not my patient."

I didn't talk to Rosario, after all. There wasn't much point in it, I had already said everything I had to say to him. I walked out of that hospital around eleven that morning wearing crusty hiking boots, filthy blue jeans with blood spatters down the left side, and one of those blue short-sleeved shirts that doctors wear. Nobody said anything, though. Mainers are like New Yorkers that way. They ain't gonna let you know, either way. If they're impressed or intimidated, they don't like to let it show.

There were lots of minivans in the parking lot. I wandered around carrying my paper bag full of crap until I found mine. I hadn't been impressed with it before, but it sure seemed luxurious now, spacious, smooth, and comfortable, especially compared to the Subaru and Louis's Jeep. I stopped at McDonald's, put a coffee in the cup holder and some food in the nifty little tray, and went to a drugstore to fill my prescriptions. When that was done, I gassed up the van and headed for Louis's house. I was still getting used to the emptiness of this place. I come from a world where the streets are numbered and lettered, where they bisect in more or less predictable ways, where they're lined with houses and buildings, where green spaces are fenced off from everything else. You miss something, you can turn at the next intersection, go around the block, and see it again. Maine isn't like that, though, at least not the part of it where I was. The roads roll with the contours of the land, they swing around the hills and meander along the rivers. I suppose you could get tired of it after a while, but I was still new, and I passed the trip back in silent wonder.

It was a dismal house without Eleanor or Louis in it. I thought I had become fond of the place, especially the kitchen, but as I stood next to the woodstove, it just felt like an empty room in a poor man's house, the house itself just an old building nearing the end of its life, with doors that leaked cold air, windows that rattled in the wind, and a field mouse scratching in the cupboard. I could see it standing empty in a year or so, all the people gone, the sounds and smells that gave this place life surviving only in the dimming memories of those few like me who had paused here, then moved on. It's a fight to remain upright, though I don't always remember that. I tend to act as if it were my divine right to stand where I choose, to conduct my business as I see fit. This house was not young, though, and it was probably far past such rash assumptions.

My phone was out in the car, recharging, so I called Bookman from Louis's phone. "Be right there," he said when he heard my voice, and he hung up.

I waited for him outside.

He turned his police car into the bottom of Louis Avery's driveway and drove casually up the hill. He stopped next to Louis's Jeep, where I was sitting on the tailgate. He rolled down his window.

"Hey," I said.

He pursed his lips, looked at my bandaged shoulder, and shook his head, as though he were slightly disappointed in what he was looking at. "Get in," he said. "Take a ride."

I didn't move. "Okay if I ride up front? I hate back seats." Particularly, I didn't need to add, when the doors didn't have handles on the inside.

Bookman permitted himself one tiny, wry smile. "Come ahead."

I walked around the front of the car and got in. Bookman dropped the gearshift into reverse, backed around, and headed down the driveway. "You don't look so hot," he said.

"They gave me something for infection," I told him. "Stuff is giving me the screaming shits."

"Antibiotic," he said, nodding. He turned out of the bottom of the driveway and pointed the car back toward Route 1. "Eat some yogit, when yaw done with the medicine. Get some good bugs back into yaw system." He accelerated as he talked, and within a hundred yards, we were way past legal. The stop sign at the intersection with Route 1 arrived in record time. Bookman braked, stopped at the sign, stopped completely, sat there for a minute.

"Yaw boy," he said, looking straight ahead, "don't like unifohms much."

"I know. Don't take it personally."

He didn't move, just sat there looking out the side window.

"After his mother died, the state took him. Since then, most of his encounters with you guys have been unpleasant."

"That so," he said. He pulled out onto Route 1, accelerated calmly and undramatically up to about ninety. "Why'd they take him? Yaw inlaws rathah have him in fostah cayah than living with you?"

I had to think about that one, but after a couple of seconds I remembered the bullshit story I'd given him about Nicky's mother and the Russian Mafia. "I don't know," I told him. I had the impulse to trust this guy, but I reminded myself that no matter what I thought about him, he was still a cop, and I was still . . . whatever. "I'll tell you the truth," I said, thinking I would tell him a piece of it. "When we had Nicky, no way was I ready to be a parent. I had no idea what I was supposed to do, but I was pretty sure I couldn't do it. Then, you know, his mother died. I guess I did a lot of things wrong."

"Ayuh," Bookman said. He had us up over a hundred and ten, and the Crown Vic felt like it was floating. If it'd had wings, we'd have been airborne. "So what's changed? You any moah ready now?"

Oh, yeah. Oh, yeah, I'll be so good from now on, I promise. "You want to know the real difference?"

"I do," he said.

"Nicky's the difference."

"Yeah? Howzat."

"Back then, you know, he was just this little baby that shit his pants and cried and woke me up in the middle of the night." Actually, I couldn't remember ever having been there for that, but I'd heard about it plenty. "But now . . ."

"Yeah?"

I could feel myself getting into uncharted territory. "Now he's a person. And he thinks, ahhh . . ." Jesus. Where was this shit coming from? "He thinks, and he believes, that I'm a great guy. He believes that completely. He has this certainty, this expectation, that I'm going to take care of him, that I'm going to do the right thing. I can feel the weight of it, you know what I mean? Especially when I feel tempted to, I don't know, exceed the speed limit or something."

"How 'bout that." Bookman took his foot off the gas, and the car settled back down on the road and began to slow down.

"I don't think I can be the guy he thinks I am," I said. "But I'm trying like hell."

"Good to heah," Bookman said. "Now yaw in the same boat with the rest of us." He braked, turned west off Route 1 onto a narrow two-lane road that headed uphill into some woods. I didn't see any other cars around. The trees hung low over the road and visibility was poor, so Bookman held it down to eighty. "Glad you nevah shot them Rooskies," he said.

"I don't know what difference it would make," I told him. "There's plenty more where they came from."

"So what's yaw ansah?"

"I guess I have to move on. Find a quiet place somewhere. . . ."

"Ayuh," he said, peering ahead. The trees opened up, there were some big empty fields on one side of the road, and you could see straight up the road for a half mile or so. Bookman cranked it up a little higher. "You showah there ain't no way you can do this legal?"

"I've got an appointment with a lawyer tomorrow, in Manhattan," I told him. Another small piece of the truth. "I don't know if anything is going to come of it."

"Don't hurt to try," he said. "You can leave Nicky with us if you like." He looked at me, and I thought I saw something in his eyes, but I didn't know him well enough to know what it was. "He and Franklin have become fast friends. You could pick him up when you get back." He paused for a minute, shook his head. "I don't know what you two have done to Franklin, he's said mowah in the past two days than he did in the previous two yeahs."

What choice did I have? It would be a terrible idea to bring Nicky back to Manhattan with me. I hadn't even thought about what I was going to do with him. Great work, Dad. "Thank you," I said. "I appreciate that."

We rocketed up the hill, and the trees petered out as we got to the top. The road we were on ended at a T-shaped intersection. The road we were about to turn onto pierced the empty landscape north to south. Straight ahead to the west was nothing but trees covering the round and furry shoulders of what had once been the Appalachian Mountains. I could see three hawks riding the thermals, and either a turkey vulture or a black vulture far to the west. They were all too far away to identify, even with glasses. You can tell a vulture from an eagle or a hawk, though, because turkey vultures and black vultures almost never flap their wings, they tip side to side, taking full advantage of every slight difference in the air currents.

To our right, a vehicle crested the hill, heading south. It was a big Chevy Suburban, new and shiny, four-wheel drive, the kind of thing you see frequently in places like New Jersey but rarely up in this part of Maine, unless it is driven by tourists. The driver apparently did not notice us, because he barreled down the deserted road at a speed that, while it did not rival Bookman's preferred rate, was still surely far above the posted limits. He picked us up, finally, when he was a couple of hundred feet away. You could see the nose of the thing dive as the driver braked, even though he had to know it was too late, and that he was dead meat. Bookman sat there and watched the guy go past, and then he turned right and headed north.

I was surprised. "Ain't you gonna go get that guy? Give his ass a ticket?"

"Bet you think I live for that." He ramped the Crown Vic back up to warp factor one. "Ain't that right? Nobody out heah, he wants to go sixty-five instead of fifty-five, why should I cayah?" He looked over at me. "Tell me, Mistah Williams. What do you think my job is?"

Now there's a loaded question. I gave him the textbook answer. "Enforce the law?"

"That so? Make everyone go fifty-five? Make showah nobody undah twenty-one drinks a beer or two? All that shit?"

I looked at him, curious. "That was my assumption."

He drove on in silence for a few seconds. "Tell you a story," he said. "The lobstahmen up here use the honah system. Did you know that?"

"I got no idea what you're talking about."

"Think about it," he said. "Yaw out theyah on yaw lobstah boat, pulling yaw traps. Nobody in sight, yaw all alone. Now, each lobstahman has his own colors, so he can tell which buoys ah his. You get it? No policemen watching him."

"So you're telling me nobody steals lobsters from the other guy's traps."

"I ain't telling you no such thing. But when it does happen, they don't call me. They handle it."

"Yeah? How's that?"

"The traditional wahning is to burn down the guy's bahn. If it still keeps up, they burn down his house. Then, last, well, you can probably figure that out."

"How often does that happen?"

"It has happened, but not in yeahs, not up heah. But what I'm trying to tell you is that things ah different up heah. Everything runs along just fine without my thumb on the scale, most of the time. Oddinary people, they know I ain't gonna bothah them if I don't need to." He shifted in his seat. "I know most everyone up heah," he said. "I know who drives fifty-five and who don't. I know who grows dope in theyah woodlot, and I know who smokes it. I know Louis Avery don't have his Jeep registered, and that the law puts limits how fah you can go from the bahn on a tractah. But I also know that Louis is doing the best he can, and that he's got to get to Lubec to get his groceries on occasion. Do you undahstand what I'm trying to tell you?"

I wondered, and not for the first time, how much this guy really knew about me. "I think I catch your drift."

"That's good," he said. "This is just what I'm trying to teach Hopkins. I been trying to explain to him that there are reasons for the things I do, the things I don't do, and the way I try to treat people. You, for example, and yoah boy. But don't think, if a fella is going around stepping on othah people's toes, that we won't do what we need to do."

"That why you put Louis in jail?"

"No," he said, shaking his head. "No. I put Louis in jail because without Eleanor keeping him straight, he ain't nothing but trouble."

"Can I bail him out?"

"Why?"

It was a stupid idea, half of my brain knew that absolutely, but the other half had already decided. "He doesn't need to be in jail, he needs to take care of Eleanor."

"Yeah, I know he does, but the rest of us don't need him ramming around drunk and raising hell."

"I think I know why he was doing that."

"That so?"

"Yeah. She needs an operation, and he can't pay for it."

"Heard that."

"Well, I think I can help him out with it."

"That so?" He looked at me appraisingly. "How you gonna do that?"

I didn't even want to say it out loud. "I can help him out. Trust me, okay? You gonna let me bail him out?"

He thought about it for a minute. "All right," he said, and he looked back over at me. "Go get him, if you want to."

"How much is bail?"

He shook his head. "Don't worry about that. I'll call and tell them to release him to you. Go get him."

Nicky, of course, was overjoyed to see me. He came charging across Bookman's front yard and nearly knocked me over. I was beginning to feel a little light-headed, and my shoulder was throbbing. I had to turn to shield it from his exuberance. Franklin ambled over, too, shook my hand, and watched as Nicky told me excitedly about the fish that he had caught, and that Franklin had thrown back. "Pickerels are too bony," Franklin rumbled. "Can't eat 'em." I was vaguely conscious of Bookman and his wife standing and watching the three of us. Nicky was the embodiment of something Franklin would never be, and I felt a little of the pain that caused. I was on my knees in the grass of their front lawn, looking around at their house and their station wagon and their dog running around, barking his ass off. I realized then that I was taking something from them. It was the same old thing, you know, I didn't have it myself, so I stole it from somebody who did. I had been stealing it from Louis and Eleanor, and now I was going to take it from Bookman and his wife, and Franklin. You got no choice, I told myself, but that sounded pretty hollow.

None of the drivers going by recognized the minivan, and nobody waved to me. I kinda missed the Subaru for that reason. I pulled out around in back of the municipal building, got inside without seeing Hopkins, or anyone else I knew.

Bookman had been good to his word, he'd called ahead, and a deputy was waiting for me. I stood behind the guy when we got down to the cell. I watched Louis through the glass. I held a finger up to my lips when we made eye contact, and he gave a little nod, like he understood. He took it seriously, too, because not a single word escaped his lips until we got outside the building.

"I didn't mean to do it."

"Cut the bar in half?"

He grimaced. "Not that. The other. Get tanked up, drive around with Nicky in the truck with me."

I'm always paranoid around police stations. "Shh. Wait until we're in the car." He went down the stairs in that halting way common to young children and old men, right foot down one step, left foot down onto the same step, then right foot down onto the next step, left foot down onto the same one, and so on. "Louis, you all right?"

"Little stiff," he said. "Nothing to do in theyah." He got to the bottom of the stairs, looked up and squinted. "Getting tossed into the drunk tank didn't seem so bad back when I was eighteen or twenty. This time, I didn't think I'd ever get out again."

I shook my head. "Things have changed a lot since then, Louis."

"Not enough," he said. "Not near enough."

We got out back and he climbed awkwardly into the minivan. He winced when he slammed the door. I hadn't asked anyone how long he'd been in there, but I didn't think he could still be hungover. I was pretty sure he was feeling lousy, but it had to have more to do with Eleanor than with booze.

"Is he all right?" He asked the question without looking at me. "Is Nicky okay?"

"Yeah, he's fine, Louis. He's staying with Bookman. Him and Franklin go fishing every day. He didn't say anything about what happened with you two, and I didn't ask. I figured, if it doesn't bother him, no point in bringing it up. Let him forget about it."

He nodded. Louis was silent for a long time after that. He looked out his window as we drove out of Eastport, and he didn't say anything until we reached the long causeway that connects the island to the mainland. "Nice cah," he finally said, rubbing the soft cloth of the seat.

"Not bad," I said.

"Buy her new?"

"Used."

"Pay cash?"

"Yeah. Fifteen grand."

"Hmm." We rode in silence for a few minutes. "I hate cah payments," he said finally. "I hate payments, period."

"Yeah, me too."

Four herring gulls were chasing a fifth, who apparently carried something edible in his beak. He swooped and dived to escape them, and they chased him with a skill and determination that were truly impressive. One of the pursuers finally induced the fleeing gull to drop what he was carrying, and one of the other gulls dived down and snatched it out of the air. Immediately that one took off, fleeing in a new direction, with the other four hot on his tail. The calories each of the birds was expending in the chase had to far outweigh the value of the prize, and besides, why didn't the lead bird just swallow it down? I guess that would end the game, though. You've got it, I want it, I've got it, you can't have it . . .

"I coulda took a job at the mill," Louis said. "I coulda went to work for the Calders. Coulda had benefits. Health insurance and all. But I was selfish, I didn't want to do it."

I didn't know what to say to that, so I kept quiet. I didn't have health insurance, either, hadn't even thought of it. It had never occurred to me that I needed it. Something else to put on the list.

"I thought it was a lousy trade," Louis said. "Take the most precious thing you got, your life, and give it up to some company. And what do they give you back? Enough money, and bayahly enough, for you to buy some of the things you see on yoah television. Frozen vegetables. And a new pickup truck. Does that make any sense to you?" He didn't wait for an answer. "Spend every day of my life in some stinking hole of a factory, take the money they pay me, go to the stowah and hand it ovah to someone who gives me back a bag of frozen vegetables. I can grow better ones myself, thank you very much. And Eleanor can put them by." We reached the end of the causeway, where it connected to the Passamaquoddy Reservation at Point Pleasant. Small houses dotted the landscape on both sides of the road, and a large red church stood off on a hillside.

"That's what I thought," he said, and he looked over at me for the first time since we'd gotten into the van. "I didn't figure on insurance, though. Didn't figure Eleanor was gonna have to die because I didn't have forty thousand dollars."

"I think I can help you out with that, Louis."

He didn't take me seriously. "Yeah? You got forty thousand dollars you ain't using?"

"I want to buy an option on that piece of land you got up in Eastport. That ought to be worth something."

He still wasn't listening to me, not really. "You know Sam Calder, that son of a hoah, he'd offered me fifty for it, but when he found out how much I really needed the money, he decided he didn't need to buy it aftah all, he just needed a right-of-way to cross it. Twenty-five is all he'll give me. And his boy will give me twenty-six. And no matter which one of them I give it to, they'll have something fuming up theyah before I'm cold in the ground."

"Maybe so, Louis. But not if you sell me an option on it. I'll give you fifty for it, just like Calder's original offer."

He turned slowly, looked at me. "Yo-ah serious, ahn't you."

I nodded. "Yeah."

"You a rich man?" he asked me. "I didn't figure you for one."

"Being rich is kind of a fluid concept, Louis." It was my turn to think for a minute. I hadn't considered myself a rich man, either. "Put it this way: paying you fifty grand for an option isn't gonna put too big a crimp in my situation."

"I'd be saying no," he said. "If Calder can't build his tanker port, there won't be no new jobs at it."

"You been out there on the bay, haven't you?"

"Yeah," he said.

"You want 'em bringing loaded oil tankers in there? Picture a bunch of old trucks with lousy brakes, overloaded, sitting at the top of a steep hill. You might get most of them down, but sooner or later one of them is gonna get away from you."

"Oh," he said, "you don't have to convince me. I'd set fiyah to the whole state if it'd get Eleanor out of that hospital whole. It's just that I didn't want to have to be the one to decide whether that place got built or not."

"You don't have to be."

"No?"

"No. First of all, it's just an option. Call it the right of first refusal. Something else happens to put you in dire need, you can still dump it. Okay? We'll make the deal run until your son Gerald moves up here, and then you can give it to him, let him figure out what to do. Besides, the property might be worth a lot more by then."

Louis nodded his head. "Might," he said.

"There's only one condition," I said.

"What's that?"

"You gotta take the money in cash."

He looked over at me. "Why in cash?"

"That would make it easier for me, Louis. If I had to write you a check, it would take too long to set up. Besides, then you'd have to deal with the taxes."

"You get paid in cash often in the computah business?"

"Louis, you used to be different, Bookman told me so. Said before you found religion, you used to raise hell, but then something happened to you, and you changed. Am I right?"

He nodded. "Ayuh."

"I, ah, I guess I pulled a lot of shit in my life, Louis, but I'm different now. I'm trying to do something good, for once in my fucking life. Why you trying to make it hard?"

"Oh, I'm not," he said. "I'm sorry, Manny. None of my business where you got it from. I appreciate what yo-ah doing, I can't tell you how much." He took a deep breath, straightened up a little bit. "Where should I say I got the money from?"

"I don't think anybody will care where you got it. Tell 'em you had it buried in coffee cans under your barn floor."

"You know, I nevah thought of that," he said. "Maybe I should go dig around undah theyah, see what I find." It was an attempt at humor, but it didn't hide the sadness in his voice. He'd never believe I was a computer programmer, never again.

When in doubt, ask a lawyer. There was a guy who practiced in Lubec, had a sign out in front of his house. His name was Weaver, and Louis and I decided to stop and see him on our way past. It just happened that Weaver was tied up with old man Calder and some other guy, so we sat in his kitchen and waited. At least he had coffee going, or his wife did. She seemed very nice, much more cheerful than anyone ought to be. She was short, round, and happy, there were pictures of her and her husband everywhere, and the two of them could have been bookends. I got a chance to talk to her for a while because Louis was still a little stunned. It struck me then that he wasn't out of the woods yet, that regardless of his financial situation, Eleanor was still in the hospital. Mrs. Weaver tried to engage him, asking him how Eleanor was holding up, but Louis had retreated to some monosyllabic alternate universe. She gave up on him after a while, and she and I sat in the kitchen and listened to her husband doing what lawyers do. I could hear him, not the words he said but the sound of his voice, measured and reasonable. The guy with Sam had a voice that was a little higher and a little more strident, and Sam himself was off the chart. He either started or finished every one of his sentences with "Goddammit, Weaver." Mrs. Weaver and I sat drinking coffee in her kitchen and listened to him. I found my mood rapidly improving, watching Mrs. Weaver giggling every time Sam said something in the other room.

"You know," she said to me, "Mr. Calder has always been such an unhappy man. You would think, with all his money, he could have anything he wants, but I can honestly say that in all the years I've known him I can't remember seeing him smile." She glanced over at Louis, but he was still in a world of his own.

"Takes more than money, I guess."

"Well, you know, that's true," she said. She pitched her voice low and leaned across the table to be heard. "Mr. Weaver and I don't have a lot, but we enjoy life, do you know what I mean? We both like to play golf. I may never be that good, but my husband is actually not bad, you know, he's got a nice tight swing and he stays in the fayahway mowah than just about anyone I know. But what I mean to say is, we enjoy life. We have a time-shayah in Noth Carolina, and we go golfing down theyah for two weeks every yeah, and we take other vacations when we can affodd it, we've played everywayah from Florida to Banff, you know, and of course we play around heah. There's a nice little course right over to Campobello. But Sam, he hardly evah even takes a day off." She leaned closer. "Tell me," she said. "Can going to business be that interesting? Can it be so much fun that it's all you want to do? And if it is, how come everyone that does it looks so unhappy?"

"I don't know the answer to that one." I stopped, and she and I listened to Sam launching into a tirade, but after a strong start he lost steam. "I can tell you that I used to enjoy my profession a lot more than I do now." I watched Louis out of the corner of my eye, but I might as well have been speaking Swahili. "I used to think being good at something was worth whatever price you had to pay for it. It's like playing a game, I guess. You want to win, even if there's no prize. There was something in me that needed that. But you know, after my son's mother died . . ."

She clucked her tongue. "Sorry to heah that."

"Thanks. But I've had to spend a lot more time with my son recently, and it almost makes me wonder why I was so interested in what I was doing before. You know, I've never played golf. I don't think I've ever even held a golf club in my hands. I used to wonder about people who played. Like, What could they be thinking?"

She laughed softly. "Oh, I know what you mean," she said. "When my husband first wanted me to go, I thought he was crazy. I agreed to try it, though, and I went and took some lessons with him. It was so funny, at first, half the time I would miss the ball altogethah. But you know what? All it took was one good shot. The first time I swung that drivah and heard that smack that you hear when you've struck it well, Lord, I stood theyah and watched it fly. . . . That was all it took. I've been hooked evah since. You know, you should try it sometime. I bet you'd like it."

We listened to Sam Calder through the walls of her house. "Now, goddammit, Weaver . . ."

"You suppose he'd be happier if he played golf?"

"Oh, you know," she said, "it wouldn't have to be golf. But you ought to have something that you can do, just because. You've got to have something in your life that makes you smile."

A while later, I looked out of Weaver's kitchen window and saw Sam Calder Sr. and the guy who was with him go stomping across Weaver's front yard towards Sam's Mercedes. They stopped for a few seconds to stare at the minivan before continuing on. Weaver came back into the kitchen a few minutes later, and his wife made introductions. He offered to take Louis and me into his office, but that hardly seemed necessary—his wife was going to hear it all anyhow, though I didn't say that. I explained what Louis and I wanted to do, and it turned out he had contract templates loaded in his word processor, all he needed to do was fill in the details and change some shit around. We wound up signing papers about an hour later, and Weaver had some advice for Louis on handling the money once he got it. Weaver's fee was a hundred and fifty bucks, and I had to fight with Louis to pay it out of my end. I won, finally, but it was a struggle.

When we got back to Louis's house, he stared at his Jeep with a funny look on his face. I thought I knew what it was. I've done it myself, and it's worse when you do it in the city, you get fried and park your car on the street someplace, and then in the morning you can't remember where you put it. You spend a couple of hours, or days, sometimes, wandering around the neighborhood looking for it, and when you finally find it, you stand there staring at it, thinking, Shit, I don't remember this at all. But there it is, you know, and your key fits and all that, so it had to be you who put it there, and it's a strange thing to realize that you were behind the wheel but someone else was driving.

"C'mon, Louis," I told him. "It's all right." He shook his head and followed me into the kitchen. "I gotta make a run down to Manhattan," I told him once we were inside. "I should be back in a couple of days. You gonna be all right?"

I watched him stand there, breathing, looking at the wall. "You know," he finally said, "when I was in that cell, I felt like I was back where I belonged. I felt like I had just been playacting all these yeahs since the last time I was locked up. I've been pretending that I was grown up, but it was all for show."

"That's fucked up, Louis. Eleanor needs you now, you gotta be there for her. You think you can do that?"

He nodded. "I'll be all right."

I went upstairs and grabbed one of my duffel bags. The other one, the one that held my laptop, my birding stuff, and the money, I left where it was. I did grab five bundles out of it, though, fifty grand. It seemed such a meaningless thing, like I was giving someone some of my extra socks. I took them downstairs, laid them on the kitchen table, where Louis was sitting down. His friend Jim Beam was nowhere in evidence. Louis let out a big sigh when he saw the money, like he'd been holding it in ever since I'd picked him up.

"Manny," he said. "I don't know what to say."

"You don't need to say anything."

"I don't know why you're doing this," he said.

"I've made a lot of mistakes in my life, Louis. Made a lot of poor choices." I had always taken care of myself first. I had the feeling that if I got started telling him about that, we would be sitting there for hours. "Maybe this'll make up for a couple of them."

"Maybe it will." Louis's voice got husky, and he got that Sunday-morning look in his eye. He stood up, walked over, and took my hand in both of his. "I'll pray for you, son, you and Nicky both. I'll pray that the Lord forgives you, and that he sets you on the right road."

"Thanks, Louis." His gratitude was making me itchy because I still had no real appreciation for money. I wasn't giving him something I had worked for, it didn't feel like I was doing anything more significant than passing on a pair of shoes that didn't fit me anymore. "I appreciate that. You want my advice, I would take the money up and give it to Weaver, let him handle it for you. You can't just go and lay it on the hospital, you know what I'm saying? You gotta make them think you had to sell your firstborn to get it, every step of the way. You need a ride back down there? You need a ride down to the hospital in Machias?"

"I can make it," he said. "You go on and do what you need to do. Thank you, Manny. Thank you for everything."

I almost forgot about Gevier's money, but I noticed his invoice lying on the floor of the passenger side of the van when I threw my duffel bag inside. It wasn't a lot, not to me, but I don't think money ever means much of anything to a thief. It had never mattered that much to me if I was broke, because I knew how to get what I needed. You take a guy like Gevier, though, even though he was obviously a bright guy and knew his profession, if no one came into his garage for a few weeks, or a few months, he could wind up in a hard way pretty quickly. It struck me then that I'd had the unearned luxury of not needing to worry about finances most of my life, on account of being a crook, while more or less normal guys like Gevier and Louis probably had to expend a lot of mental energy sweating how they were going to make it. Of course, neither one of them was likely to get locked up for pursuing his chosen profession.

Now that I had Nicky, I couldn't afford that risk any more, either.

Jesus.

I drove over to Gevier's house to pay my bill.

I didn't expect him to be there, and he wasn't. Eddie answered the door. She didn't say anything, she didn't even look at me, she just stared out past me at the minivan. Sometimes I have this effect on people, and I've never understood it. I don't growl, I don't flex my muscles at you, I even try to smile sometimes. Maybe it's just a size thing, you know, maybe some people are afraid of me for the same reason I'm afraid of Louis's horse.

I'm not really afraid of the horse, okay, I just don't like it. Anyway, Eddie hadn't been afraid before, either of the times I had met her. Her father and Louis had both been around the first time, but I couldn't see that making too much of a difference, and I thought we'd done great when Nicky and I met up with her out in Louis's pasture. When a person is scared of you, though, you can sense it, you can see it in the way he looks at you, the way he moves, the way he sits, everything he does. I'll tell you something I would never be able to admit if you and I were standing someplace having a conversation: it hurts every time it happens. It's like being slapped in the face. You think you can get used to it, right, you think you have a thick skin and they can't really touch you, but then you see that look again, and you think, Come on, man. I ain't a bad guy. And even if I am, you don't know it yet. But you're on the outside again, and there's nothing you can do to make him let you in.

She did, though, she stood back from the door, held it open, waited for me to come inside. "He's not here," she said.

"He's still at work, right? I just came by to pay up." I held out the bill, and she took it from me with a shaking hand. This kid is afraid, I thought, really afraid. Something must have happened, something that shook her up. I wondered what she thought I was.

"I couldn't stand it if he had to go back to jail," she said. "They'd send me away somewhere, we'd be locked away from each other, and I can't stand the thought of it." She started undoing the buttons on her shirt. Her cheeks were flaming red, and she still wouldn't look at me.

"Eddie, stop." She had all the buttons open and she shrugged her shirt back off her shoulders. She had no bra on underneath it, and, I suppose, no need for one. I turned away, put my hand on the doorknob. "I gotta go."

"Why can't you just leave him alone?" I heard panic then, and her voice rose in pitch, loud, uncomfortably close to hysteria. "I'll do whatever you want me to, if you'll just go away afterward, and leave my father alone."

I didn't turn around. "Eddie, put your shirt back on."

"He didn't do anything! He's just a mechanic now, don't you understand that? He fixes cars for a living!"

I kept my back to her. "Eddie, I ain't made out of stone. If you put your shirt back on, I'll stay and talk to you." I listened to the sound of her breath, angry little huffs in and out.

"All right," she finally said. I turned around to see her standing, rigid, her face still red. Her shirt was on, though. She had buttoned it all the way up to her chin. At least she was making eye contact.

I walked past her. "Sit down," I told her. "Over there." She took a chair, and I sat down across the room from her. "Eddie, I don't know what the hell you're talking about. Your father fixed my van, and I came by to pay the bill. That's all I know."

She glared at me. "You can stop pretending. Thomas Hopkins told me who you really are."

"Did he now?" My stomach did a kind of a roll, but it stopped, because I didn't think Hopkins knew who I was, for one thing, and it didn't fit with Eddie's worries about her father, for another. "What did he tell you?"

She looked at me, anger and defiance plain on her face. "He said the DEA sent you up here to break up the Oxy trade. He told me you didn't even care if you got the right guy, that you knew my father used to be a chemist, and you were going to hang it on him."

It was almost funny. "Fucking Hopkins." The guy was poisoning the waters, I guess. "And you believed him?"

"You wouldn't tell me the truth, anyway."

Maybe not. "Look, Eddie, I am the furthest thing in the world from any kind of cop, okay? But I just came by to pay my bill. When I'm done here, I have to go out of town for a couple days to take care of some business, and when I'm done with that, I'm going to come back up here, pick up Nicky, and be on my way. I got nothing to do with the DEA, and I couldn't care less about the Oxy trade."

Her face seemed to crumple. "Hopkins said you thought my father was the chemist who figured out how to counterfeit OxyContin. He said there's a lab in India someplace where they're making it now, and that they're bringing it in through Canada."

I shrugged. "Well, that may be true, but I always figured, you want to put a needle in your arm, it's your business. Nothing to do with me."

She leaned forward in her chair, covered her face with both hands, and began to cry silently. It was relief, I guess. After a couple of minutes she stopped, but she didn't uncover her face. "You must think I'm a fool," she said, her voice muffled.

"No."

"I'll be right back." She stood hastily and stomped out of the room. I could hear water running, and then she lost it again, I could hear her going on, "hoo-hoo-hoo," crying like a little kid. She came back about ten minutes later. She had washed her face, tied her hair back, tucked her shirt in. Probably had on a pair of cast-iron underpants.

"I'm sorry," she said, standing next to her chair, flustered. "I thought . . ." She gestured with a fluttering hand over toward the door, where she'd been standing when she'd taken off her shirt. "I was afraid of you, you know. . . ."

"Sit down," I told her. "Let's move on from there, okay? Let's just, like, go forward. Can we do that?"

She glanced at me, and she blushed again and looked away. "Okay," she said, sitting down. "Yeah, sure."

"You must love him a lot."

"All I have is my father." Her eyes clouded over. "Why would Hopkins say that stuff about you?"

I told her the whole story of Hopkins and me, the traffic stop, the convenience store where he'd been smacking his girlfriend around, the complaint Bookman made me sign, the fight at the VFW, Bookman suspending Hopkins for the fight at the VFW, all of it. "Next he'll be sneaking over at night to let the air out of my tires," I said. "I caused him some trouble, or he thinks I did, and he wants to return the favor. Nothing he would say or do at this point would surprise me."

"What a dick," she said. "Listen, I'm sorry. It's just that I've been under so much stress lately. I'm trying to figure out what I should do, and I worry about what would happen to my father if I left, you know, and then this. . . . I couldn't stand it if he had to go back to jail."

"I understand, believe me."

She looked at me. "If Nicky were in my position, would you make him go away to school? Will you do it when he gets old enough?"

I hadn't thought about it. "I don't know. I guess I would want him to go. Not to get him away from me, not to get rid of him. But you know, I've made a lot of mistakes in my life, and I don't want Nicky to make the same ones. I want better things for him. I'm sure your father wants better things for you than what he can give you."

She thought that over. "Do you remember what you said, back when I told you I didn't fit in up here?"

"What'd I say?"

"I told you I wouldn't fit in down in New York City, either. You made a joke. You howled like a wolf, and then you told me you could get me around that in ten minutes."

"Oh, yeah." She sat there staring at me. "All right," I told her. "Easy enough. First of all, you don't have much of an accent, so you don't need to worry about that. Second, don't go by the name Edna. Nicky was right. Call yourself Eddie. All right? Eddie Gevier. Lose those flannel shirts, but just keep that one on for now, okay?" She grimaced at me. "Wear black jeans everywhere, and sneakers, those old-fashioned Chuck Taylors are good. Sunglasses, no jewelry. T-shirts, black leather jacket for winter. Okay? That'll get you through the first year. Next, stay out of places you don't belong. Don't smoke dope, don't drink more than two beers. Never tell anybody anything about yourself. Nobody's got your back, so you got to look out for your own self. If you go out, go with a bunch of other females. Keep your mouth shut and sit near the door. Never carry money in your wallet, keep it in your pants pocket. Never date a guy more broke than you. Never believe a guy when he talks shit to you."

"You think men are dogs?"

"I know it." I looked over at her. "Guys will do or say almost anything to get into your drawers."

"You didn't," she said. "You had the perfect chance and you didn't take it."

"You can't go by that, it was just a moment of weakness."

She stood up, and so did I. She watched me count bills out of my wallet. I handed them to her. "Thank you," she said, "for not, you know . . ."

I looked at her, remembering. God, I couldn't help it. "Don't mention it. You love him that much?"

Her face wrinkled, she took three steps across the space between us and wrapped her arms around me. It was a chaste hug, though, all arms and shoulders, not the full-body squirm you get when they really want you. "Come on," I said, patting her back. "Don't start up again."

"All right." She separated herself from me. "I really should do it, right? Go away to school, I mean."

"It's your call."

"I know it would be stupid not to. I just hate being alone again."

"I know what you mean. You can take it for a semester, though. So can your father. I gotta go, Eddie, I want to make it to Boston tonight. You gonna be okay?"

She nodded, put the money in her pocket. "See you."

I called Bookman's house from my cell phone. Bookman wasn't home, but his wife answered and I talked to her for a while. She told me how much she liked having Nicky, even if it was only for a few days, and how much Franklin enjoyed having him there. I could hear that mixture of joy and sadness in her voice, her happiness that Franklin had someone to play with, her sorrow at being reminded of her son's limitations. She put Nicky on the phone, and he bellowed in my ear about the yellow perch he'd caught, and how you couldn't eat yellow perch, either, how they tried to stick you with their fins when all you wanted to do was take them off the hook and let them go, and Franklin had caught a bass, a great big one, but they let him go, too. "You have to use worms, Poppy. You have to stick them right on the hook. Do you think it hurts them?"

"I don't think so, Nicky. I don't think worms can feel anything." He talked to me a while longer, but then he ran out of steam. I made him promise to be good, and I listened to him hang up the phone. I had to remind myself again why I needed to do this, leave Nicky with someone and drive away.

Information gave me Thomas Hopkins's telephone number and

placed the call for me. His answering machine was on. I listened to Hop's voice say, "You know what to do," then I heard the beep. I thought about the bullshit story he'd told Eddie Gevier, but I couldn't think of any useful message to leave the son of a bitch, so I hung up. I needed to talk to him, though, because there were too many things going on for me to waste time thinking about Hop and his stupid schoolyard shit.

I started falling asleep behind the wheel just north of Portland. The second or third time it happened I got off at the next exit and bought a couple cups of coffee. I don't know why, but I couldn't bring myself to stop there for the night.

The coffee wore off before I reached Massachusetts. Maybe it was coincidental, or maybe it was just because I knew where the fucking place was, but whatever the reason, I wound up back at the same motel Nicky and I had stayed in that first night, on our way north. Different room, at least. I wondered how Nicky was, what he'd had for supper, if he was asleep, all of that. For a guy who always thought he had it together, I had to admit that my shit was spread out all over the place. My money was in New Jersey, my kid was in Maine, and my ass was in Massachusetts. I was beginning to feel like I was losing control. I wanted to call Nicky again but I didn't. What could I tell him that I hadn't already, just a couple of hours earlier? Nicky, I promise to do better than this. . . . He wouldn't understand, and anyhow, it was myself I needed to make that promise to.

I've never been much for praying. Like Huck Finn, I always got either the hooks or the string, so I gave up on it. I used to think I had a lot of this shit figured out, you know, why people do certain things, why it was all right for me to be what I was, and all that, but you add a couple more pieces to your equation and suddenly the answers start coming out all different. I could see houses up on the hill behind the motel, just ordinary places with trees around them, places where regular people lived. I tried to picture Nicky and me up there inside one of them, the minivan parked in the driveway, Nicky going to school, me cutting the grass. . . .

What a thought, man, what a life. What a fucking world.

9

The pain in my shoulder got me up early. I felt hungover from the night before, but it was unearned because I hadn't had anything to drink. I guess I woke up feeling sorry for myself, but going around wishing things were different than they are is a loser's game. Shit will always be shit, no matter how you try to dress it up.

I got out of that motel and hit the road. I stopped for a truly abysmal breakfast on the Mass Pike. I just had a couple hours to go. First thing I noticed when I got close to New York was the traffic. I picked up on it when I was still about an hour away from Manhattan. It wasn't like I expected people to wave at me the way Mainers do, but Jesus. There must be a certain ratio of cars to asphalt beyond which people lose their minds. A lady in a big red Ford Excursion on the Connecticut Turnpike must have missed her stop, so she bet her life and the lives of the children she had riding with her that I would be quick enough to miss her when she went flying across two lanes and cut me off to make the exit ramp. She won her bet, that time, anyhow, but I couldn't help seeing a munched SUV full of dead kids somewhere in her future. Funny thing was, that was nothing compared to the sick shit I have seen people do with their cars, and have done myself, but when I lived here, I never thought about it twice. I used to think everyone was like that.

The other thing that struck me was that I didn't know anybody. Didn't recognize anybody in the other cars, didn't know the woman in the toll booth at the Triborough Bridge. I would go on my way and none of them would have any reason to think of me ever again, unless I managed to make the six o'clock news. I used to like that feeling, but this time I wasn't so sure. I could get back into it, though, if I stayed long enough, I could feel that, too.

I went across the Triborough and took the FDR southbound down the East Side of Manhattan. The FDR is a great road, it hugs the water all the way down to Manhattan's southern tip, and it's a terrific place to kill yourself. You've got to hit it at the right time, though. During rush hour, which isn't an hour anymore, it's more like three hours in the morning and at least that much during the evening, it's too choked with cars to be much fun, you wind up spending most of your time sitting and waiting. But catch it right and it can be beautiful, an adrenaline junkie's dream, you can crank it up and really wail, like the world is butter and you're the hot knife. I'm not saying you should do this, okay, but it's better if you do it in somebody else's car, because once you get beyond a certain speed there's zero tolerance for error. I remember once I was in someone's Camaro, seriously hauling ass, and I hit this one section where the road curves to the right just as it rises up on legs and goes elevated for a while. I cut into the right lane to get around a commuter van just in time to round that curve and find some putz broken down in the lane right in front of me. It was too late to stop, too late to duck back behind the van, too late to do anything except stand on the gas and go for it. I missed them both, I don't know how, all I can remember is that the guy who'd been standing out behind his car suddenly had to run for his life. I have this image frozen in my memory, him going over the fence. Man, what a rush. I lived on it for months. Only recently have I begun to wonder if the guy was all right, because it's a long way to the ground, right in that spot.

Too many cars for that now, plus, I wouldn't try it in the van. Well, I would have once, but no more. You get too much riot serum in your bloodstream when you're young, and not enough when you're old. I don't know whose idea that was. I do know that you can feel yourself changing as you get older, if you pay attention. That's assuming you survive the insanity years, the years when your blood runs too high and too hot and you can't hold back. When you feel yourself start to grow up, do you mourn the passing of that craziness or do you thank God that you survived it? And was I different now because of the time that had passed by or was it because of Nicky and Bookman and Louis and Eleanor and all the rest of them? I didn't have to worry too much about my driving this time, though, I stayed in the left lane behind a gypsy cab. He would move twenty feet up and stop, and I would move twenty feet up behind him and stop, and so would the guy behind me, the guy behind him, and so on.

Once you get to about Ninty-sixth Street you can see where the Harlem and the East Rivers come together at Hell Gate. There's a tiny island out in the middle of the water there, and then you go another ten blocks or so before you get to Roosevelt Island. Roosevelt Island is like a big battleship moored right in the middle of the river, and the northern ninety percent of it is all built up with apartment buildings and so on, but the southern tip is overgrown and wild. There's an old stone building there, slowly falling into the weeds, looks like King Arthur's castle but it used to be the hospital where they kept Typhoid Mary. That's what a guy on the Circle Line told me once, anyhow, and just south of Roosevelt is a birdshit-encrusted rock known as U Thant Island. It took me almost an hour to get from Hell Gate down to U Thant, where a bunch of cormorants were standing on the rocks hanging their wings out to dry. They call them shags up in Maine, they're dark brown, greasy, duck-looking birds, and instead of flying over the water and plunging down in when they see a fish, they sit low in the water with just their necks sticking out, and they dive under and fly around under the water after fish. It's amazing, when you think of it, this bird can swim faster and maneuver better than a fish can, but there you go. Mainers have told me they catch them in lobster pots once in a while, the cormorant goes in there after the bait and then can't get out. I don't know if that's true or not.

I started to wonder where I was going to dump the car, then I remembered, This one is mine, I can't dump it, I have to park the fucking thing. Not only that, but now I got to worry about the stuff I've got inside it, too. When I was a kid, I would bust your windshield to steal a cool pair of sunglasses. Not so goddam funny when the shoe's on the other foot.

Coming back to New York City is like going back with an old girlfriend. There are really no new places for you to go, but then, you already know your way around, and you wonder, is she the one for me after all? Twenty-eight years I lived here, except for when I was staying in the barbed-wire hotel, and I been everywhere from Rikers to Lincoln Center. Tell you the truth, I never thought I'd leave, and now here I was seeing the place different. I got off at Houston and went over to Katz's for a pastrami sandwich. I couldn't have been inside that place for more than ten minutes, and I got a parking ticket right out in front of the place. There it is: Welcome back, dickhead, here's a home coming present. Sixty-five bucks.

Yeah, sure. Try and get it.

I wound up in the Holiday Inn on Fifty-seventh Street over on the West Side. It's kind of an out-of-the-way place for Manhattan, which is a weird thing to say. How can you be out of the way when every square foot of ground has some asshole standing on it? But the place is a long way from the theater district and all the stuff that goes with that, which was okay by me. I felt a lot better when I had my bag locked in a room and the van in the garage next door. I sat in a chair in the lobby and called Buchanan.

"Mohammed," he said, sounding all happy. "You want to come to my office or should we meet someplace?"

"Let's meet someplace," I said. I suddenly remembered that movie where Tommy Lee Jones was chasing Harrison Ford, and I lost my enthusiasm for going out. Those guys had followed me all the way up to Maine, chased me through the woods. "How about the Holiday Inn on Fifty-seventh Street? Over on the west side. Tell them at the desk you're there to meet the Baker party."

"All right," he said. "I have to get some stuff together. Give me an hour and a half."

* * *

I rented a conference room. The hotel went all out, they put two urns of coffee in the place, one regular and one decaf, plates of pastries and doughnuts, two long tables with paper tablecloths, nice soft chairs all around. I had a couple of cups of decaf while I waited, ate all the poppy seed Danishes out of the pastry tray. Try finding those anywhere north of Bangor.

Michael Timothy Buchanan knocked on the door, opened it a crack, and stuck his head in. "Wow," he said when he saw me. "Very corporate. Coffee and doughnuts. That's the only reason anyone really goes to meetings, you know." He came the rest of the way in, locked the door behind him. "You check those other doors?"

"Yeah, I think we're cool."

He looked at me. "Getting cold feet?"

"No. Why?"

He sat down, put his briefcase on the table in front of him. "You and I have worked together before, but not with this kind of money. It's not unusual, in these situations, for people to start worrying. Demanding guarantees and assurances. These transactions, by their very nature, require a certain amount of trust. I lose a certain amount of business because the parties involved get right up to the threshold and discover that they can't muster the faith in me to go through with things."

"I can see that. You want some coffee?"

He nodded.

"Regular or decaf?"

"Why drink decaf?" he said, sneering. "What's the point?" I got his coffee, left it in front of him along with a small pitcher of cream.

"I checked you out a long time ago, Buchanan. Scary how easy it is to do that, don't you think? I know where you live, I know your Social Security number, I know what you paid in income tax last year, I know how much your house out on the Island is worth. I don't figure you're going to run for something under two million. And I figure, you know I could find you if you did."

He sighed. "The Internet?"

"Yeah, some of it. But people who work in banks and credit bureaus are as easy to scam as anyone else. Just a few phone calls."

"You've been wasting your talents, Mohammed. So we're on, then?"

"Yeah."

"Good," he said, and he opened his briefcase. It took about two hours, which made it late afternoon by the time we wrapped it up. He'd set it up like I'd asked him to, half in my name and half in Rosario's. I signed for myself with my right hand, and I signed for Rosario with my left. I got a half a smile out of the guy when I did that. We agreed to meet the next morning, out in Hackensack, New Jersey, at the storage place where I'd stashed the money. He grimaced at the idea—God, New Jersey—and then he left without saying good-bye.

I tried Hop's number again that night, just before I went to bed. I used the hotel phone, just in case he had caller ID, though I didn't know what difference it made. I got the same terse message, the same mechanical beep, and I sat listening to the silence until his machine disconnected me.

10

I checked out of the hotel in the morning and drove the minivan out to Jersey. I had a funny kind of awareness, I don't know where it came from, but all of a sudden I was looking at the city like a tourist. All my life I'd been committed to the place, as if New York City were the only place in the world where I belonged, the only place where I could be myself. It changed that morning, though, and everywhere I went I looked at familiar streets and buildings through new eyes, wondering if I would ever get back that way again. When you live so long in one place you build up an intimate knowledge of where everything is and how it all really works, and it seemed to me that morning that I was kissing it all good-bye somehow. It's like when you're breaking up with a woman: you know you're going to leave her, but she's still got whatever it was that hooked you in the first place, and you watch her with a little more focus, a little more intensity, trying to fix in your memory the image of that long hair or that soft voice or that perfect ass, because you're about to take a step that you can't take back and you wonder if you're ever gonna stand in that particular spot again. I got on the West Side Highway and I swear to you the Hudson River never looked so beautiful before. For the first time in my life I noticed that the tide was in. The river was high, and the early-morning sun made it look blue and warm, as pretty as the day Henry Hudson first put his boat up in there. When I went past the Seventy-ninth Street boat basin I could feel something pulling at me. I had never given sailboats a second glance before, but that morning they all looked as gorgeous as if they had come from God's own hand. I envied those fortunate souls living aboard, surrounded by beauty and freedom and cool autumn air. It was just an illusion and I knew it, that's what gives a dreamer that ache in the pit of his stomach, because you know the guy in the sailboat is worried about his bilge pump and his engine and what the salt air is doing to his wiring, plus the poor bastard still has to get his ass out of bed and go to work like everyone else. And you know that, right? And you know that you can't afford to let some dream suck you under, but sometimes they look so goddam beautiful.

Traffic leaving the city was relatively light, especially when you compared it to everybody lined up trying to get in. I felt curiously unsteady, as if I were one of those sailboats in the boat basin I had just passed and someone had cut me loose. This place was all I was used to, this one little corner of the world, the one place where I knew I could survive, and here I was putting my back to it, driving away. This must be what Eddie Gevier had felt the day before, this strange sensation that things are sliding on you, that you're about to cut yourself loose from the only safe place you've ever known. It's one thing to tell yourself up in your head that safety and security are illusions, but it's another thing altogether to let go of them only to find that, as illusions go, they were comfortable as hell.

I got out there early, Buchanan wasn't supposed to meet me until ten, so I drove around for a while. I saw one of those doc-in-a-box places and went in, had the guy look at my arm. There was no fooling this guy, he laughed when I told him I got it in a car accident. "Yeah," he said. "Sure. What happened, the other driver decide to cap you? Well, there's no infection, it looks like it's healing normally." He walked me back out to the front desk, told me to watch my ass and to finish taking the antibiotics.

I bought a cup of coffee, took it over to the storage place, and sat waiting for Buchanan. It was a nice little speech he'd given me the day before, but if something bad was going to happen, it would be here, at the transfer point. I had left the pistol I'd taken off the Russian up in Maine, rolled up in my vest, but I knew a guy over in Canarsie who sold guns. I wasn't going to drive all the way back over into the city to get one, though, and besides, it was too late. And it's karma, you know, whenever you buy a handgun you are tempting fate. Certain things you do, I think the universe piles up the odds against you, and buying a handgun is definitely one of those things. I always thought that a burglar who carried a gun, particularly if he was a pro and not just some stupid kid, was betting against himself. The idea is that you're smart enough and good enough to get in and back out again before anyone knows you were there. Some B&E guys that I know, first thing they do when they get into your house, okay, they stop in the kitchen for a nice big knife. I never did that, either. It was right at that point that I realized I wasn't even a burglar anymore. I missed it a little bit, but nowhere near as much as I missed Nicky.

Buchanan showed up about a half hour late. This big black stretch limo pulled in and stopped at the gate of the storage place, and I saw the guard point down in my direction. The stall I had rented was near the end of a row of ground-level walk-in closet-sized cubicles, with another row of identical cubicles about twenty feet away. To my back was a chain-link fence, with barbed wire on the top. In other words, I was at the back of an alley, with no place to go. The limo stopped at the front of the alley, blocking the way. I got out of the van and waited. The limo driver got out—the dude actually had white gloves on—and opened a back door. Buchanan got out, looked around, walked down to meet me, leaving the car where it was. He was carrying a thin attaché.

If Rosario had been here, he would have been carrying. Not only that, he would have put a round or two through the limo windshield just to show them he was serious. My heart was thudding in my chest, I felt like its motion was shaking my whole body. Every instinct I had was yelling at me to run, but I didn't. I walked over to my stall, unlocked the door, opened it up.

Buchanan and I stepped inside. I hung back for just a half second, to get another look at the limo, but it stayed where it was, doors closed. I decided I was safe enough for now. Buchanan had no way of knowing whether I was carrying or not, and whoever was in the car couldn't see what was going on inside the little storeroom. As a matter of fact, Buchanan was as much at risk as I was, and if he was nervous, he didn't show it.

A single bare bulb hung from the ceiling of the place. I pulled the string, and Buchanan held up a hand to shield himself from the harsh light. His eyes adjusted after a minute or so, and he looked at the two big green bags lying on the long table that was against one wall. The storage facility was backed up against the Hackensack River. The river is biologically active, they say, regaining life, but it looked and smelled like a fucking sewer.

Buchanan ripped open both zippers. He counted the bundles first, then took one bundle out of each bag, one fat one and one skinny one, and he counted each bundle. He counted money the way they do at the track, fingers and bills moving faster than I could follow. He seemed happy with the count. He stuffed the bundles back where he'd gotten them, zipped both bags back up. He patted the last one unconsciously, then picked his attaché up, plopped it on the table, and opened it. He had a thin Sony laptop inside. He opened that, too. It was already running.

"I took the liberty of setting up the transaction," he said. He was looking at the screen, not at me. He had my brokerage account up. "You made some money on Pfizer," he said. "Did you know they were buying Pharmacia?"

"Been in the papers forever."

"Well, they got final approval yesterday," he said. "You got a nice little bounce. Okay, look here. There's the stock you're buying, it's OTC. Here's how much you're buying. All you have to do is okay this transaction and you dump everything you're holding now and buy the new stock with the proceeds."

"All I do is hit 'OK'?"

"That's it."

"You on-line?"

He nodded. "Wireless."

"How you doing it? You got a cell phone modem?"

He shook his head. "Too slow, and too unstable. This is called

Express Network. I got it from Verizon. It runs at about a hundred forty-four K. It's good as long as I don't get too far outside of Manhattan, and you know how often I do that."

I walked over, looked at the screen, used the cursor to click the 'OK' icon. Twenty seconds later, the screen changed, showing my transactions, asking if I wanted to print out verification. Buchanan took a silver pen and a notebook out of the inner pocket of his suit jacket, wrote down the confirmation number, and handed it to me. He looked at me for a couple of seconds.

"Log in to your service provider," he said. "Check your account page yourself. You should even get confirmation via e-mail, you can check that, too." I did both of those things, then called up *Playboy*'s Web site. I didn't figure he could fake that, and there was no way he'd know ahead of time that I would look at it. I shrugged.

"All right," I said.

Buchanan stepped out into the alley, held his left hand up in the air, and waggled his fingers. A second later I heard a car door slam. Buchanan stepped back inside the storeroom, closed his laptop, and shut it up inside the attaché. Two ironheads came walking into the storeroom behind Buchanan. If he was setting me up, this was bad; I might have been able to handle one of them, but not both. They weren't meatballs, though, they didn't have the look, and one of them had a little gray around his temples. My guess was that they were retired cops. Whatever they were, they didn't look at me, or at Buchanan, either. They grabbed one bag each, stood up under the weight, walked out. Buchanan did not bother to watch them. He waved his hand to catch my eye.

"Your funds," he said, with a small grin, "are now in escrow with me. The FDA will do a press release three days from now. Now, you want my advice, here it is: This company you just bought into is way too small to handle production and distribution of this new drug, never mind sales or promotion. One of two things will happen. Either they'll partner with one of the bigger pharmaceuticals, or they'll sell out. What you should do is ride the initial run-up, then sell half your holdings. If they become a takeover target, the stock price will skyrocket. Don't be too greedy, sell it off gradually. You with me?"

I was still reeling. I had just watched two jamokes that I had never seen before walk out with about two million bucks. All of the account numbers and balances and Web pages could not compete with that kind of an impact. "Yeah," I said. "I got you."

Buchanan stepped up, put a hand on my shoulder. The unbandaged one. "Mohammed," he said. "You've done well here. In less than a week, you'll know exactly how well. Now you have the opportunity to go off somewhere and live a nice, quiet, normal life. Don't blow it." He picked up his attaché and walked out. I stayed where I was, listened to the limo door slam, and then I heard the crunch of gravel under tires. A quiet, normal life? What would that be like?

I got back in the minivan, sat there thinking about it. I remembered that lake up in the woods, the place where Nicky and I had gone walking. All the things I had then thought unattainable were now within my reach. It was a frightening thought, I guess because I realized that if I wanted it to work, I would have to turn my back on everything I knew. It's not so easy, when you're a survivor, to let go of those tools you have used to stay alive, no matter how dark they are. The thing was, survival was no longer my sole objective. Now I wanted more. I called Bookman's house while I was sitting there. His wife answered, so we talked for a few minutes. She told me the boys had already had lunch, and that they and the dog had gone off to the stream. "Yoah son is so sweet," she said to me.

"I really hope he hasn't been too much trouble," I said.

She laughed at me. "He's teaching Franklin so much, just by being with him, and by talking all the time. We paid for therapy for years," she said, "but no one ever got neah the results yoah son has."

I told her I was glad to hear that, asked her to tell Nicky I'd see him tomorrow. I started the van up, left my storeroom key with the guard at the gate, and headed north.

I called Hop from Route 84 in Connecticut. I was surprised when he answered the phone—I had gotten used to his answering machine, getting him in person took me off guard. I didn't say anything at first.

"Who is this?" he said. I had a feeling he already knew it was me, either that or he always sounded pissed off on the telephone.

"Just your friendly local DEA agent. What is your fucking problem, Hoppie? What good did it do to scare Edna Gevier half to death with a bullshit story like that? What did that accomplish?"

"You should never have come up heah." He snarled the words into the phone. "Why didn't you stay where you belonged? You ought to just go on about yoah business and get the hell out of my life. Yoah messing with the wrong man."

"I got every intention of doing that, Hop, but I don't need any trouble from you in the meantime."

"You don't know what trouble is," he said, and he hung up on me.

Maybe I should have called Bookman, I don't know. I didn't, though. Complaining to Bookman about Hop's penny-ante antics seemed too petty, and I guess I didn't want Bookman to think I was a crybaby, and besides, he still seemed to think he could turn Hopkins around. I was surprised to discover how much I cared about what Bookman thought of me. And how much harm had Hop's story done, anyhow? Scared Eddie a little bit, gave me a minor thrill, though I felt guilty, remembering how she'd looked, standing shirtless in her kitchen.

The hell with it, I told myself. Let it go. Another day or two and this will all be over.

I had intended to make it back to Louis Avery's house that night, but by the time I had gotten done with Buchanan it was almost noon, and it's a bitch of a drive. I was beat by the time I hit the Mass Pike. I kept pushing until I got over the Maine–New Hampshire border, then stopped at a little motel on Route 1. They had a restaurant attached, with big windows looking out over a saltwater marsh. I went out on the deck behind the restaurant after I ate, stayed there watching until it got dark. There was a tern working the channel that ran up the center of the marsh, I couldn't tell for sure if he was a royal tern or a common tern, but he would hover in place, then dip down for whatever it was he was eating. A lot of terns have the same coloration as herring gulls, gray wing backs, white body, but they have a little black yarmulke and a long forked white tail. They're beautiful in the way a painting can be, once in a while you see one, there's not a thing about it you could change without making it less perfect than it already is.

I don't know why, but I felt better being in Maine. They must put something in the air that makes you feel like you need to come back to the fucking place.

11

Look at any map of the state of Maine and you will notice that the farther south and east you go, the more crowded the map gets. From Portland on south the place is particularly thick with stuff. Towns, villages, roads, outlet stores, inns, beaches, gas stations, retreats for former presidents, and giant statues of Paul Bunyan standing by the side of the road. This is not really Maine, not anymore, it is more like Massachusetts North. It's a nice enough place to visit, you can stay in a motel with knotty pine paneling, eat lobster meat on a hot-dog roll, and your kids can play in the surf. You might even get bitten on the ass by a stray blackfly, if you are lucky, just to lend your vacation the tang of authenticity. It's a nice drive, too, as long as you're not in a hurry. I was, though, so I stayed on Route 95 all the way up to Bangor.

It would be tempting to say that Bangor is in the middle of the state, but it is somewhat south of the center. It is the jumping-off spot, though, and there's a whole lot of very sparsely inhabited space north and west of the place. Route 95 does continue on from Bangor, but not exactly north. It sort of leans over to the right as you go up, and it crosses into Canada at Houlton. Houlton, however, is a long long way from the northern tip of the state. If you want to go up there, you should fly if you can, because it is a long-ass drive. I'm told they grow potatoes up there.

I left Route 95 at Bangor and took Route 9, which is basically a two-lane road that roughly parallels the coast, but it runs about thirty or forty miles inland. It would be a longer trip to get to Louis's house that way, but a faster one, because by staying away from the coast, you're less likely to get stuck behind some fat, slow hulk of a Winnebago. Route 9 takes you through the real deal, too. Thick woods, brown rivers, no outlet stores, and no statues of Paul Bunyan. I did see one guy hitching southbound, he had his T-shirt off and he was waving it around his head energetically to keep the bugs from eating him. I stopped and let him use my bug spray, offered him a ride, but he declined, he wanted to go south. He'd had enough, I guess. Probably headed for Kennebunkport. I saw a lot of "Moose Crossing" signs, and I looked hard, but I did not see a moose.

I had my phone on the seat beside me. It had been a couple of hours since I'd gotten a signal, but at the top of a big hill about fifteen miles from the northern end of Route 9 I noticed that two of the little signal bars were lit up, so I pulled over and called the hospital in Calais.

"I'd like to speak to one of your patients," I told the lady who answered the phone. "First name Rosario. Last name Colón, he was in there with a collapsed lung. Can you ring his room for me?"

"I know who you mean, sir," she said. "I'm afraid he's not in this hospital anymore."

That seemed an odd way to say it. "Not in that hospital? What do you mean? He didn't croak, did he?"

She cleared her throat. "I'm afraid I don't have any more information, sir. If you would like to give me your name and phone number, I could have someone get back to you. . . ."

Yeah, right. I broke the connection, sat there thinking about it. She already had my phone number, or could probably get it easily enough. I didn't think that mattered too much, it's not a crime to make a phone call. Plenty of people must have seen the two of us together, anyhow, when they brought us in. The question was, what had Rosey done? He must have pulled something at the hospital, and it had to have been something good, too, because that woman on the phone was not going to tell me about it.

Fucking Rosario. I should have known that he couldn't take the waiting. God, all he had to do was lie there. I had figured on him being sick enough, I thought that would override his paranoia and keep him safe in bed. I had left him there with no money and no clothes. What else could I have done? Tie him to the bed? He couldn't trust me, though, so he had gone looking for an edge. I knew it.

Bookman would know what had happened, but I didn't want to talk to him. I tried Louis's number but there was no answer, not that I'd expected one. Louis was probably down in Machias trying to atone to Eleanor for his sins. She would forgive him, I was sure of that, she loved him too much to do otherwise, but I was also sure that she'd make him work for it. I called Bookman's house, talked to Mrs. Bookman for a few minutes, but Nicky and Franklin were out somewhere, and so was her husband.

I got out of the van and stomped around in the weeds for a while, cursing my luck. An eastern mockingbird flew up to the top of a dead tree and sang to me. He was loud, man, and he was into it. As I stood there watching he spread his wings and jumped straight up in the air, singing, flapping his wings and then settling back down onto his roost without missing a note. Damn, he had nothing to worry about but singing, that and driving the other mockingbirds out of his territory. No wonder he was happy.

Who the hell could I call? Eastport and Lubec were far away enough from Calais that most people there would probably not have heard about, or paid much attention to, whatever had gone down at the Calais hospital, so it probably wouldn't do me much good to try Hobart or Roscoe or any of the other people I knew.

I'd left the motel around seven that morning, and I'd been on the road for about five hours. I still had time, though. It might cost me an hour or so, but I could head west instead of east when I got to the end of Route 9, go up and talk to Mrs. Johnson. Maybe she'd know somebody.

It wasn't all that far from the end of Route 9 up to Mrs. Johnson's house in Grand Lake Stream. At least it didn't seem so to me. It took me about thirty minutes to drive it, not bad when you compare that to the duration of a subway ride from Park Slope to midtown. You take Route 1 north, and you turn off of that onto a narrow two-lane strip through the woods to get there, and it seems like a longer drive than it is because you don't pass much of anything besides trees once you've made the turn. It's almost like you're going back in time, or maybe that's not it at all, maybe you're going sideways, somehow, journeying to some separate place that's only distantly related to the world you came from. The tires on the minivan made a hypnotic thrumming noise that silenced the debating team inside my head. I passed that first sign after a while, the one that says "You Have Just Entered," and still nothing, just more trees, then a while later I passed a camp back up in the woods, and finally a bridge across a stream, and the tackle store, and not a hell of a lot else, a few scattered buildings that catered to the fishing addicts who fly in periodically for their fix.

There was a scar on the pine tree I had hit with the Subaru, but not a big one, considering the damage I'd done to Hobart's vehicle. A piece of bark was missing, maybe ten inches wide and two or three high, the exposed wood just a little punky from the impact, weeping sticky pine sap. I parked the minivan next to a GMC pickup in Mrs. Johnson's front yard. A tall kid came out of the house, he was a couple of inches taller than me, but skinny, long dark hair, dark eyes, ropy, corded muscles in his arms. "Hey," he said, extending a hand.

"Chris Johnson?"

"Yeah."

"Your mom around?"

He blinked at me in surprise. "She went on downstreet," he said. He was curious, I could tell, but he didn't ask. "You want me to go get her?"

"You think she'll be long?" I said. "Is it okay if I wait?"

"Sure," he said. "She should be back in a few minutes. Get you a cup of coffee? Beer?"

"No, thanks. I'm good. They told me you were up in the Allagash, but nobody told me what it was."

"Allagash Wilderness Waterway. You never been?"

"Never even heard of the place."

"Oh, man," he said. "You should go. Little crowded, right now, we seen other canoes almost every day we was up there, but still . . ." He shook his head. "I got pictures. You wanna see 'em? Better than me trying to tell you what it's like."

We were still looking at the pictures when Chris's mother came walking up the road. She just glanced at the minivan, but then she saw me talking to her son. "Hey, Coyote," she said. "You come back to tell me some stories?"

"I came back to ask you a question. I owe you some money, too."

"That's right, you do. Some businessman I would make, huh?"

Chris glanced at me, then at his mother. I guess he thought his mom and I were an odd combination, and maybe we were. He shook his head, suppressing a smile. "I'm going back inside," he said. "Nice to meet you, Manny."

"Same here. Thanks for showing me the pictures."

I told Mrs. Johnson about Rosario leaving the hospital.

"He's that man you carried out of the woods," she said. "Do you still have that cell phone?"

I got it out of the car and gave it to her. She made some calls, speaking, as she had done the first time, that strange language. All I understood were the names and an occasional sentence in English, like, "Oh, no, John, are you telling the truth?" I had no choice but to wait, so I leaned back against the van and tried to relax. There was a bunch of cedar waxwings feeding in some juniper bushes across the road from Mrs. Johnson's house. At first I saw only a couple, and I thought they were female cardinals—waxwings have a similar crest and a sort of subtle reddish tan coloring—but the longer I looked, the more of them I saw, there had to be twenty or thirty of them, and cardinals never flock together like that. Waxwings do, though, certain times of the year they forget their territorial impulses and get together to feed in bunches. I wonder if they do it because they enjoy each other's company. Ornithologists and other scientists will tell you that's bullshit, that birds don't enjoy or not enjoy, for them there's only instinct. I'll tell you something, though, they don't know, either. They're just giving you their best guess.

Mrs. Johnson shut the phone off and handed it back to me. "Do you remember my friend, the doctor?"

"Yeah," I said. "Absolutely."

"Well, he told me that your friend is crazy. Yesterday morning your friend got up out of bed, disconnected himself from the tubes and machines, went down to the hospital loading dock, and stole a station wagon."

"Station wagon?"

She shook her head. "My doctor friend told me that they have a walk-in cooler down behind the dock, and when someone dies in the hospital, they just put a shroud over them, tie a tag on their big toe, wheel them in there on a gurney, and leave them there. When the man from the funeral parlor comes to get them, he just backs his station wagon up to the dock, goes inside to fill out the paperwork, then brings his gurney into the walk-in box, and they flop the dead person from the hospital's gurney onto his, and he loads up and goes away. Just like someone picking up a load of frozen hamburgers."

I waited for her to go on, but she didn't, she just stood there looking at the ground and shaking her head. Rosario on the loose. It was a good thing Nicky was with the Bookmans. "So what happened? Rosario stole some undertaker's van?"

"Oh," she said, looking up. "Sorry. The man from the funeral parlor had his wagon all loaded when your friend found him. Your friend had a knife, and he made the man drive around the block, and then he stole the poor man's clothes, left him standing there in his boxer shorts. And then he left the dead person in the McDonald's parking lot. The police found it there, the gurney with the body on it. Oh, and I almost forgot. You remember that Russian, the one that hit his head on a rock? They found him dead in his hospital bed. My friend says it looks like he was strangled." She clucked her tongue. "What do you think happened to your friend, Coyote? Did he lose his mind?"

"No." I looked over at her. "Did you ever know somebody who was so sure that everybody was going to screw them that they almost made it happen?" She nodded. "Well, Rosey is like that. He's so afraid, he thinks so much about everything bad that could go wrong, that he winds up doing something so crazy that it seems to attract bad results. It's like if you have to buy tires for your car, but you're so sure the tire guy is going to screw you, you go in there and treat him bad, you yell about every dollar it's going to cost you, you force the guy to screw you just to cover himself. You know what I mean?"

She was nodding. "He calls up the evil spirits. You believe in spirits, Coyote?"

"No."

"Don't be so sure of yourself. So what is he going to do now?"

"He's looking for something he can hold over my head. He thinks he's going to have to force me to give him his money. And the only thing up here that I care about is my son Nicky."

"You'd better go get him, then," she said.

"He's in a safe place."

She shook her head. "Go get him."

"I'm on my way. Listen, I figure I owe you four hundred bucks, let me give you that."

"I only took you out one day. That's a hundred."

"Yeah, but you sat with me two days in the hospital, and if you hadn't known that doctor, my life would've gotten a lot more complex. So I owe you for three days, plus you gotta get a tip."

She was shaking her head. "A hundred dollars," she said firmly.

"Mrs. Johnson?"

"Yeah?"

"Please."

She stared at me for a minute. "All right. But you've gotta come back and tell me how this comes out."

I was surprised, the minivan broke one hundred, no problem. I kept my foot on it all the way back to Route 1. I passed only two other cars, they were going in the opposite direction, and they seemed to be crawling.

It was much tougher going once I got southbound on Route 1, there was lots of other traffic. Not too many tourists, though, mostly Maine plates, cars and pickups and a lot of pulp trucks hauling big logs. Then, of course, everybody had to slow down to go through Calais, and there were some traffic lights and so on. But I don't think it mattered. If I had been able to keep my speedometer needle buried the whole trip back, it still would have taken too long. Once I got through Calais, though, Route 1 followed the St. Croix River on its way to Passamaquoddy Bay, and it's only a two-lane road, without a lot of places to pass. I got stuck behind a UPS truck, which was a good thing, I suppose. The guy was moving pretty fast, not fast enough for me, though, but a state cop passed us heading north while I was still looking for a space to get by. It got me thinking that Bookman might be the county sheriff, but he wasn't the only police authority up in this place, they have staties and even some town cops, so I cooled out a little bit and stayed behind the UPS guy.

I could understand Rosario sweating about his money. I could even understand why he would want to wax the Russian, especially after the hurt that the Russian had put on him. And it was not in Rosario's nature to trust anybody, not even me. He might be able to do it for a couple hours or a half a day, and if the two of us had a job going, he might even restrain himself for a couple of days, long enough for us to be able to do what we needed to do, but that was the upper limit. Even after I had saved his ass, carried him out through those woods, he just knew I was going to screw him unless he had a stick he could hit me with. Or it could have been that he was just more comfortable that way, I don't know. I read someplace that LBJ was like that, that he wouldn't trust you unless he had a gun stuck in your ear.

The thing was, the more I thought about it, the more I was convinced that Rosey was going to spoil Buchanan's deal for both of us. He was attracting way too much attention, and the cops were bound to get him sooner or later, and when they did, he would turn back into the aggrieved party, he would tell them how I had fucked him out of his money. That would get them looking, and from there it was just a short hop to the SEC, and I would be broke again. And worse than that, Bookman already had Nicky. I started adding it up: There was the initial heist, and stealing money is against the law, even if you steal it from bad guys. Then there were those three dead guys in the Dumpster, the cops would try hard to get me as an accessory to that. On top of that, I had snatched Nicky, I didn't know if they would call that kidnapping or not, but they'd get me for it either way. And now there was a dead Russian in the Calais hospital, not to mention the stiff that Rosey had dumped in the McDonald's parking lot.

First things first, I told myself. All you gotta do right now is get to Nicky, then you can figure out what comes next.

I pulled into Bookman's driveway. Their dog went ape shit, he came running over to the minivan, barking and showing his teeth. I opened the door a crack and he jumped back, started running around in circles and generally making as much noise as it is possible for a dog to make. Stupid mutt. He was afraid, I guess, but he was trying like hell to do his job. The front door to Bookman's house opened and he came out, down the steps and into the yard. The dog was more afraid of him than he was of me, and he began making larger circles, avoiding Bookman altogether, barking the whole time.

Bookman did not seem his normal imperturbable self. "Scruffy!" he bellowed at the dog. "Get over here!" At once the dog stopped barking and running. He flattened himself down as close to the ground as he could get and still be able to walk, and he went slinking over toward Bookman, his ears flat back on his head. "Be quiet!" Bookman thundered at the dog. He pointed in the direction of his backyard. "And get outta here!" The dog looked at him, glanced back at me, and did his crab walk back toward the rear of the house. He stopped when he got to the back corner of the house, and lay down in the grass, watching the two of us. Bookman turned and looked at me, visibly struggling to regain his composure. It was going to be my turn next. "Fuckin' dog," he said, but it was unclear whether he was talking about me or Scruffy.

Behind him, the front door to his house opened again, and Mrs. Bookman came out carrying Nicky's knapsack. Bookman heard her, but he didn't even turn around. Instead he dropped his shoulders, looked straight up at the sky, sucked in a big breath, held it, blew it out. She marched right past him, came over to me, and thrust Nicky's knapsack into my hands.

"I'm going to miss him so much," she said. "We all will. Especially Franklin." Behind her, Bookman stared at the ground, shaking his head. She turned and looked at him. It was obvious that the two of them had discussed what they should do about Nicky and me, but it was just as obvious that Mrs. Bookman had reached her own conclusions, which were not subject to debate. One thing I've noticed about women, you can't tell them what to do, particularly the good ones. They won't listen, especially if they think they know something you don't. She turned back to me, reached out and squeezed my arm. "That child is going to be something special," she said. She turned away then, headed back to her house. She stopped in front of her husband. "Taylor," she said firmly. "Go get them."

He had the barest hint of a smile on his face. "Yes, deah," he said. She glared at him for a second, and then she went back inside the house. Bookman stared at me until he heard the front door slam. "Women," he said. "If Mama ain't happy, ain't nobody happy."

I didn't dare to smile. I turned away instead, silently thanking whatever goddesses had interceded on my behalf, and I stuck Nicky's knapsack into the minivan. "Come on," Bookman said. "Theyah down over the hill, fishing." He looked at me. "Listen," he said. "That boy belongs with you. You understand me? The thing is, there's plenty of people think they know bettah than you. The state, the teachahs at school, the ministah at yaw church, they all wanna tell you what's best for yaw kids. You got any goddam brains at all, you'll take that boy fah away from heah. You keep mucking around, yaw going to lose him."

"I hear you."

We walked out past the cars, out toward the back of Bookman's house. He paused when we got to where his dog was laying in the grass. Bookman pointed his finger down at the dog. "Stay," he said. The dog stared back at him, watching intently with big brown eyes. "Stay, damn you."

There was a neatly mowed patch of green lawn out behind Bookman's house, and a field of tall yellow grass behind that. A rock wall bordered the far side of his property, and some big maple trees grew along the border, along with some smaller trees and puckerbushes. We followed a path that paralleled the wall. It led up a long hill behind the house.

"You know how I wound up with that fucking dog?" Bookman said.

"No idea."

"Someone driving past the house," he said, "must have chucked him out the windah when he was a puppy. Franklin found the stupid thing. It was hurt, naturally, and nothing would do but I had to take it to the vet." He shook his head. "Cost me over a hundred bucks to fix up a fifty-nine-cent mutt, but Franklin was in love with the goddam thing, and my wife wouldn't have it any uthah way." He walked a few paces in silence. "So now I'm stuck with him," he said. "I still think about shooting or drowning him 'bout once a day, though. Do you undahstand where I'm going with this, Manny?"

"I think so."

"You and that goddam mutt have got a lot in common."

"That's what I thought you meant."

"The dog," he said, "earns his keep, I guess. Bahks whenevah someone he don't know comes around. He is, mahginally, less trouble than he's worth. But there is a limit, if you know what I mean."

"I get it."

"I found out what you did for Eleanor Avery," he said.

I had forgotten all about that. "Okay."

"You keep surprising me," he said. "First by being bettah than I thought you were, then by being worse. How come you never told me about this other character? The one caused all that trouble up to the Calais hospital?"

"I was trying to get rid of him," I said. "I was going to pick him up this morning, as a matter of fact. I had intended to put him on a plane today, but I found out he had kicked over the trash cans while I was down in Manhattan."

"What's his name?"

I thought briefly about giving him a phony name. If the cops got Rosey, then the master plan Buchanan and I had put together would still come crumbling down. I couldn't do it, though. Not after what had just happened. I still had some cash in my duffel bag over in Louis's house, I could settle for that, as long as I got to keep Nicky. "Rosey," I told him. "Rosario Colón."

"Do you have any idea what Mr. Colón is going to do next?"

We had reached the crest of the hill, and the field fell away in front of us. The rock wall, the trees along the border that it made, and the path through the tall grass sloped gradually down to a stream at the far end, maybe a hundred yards away. There was an enormous beech tree at the far end of the field, right next to the road that ran along the bank of the stream. The tree had to be four feet thick at the base. A raven flew out of the top of the beech tree, cawing sharply as he went. Telling his friends, Watch out, palefaces coming. There was a green station wagon parked under the tree, with one of its back doors open. Rosario stood next to the car, and he had Nicky by the hair.

12

"Oh, shit," Bookman said. I took off and left him there. I could hear Nicky's sharp cries, faint in the distance, I could see him struggling in Rosario's grip. It didn't do him any good, of course. Rosey tossed him into the back of the station wagon and slammed the door closed. He turned and headed for the driver's side, and as he did so he must have caught the motion out of the corner of his eye, because he turned and looked in my direction. It was too far to tell for sure, but I thought I saw him grinning, I thought I could read triumph in the way he stood, looking in my direction. I was moving as fast as I possibly could, but I was too far away. He had plenty of time, and he knew it. So did I, but I kept on anyway. What else could I do? I heard Bookman yelling behind me, I heard a pistol shot. He couldn't run, he was middle-aged and out of shape, but he was doing what he could, I guess. The pistol shot was just an empty threat, though, he was too far away to hit anything, and he wouldn't take a chance on hitting Nicky anyhow.

Franklin came lumbering up the stream bank behind Rosey. He dropped the two fishing rods he was carrying and he wrapped his hairy arm around Rosey's throat. I couldn't run any faster, I couldn't do anything but keep going. Just hang on to him, Franklin, I thought, just hold him there. . . . But there was no way. No matter what he looked like, Franklin was a gentle soul, a little boy. Rosario broke his hold, turned, and crashed an elbow to Franklin's jaw, and Franklin melted down into the grass at the side of the road.

The passenger door on the far side of the station wagon popped open and Nicky flew out, running for all he was worth. Rosario looked around wildly. Nicky disappeared into the weeds down at the water's edge, and I was bearing down, getting closer. Rosario was not afraid of me, but he had to know that I could hold him up long enough for Bookman to chug down there and shoot his ass. He had one option left, and he took it: he humped Franklin's inert form into the station wagon, walked calmly around to the driver's side, got in, and took off. It took me another ten seconds to get there. I got to the street in time to see him hit the brakes once, just before he went out of sight. I stood there, leaning over, my hands on my knees.

"Shit!"

I could see it again, Nicky jumping out of the far side of the car, taking off into the underbrush. I was inordinately proud of him, even though that resourcefulness had nothing to do with me, it was just a product of the need to watch out for yourself from an early age. Still . . . "Nicky! Nicky, come on out! It's okay, he's gone now." He didn't, though, he stayed where he was. Behind me, Bookman came huffing down the hill. He tried to talk in between big gasps of air.

"Was . . . that . . . guy . . . Was that . . . him?"

He sounded like he was having a heart attack. "Yeah, that was him. Gimme your keys."

"Huh?"

"Gimme your car keys. I'm gonna run back up to your house and bring the cruiser down here. See if you can get Nicky to come on out."

He nodded, red-faced, fished his keys out of his pocket, and handed them over.

It had been a while since I had driven anything like Bookman's cruiser. Crown Vics aren't real popular anymore, especially in the city, where you've got to worry about parking them, but you've got to wonder why we gave up on those big American sedans. Detroit puts a lot of extra stuff into cop cars, too, big fat antisway bars, good strong engines, serious rubber. I hauled ass out of Bookman's driveway and left a set of smoking black adolescent streaks on the road in front of his house. Detroit could do it if they wanted to, take a platform like the Crown Vic, spend the kind of serious attention on it that they're gonna waste on whatever isn't going to measure up to next year's BMW 3-Series. Quit being copycats, man, quit trying to be something you ain't and do what you know how to do. Give me a new Goat, man, put an active suspension under it, with quad discs and ABS brakes. . . .

When you need a distraction, anything will do. I didn't want to think about Rosey and Franklin, and I didn't want to think about what I had decided to do when I was running up that hill, because I felt lousy about it already. But your kids come first, isn't that the way it's supposed to work? Aren't I supposed to take care of him, isn't he my first priority? All I needed to do was get Nicky back, Franklin was not my problem. His father was the county sheriff, for Chrissake. Rosey probably wouldn't hurt him anyhow, once he knew I was gone. He would realize that it would do him no good to hang on to Franklin and no harm to let him go. He would dump him and take off. I mean, he'd leave him somewhere where he'd be found, right? Franklin would be okay.

I came tearing down that road by the creek, stomped the emergency brake and laid a beautiful bootlegger's turn on Bookman, pointed the car back in the direction Rosey had taken. I jumped out, left the door open.

Bookman was still catching his breath. "He wouldn't come out," he said. "Not for me. He's down along the creek there someplace." He got into the cruiser, slammed the door. "Manny," he said. "This guy Rosario. Is he flying blind here? Did he do this on impulse, or does he have someplace to go?"

It made me sick to have to answer. "He's too smart to just jump at it. He's got something set up, he's got someplace to hide, I'd bet on it." Bookman looked at me for another half a second, then went tearing off down the road.

* * *

It took me fifteen or twenty minutes to find Nicky. I couldn't blame him for not trusting me—the kid had been through a lot of shit since the day I picked him up outside the Bushwick Houses. He was hiding back in under a raspberry thicket. I couldn't get to him, but when he saw me standing there, he came out, looking pale and shaken. He didn't say much at first, but then the questions started.

"Who was that guy, Poppy?"

"He was a bad guy, Nicky, but he's gone now."

"Where's Franklin?"

"Franklin is okay, Nicky. C'mon, we gotta go."

"Did that guy hurt Franklin, Poppy?"

I didn't want to lie to him, but only because I wasn't sure how much he'd seen. "Well, he knocked Franklin down, but I think he's going to be okay. C'mon, Nicky, we got to go." He seemed to calm down then, and the two of us clambered back up the stream bank onto the road. I made a tactical mistake, though, I led him back up the same way I had gone down, and forgot about Franklin's fishing rods. When Nicky saw those rods lying in the grass he pitched a fit.

"Poppy!" he yelled, and he started crying. "Poppy! What happened to Franklin? Where's Franklin, Poppy?"

Ah, Jesus. "I think he went with Rosey, Nicky. I think he went with that guy."

"Is he gonna hurt him, Poppy?" He wouldn't look at me, he just stared down at the fishing rods lying by the side of the road.

"Nah, he'll be fine. C'mon, Nicky, we gotta go."

He didn't move. He looked up at me then, his face white. "Are you gonna go get him, Poppy? Are you gonna go get Franklin?" He was doubting me for the first time, I could hear it in his voice, he knew what the right thing was but he wasn't sure I was going to do it. My free pass was over.

I knelt down to put my face at his level. It wasn't his tears that got to me, not really, it was that doubt in his voice, it was that implied judgment. Maybe I wouldn't have done it in the end, anyhow, I don't know. Maybe I wouldn't have taken my kid and my money and run off, leaving Bookman holding the bag.

I'd been ready, though. All I had to do was put Nicky in the van, pick up my stuff at Louis's, and take off. Kneeling there, looking at my son's face, I realized that he would remember it if I did, that for the rest of his life, this event was going to color his perception of me, no matter what else I did.

Yeah, but . . . I could hear the inner voice. Every extra minute I hung around this place lengthened the odds against me. Every second that ticked by gave Bookman another chance to reevaluate his judgment of who I was, and whether it might not be better, after all, for Nicky to go back into foster care. And I had it, you know, I had it all right there in my hand, I had Nicky, I had the money, all I had to do was take it and go. Nobody in the world was watching me, except for my son.

"I'll go get him, Nicky, I promise." Maybe it was the right decision, I didn't know, but I couldn't escape the feeling that I had scored big at Vegas, and instead of taking my winnings and leaving, I had just pushed it all back up there on black, my life with Nicky, the money, even my freedom, and I was waiting for that stone-faced croupier to spin the wheel one more time. By the time we got back to Bookman's house, though, I was ashamed of what I'd been ready to do. Thanks for taking care of my kid, Mrs. B, and oh, by the way, this buddy of mine just abducted Franklin, but he's an okay guy, really, I think everything will turn out all right, and pardon me, but I gotta run. . . .

I was surprised to find Louis at home. I'd been sure that he would be in Machias at the hospital, seeing to Eleanor. "Hi, Louis. How is she?"

He was nodding. "She's going to be all right. They're going to operate tomorrow, thanks to you."

"Nothing to it, Louis. I'm really glad I could help. I just need to run upstairs and grab my stuff. Nicky, stay here, okay?"

It took me only a few minutes to pack up. I didn't know what was going to happen with Franklin, but I wanted to be ready to haul ass as soon as he turned up. It's an old trick: if you think you're gonna have to take off in a hurry, you fill up your gas tank, and you back your car into your parking space instead of nosing it in. Nicky wasn't sure of me yet, though, because he ratted me out to Louis while I was upstairs. Louis looked at me oddly when I came down carrying my bags.

"Manny, what is Nicky talking about? Did something happen to Franklin?"

"Yeah. There's this guy, his name is Rosario, and he's been after me for a while. He was trying to grab Nicky, but Nicky got away so he took Franklin instead."

It didn't take a genius to figure it out. I watched as Louis wrapped his mind around it. "All right," he said after a minute. "So what do we do now?"

"We wait for Rosario to call us," I told him. "He really doesn't want to hurt Franklin, he just wants his money. He'll get in touch."

"Does he have my phone number?"

"No, but he's got my cell number." I felt for the cell phone, but I remembered I had left it in the van. "Let me go get my phone," I said. I took my bags with me, dumped them in the van.

There were three messages in my voice mail. I listened to the first one on my way back into Louis's kitchen. It was Bookman, he'd gotten a radio call about a high-speed chase somewhere west of where we were, he thought the time frame was about right, and he was on his way to find out if it was Rosario. The second message was from Rosey himself, and he sounded like he was ready to burst into flames.

"Answer the fuckin' phone, Mo, answer the fuckin' . . . Goddam you, Mohammed! Answer the fuckin' telephone!" He got louder as he went. "Don't you do this to me, Mo, you fuckin' piece of fuckin' shit, Mo, answer the muthafuckin' phone!"

The third message was from Rosey, too. He sounded almost sheepish. "All right, all right, voice mail, I know you couldn't hear me. But I'm gonna call you back tonight, you fuck, and you better fuckin' pick up. You hear me?" He sounded like he was outdoors, and he was shouting just a bit to compensate for the ambient noise. "You better fuckin' talk to me, Mohammed, I got this fuckin' retard here, and he's not looking so good. I don't wanna kill him, Mo, but you fuckin' know I'll fuckin' do it, so you better answer your phone tonight. I'm gonna call you, maybe. . . ." He paused, looking at his watch or something, I guessed. I could hear a low drone in the background, it almost sounded like he was riding on a bus, it was a steady hum of some kind of engine. Not a bus, though, because it didn't sound like a diesel. Then, on top of that, another tone, lower and deeper, maybe two seconds in duration. "I'm gonna call back eight or nine tonight," he said. "You better fuckin' answer, Mo. I want my fuckin' money."

Louis was watching me. "Was it him?"

"Yeah. It was him, all right." I erased the first two messages. "Do me a favor, Louis, listen to the background noise in this message, tell me what it sounds like to you." I started the message running again, handed the phone to Louis.

"The boy don't sound happy," Louis said.

"Forget him, Louis, what's the noise he's yelling over?"

"Outboard motor," Louis said.

"What? He's on a motorboat?"

"Outboard," Louis said, nodding. "Oh, wait. That's the foghorn up in Indian Road."

He was losing me. "What?"

Louis handed the phone back to me. "Play it again, so I can be sure," he said. I did it, watched him listening to the message again. "Yeah," he said. "That's an outboard motor. Indian Road is the channel over on the Canadian side, across from Eastport. Runs between Campobello and Deer Island, I think. That low honk, that's the foghorn from up there. You can hear it when you take the ferry across to Deer Island."

I couldn't believe it. Fucking Rosario, he'd left the hospital with no money, wearing a bathrobe and a pair of paper slippers, for chrissake, and now he was on a boat? The guy spent his whole life in Brooklyn, what the hell could he know about boats? "All right. Louis, why don't you call the sheriff's department, see if they can relay a message to Bookman, because it sounds like he's chasing the wrong guy. Maybe I should head up to Eastport. Maybe I can figure out what to do from there."

"Maybe so," he said. "The thing is, Manny, if this guy is hiding someplace up within earshot of that foghorn on the Canadian side of the bay, you could look for him for six months and still not find him."

"Oh, shit, Louis."

"Ayuh," he said. "And heah's the other thing. This fella didn't have no boat of his own, he couldn't have. And even if he did, how's he know where to hide? I think someone must be helping him, Manny."

I remembered the last thing I'd said to Bookman before he took off in his cruiser. "Yeah, you're right, Louis. I think he set this up ahead of time. He found the place first, then he came looking for me and Nicky."

"How could he'a done that?" Louis asked. "He hasn't had much time." He shook his head. "How did he know where to look for you in the first place?"

"I don't know. For a while I thought it was Bookman, because he's the only guy who knows anything about what I'm running from." I looked over at Nicky, wondering how much of this, if any, he understood, and how careful I was going to have to be with what I said. "He had me pegged that day I went up to his office, but he decided to let me slide. He had enough information, I think, to call somebody down in New York and put this thing in motion, but I couldn't believe that he would do it. The problem is, nobody else knew enough about me."

Louis was shaking his head. "Nah. Wan't him, that ain't the way Bookman does things. He might throw you in his cah trunk and ride you around for a couple hours to make you a little more cooperative, but he'd never have some other guy put the dogs on you. Bookman don't do business out the back door like that. But I'll bet you he told Hopkins what he knew."

"Hopkins! Why the hell would he tell Hopkins?"

"Hop's his number one apprentice. He's been trying to teach Hoppie how to act for a couple yeahs now. I can see Bookman telling Hop why he was doing things in a certain way, trying to make him see right. Problem is, you can't change the way a boy was raised. I'll bet my house, Hoppie was smart enough to figure out how to put your tail in a sling, and mad enough to go through with it."

"Son of a bitch! Son of a—"

"Now you just wait." Louis was holding up a finger. "Won't do you no good to go chahging around like a deer in the rut. You just wait right there." He walked off into his dining room, and I could hear him pick up the telephone. "Hello, Brenda," he said, but after that he pitched his voice too low for me to hear what he was saying. A couple of minutes later, he hung up and came back into the kitchen. "Brenda says Hop ain't working. She says he's at home."

"Great!" I turned to go.

"Hold on, now," Louis said. "Hold on just one more minute."

"What is it?"

"You're not gonna be able to beat it out of him," Louis said. "You're gonna have to talk him into helping you. Catch more flies with honey than vinegar, anyhow."

"Oh, great."

"And anyway, I bet you don't even know where Hop lives."

"Where's he live, then?"

He had to draw me a map. It was only about eight miles from Louis's house up to Hop's trailer, but the route was convoluted and the directions too complex for me to hold them in my head. I found the place, though. The trailer itself was okay, I guess. If a trailer was what he could afford, who was I to think less of him for it? The location was another thing altogether, though. Hop's trailer was situated about ten feet off an unpaved road, across from a blueberry field, which was nothing but an expanse of low brush stretching far back to a distant tree line. Behind the trailer, the hillside had been gouged out by someone who had carted away the underlying sand, and behind the sand pit, the forest had been ripped away, leaving a stubble of small trees growing up through the huge piles of brush that rendered the place impassable. I was amazed at the poverty of spirit required of anyone who would choose to put his house in that particular spot, especially in such a sparsely populated region, where other, more attractive alternatives abounded.

I parked the van behind the pickup in the sand between the trailer and the road. I was looking up at Hop's satellite dish and thinking about what Louis had said I had to do, when the door to the trailer opened up and Hop came out. He wasn't in uniform, but he did have a gun in his hand, and he was pointing it at me. His black eyes were getting better, the swelling had gone down, but he still had a bandage on his nose and he had a lot of discoloration. It was starting to fade to yellow around the edges, but all in all, he still looked like creamed shit on a stick.

"You no-good son of a hoah," he said. He sounded pissed off, but it was impossible to read anything in that ruin of a face. He looked up and down the road, but the gun never wavered. "I ought to blow yoah head off, right heah in my front yahd." I could see his jaw muscles working. "Only reason I ain't doin' it is I got no time to hide the body."

"Why be mad at me, Hop? If you hadn't come after me that night at the VFW, I'da never touched you."

Hop came down off the steps to his place and stood off to one side. "I don't care about that," he said. "But you had to go and swear out a complaint on me, didn't you? None of this would have happened if you had just minded yoah own damn business. I nevah hurt Brenda, anyhow. Not really." He glanced up and down the dirt road again, then waggled the gun at me. "Inside, you son of a hoah. Get inside."

"Yeah, sure." I didn't move. "It was Bookman, anyway. He made me do that. He needed a stick to hit you with, so he kind of insisted. I'da never set foot in that police station otherwise."

"Goddammit!" It must have dawned on him just then how Bookman had manipulated him. He wasn't pointing the gun at me anymore, not exactly, but he looked like he badly wanted to shoot somebody, or at least smack him around with his pistol, and I was the only candidate. I didn't stand a chance against him, not with my wounded shoulder. All he had to do was put the gun down and come after me and it would have been all over. He didn't, though. He stood there shaking, and after a minute he deflated like a balloon with a hole in it, his shoulders sagged, and he pointed his gun at the ground. "Goddammit," he said, but without any spirit. "Bookman told me . . . he said you hated a man that would hit a woman. . . ." He glanced up and down that dirt road one more time, but there was fear in his eyes this time, and defeat. "Ah, fuck it. I got no time for this," he said, shaking his head. "I got to get outta here. What the hell do you want?"

"Are you the guy who ratted me out to the Russians?"

"You wanna talk to me," he said, "you better come inside. I gotta finish packing."

The inside of Hop's trailer smelled a little funky, but I didn't say anything about it. He had a big swollen suitcase on the floor by the front door, and another one open on a couch. He took a look back at me, dropped his pistol into the suitcase, went off for more shit. "Why did you rat me out, Hop?"

He was digging around in his kitchen cabinets.

"You were ruining my life, you ahshole! I had everything going for me before you came along. Then all of a sudden Bookman's writing me up, my girlfriend won't even let me smell it anymore, and my friends all laugh whenever they see me." He gestured at his nose. "I'm never gonna look like I did before. Bookman said you was trying to stay away from the Russian Mafia, but he didn't say why. I know a guy on the NYPD, and as soon as I said the word 'Russian,' he knew who I should call. I figured, I call these guys, they come up here, you get one sniff of them, and you'd be gone and out of my life forever."

That answered that. "You know a guy named Rosario Colón?"

Hop came out of his kitchen with two more pistols and a box of shells. "He came heah to the house two nights ago. He told me that you and him took five million dollars from some Russian gangsters. Is that true?"

"Five million bucks? Are you kidding me?" I didn't feel like explaining myself to this dickhead. "They had my kid. I took the kid back, and I stung them a little bit while I was at it, but it was nothing even close to five million."

"Figures," Hops said, turning and peering out his front window. "Another lying bahstid."

"What did Rosario offer you?"

Hopkins looked back over at me. "Said he'd give me a million in cash if I gave him a place to hide, and if I helped him set you up. Then he changed it to half a million."

I decided to play a hunch. "You never figured he was gonna grab Franklin instead of Nicky."

"I nevah figured he'd take either one of 'em! It was you he said he wanted." He looked out his front window again. "All I evah did was make one phone call, I nevah meant for any of this to happen. I didn't even tell them wheyah you was, I didn't give them yoah name or anything. Just said the guy they were looking for was around heah somewhere. I thought they'd come up heah looking for you, you'd get wind of it and take off, and that would be the end of it." He looked down at the guns in his hands. "When Bookman finds out I was paht of this, he'll kill me. I'm not shitting you a pound, mister, even if he gets Franklin back, I'm as good as dead. I'm leaving right now, this minute."

The law of unintended consequences had bitten us both. "Rosario would never pay up, anyhow."

"Maybe not." Hopkins dumped the pistols and the ammo box into his suitcase and closed it up. "He didn't tell me that he'd killed the Russian up in the hospital, I found that out after. And he didn't tell me he was gonna grab Franklin and hold him hostage. I nevah signed on for that."

"Where's he keeping Franklin?"

"Why should I tell you anything? Fuck you. This shit is all yoah fault. I'm gonna have to start all over someplace with nothing, and you want me to help you? Fuck you, ahshole. I already did you a favah by not putting a bullet in yoah head. That's all yoah getting outta me."

God, you're cutting me to the bone, here. "I think I got about eighty grand left. Tell me where Franklin is and it's all yours."

He looked out the front window again, torn. He shook his head. "You'll never find him, not even if I tell you where he is, and I got no time to show you. I don't even have time to wait for you to go get yoah money. I'm telling you, when Bookman catches up with me, I'm dead. Don't you undahstand that?"

"Come on, Hopkins, do something good for once in your life. I'll put

Louis Avery on the phone, you can tell him where the place is. I got the money out in the car." He looked at his suitcase, where his weapons were, but I had nothing to worry about. Hopkins was beaten, he would never go up against me again. I picked up his suitcase. "C'mon, grab that other bag. My phone's in the car, too. You tell Louis, I give you the money, and we're both outta here."

"Go on, then. Go."

I got my telephone, called Louis, put Hopkins on the phone. "Louis," he said. "Do you remember that camp my fathah used to have ovah on the Canadian side, on Deah Island? Well, that's wheyah he is. I give him my boat to run back and foth." A minute later he handed the phone back to me.

"Hi, Louis."

"Hello. Sounds like you done okay."

"Maybe. We'll find out when we get Franklin back. Do you know this place? You know what he's talking about?"

"Ayuh," Louis said. "I'll call Hobart, get him to give us a ride over there. You remember where he keeps his boat?"

"Yeah, I do, but this might get ugly, Louis. I'd feel a lot better if I knew Nicky was safe with you. Does Hobart know this place?"

"I undahstand," he said. "Hobart used to play cahds ovah theyah with Hoppy's old man. I'll call him, get him to meet you at the boat. You sure you remembah where he keeps it?"

"I remember. I'll call you when I know something."

I opened the back of the van and fished out the paper bag with the money in it. Hopkins took it, peered inside. "You know," he said, "I'd give this back if I could have my life back, the way it was. Now I'm nothin' but another criminal."

"No, you're not. You're half as smart as Bookman thinks you are, you can still be what you want to be."

He stared at me, and for a second I thought I saw some of his old swagger in the set of his shoulders. "What do you know?" he said. "Move yoah goddam van."

13

The fog came out of nowhere, or maybe it came straight down out of the sky. One minute we were okay, chugging across a gray ocean on a gray day, and the next minute I could no longer see the shore, the islands, or the birds. I could see the surface of the water for twenty-five or thirty yards through drifting eddies of gray smoke, and that was all.

I was up next to Hobart, watching him steer the boat. He did not seem to notice the fog. Hobart had always impressed me as a guy who was past giving a fuck, and right now that did not seem like a good thing.

"You know where the hell you're going? How can you know we aren't headed out to sea?"

He looked at me pityingly. "We're in a bay, you idiot. There's land all around."

"Serious. How can you navigate in this soup?"

"Soup? This is nothing. This is a nice, friendly fog, give you plenty of wahning before you run into something. I seen it so thick, you'd think you had a gray wool sock pulled right down over your head." He looked at me. "Don't worry, Manny. I been out on this bay almost forty years. I can do this in my sleep."

"All right." I tried to relax and give in to it, but it's hard for me to give up control. I've spent most of my life playing the underdog, and when the odds are against you, you survive through intensity. You pick up on things the other guys miss, you manipulate the data, you use every ounce of influence and control you can muster. And after years of that, how can you just get on a plane, sit down and trust blindly that the pilots, the mechanics, the air traffic controllers, and all the rest of them know what the hell they're doing, and are paying attention? Hey, how much gas you got in this thing, buddy, did you check? You had a couple cups of coffee this morning, you feeling all right? After the plane is in the air, though, it's too late for all that, all you can do is sit there in your seat like a cow in a boxcar, wondering if this was the misstep that's finally going to bust you into steaks and hamburger. I watched Hobart driving his boat, cocking his head to listen to the bells and the foghorns making their mournful racket: "Don't get too close, brother, there's some shit over here that will eat you up." I forced myself to turn away. Don't stand there like a moron, I told myself, and don't ask the guy a bunch of asshole questions. Don't distract him, leave him alone. Worry about something else.

Hobart glanced at me, swung the boat over to his right. "Manny."

"Yeah."

"You got a watch?"

"No. I don't wear one."

"Too bad. You'll have to count. Thirty seconds from right now, you'll see Friar's Rock on your right."

"Oh, yeah?" I tried to trust him but I couldn't do it, I counted, and twenty-eight seconds later it loomed out of the fog, a man in a granite robe at the foot of a cliff.

"Feel better?"

"Don't take it personal," I told him. "It's my nature to sweat the details."

"Heard you totaled out the Subaru," he said.

"Yeah, I did. What do you figure it's worth?"

"Ahh," he said, waving his hand. "We can settle up later." He didn't care about it, you could hear that in his voice. Maybe he just figured he was too close to the finish line to worry about things like that.

The wind picked up after we passed Friar's Rock, and when we got into the wide space of the bay between Eastport and Lubec, visibility improved. I could see a harbor seal in our wake, looked like a man's head floating in the water. I could see the dark shadow of land through the gray mist, and I could see the public wharf in Eastport. A small boat came zooming out around from behind the wharf, it looked a little shorter than Hobart's boat, and a whole lot faster. It was open, it had no cabin, just a little seat with a console that held a steering wheel. It had an outboard in the back that threw up a rooster tail. There was just one guy in the boat, but he was coming fast.

"Oh, shit," Hobart said. He gunned his engine, for whatever that was worth, and he spun the wheel and turned us north, toward the fogbank that still covered the water on the Canadian side.

"What?" I said.

"You think we'll make it?" he asked. There was no emotion in his voice. He might have been asking for change of a quarter.

"Think we'll make what?" I had been daydreaming, watching the water, mooning about being out of here, my troubles finally over. I wasn't thinking.

"That fogbank up ahead," Louis said. "We gotta get up in theyah before whoevah that is in Hop's boat catches up to us."

"Are you kidding me?"

Just then I heard it, sounded like a supersonic insect going past, up over our heads, made a *vvvvvvvvv* sound. There was no bang to go with it. "What's he got?" Hobart asked calmly. "My eyes ain't what they used to be. Can you see it?"

I tried to pull myself back into the present. "Not really," I said, squinting. It was Rosey, all right. "Semiautomatic with a long barrel, target pistol, I think. And I didn't hear any noise, so I'd guess it's probably a twenty-two with a suppressor on it."

I heard that noise again, only this time it ended with an impact sound, and the bullet blew a hole in Hobart's windshield between him and me. "Damn good shot, too," Hobart said, still in that calm voice. He looked at me. "Wise man might set down, make himself a bit smaller."

"He won't shoot me. If he kills me, he'll never get what he's after.

He'll shoot you, though. Do it in a second. Why don't you let me steer? Scootch down on the floor there, so he can't see you."

Hobart shrugged. "Fuck it," he said.

"No, no way. Get on down, there."

"All right, all right," he said. "Ain't a floor, anyhow. It's a deck. You bring any ordnance?" He moved aside so I could take the wheel, grunted as he sat down.

"Yeah," I said. "I picked up this forty-five a while ago, but I won't be any good with it until he gets within about an arm's length. I shoulda got some ammo to go with it. I think there's six or seven rounds in here. You ever shoot a pistol?"

"Been a while," Hobart said. A few more of those high-speed bees went on past, but to our left this time. I figured Rosario was just firing out of frustration. He wouldn't hit me, but he had the pistol there in his hand, and he had to shoot at something. The fog was closing in on us, and a minute later I could not see Hopkins's boat anymore, or much of anything else, either, only this time I was glad for it. Hobart had me go straight on for a few more minutes while he watched the currents sweep past the side. It seemed that we passed over some kind of nautical dividing line, and suddenly the current that had been rolling up into the bay reversed course. The water began carrying us back the way we'd come. "We'll see how bright the boy is," he said to me. "Pull back on the throttle, there." I did, and the engine faded to a low rumble.

I could hear the son of a bitch, but it was hard to tell where the sound was coming from. We drifted in the gray dampness for about five minutes. Hobart looked at his watch and then peered out over the nose of the boat. "We gotta crank up here," he said. "We don't wanna run into them salmon pens back there. Now the question is, do we wanna make a run for home or do we wanna get where we're going? Yoah boy, he's got the speed on us, plus, we turn back, he knows wheyah we're headed. Probably got a fayah chance to cut us off before we get theyah. We go on like this, he might find us, and he might not. Or we might try to beach this thing, make a run for it. What do you wanna do?"

"I don't want to get either of us killed, but I'd love to get this over with. What are our chances of getting by him?"

"Well, let's see what we can do," Hobart said. "If we can sneak past him up to Indian Road there, we'll probably make it."

I saw square shapes in the water behind us, a symmetrical grid of lines in the water that marked off spaces that were about twenty by thirty feet, with nets rigged over the top, a couple of feet off the water. You couldn't see the cages, which were sunk below the surface. There were silvery shapes jumping inside, they looked to be about ten inches long. "Damn," I said. "If I was a seagull, I would sit right there and drool."

"Seagull is smahter than you," Hobart said. "He won't sit mooning about what he can't have. He knows he can't get his breakfast heah, so he'll go somewheyahs else. Turn us to port, and crank her up. No, port, goddammit, left. Your other left. That's better. Now shove the throttle back up." The fading buzz of the outboard motor on Hopkins's boat changed tone and began getting louder.

"I think he hears us."

"Well, I didn't think he was deaf," Hobart said. We held course away from the salmon pens. I was beginning to lose my sense of direction, but Hobart seemed to know where he was going. We passed another one of those invisible dividers in the water, and suddenly we were caught in a current that was ripping in the opposite direction. "Shut her down," Hobart said. I pulled the throttle back and we drifted again.

"You're using the currents," I said. "You know where they are and where they're going, and he doesn't."

He gave me the ghost of a smile. "If you have to be slow, you better be smaht."

I listened to the sound of Hopkins's outboard as it gained strength, faded, then gained strength again as Rosario zigzagged over the water looking for us. We passed through a stretch of water where a cloud of seabirds sat on the surface, feeding. Even with a nutcase like Rosey flying around the bay after my ass, that old curiosity itched at me. "What are they eating?"

Hobart looked over the side. “Eyeballs,” he said.

“Say what?”

“Eyeball herrings.” He held a thumb and forefinger about an inch and a half apart. “’Bout so big. Usually, what we get up in here are bricks, seven or eight inches long.”

I looked over and I could see them, just quick specks of moonlight in the cold water. “These ones are baby herrings.”

“Yeah.” He cocked his head, listened to the outboard. “Stand by that pistol, son.” We didn’t see the boat, though—apparently Rosario changed direction just a little bit too soon, and the sound faded again.

“Pretty slick,” I said to Hobart.

“Oh,” he said, “this’ll do for now. We get to Indian Road, though, we’re gonna have to turn her back on. We don’t lose him by then, might be a different story.”

“What about finding a place to hole up, wait until he gets tired of this, or else has to go get gas?”

“Well,” Hobart said, and he put a world of doubt into that short syllable. He peered up into the sky. “This fog here ain’t sticky enough. She’s gonna burn off soon.”

“Oh, shit.”

“ ‘Oh, shit’ is right. Looks like yoah boy means to have it out with us right now. Guess you ain’t the only one tiyed of the suspense.”

We drifted like that for another twenty minutes. Hobart had me start up the engine once to reposition us in the current, and we both sat and listened to Rosey’s mad search. The sky overhead was beginning to get perceptibly lighter, with patches of sun reaching us now and then, and a breeze began to tear at the fog’s subtle fabric. “Well,” Hobart said. “We gotta turn heah to get up Indian Road. It’s now or nevah.”

Suddenly, just in front of us, I heard something unlike anything I’d ever heard before. I guess it was sort of like a cross between a waterfall and a cement mixer, a kind of watery grinding roar but with a timbre that you wouldn’t associate with a fluid substance. “What the hell is that?”

“Crank up, son, crank up. Turn us hard to starboard. That’s the Old

Sow, Manny, and we've got just about close enough." We began to make some progress against the current, but I could feel the English imparted by the whirlpool, unseen in the water behind us. Up ahead, I could see Hop's boat cutting through the diminishing gray smoke. He was farther up Indian Road than we were. Rosario, behind the wheel, turned and looked in our direction. It was probably my imagination, he was probably too far off for me to say for sure, but I swear I saw him grinning. I think he loved this kind of shit, I think he loved shoving all of his chips up to the line and going for it. Hop's boat heeled sharply and headed back in our direction.

"Stay down, now. He shoots you, I'll never find my way back." I veered off just a touch, cocked the revolver, took aim, and fired. The recoil pushed the barrel upward. The boom the gun made seemed loud enough, but the sound was swallowed up in that vast space. I reaimed and fired again. I doubt if I hit anything, but he turned away briefly. Wanted to think it over, I guess.

Hobart had me throttle his engine back until we were just holding our own against the current. He looked at the pistol in my hand, evaluating. "You any good with that thing?"

I shook my head. "If I hit anything, it'll be by accident."

"Hmm." He looked out at Hop's boat again. "Well," he said. "You feeling lucky?"

"What do you mean?"

Hobart looked at me, shook his head. "Well, they tell me I'm a rash old bahstid," he said dryly. "How about you? How's your luck been running lately?"

I realized then what he meant, and I looked out at the swirling currents behind us. "Flood tide, am I right? You wanna play chicken? Sure. Let's find out how bad he wants it."

"Better let me take the wheel, son." He clambered to his feet, and I stood directly behind him so that Rosario could not hit him without hitting me. Hobart grinned.

"You are a rash old bastard. You love this shit, don't you?"

"Don't it make you feel just a little bit more alive than you was?" he said.

"No." I still had Nicky to worry about, and I was finding that I didn't like taking chances as much as I had in the past. Rosey fired again, we heard the round go by overhead. Hobart spun the boat around again, but he didn't point us exactly in the direction of the current, he headed about ten minutes on a clock face across the flow, farther out into the bay. The discrepancy cost us some headway, and Rosey gained ground on us quickly. Two more rounds went buzzing past. I was careful to stay between Hobart and Rosey.

"Give him another one," Hobart said. "Give him something to think about." I aimed as best I could and fired off another round, but Hobart's boat had taken on an odd, sideslipping kind of motion, sort of like a car losing traction on an icy road. Rosario changed direction, though. I guess he intended to pull up on a parallel course. I had no doubt that he would kill Hobart and Franklin, but he couldn't kill me until he got his money. That was the theory, anyhow, but Rosario could be irrational at times. "Save the last couple rounds," Hobart said.

"You want to try?"

He shook his head. "No need. Just give her a few minutes here."

"All right." Rosario was much closer now, maybe eighty feet to our right and roughly beside us, heading west. Behind him I could see Deer Island, cool and green, now with just a hint of gray in the air over the treetops. Rosey cut his speed down to almost nothing. Where he was, the current was running up the river, and where we were, it ran the opposite direction. Hobart had the boat nose into the current, and we were fighting to make progress. There was a streak of foam in the water going past Hop's boat, marking the division between the two opposing currents. I looked at Hobart. "Looks like he's using your trick against you."

Hobart smiled again. "Maybe," he said. "We were nevah gonna outrun him anyhow. I told you, when yoah slow, you have to be smaht."

Rosey was bellowing across the space between us. "Mohammed," he yelled. "I just want whass mine. You come with me, and he can go pick up that retard and take him home."

I looked at Hobart. "We been smart enough?"

"Ayuh," Hobart said. I noticed then what he had been waiting for.

The water between the two boats was churning insanely, and a big mound of water boiled up behind Hop's boat, swelling up about the height of a man above the surface of the bay, and about ten or twelve feet across. Rosey, startled, gunned his boat away from it, closer to us, and it was suddenly plain that that had been the wrong thing to do. The current seized him, spun him around, and pushed him into a long arc that would bring him within about twenty feet of us. In the center of that arc, the water disappeared, I mean it just fell away, there was suddenly a hole in the water. In the space of ten seconds, the hole grew to be thirty-five or forty feet across. I could hear that grinding roar, too damn close this time, and the insectile whine of Hop's outboard was barely audible over it. By the time Rosey got the nose of the boat pointed outward, he was sliding down over the lip. "Holy shit," Hobart said.

The thing was pulling at us, too. Hobart had changed direction while I was watching Hop's boat, he had his throttle jammed forward, but we seemed to be going backward in the water. Rosario passed close by us once, close enough, anyhow, for me to see his face, white with fear. He was gaining ground, though, the Old Sow looked like she might let him go. "He might make it," Hobart said. "He gets clear of that, we're in trouble."

"Maybe so." When he passed us again, he was pointing the gun straight at me. I guess he wanted my company on the way to hell. He fired, but the Old Sow was pulling at Hop's boat, spoiling his aim, and I heard the bullet whisper past my head. I pointed the .45, cursing myself for not ever having learned how to shoot. I fired off two more rounds. I don't know if I hit the outboard or not, it was what I was aiming at, but I didn't see pieces fly off it the way they would have in the movies. I must have gotten lucky after all, though, because Hop's engine coughed and died, and the boat slid slowly backward over the lip.

The Old Sow was drifting lazily downriver. I saw Rosey pitch off the front of Hop's boat, I saw his face, contorted, his mouth open wide, but I couldn't hear him screaming, all I could hear was the Old Sow grinding. A minute passed, and Hobart's boat began to move away toward the far shore. The sound tapered off as the whirlpool moved downstream, and then the hole in the water seemed to shrink, and it was gone. The noise started up again, though, as the Old Sow re-formed about a hundred feet behind us. Rosario and the boat were both gone, swallowed up as if they had never been there. The bay went on doing what she'd done for millennia.

"She ain't done yet," Hobart said. "Jesus. That was the biggest one I ever seen. Let's get the hell away from here."

"Good idea." I wiped the Russian's gun off with my shirt and pitched it over the back.

15

I guess everything looks beautiful after the bullet with your name on it has gone past your ear without hitting you. The sun came out and burned off the rest of the fog as Hobart piloted his boat up Indian Road. I didn't know what I was looking at, islands, mainland, river, bay, ocean, whatever, it didn't matter. I even quit trying to identify birds, I just watched. The noise of my breath echoed inside my empty skull, I had no words for questions or opinions. There were a few small houses, cabins really, on the shore of whatever landmasses we were passing. Each one looked more painfully beautiful than the last. How could anybody who lived in a place like this ever be unhappy? For that moment, the land, trees, rocks, water, birds, fish, even Hobart's lobster boat with the hole in its windshield, seemed like a painting in a museum or maybe like something out of a dream. How could anything in real life be so perfect?

Hobart steered us up into a narrow rock-lined finger of ocean. An A-frame cottage sat high on a ledge, up near the tree line. A short wooden pier stood on what looked like a collection of old telephone poles, rotted black and covered with seaweed and barnacles. A herring gull sat on top of one of the poles. I think he was a herring gull, I wasn't really sure, but he pointed his head at the sky and called when he saw us coming. "Go away," I guess he was saying. "Go away and leave us alone." We kept coming, though. The gull spread his wings, lifted his feet, and the wind raised him up. He wheeled and soared away without ever once flapping his wings.

Hobart tied up next to a wooden ladder nailed into one of the poles. "You think you need a hand?" he said. Bullets and whirlpools didn't scare him, but he didn't look like he wanted to climb up onto that pier.

"If I need you, I'll yell."

Walking from the pier up to the cabin, I actually wondered what it would cost to buy the place. I even stopped and looked out behind me, over the water. Why is it that you can never seem to hang on to something like this? You just get a moment, now and then, and then that moment passes on and you're left with just that ache, just that hunger. What would get done, a voice in my head asked, what would ever get done if everyone found a place like this, and never left it?

Yeah, but what would need to get done?

Franklin was tied to a chair in the middle of the floor in the A-frame. He squirmed in discomfort when he saw me. "Holy shit, Franklin, am I glad to see you."

"Don't cuss, Manny," he said, not surprised at all to see me. "Cussing isn't nice. Hurry, I gotta go pee."

Franklin didn't seem to like the boat ride, he sat down and held on grimly the whole trip back. It was a trip, too, getting him down that goddam ladder into Hobart's boat. "How are you feeling, Franklin?" I asked him. "Are you okay?"

He glanced at me for about a half a second. "Headache," he said.

"Let me see," I told him. "Let me see where he hit you." Franklin held his chin up for inspection. "I don't even think you're going to have a bruise, Franklin."

Hobart chuckled. "'Bout like punching a piece of wood," he said.

We stopped and picked up Nicky and Louis on the way. I wanted Nicky to see with his own eyes that Franklin was all right, I didn't want to have to keep reassuring him about it for the next ten years. I don't know what their bond was, they didn't talk too much, they just sat side by side in the back of the van. Nicky asked Franklin questions in a voice pitched too low for me to hear, and Franklin patted him on the shoulder and gave him one-word answers. Nicky still seemed a little shook, but maybe that was because he knew that we were leaving. That was the plan, anyhow. I didn't know what Bookman was going to think of it.

I called his office from my cell phone, left a message that I had Franklin and was headed for his house. He got there before we did, and he and his wife were both standing out by the rear of the cruiser. Their stupid dog started running around, barking, when he saw me pull into the driveway.

Bookman's wife came out and hustled over, she hugged Franklin and cried on his shoulder, while he looked embarrassed. "Ma," he said. "I'm okay." She let go of him then, and came over to give me and Nicky both a hug.

"That's twice you brought my son back to me," she said. "Thank you so much. Thank you." She smelled really nice. I couldn't remember anyone ever hugging me like that before.

Bookman ambled over. "Do you know where the two of you are going now?"

"Not really. Canada, I guess."

"That's probably smaht," he said. "Don't cross in Calais, though. There's another place to cross, just beyond there. It's a quiet place, nobody uses it, just the locals. The customs guy won't even get up out of his chair, he'll just wave you through. Hold on for one minute, I'll write out the directions for you." He looked at me for a couple of seconds then, with those bland eyes in that still face. Then he turned away and went off to get a pen and a piece of paper.

I said good-bye to Louis while Bookman was inside his house. It hurt me as much as anything I could remember. I didn't know what to say, I didn't even know if I could talk. Louis took my hand in both of his, the same way he'd done when I gave him the money. He squeezed, hard. "Yoah gonna be all right, Manny," he said. "You take good care of that boy."

"Say good-bye to Eleanor for me." I didn't recognize the sound of my own voice. "Tell her, I don't know . . . Tell her Nicky and I are gonna miss her. Tell her, we get where we're going, we'll write. Okay?" I had to swallow. "Tell her we all came out all right."

He nodded and turned away, and I wiped my face on my shirt.

Bookman was right, the guy waved us through. I stopped in St. Stephen, the town on the Canadian side, and bought a map. It looked like a long drive to Montreal, and a longer one to Vancouver, but I had plenty of time. My ATM card still worked, too, so we had gas money. I got to thinking about that, so I turned around and went back to St. Stephen and used the computer in the library to check a few things. I had an e-mail from Buchanan, and I saw in the news that the FDA had approved a new boner drug. I watched my stock soar over the next week, I kept stopping every time I saw a place that had Internet service. Nicky didn't seem to mind. Once, I found a motel with an indoor pool, and Nicky thought he had died and gone to heaven. All of his troubles seemed forgotten then, and he did his best to drown the both of us.

I guess I won, after all. Rosario lost, that's for damn sure. It wasn't because I was smarter than he was, though. If I won, it was because a few people had taken pity on me, taken me in and looked out for me. Louis and Eleanor, Bookman, Mrs. Johnson, Hobart . . . Rosario had linked up with only one guy, Hopkins, and all they had shared was trouble. Maybe, in that part of the world, you can't make it on your own. Maybe you've got to have help.

I've never been able to get that cabin out of my head, though, that A-frame on the coast of Deer Island. There was something there, man, I felt something in that place that I've never felt since. Maybe it was just the moment, I don't know. That's the way it goes in paradise, I guess. You don't appreciate it when you're in it, you don't understand that you're going to have to leave someday, and you don't know the price of admission until after they've thrown you out.